THE AUSTEN INTRIGUE

JULIA GOLDING

One More Chapter
a division of HarperCollins*Publishers* Ltd
1 London Bridge Street
London SE1 9GF
www.harpercollins.co.uk
HarperCollins*Publishers*
Macken House, 39/40 Mayor Street Upper,
Dublin 1, D01 C9W8, Ireland

This paperback edition 2025

1

First published in Great Britain in ebook format
by HarperCollins*Publishers* 2025
Copyright © Julia Golding 2025
Julia Golding asserts the moral right to
be identified as the author of this work

A catalogue record of this book is available from the British Library
ISBN: 978-0-00-877084-6

This novel is a work of fiction. Any references to real people, places and events are used fictitiously. All other names, characters and incidents portrayed are a work of the author's imagination and any resemblance to actual persons, living or dead, events or localities is entirely coincidental.

Printed and bound in the UK using 100% Renewable Electricity
by CPI Group (UK) Ltd

All rights reserved. No part of this publication may be reproduced, stored in a retrieval system, or transmitted, in any form or by any means, electronic, mechanical, photocopying, recording or otherwise, without the prior permission of the publishers.

Without limiting the exclusive rights of any author, contributor or the publisher of this publication, any unauthorised use of this publication to train generative artificial intelligence (AI) technologies is expressly prohibited. HarperCollins also exercise their rights under Article 4(3) of the Digital Single Market Directive 2019/790 and expressly reserve this publication from the text and data mining exception.

Julia Golding is a multi-award winning writer for adults, young adults and children. She also writes under the pen names of Joss Stirling and Eve Edwards. Over a million and a half of her books have been sold around the world with best selling titles in a wide range of age categories, such as *The Diamond of Drury Lane* (children), *Finding Sky* (YA) and *Don't Trust Me* (adult). Regency Secrets is her latest series for adults, which began with *The Persephone Code*. She is also Director of the Oxford Centre for Fantasy which uses the inspiration of Oxford Fantasy writers such as Tolkien, C.S. Lewis and Lewis Carroll to inspire new creativity.

In 2019 she was writer-in-residence at the Royal Institution, the home of science. She can be found taking an early nineteenth century perspective on modern life in her Jane Austen podcast 'What Would Jane Do?'.

She is also a screenwriter, working on a number of feature and TV series concepts, featuring strong female leads.

Former British diplomat and Oxfam policy adviser, she has now published over sixty books in genres ranging from historical adventure to fantasy. Read carefully and you'll spot all sorts of material from her diplomatic and Oxfam careers popping up in unexpected places. She has a doctorate in English literature from Oxford.

www.goldinggateway.com

facebook.com/jgoldingauthor

Also by Julia Golding

Regency Secrets

The Persephone Code

The Elgin Conspiracy

The Wordsworth Key

The Austen Intrigue

For Katy Macfarlane, podcast partner and the best dressed nineteenth-century lady I know!

Chapter One

24 July 1812

Chawton

Mr Henry Austen was a banker with a broad idea of friendship, or so his wife, Eliza, informed her sister-in-law Jane in her most recent letter. The fourth oldest brother in the Austen family had developed a wide circle of friends in the city, both those in trade and those of inherited wealth. Prejudice went both ways, with one group sneering at the other for being idle, the second regarding working for a living a shameful thing. However, Henry refused to entertain such small-mindedness; indeed, he went further. He had not hesitated to take on more outré acquaintances, such as Eliza's French connections, not even when Comte Emmanuel Louis D'Antraigues presented himself in England with an opera singer for a wife.

'*You will remember them,*' wrote Eliza to Jane. '*I took you to tea with them in March last year when you were correcting the proofs of* Sense and Sensibility *– they were the family who had the grand house in Queen Anne Street.*' Perhaps it would have been wiser not to read that sentence aloud, thought Jane, regretting her haste, but Eliza's letters were always so deliciously entertaining. Jane had a tendency to gambol through them like a puppy falling over its paws to reach a treat.

'You did not have tea with an opera singer!' exclaimed Cassandra, pausing in buttering her toast. Her eyes rounded in shock beneath her lace-trimmed cap, dark curls framing her pink cheeks. Even at thirty-nine, Cassie had lost none of her good looks and retained a youthful bloom. She had always been judged the most handsome of the Austen daughters. The sun certainly seemed to think so, bathing her in summer light as it came through the windows, making her its particular favourite.

In the shadows by the grandfather clock, Jane had to content herself with being the wittiest – and giving her own name to the most beautiful of the sisters in her next novel. Cassie had laughed at that little revenge. But back to the events in London…

'I did call on them with Eliza. They were very pleasant.' Jane had enjoyed her time in Henry's home, 64 Sloane Street, seeing her first novel through the press. Her brother and sister-in-law had been so kind, introducing her to their friends, holding lavish musical parties, and helping to keep the reason for her visit quiet with a round of morning calls. The book had come out with the demur byline of *Published by a lady*, a charming secret identity that only the closest to her knew. It had been exciting to be in London on false pretences, like being a spy in enemy territory. The good wives of Chawton would swoon if they knew one of their number had dared to become a public figure – an authoress!

Cassandra shook her head slowly as if she couldn't believe it. 'Miss Jane Austen from Chawton village took tea with a French *comte*?'

'And a *comtesse*. Antoinette-Cécile Clavel, formerly a famous soprano at the Paris Opéra.' It was fun to tease her sister. Cassandra hated being left out of family events.

'And yet you did not write to tell me about the *comtesse*'s past?' Cassandra looked more scandalised at the omission than the visit because the sisters told each other everything.

Almost everything, Jane corrected herself. Everyone needed privacy. Living so that every whim and flaw was exposed to public attention resulted in shallow characters such as those who were counted as famous these days – not to mention the disgrace that followed whole families when one of them became notorious.

Publishing her books was not without risks to the Austen clan, Jane thought ruefully, particularly if someone influential decided to object to their content.

Jane glanced at her mother whose mouth was already set in a disapproving line. Her new independence had not found favour with every member of her family. 'I did mention it, Cassie – in my letter about Eliza's musical party.' She had bundled it in at the end, hoping her mother didn't notice. 'True, I may have left out the detail about the opera singing but only because I did not think Henry and Eliza wanted that bandied about.'

'Oh,' said Cassandra, understanding. In other words, the less Mrs Austen knew about her son and daughter-in-law's circle in London, the better. They dined with so many more people than the restricted society of a country village and some of them were decidedly ... uncommon.

'The *comte* and his wife were charming. Even the Duchess of York approves. Her Grace was the one who suggested the *comtesse* set up a singing school,' continued Jane.

'A singing school!' snorted Mrs Austen, stirring a spoonful of sugar into her tea as if it had personally offended her.

'Mama, French émigrés need a way to support themselves now their ancestral estates have vanished like the morning mist, in the blaze of the revolution. They can't all marry out of their difficulties like Eliza.' Not that the D'Antraigues had seemed short of funds. Odd that, now she thought about it.

'It is not your cousin's fault her first husband was guillotined!' said Mrs Austen.

Jane sighed inwardly. Her mother was apt to take what she said the wrong way. 'I never said it was. I love and admire Eliza, and I consider her friend the *comtesse*'s singing academy a brave attempt to reestablish a life in the margins of the court.'

As Mrs Austen didn't have a response to that, Cassandra waved her piece of toast. 'Read on, Jane.'

Her eyes went to the next line and the bottom fell out of their morning. 'Good Lord.' This was horrible and would bolster every prejudice their parent had against the diversions of a life in town. 'Perhaps we should finish the news later?' The clock began striking a doleful nine. 'Look at the time: I have stockings to mend.'

Cassandra was having none of that. 'Jane!'

Resigned, Jane cleared her throat. '*However, Henry's generosity might have a sting in its tail as the* comte *and* comtesse *were stabbed to death yesterday by a manservant, a deserter from the French army that they should never have trusted near them.'*

There was a deathly silence.

'Clearly not,' said Mrs Austen. 'That's the French for you.'

Cassandra set down her toast. 'That is not something one usually hears at the breakfast table.' She fixed Jane with her sternest look. 'One does not expect such things to happen in England where we have laws, and magistrates, and decency.'

'I imagine the late Prime Minster thought very similarly before he was assassinated,' said Jane. 'By an Englishman.' Still, she found it profoundly shocking that someone she had visited had met with such a violent death. It went far beyond her experience.

In the silence, the blackbird sang on the lawn, untouched by war and murder. The roses danced in the light breeze and the hollyhocks in the border bobbed their curtsies.

'Read on,' said Mrs Austen.

Jane tore herself away from the peaceful world of the garden and back to the violent one of the city. 'I thought you didn't approve of French opera singers, Mama?'

'This is not approval. The count and countess were friends of your brother. We will pray for them, poor souls.'

Not to mention that Mrs Austen was wildly curious, as were Jane and Cassandra, to find out more. Death held a horrible fascination and, sadly, at a distance it could even be entertaining, though Jane was depressed by what that said about the human condition.

'Henry and I are both at a loss to explain why such a violent end befell two worthy people who came to England for sanctuary. Poor Julien, their son, is left all alone. The rumour mill is grinding but the perpetrator shot himself after he killed his employers so the story will

smoulder, producing a lot of obscuring smoke unless we can find someone who can investigate and blow it away.'

'Why must Henry and Eliza be like this?' said Mrs Austen. 'Why not let sleeping dogs lie?'

'I would say the dog in this case wasn't so much sleeping as being slaughtered,' muttered Jane. 'I fully sympathise with the frustrations of not knowing the end of the story,' she said more plainly. Not that she'd ever use such material in her own novels. She thought of her writing as miniatures painted on ivory with a fine brush, depicting the world she knew best, not vast bloody canvases like those painted by historical artists.

'As with Mozart and the incomplete chord – one has to get up and finish it,' said Cassandra.

'Exactly,' agreed Jane, skimming the rest of the letter. This she would keep from her mother: her sister-in-law wrote that she was concerned Henry's reputation might suffer as it was known that he had been close to the D'Antraigues – and trust was what underpinned a financier's affairs. Henry wanted the matter cleared up and tidied away or his business was at risk. Ah good: they had a solution. 'Eliza writes that Henry has an idea. Frank told him on his last leave that he knows someone who investigates this sort of thing.'

'This sort of thing!' Mrs Austen's cap ribbons trembled. 'How often does this sort of thing happen among Henry's acquaintances?'

'Not very often, one would hope. He has written to Frank to find out their address in London.'

'Who does Frank know?' asked Mrs Austen querulously. She claimed that many of her grey hairs were down to her two sons who were rising in the ranks of the navy. Frank and Charles were constantly doing battle with the French – and now they had the Americans to fight too! Frank, the son born between Cassandra and Jane, a captain in the navy, was somewhere in the Channel on HM *Elephant* so the letter might take some time to reach him. 'How does he know anyone in London who investigates murders? He's been at sea for most of the last ten years!'

Jane read through the rest of the letter. 'And it is at sea that they met. Frank knows a military surgeon, Dr Jacob Sandys, brother to Viscount Sandys.'

'Jacob Sandys? Why is that name familiar?' asked Cassandra.

'Because he is the man whose life Frank saved at the evacuation from Corunna.' Jane folded the letter away. Perhaps now, she thought, it would be Jacob Sandys's turn to save the Austens.

Chapter Two

18 August 1812

Bruton Mews

Dora surveyed her little room with satisfaction. Two doors down from their office, she had taken lodgings with a retired wigmaker. There was far less call for wigs – only judges, priests and footmen continued to wear them – so Mrs Jones had given up the trade and let out rooms instead. Yarton, Lady Tolworth's inestimable butler from the big house across the way, had arranged everything. Dora's bedroom was on the first floor and looked out onto the cobbled mews. Right now, she could see Kir, their office boy, playing football with some off-duty servants from Lady Tolworth's house. He had free passage between both establishments – the investigative agency and the grand house the lady kept – and was taking to his new life as if born to it. Rescued from life as a camp follower in the border town of Berwick, the orphaned Kir had even begun to develop a London accent, dropping his Scottish one.

Children, mused Dora, were like the chameleons on display at the Tower Menagerie, able to change their colour. They sensed when it was easier to fit in than stand out.

Moving away from the glass, she prowled her den.

'A room of my own,' she murmured. She touched each object she had unpacked: her small library of novels and plays, the commonplace book she had created with her late brother that contained samples of handwriting from many famous people, her grey great coat and scarlet redingote hanging on pegs along the wall. They were joined by a few reluctant bonnets and a row of happier hats. Bonnets were such stupid things, their only advantages being that they did not fly off so easily when chasing a villain and they were a good disguise as they hid the wearer's features. On the whole, she preferred hats and was gathering a selection between which she could alternate when tailing someone. Luckily there was plenty of space for them. She guessed the pegs had once been used to display the huge variety of wigs the previous generation had thought indispensable, puff balls like clouds with birdcages and boats as ornaments. How tame the present generation was in comparison, wearing their own hair with nary a sniff of powder.

After a month of travelling in the north, it was good to be home.

The thought took her by surprise. When had London become her home? She had been raised in Liverpool and, after quitting her father's house, travelled with a troupe of players on the northern circuit, offering Shakespeare plays and

Restoration comedies to agricultural labourers and the workers in the new manufactories. She was still learning her way around the streets here, still finding the size of the city daunting.

She gazed over the slate roofs to the murky blue skies, cooking fires dulling the summer's day.

Perhaps it wasn't the city but the person who lived here that gave her a sense of being settled. It had become home when she had thrown in her lot with Jacob Sandys, she acknowledged. Also, thinking more practically, the capital was the best place to start an agency dealing with private enquiries, which meant she was unlikely to have to pack up and move on for some time. That was a very pleasant prospect because her life for the last five years had been nothing but shifting from place to place.

Two sharp whistles came from the mews. That was Kir's signal that a customer was approaching their office. As Jacob was at his bank this morning dealing with the financial consequences of his father's death, she was in charge of greeting new clients. Quickly straightening her gown and checking her hair in the mottled mirror – it would do – she hurried downstairs.

Opening the door to their office, she found Kir had already done his job and seated the visitor in the chair opposite the desk. The caller looked to be in his middle years, a handsome man with a long face and intelligent eyes under dark brows. When he stood up on her entry, he revealed himself to be of above average height and with the lean build of a sportsman or soldier. His clothing was impeccably cut, showing an almost French flair in the details on cuff and collar – an attractive man, used to female attention.

'Ma'am.' He bowed politely.

She approached, holding out a hand. This was business, not a ballroom, so he could greet her as a fellow professional. 'I'm Miss Fitz-Pennington.' He shook her hand with a bemused smile at her forthright ways. 'Please do take a seat.'

Obediently, he sat. 'Is Dr Sandys away, Miss Fitz-Pennington?'

'He has business in the city. We are partners in the agency so speaking to me is like speaking to him.'

That made him smile more broadly. 'I assure you, good lady, no gentleman would consider talking to you as akin to talking to a man. You are far prettier than your partner, I would wager.'

Her visitor was a gallant. That wasn't a problem: she could deal with flattery as long as it didn't become an affront.

'You are too kind, sir. Might I trouble you for a name?'

'Of course.' He handed over his business card. 'Henry Austen of Austen, Maunde & Tilson.'

Banking and Investments read the card. She had not thought him a banker; he seemed too fashionable for such a sober occupation.

'What can we do for you, Mr Austen?' She was conscious of Kir coming to stand silently at her elbow. Her colleagues in the agency made a point of not leaving her on her own with new male customers, an endearing if somewhat annoying state of affairs when even a boy of nine felt obliged to guard her. Perhaps they were pandering to the sensibilities of men who would feel safer with a chaperone? That was an amusing thought.

'My brother, Captain Austen, recommended Dr Sandys as a reliable man for a delicate matter.'

Dora sighed internally. She had initially rather liked this man, but 'delicate matter' was usually code for some kind of marital intrigue. 'We promise our clients discretion.'

He studied her for a moment, as if pausing to make up his own mind about her. 'Very well. It's about my wife's friends.'

Oh, dear – that tired old story. 'You don't approve of them?' She flipped to a new page in the notebook they kept for open investigations.

'What?' He looked bewildered by the remark. 'No, no, nothing like that. You see, they've been murdered. Mrs Austen and I want to see justice done.'

Dora's pulse leaped, jolted out of the expectation that this would be some tawdry marital affair. 'Murdered? I assume the authorities are involved?'

Henry crossed his leg over one knee and flicked off a thread that clung to his thigh. 'Indeed. The murderer killed himself on the scene so they do not think any further action is required. An inquest was held the following day – there were witnesses so they had no doubt that they had the right man.'

Dora spread out her hands in a helpless gesture. 'Mr Austen, I'm struggling to understand what we can do to help.'

He sighed. 'I'm sure your partner would comprehend my situation.'

She held his gaze. She couldn't conjure up Jacob so Mr Austen would have to do with her 'slowness' to grasp his issue. She rather thought the fault was with him for failing to explain. 'I'm sure he would. Please put it in plain terms that a mere female can understand.'

He gave a grimace of apology. 'I'm sorry. Let me start again. You are aware, I presume, that people in my station live and die on the breath of scandal? Ladies who stray from the marriage bed are sent to a country cottage to serve a life sentence of disgrace; gentlemen are challenged to duels for a difference of opinion and sometimes die of their injuries, but businesses such as mine rise and fall as faith in their operations waxes and wanes.'

Dora was beginning to see the outlines of his problem. Mr Austen was a banker. The last thing a bank wanted was a run on its funds, everyone demanding their money at the same time. That always resulted in bankruptcy. 'You believe your own credit with the ton might suffer if this matter is not resolved?'

He gave her a wintry smile. 'Exactly.'

'But if the magistrate declared the case closed, why reopen it?'

'The authorities might be done with the matter, having given their verdict of insanity on the part of the perpetrator—'

'Like they did with the man who shot the Prime Minister,' murmured Dora, who with Jacob had witnessed both the crime and the punishment that befell John Bellingham three months ago.

'Indeed. But the gossipers have been hard at work adding two and two and making five thousand. My family were frequent visitors at the *comte*'s house in Barnes Terrace, as well as the one in Queen Anne Street.'

'They kept two houses in the capital?' Dora picked up her pen again.

'The one in Barnes is more of a rural retreat, on the Thames near Richmond.'

To afford houses in two such prized locations the Frenchman must have had money coming from somewhere.

'Your reputation is entwined with that of the late *comte* and his wife?'

'Just so, particularly in view of the fact that my wife is the widow of the Comte de Feuillide.' Dora raised a brow. How had an ordinary Mr Austen managed to land so exotic a bird for his wife? 'We are well known to be intimates of the French émigrés who have settled here,' he continued. 'They come to our social gatherings and we go to theirs. Few members of society cross the divide as we do.'

Dora pieced together what he was not saying. 'The inquest gave its verdict, but rumour refuses to accept it. In the absence of a full investigation giving a more satisfying motive than insanity, speculation has spun out of control and is threatening to suck you into the whirlpool. Do I have that right?'

'Correct. The summer has given us a respite, but come the autumn when society returns to the capital, there will be a reckoning. The future of my bank and the good name of the Austen family is at stake.'

'And you would like Dr Sandys and me to investigate—'

'*Quietly* investigate.'

'But of course – *quietly* investigate why your friends were murdered and provide a motive that will shut down the gossipers and keep the Austen name out of the scandal before the month is out?'

Henry nodded. 'It would be better for us if it was found to be a crime of passion – the servant struck by unrequited love for his mistress or something of that nature. That would be counted as eminently French and romantic and the story would settle there, far from any dealings in the city.'

'We won't make anything up to please a client,' Dora warned. 'We don't spread fictions.'

He gave a bark of laughter. 'Do not be concerned: I have a sister to do that.'

'I'm sorry – I'm not following you.'

'Never mind – a family joke.'

Dora was beginning to find him a little annoying. 'You won't help our investigation if you continue to talk in this enigmatic fashion. We need to know what you know at the very least.'

Henry got up and replaced his hat, tapping the crown to settle it on his head. 'Speak to Dr Sandys to see if he agrees to take the case then send the contract for your services. Once that is signed, I will tell you what I know.'

'Everything?' asked Dora, accompanying him to the door.

'Everything,' he agreed. 'Good day.'

Chapter Three

Coutts Bank, The Strand

Mr Jefferson, Jacob's personal banker, closed the ledger. 'In summary, Dr Sandys, your private funds are in a healthy condition. You've not been drawing down on them, I notice.' The man's white whiskers bristled with pleasure at this evidence of praiseworthy parsimony. Like the dragon of Norse myth, the banker did not like to see gold leaving his hoard.

Jacob Sandys tapped his fingers on the arms of the visitor's chair. No expense was spared on the furniture of this office; the chair had Moroccan leather upholstery and the walls oak panelling. Burgundy satin curtains swaggered at the windows. Coutts only dealt with the aristocracy – tradesmen or East India Company Johnnies need not apply. 'Happily, I've been earning money from my investigations.'

'Ah, yes.' The sniff was not quite disapproval but approached it. 'Your brother did mention something of the sort. Will you need funds to invest in your venture?

He suggested you might consider employing investigators to do the work for you and you might be contemplating standing for a parliamentary seat.'

This had to be the latest plan coming from the viscount to drag his brother back into respectability. Was Arthur really spreading this rumour around town?

'An interesting idea but not one I am pursuing at this time.' See, thought Jacob, I can be diplomatic when required and not betray to one of London's chief gossips that the Sandys brothers do not see eye-to-eye on Jacob's future.

'You were left additional properties under the terms of your father's will,' said Mr Jefferson, changing the subject.

Jacob's grief for his father swept through him. He'd received the news when staying at his cottage in the Lakes only three weeks ago, further pain added when he discovered his older brother had not sent for him to attend the deathbed for fear of Dora 'polluting' the family seat with her presence. He was still smarting from that double blow.

'I was. I have not yet had a chance to visit them but my brother's steward is keeping a weather-eye on them until I have the time. If I need to draw on my investments to repair or improve them, I will in due course let you know.'

'Naturally. We at Coutts are always ready to help in such matters. I can recommend people who have experience of land management, should that be required.' The banker seemed happier to be on familiar ground. Estates were something they understood at Coutts.

'Thank you.' Jacob stood up to go. 'What news on the financial markets?' Gossips had their uses, particularly for anyone with investments in riskier ventures.

Jefferson rose to conduct him to the door. 'There isn't much happening over the summer, as you might imagine. There are troublesome delays in the Indiamen coming back to port – storms in the Atlantic, they say at Lloyds.'

Jacob had stakes in some shipping companies. 'Any losses?'

'None confirmed. Also, the bank of Austen, Maunde & Tilson is looking a little shaky.' Jefferson smiled briefly. 'Happily, it is too small a house to affect the rest of us so no need to ring the alarm bell as yet.'

Jacob frowned. He didn't personally have dealings with the company, but he knew a brother of one of the partners. 'In what way is it shaky?'

Jefferson lowered his voice to a conspiratorial tone. 'Whispers about involvement with the French, that kind of thing.'

In a time of war, one had to be very careful to be above the taint of collaboration. It sounded like someone at the Austen bank had been foolish. 'How interesting. Good day to you, sir.'

Tapping his hat brim, Jacob left the office and headed out through the banking hall. His passage did not attract much attention. He had no lofty title to garner respect, and his holdings were modest by the standards of the biggest accounts in this place. Had he been with his eldest brother, he would have witnessed genuflections to the greatness of the Sandys name.

Stepping out onto The Strand was to enter a squall after the becalmed halls of finance. Hackney cabs rattled past, loaded with the well-to-do; wagons pulled out of Covent Garden at the end of the morning's fruit and vegetable trade, rumbling back to the market gardens on the fringes of London; pedestrians jostled for a place on the pavement, beggars holding out empty palms on the corners, pickpockets weaving between legs looking for an unsecured purse or handkerchief. Flipping a shilling to a wounded veteran (or so the man's sign claimed – one had to be cynical about these things), Jacob turned in the direction of the Haymarket, cutting through a backstreet so he could avoid the congestion at Charing Cross. London was a flourishing city that hadn't kept up with the number of people and vehicles swarming into it, feeling somewhat like a hive about to burst. It made him miss his quiet cottage in the Lakes.

Not so quiet, he reminded himself. Dora and he had returned from there a few days ago after a busy week solving the murder of a magistrate and a string of violent attacks on young men. His brother the viscount had been shot in the business and come to town to consult his doctors. Jacob really should send a note to see if his recovery was progressing satisfactorily.

Striding over a pile of horse droppings, he crossed the road to Piccadilly. He tapped his hat brim to several acquaintances heading for the gentlemen's clubs of St James. He'd ceased frequenting his club since setting up the business with Dora, preferring to spend time with her, but he should probably make himself go back to Brooks as it was a fine place to gather intelligence. He could ask around about that bank business. If panic spread, contagion in the markets could bring many of the smaller banks to their knees. No one would escape the financial ramifications.

A drink with old friends or a chance to see Dora? With a wry smile, he turned for Bruton Mews. Dora won every time.

He found Dora at the desk writing in their case notebook. She looked up and smiled, her dark curly hair bronze-tinted by the sunlight that came in through the door with him. Approaching the desk, he kissed her and ran a finger appreciatively over the warm brown smoothness of her cheek, feeling the tug in his belly of his attraction to her. Dora's mother had been a planter's daughter in the West Indies, so her heritage imported a richer skin tone than was commonly found among the pallid ladies of the ton. The sun in the Lakes had darkened it further as she didn't hold with poke bonnets and parasols.

But he couldn't act on that attraction now. He was a grown man, not a callow youth who thought of nothing but sex. True, he admitted privately, he thought of it, but he could move on to what they needed to do.

'All well?' he asked, taking a seat at the desk beside her.

'I've been enjoying my new room.' She turned the notebook so he could read the latest entry. 'And we have a new client – that's if you agree we should take him on.'

Jacob scanned the notes and felt that stir of excitement at the beginning of a new case. Solving puzzles had become his new addiction, though it was proving as dangerous as his old reliance on opium. 'How strange – I was only half an hour ago hearing rumours at Coutts that Austen, Maunde & Tilson were looking doubtful. It appears Henry Austen is apprised of the gossip and taking action to prevent a collapse.'

Dora grinned. 'Then I suggest we get payment up front.'

He tweaked a ringlet. 'Mercenary lass.'

'We aren't running a charity, Jacob.' Tugging her hair free with a smile, she got up and walked to the cupboard where they kept copies of their contract, filled out by an expert copyist they'd hired for the purpose. She flourished one at him.

'Shall we? I'd like to meet this French wife of his. She sounds entertaining.'

Jacob added Henry's details and put in their charging rate. 'I don't believe she is French. Eliza Austen, if memory serves, was born in India. Rumour has it that she was the love child of the then governor, Warren Hastings.'

'India? Good lord: she's even more exotic than French.'

'Her mother was one of the fishing party ladies who went out there to find a husband.'

'Sounds like she found both a husband and a lover.'

'Don't quote me on that. It is purely a rumour. Anyway, Eliza then married a Frenchman, was widowed, and came home to fascinate the Austen brothers, her cousins.'

'How do you know all this? She's not a former amour of yours, is she?'

'Hardly.' Jacob chuckled at her mock-scowl. 'I don't tangle with married ladies.'

'Apart from Lady Tolworth.' Dora flicked a glance to the house across the mews where his former lover resided.

'Only when her late husband was already half dead. You're distracting me.' He pulled her on to his knee. 'Teasing me unmercifully for a past before you came into my life. You're the only lady I tangle with now.' His fingers danced over the soft skin of her midriff, kept from him only by a summer-weight muslin dress and shift.

'Then how do you know about Eliza Austen?' She played with his cravat, pulling the ends from his shirt.

'Henry's brother Frank is a friend – one to whom I owe a great debt. He was full of his wonderful sister-in-law and the stories she could tell.' He frowned. 'Or was that his sister? I might be getting mixed up.'

Dora glanced at the contract and grimaced. 'You know Frank, so that is why you are charging the friends and family rate for this task. I'll have to teach you to be mercenary like me or we won't turn a profit.'

He squeezed her tightly, enjoying the weight of her on his lap which was doing delicious things to his desire for her. That fire never went out, always ready to flame into passion. Sadly, this was the middle of the working day, and they had business to conduct. 'Never fear, we are doing well enough. I have that confirmed by my banker who wondered why I was leaving my savings intact. The petty crimes that Alex has been settling in our absence have meant a steady flow of income, far more lucrative than solving a murder.'

'Yes, Alex is proving to be worth his weight in gold.'

Their deputy was a former army officer, Alex Smith, who had left his regiment under a cloud when it emerged that he'd lodged sensitive military plans with the Hellfire Club as the price of his entry to that secret society. He'd been Dora's brother's lover before Anthony was murdered a few months ago, an event that had brought Jacob and Dora together for the Hellfire Club investigation. Many would consider belonging to the club a misstep but, with Alex and Anthony's love being counted a capital crime by the law courts, private societies had been the only safe place for Alex and Anthony to conduct an affair. Pitying Alex's situation and also mourning Anthony, Dora and Jacob had given him a second chance and he was proving an adept and reliable investigator.

Which reminded him…

Reluctantly ushering her off his lap, Jacob went to the stairs and called:

'Smith, are you up?' Alex had been on night surveillance of a cheating servant.

There came a grumpy 'I am now' and Alex appeared at the top of the stairs in his dressing gown. Golden haired and with the physique of a Greek god, he was a most useful employee to charm the ladies – and the gentlemen who wished to emulate his social allure. He stomped down the stairs, yawning, hair going every which way, jaw showing his pale stubble. 'Morning, Dora.'

'I believe you will find it is afternoon,' she said pertly as he dropped a brotherly kiss on her cheek.

'Pedant.' He collapsed into the visitor chair.

'Slugabed.' The usual exchange of gentle ribbing over, Dora fetched him a mug of tea and a bread roll from their larder. 'We're going out and leaving you in charge.'

'Thank you.' He raised the cup to her. 'Did I hear voices earlier?'

'New client,' said Jacob. 'Henry Austen. Do you know him?'

Alex's eyes lit up in recognition. 'Military chap before going into banking?'

'That's the one.'

'If I recall correctly, he was paymaster for the Oxfordshire Militia and made the right connections there for his new profession.'

'Then he never served abroad,' noted Jacob adding that to the client file. 'He's probably not been to France or the Peninsula.'

'He got as far as Ireland, but I don't think he saw action,' agreed Alex.

'It always amazes how you upper class types gossip about each other!' said Dora.

'There are fewer of us than there are of your lot,' said Alex with a smile.

She pretended outrage. 'Who am I? The common as muck type?'

'You said it, not me. Besides, the Austens are a respectable family from Hampshire with relatives in town. Of course we all know them! I'd say they are fairly unremarkable apart from the two sons rising in the navy – oh, and one was adopted by a noble family, lucky beggar.'

Jacob added the details to the notes. 'I'd heard of Edward's good fortune, but it's Frank Austen I know best. He's the captain who pulled me out of the water at Corunna. I think I bled all over him, but to be honest my memory of the retreat is hazy.' That night in 1809 had been a turning point in Jacob's military service, leaving him with a scar that ran from chest to hip.

'Indeed? I've not met him. He sounds a fine man. He isn't out and about in society like his banker brother, Henry, and his wife.'

'Could that be because Frank is too busy defending the realm?' said Jacob laconically.

'You might have a point.' Alex grinned and took his empty plate to the little larder for Kir to wash later when the lad came to do his office-boy tasks, and then he tucked in his shirt, evidently thinking the day should get started for him. 'Aside from Frank and the younger one – what's his name? I forget. Charles or something of that sort – the most interesting person in the Austen clan is undoubtedly a woman.'

'One of Henry's sisters?' asked Dora.

'Not them. They are your usual boring spinsters, living with their mother in some village, entirely forgettable.' He went to the map of England they had pinned up on the wall and examined Hampshire, which lay to the south-west of London. 'Near Winchester, if I recall the details. Edward Austen, the lucky one, has a property that way.'

Dora scowled. 'Alex, you shouldn't talk like that about us spinsters.'

He turned to her with a mischievous grin. 'You, my dear Dora, hardly qualify for that title.'

'I mean,' said Dora, approaching to clip him around the ear lightly, 'that single women should not be dismissed just because we are unable to have careers in the navy or army. Or because we don't get adopted to inherit estates.'

'Who do you have in mind?' Jacob asked before Alex wound up Dora any further. He'd doubtless made his comments about spinsters to elicit that exact reaction from her. Alex took his role as her adopted brother seriously. Siblings had to torment each other, then turn on the rest of the world when they were threatened.

'He's going to be talking about the exotic widow, of course,' said Dora with a grimace.

Alex folded his arms and leaned against the sideboard under the map. 'Yes, I was talking about Henry's wife, Eliza. She's a cousin of the Austens, her mother being the sister of their late father.' He wrinkled his nose. 'I don't hold with cousin marriage, but families like Henry's seem not to have a problem with it. Eliza is wonderfully spirited, despite the hard knocks life has dealt her.'

'What hard knocks?' asked Dora dubiously.

'A husband guillotined; the son of that marriage dead at fifteen or sixteen some years ago.'

'Poor lady.' Dora sobered at the mention of the lost child. His Dora had a heart the size of Hampshire.

Alex put an arm around her shoulders and squeezed. 'The only bright side is that Henry and Eliza have no other children so they are free to rattle around London without worrying about the funds to send the infants to school or provide a dowry. And that's exactly what they do – gad about town to parties, late nights, trips to the theatre. They are great fun, and I think you'll enjoy making their acquaintance.'

'We aren't going to them to make friends but to save them from financial disaster,' reminded Jacob.

Alex released Dora, fetched her bonnet from the peg by the door and held it out. 'But it might be a pleasant side benefit, might it not?'

Chapter Four

64 Sloane Street, Knightsbridge

Henry Austen rose from behind his desk when the maid showed Dora and Jacob into his study. The room was gloomy after the street. Afternoon sunlight slanted through the bow window so he'd pulled the curtains to reduce the glare. Dust motes danced in the gap.

'Thank you for coming. I take it this means you've accepted the case?' He shook Jacob's hand and insisted on bowing over Dora's.

'We have,' said Jacob, placing the contract on the desk. 'Would you care to review our terms?'

Waving them to a chair, Henry read through the document with laudable care, which Dora found reassuring in a man who was responsible for other people's money. He raised a brow when he came to the amount and looked over at Jacob.

'I owe your brother a debt,' said Jacob.

'Thank you.' Henry nodded and signed the bottom with a flourish. 'Frank will appreciate the gesture, though he has always said he was doing no more than his duty.'

'Few captains would wade into the surf to haul a bleeding man off a beach.'

Dora was liking the sound of this naval Austen and hoped she would get a chance to meet him.

Their client grimaced as he blotted his signature. 'Please don't tell my mother and sisters about that. He has them convinced his duties are nothing more than nannying trading vessels along the coast, with rarely a shot fired in anger.' He passed the contract back. 'Has Miss Fitz-Pennington explained the case?'

'She has,' confirmed Jacob.

Henry drew a sheet from the top drawer in his desk. 'In preparation for your visit, I made a note of what we learned at the inquest. There were witnesses who may know more. The coroner rather hurried through it, thinking there was no one alive to prosecute.'

Jacob took the paper, glanced at it, then passed it to Dora. 'Mr Austen, what are you hoping we can achieve by looking into this? You told my partner you wanted to know what drove the servant to the killing, but would it not be better, as she suggested, to let the matter drop? Your bank could do without more bad publicity, particularly should we find out things that do no credit to the victims, and by extension to yourself.'

The lines around Henry's mouth deepened, frown lines on his brow aging him beyond his forty-odd years. 'Then you've heard the rumours? I'm not sure more damage could be done, Dr Sandys, but I'm hopeful some good can be salvaged if we find out the truth. The *comte* and *comtesse* were fine people. I for one don't believe the bad things being said about them and they do not deserve to have their reputation smeared by the speculation that has been swirling since they are no longer here to defend themselves.'

'What speculation would that be?' asked Dora.

Anger flushed Henry's cheeks. 'That they were feeding information to Napoleon's ministers and using their connections to find out secrets about the relations between the Prince Regent and the government.' Henry wiped a hand over his mouth as if the words were leaving a bitter taste. 'There are rumours of bribes.'

'Ah. Now I think I understand. They would need a source of funds for bribes. Were they clients of yours?' asked Jacob.

Henry nodded. 'Not exclusively, but yes, we had dealings.'

'Are you prepared to show us the books?'

Anger turned into doubt. 'I… I would have to ask their son, but in principle I would be happy to do so, if he agrees.' A bell rang in the room next door, and Henry looked relieved at the reprieve. Dora wondered if indeed he had something to hide. 'That's my wife ringing for tea … and to remind me to introduce you. She doesn't want to be left out of this – the D'Antraigues were her friends even more than they were mine. In view of the sensitivities, we wish to be very closely involved in this investigation, as we will explain. We'd like a convincing counter-story in place for the return to the Autumn Season. Shall we go through?'

Dora had to admit to a certain excitement at meeting the famous Mrs Austen, the one Alex considered the most interesting personage in the family that already included a heroic naval captain. She was therefore taken aback to find two ladies in the drawing room, rather than one. She hesitated for a moment, trying to decide which was Henry's wife and realised she could tell by dress alone. Mrs Austen, a mature beauty with sparkling dark eyes, was in an exquisite morning gown of striped cambric muslin, elaborate pintucks, needle lace and white-work embroidery – the kind of gown that would suffer if the wearer did anything as practical as cook or clean a fireplace. The other lady, comely rather than pretty, fresh-faced with curly light brown hair and hazel eyes, was wearing a round gown similar to ones Dora owned. You could don these without assistance from a maid, thanks to the drawstring neckline. The cloth was finer than Dora could afford – grey leaves printed on a blue background – but it was of a colour and thickness that meant it would not suffer from a little housework or a walk in the country. Was the second woman a companion to Eliza Austen? Many fine ladies had dependent relatives to keep them company while their husbands were at work or at their club.

'Dr Sandys, Miss Fitz-Pennington, may I present my wife,' said Henry as the white-bedecked lady greeted them from beside the tea tray, 'and my younger sister Jane?' The other lady rose, revealing her to be taller and thinner than Eliza. She gave them a wry smile, and Dora got the distinct impression that Miss Austen had noticed her survey of their clothes and the conclusions Dora had drawn upon entry and was vastly amused by her. So much for Alex's description of the Austen sisters as dull spinsters; this one was as sharp as one of Jacob's scalpels.

Having shaken hands and taken a seat, Eliza poured the tea while her sister-in-law handed the cups around. Dora wondered how much they could discuss before the visitor from the country. Henry had already said that the details of his brother's exploits should be kept from his mother and sisters and a murder investigation was far worse.

'Are you staying in the city for long?' she asked Miss Austen politely when the initial pleasantries on the weather and state of the roads were over.

'For as long as I am needed,' the lady said enigmatically.

Henry smiled at his sister with what looked like real affection. 'Jane has come up from Chawton to assist us in our time of need.'

'Indeed, no one is aware I am from home,' said the lady with a complaisant smile. 'These summer colds can keep you indoors for weeks, do you not find?' She addressed the question to Dora.

Having to earn her own living, Dora rarely spent a day in bed ill, let alone with something as trifling as a cold. 'I suppose it might.'

'There is no one better than Jane in a crisis,' said Henry, crunching on a biscuit and chewing it with resolution.

Eliza offered Dora a plate of shortbread. 'Jane is quite the most intelligent of the Austens – we all agree on that.'

'While you are the most charming,' Jane replied.

Eliza laughed. 'Oh, Jane, I'm so glad you are here.'

'But Jane also has the advantage that she is not as well known in town as either my wife or I.'

'I am entirely unremarkable,' said Jane acerbically.

Henry smiled indulgently. 'Hardly, but if she is seen with you, no one will make the connection to us.'

Now it was beginning to make sense. Henry was delegating to his sister the job of keeping abreast of what she and Jacob discovered, rather than coming to and fro from their office himself and risking someone asking questions as to what business he had with them. Spinster sisters were frequently employed on the tasks the married ladies and gentlemen considered they did not have time to do, it being a truth generally acknowledged that sisters and aunts were at everyone's disposal.

'We will certainly write reports when there is anything to learn and send them to Miss Austen,' said Jacob, evidently thinking along the same lines as Dora. 'There's no need for her to come all the way into the West End to Bruton Mews.'

'No, no,' said Eliza. 'Dear Jane has our complete confidence and will prove an invaluable helpmate – she will be going with you as you investigate.'

'Indeed, she has as much at stake in this as we do and her powers of observation are unsurpassed,' said Henry firmly.

'Only because most of the world goes around with their eyes closed,' said Miss Austen.

'Indubitably an asset,' said Eliza. 'Would anyone like a second cup?'

Dora and Jacob emerged onto Sloane Street and turned back towards the city. By common consent, they did not discuss the case until they had left Knightsbridge and were unlikely to be overheard by anyone from the Austen household.

'What just happened?' asked Dora, unable to suppress her indignation any longer. 'Did Mr and Mrs Austen just foist on us their country mouse sister to help in a case of double murder with a seasoning of espionage, or am I in some fever dream?'

'They did,' said Jacob gruffly.

'Why? I mean to say, I know they don't know us like Captain Austen knows you, so they may not trust us, but don't they realise how foolish this is? I'm all for valuing my fellow women, but in this case, she will only get in the way. It's not fair on her to throw her into a situation for which she is not equipped.' That was what really had lit the fuse on Dora's temper – the fact that Henry and Eliza were risking their sister while staying safe themselves. 'Tell me, Jacob, what would she do if we came across a dangerous situation – and you have to admit we've faced too many of those recently to discount the possibility? What will Miss Jane Austen from Chawton do? Throw her bonnet at the villains? Give them a good telling off?'

Jacob allowed her to pace off some of her fury. He had to be sharing it. Unfortunately, the contract had been signed before this was sprung on them, so he was left trying to make the best of it. 'Is it really so foolish? Remember, the villain of this piece is already dead. We are charged to find the motive, not find more ne'er-do-wells.'

Dora snorted. 'Balderdash! If we do dig up scandal on a French count and countess, what's the betting it is going to be a very dirty business, tarnishing everyone who gets close?' Her confusion cleared. 'You know what? I think Miss Jane Austen is being sent as their man – by which I mean woman – in our investigation.'

'What makes you say that?'

'When I met him in the office, I warned Henry Austen we wouldn't make anything up, and he said he had a sister who would do that for him. I didn't understand what he meant then, but now I do. Jacob, we can't let her into our investigation: she'll twist everything we learn to make it into the pretty fiction her brother wants!'

Jacob frowned, not liking that one bit. He was even more of a stickler for the truth than she was. 'But the client demands her participation.'

'Can't we tell the client to go hang?' Dora was more than ready to throw over this investigation, no matter how interesting it had sounded at first. The conditions had become unacceptable and, besides, they didn't stand to earn very much. 'Really, it would be no sacrifice to let it drop.'

'But I owe Frank. My honour is involved. I will understand if you wish to keep out of it.'

Dora briefly glimpsed the exit from her predicament, then groaned. 'I can't, can I? Miss Austen will be expecting another female to chaperone her when out and about with you.'

'She's hardly of an age…' He let it hang delicately, but he meant that Miss Austen was long past her last prayers in the ridiculous husband hunt of the ton.

'Quite, but appearance will matter to a family like that. They engaged both of us on this case, assuming I'd be there. Dammit!'

Jacob pulled a sympathetic face. 'I'm afraid you won't be able to swear in front of her either, my love.'

'Bloody hell!'

'He did say she had an eye for detail.'

'We're the damned investigators, not her!' Dora knew she had to get her temper in check. It had to be the heat getting to her, the onset of her monthlies, and the prospect of a long dusty walk back to Bruton Mews from Knightsbridge village. Rather than give in to the impulse to growl, she said: 'Shall we hail a cab, spare ourselves the walk?'

His blue eyes twinkled at her. 'How about a cab and then an ice cream at Gunter's?'

The promise of sweet delight swiftly cooled her anger. Dora grinned up at him. 'An excellent notion.' She tucked her arm through his and squeezed fondly. 'That is exactly what the doctor ordered.'

Chapter Five

Gunter's Ice Cream Parlour

One of the benefits of their office was that it was around the corner from Gunter's at Nos. 7 and 8 Berkeley Square. The famous cake shop was a popular destination for those who wished to sample its ices in the summer, pastries in winter, and a good place to scout out female gossip and potential clients at all times of the year, or so Dora explained to Jacob when she presented her expenses for another trip for her and Kir to buy treats.

No wonder the boy was saying he liked London, thought Jacob as he held the door open for Dora.

Luck was with them. He pulled out a chair at a prime table in the window and Dora settled herself opposite his. The confectioner's was busy with the people spoiling their dinner with a late afternoon indulgence. It was a glitter of mirrors and silverware, cakes and jellies displayed on pedestals with gem-like vibrancy. He thought whimsically that it was somewhat like being inside the vault in the Tower of London where the Crown Jewels were displayed and discovering that they were edible. It was an image with which a cartoonist could have a great deal of fun, considering the Prince Regent's famous girth.

'Signorina Fitz-Pennington,' said the waiter with a welcoming smile as he trotted over with admirable efficiency. 'The usual?'

'Yes, thank you.' They both looked expectantly at Jacob.

'What's the lady's usual?' he asked with a raised brow.

'Burnt almond ice cream,' the waiter responded promptly.

'Hmm, interesting.' Jacob was tempted by the sound of that.

'If you order something different, then we can go halves,' said Dora with a gleam in her eye. He'd found her weakness and it was ice cream.

He scanned the list of offerings and picked on the most unlikely flavour just to tease her. 'I'll take the Parmesan cheese ice cream.'

Dora curled her lip, then thought better of it. 'I've not yet found an ice I don't like,' she said reflectively. 'Do your worst, sirrah.'

'Excellent choice, sir. Might I suggest you accompany that with a small cup of Italian coffee?' said the waiter.

'Oh, why not?' said Jacob.

'I'll have coffee too please – with cream,' said Dora.

Orders lodged with the kitchen, Dora and Jacob had time to look around them. The nursery-aged crowd were being ushered out by indulgent uncles and harassed maids who would have to deal with the children's excitement when they reached home. Several ladies were in earnest conversation, one displaying a ring, glittering evidence of a recent engagement. Then Dora stiffened.

'What?' he said softly.

Dora's expressive brown eyes flicked over his shoulder then back at him. 'Ruby at six o'clock.' In other words, Ruby Plum, Dora's actress friend from the Northern Players, was directly behind him. Embarrassingly for Dora and him, Ruby had recently taken up a new role as mistress of Jacob's eldest brother, thanks to an introduction they had inadvertently made in the Lakes. She was also approaching her third trimester of pregnancy – the child of an indeterminate father but one his brother had offered to raise and protect. In sum, she was a thoroughly scandalous person by most people's estimation. Jacob wasn't shocked by her, but he did find her selfishness unappealing, particularly as Dora didn't seem to mind being taken for granted. He minded for her.

'What's she doing?' asked Jacob in a low voice.

'She's debating whether to notice us.'

'Is she ashamed of us or does she think we are ashamed to be seen with her?' It was a fair question. This was a place not normally frequented by Ruby's kind of *demi-mondaine*, but then again, both he and Dora were hardly irreproachable members of society. 'What do you want to do?'

'Oh? I can do what I want, can I, and you won't be cross?' murmured Dora. They both knew she would do whatever she liked – it was a freedom she had earned. 'In that case...' She waved a hand. 'Mrs Plum! How delightful!'

Jacob turned in time to see a swift look of wily calculation pass over Ruby's pretty features before the lady moved to their table, a maid in tow.

'Miss Fitz-Pennington, it's been an age!' declared Ruby to

all the interested ears at other tables. In fact, it had been a matter of weeks since she'd left Jacob's cottage in Cumberland to take up residency in Viscount Sandys's love nest in Marylebone. She brushed a kiss on Dora's cheek and offered her hand to Jacob.

Jacob stood, bowed over her knuckles, and then pulled out another chair. 'Will you join us?'

'Only for a moment. I have errands to run. Shopping – it is so fatiguing.' Ruby sank gracefully onto the offered seat. 'You may wait for me in the shade, Betty,' she said to her maid.

Betty – who could be no more than fourteen – bobbed a curtsey and went outside, her eyes wide, taking in all the details of the high life she likely had never seen before.

'You? In Gunter's?' said Dora.

Ruby rubbed her bump, forget-me-not blue eyes alive with amusement. She had the roses-and-cream complexion that was in vogue, as well as charming ebony curls frothing around her heart-shaped face – very much a fashionable beauty. Her walking dress was of sprigged muslin with a light silk pelisse in pink – perfectly decent, but Jacob was sure Dora would tell him it was a costly garment. His Dora had a draper's eye for such things. 'I know,' Ruby said. 'Arthur would not approve but it is his fault. He sent me a pail of ice cream as a gift, and now I cannot get enough of the heavenly stuff. It's ambros— What's the word I'm looking for?'

'Ambrosia,' supplied Dora.

'Ambrosia. It's the only thing Junior appears to like.'

'Cravings are natural for a lady in your condition,' said Jacob smoothly, wondering at this thoughtfulness from his brother. Actually, on second thoughts, he didn't want to wonder about his brother's dealings with his ladylove, not when Jacob had to face his sister-in-law, Diana, at family gatherings. She did not deserve this disloyalty from her husband.

Ruby beamed at him. 'Oh, I do like you, Dr Sandys.' She cocked her head to one side. 'I don't suppose you can recommend a good accoucheur?'

'I'll send over some names,' Jacob promised, glad she hadn't asked him to be attendant at her lying-in. He had given up practising medicine unless it was an emergency and it would be in bad taste to attend his brother's mistress in such an intimate procedure.

'And they let you in here without protest?' murmured Dora. Dora had told Jacob of the many times she and Ruby had been turned away from shops and inns for the sin of being actresses.

'Oh, they are sweethearts – all of them,' said Ruby gaily, waving at the watching waiters. Even grouchy Mr Gunter smiled at her from behind the counter. 'They know people will keep coming for their exceptional ice cream even if an occasional bird of paradise alights among the sparrows.'

'Is that what you're calling yourself?' Dora's eyes glittered with laughter.

'There are worse names, Dora, which I'm sure you know.' Ruby turned her smiles on the waiter who was returning with their order. 'Oh, do tell me what they ordered, Giovanni!'

'The burnt almond and the Parmesan cheese, Signora Plum,' said the waiter, producing them with a flourish.

Ruby pulled a comical face. 'Good heavens, Dora, you really are extraordinary. Why not go for apricot or ginger if you must be different? Or the pistachio – at least that is a charming green colour.'

'I see someone else is eating her way through the menu,' said Jacob, leaning back so Giovanni could place a little cup of black coffee in front of him. The enticing odour of perfectly brewed espresso held him in rapture for a second. If Dora's weakness was ice cream, his might be a decent cup of coffee.

'*Buon appetito!*' said the waiter, with a little bow.

Ruby watched them both expectantly, like a spaniel gazing at her mistress to hand her a biscuit.

'What?' asked Dora.

'I'm waiting to find out if burnt almond and Parmesan are as foul as they sound.' Dora offered her a spoon which she refused with a delicate shudder. 'No, dear, you are my bellwether leading the flock of those of us with less adventurous tastes.'

'I already know that burnt almond is divine so I'd better try this cheese concoction.' Dora scraped a spoonful from the side of the pale-yellow ice. 'Together?' she asked Jacob.

He dug in his spoon. 'In all things.' He toasted her with his loaded utensil.

Ruby sighed. 'You two are adorable.'

In unison, they both ate their sample. It was … extraordinary. Jacob had been expecting a creamy taste, but the intense flavour of the Parmesan pushed it into a more fragrant area, countering the sweetness with a salty savour. He loved it.

'Dora?' he asked.

She was gulping her coffee. 'Tastes like smelly feet.'

Ruby chuckled with deep unladylike laughter, somehow surprising for someone of her petite frame.

'More for me then,' said Jacob.

Hesitating, Dora pushed her ice cream towards him. 'I did promise you half.'

'You know that I would never deny you anything you like.' He pushed it back and their eyes met in a charged gaze that said so much about things that had nothing to do with ice cream.

'Look at the pair of you! Turtle doves could learn a thing or two.' Ruby smiled with a hint of cynicism.

Shaking herself out of the moment, Dora turned her attention back to Ruby. 'How are you settling in at the house?'

Ruby wriggled with excitement. She was always at her happiest when the conversation turned to her. 'I'm getting new paper hung in all the reception rooms – Chinese scenes.'

'That sounds'—*expensive*—'pretty,' said Jacob.

'I'd love to see that when it's finished,' said Dora.

Ruby dipped into her reticule and pulled out a calling card. 'I'll hold a party. My parties are going to be famous.'

Jacob had no doubt about that.

Dora reciprocated with their business card. 'We're just around the corner. My room is two doors down from the office, in lodgings let by a retired wigmaker.'

Ruby read the address and sniffed. 'Dr Sandys, really? Can't you set her up in more style than this?'

Dora glanced nervously at the nearest table, but fortunately there were two strangers talking loudly in what sounded like Russian. 'Ruby, how many times do I have to explain that I do not rely on Dr Sandys for my living.'

'You're an idiot. You need me to look out for you.' Ruby turned in a businesslike fashion to Jacob. 'Dr Sandys, your brother stumped up in a fine fashion for me. I want for nothing. I'm swimming in silks and jewels.'

'How lovely for you,' he said tightly, wishing she would get the hint that neither of them welcomed these confidences.

'I realise you are a younger son so not as plump in the pocket, but you can surely do better than a mouldy old room in a mews? Not even a view of a garden square. It will not do!'

'I'm perfectly happy where I am,' said Dora with a bite in her tone.

Ruby patted her hand. 'If he's frigging you, he should pay for it. And I know he's frigging because I saw the proof in the Lakes.'

Unfortunately, the clientele chose that moment to lapse into one of its periodic silences and her last words were clearly audible to the nearest tables.

The engaged lady got up with a huff. 'Well, really!' She drew in her skirts as she passed, as if Dora and Ruby were polluting her.

'Ruby, you are the worst!' said Dora, not sounding too upset that her reputation had just been traduced in the heart of the ton.

Jacob couldn't act so sanguine. His anger rose at his brother's ladybird's carelessness. 'And how many times do we have to explain that Miss Fitz-Pennington is not my mistress,' he said, not caring that his voice carried to the fascinated listeners. 'In fact, you may congratulate us. During our recent sojourn in the Lakes with my brother the Viscount'—that should suggest all manner of respectable things—'I asked her to be my wife.'

'No!' All colour drained from Ruby's cheeks and she looked dangerously close to fainting. Jacob felt a qualm of conscience. Pregnant ladies should not be startled. 'Dora? Is this true?' Ruby asked.

Dora was looking at Jacob with exasperated amusement. 'In a manner of speaking.' She was probably remembering how he'd chosen the moment when he'd saved her from drowning in Windermere to spring his proposal upon her.

'Therefore, you may banish any idea of impropriety you thought you witnessed. You were merely seeing my transports of delight at being accepted by the lady I love and respect above all others.' Jacob knew he sounded like a prosy bore but he was too furious to care.

Dora frowned at him and said in an undertone: 'I said I would think about it, remember?'

Ruby turned horrified eyes on him. 'You aren't joking?'

'I've never been more serious in my life.'

To his displeasure, tears welled – and he didn't think they were tears of joy. 'But you can't!' Ruby wailed. For someone who so often played a part, he sensed he was seeing true emotion from her. 'You can't spoil it all for me! Dora!' She turned to her friend. 'Please, just live with him. I'll stop disparaging his arrangements for you. If you want to live in a shoebox, that is perfectly acceptable. But please don't marry him!'

Dora frowned. 'Ruby, this isn't the place—'

Ruby seized her hand and gripped it hard. 'Promise me!'

Jacob's momentary guilt had given place to anger. 'What right do you have to deny your friend her happiness?'

'Because if you … and her … if you do that, then he'll … you know what your brother will do!' Crystal tears trickled down her cheek which she dabbed away with Dora's napkin.

If Jacob married Dora, Ruby thought his brother would not continue to house Dora's best friend as his mistress. It would be too embarrassing – too complicated. Arthur wanted to keep actresses in their place as mistresses, not as society wives.

'Dammit, Ruby, this isn't about you!' hissed Dora.

Ruby rose swiftly, bumping the table with her stomach and making the cutlery rattle. 'Isn't it? Then think of the child.' With a sniff worthy of a duchess, she sailed out, beckoning her maid to join her with a flourish of her lace parasol. Jacob and Dora were left to face down the disapproval of the clients and the glee of the waiters.

Jacob's whispered curse was Anglo-Saxon and crude. 'That could have gone better,' he said aloud.

Giovanni brought unbidden two little flutes of champagne and placed them on the table. '*Per i fidanzati!*'

'Now you've done it,' muttered Dora to Jacob, while smiling sweetly as the society ladies whispered behind their hands. '*Grazie.*'

Well aware he'd set the cat among the pigeons with his bold declaration, Jacob raised the glass to the onlookers. '*Salute a tutti!*'

Chapter Six

Bruton Mews

After the excitement of the confrontation in Gunter's, Dora and Jacob retreated to the office. Dora's nerves were still humming from Ruby's departure, though she tried to maintain her pretence that it was amusing rather than alarming that her friend declared Dora was risking her happiness by seeking her own. Jacob was quietly fuming at the embarrassment, his expression set. Her lover was usually a mild-mannered gentleman, but he had a tipping point where his temper would flare – as she did. They had to talk this out, but they needed privacy for that.

This was not immediately forthcoming. When they got back, Alex and Kir were eating the dinner brought over from Lady Tolworth's kitchens while listening to Susan Napper deliver her report on the cheating maid. Susan, a mature actress with a matronly figure, had taken to investigation with tenacious skill over the past few months since they'd hired her. If there was a tedious watch to be kept on someone, Susan was the person to send. She didn't give up and appeared to have bottomless internal resources to prevent boredom. She'd told Dora she spent the time reciting all the lines from all the plays she had ever appeared in, the parts belonging to others as well as her own. As Dora knew from personal experience, the training an actor acquired in quickly conning parts for the ever-changing repertoire resulted in an excellent memory.

'She finally met her contact in the rag trade today,' Susan said, nodding to Jacob and Dora as they came in. 'You never guess what they were doing?'

'What, Mrs Napper?' Kir watched Susan with wide, adoring eyes. Susan was a hugger and Kir appreciated her warmth, regarding her as an honorary grandmother.

'They were only taking off the Brussels lace and replacing it with poorer quality stuff, expecting no one would notice, love. Who looks too closely at their petticoats after they've been purchased? Only washerwomen. If the lady's maid doesn't say anything, then it's a rare mistress who pays such close attention. They'd think it was just ordinary wear and tear making it look bad. They'd go out and buy a new one and it starts all over again.'

Dora squeezed Susan's shoulder in greeting. 'Did you get a name for the contact?'

'What do you take me for, duckie? Mrs Lamb. Lamb?' Susan crowed with laughter. 'She's a wolf in sheep's clothing if ever there was one.'

'Excellent. Please write it up and I'll take our findings to the client.' The butler in the household had become suspicious of his mistress's maid who appeared to have more money than she ought but had not known what she was doing to earn it.

'Kir, did you do your lessons yet?'

Kir wiped his mouth on a napkin in a gesture that mimicked Alex's impeccable manners. 'Yes, Miss Dora.'

She ruffled his mop of black hair affectionately. 'I'll mark them, and if you got your sums right you can go and play with your friends.'

He looked worried. 'What if I made mistakes?' Mathematics wasn't his strong suit. He was picking up reading far more swiftly.

'I'll still let you play, but we'll go over where you went wrong first, agreed?'

Looking relieved, he nodded.

Jacob had quietly been serving them dinner from the pot on the sideboard, handing her a plate of chicken casserole with summer vegetables. They joined their colleagues at the desk that served as a table when they ate. Dora made a note that they really should invest in a trestle table that could be set up for meals if this became a habit. It was nice to eat together – a makeshift family was forming around the agency.

'Where are Ren and Hugo?' asked Jacob, sitting down beside her in the chair Alex had vacated for him. Goliath Renfrew, the actor who specialised in Tom Thumb and other parts for small people, was out with Hugo Ingles, the portly player who was known for his Falstaff. With Drury Lane closed for rebuilding after the fire, there were many out-of-work actors happy to redeploy as investigators.

'They were following the husband from Harley Street. We found out that he has a mistress in Battersea and another in Lambeth,' said Alex. 'Lambeth's turn today.'

'Busy boy,' said Susan.

'Then the wife was right.' Dora frowned. It was an unpleasant case. The lady had noticed that the household finances were strained, but the husband claimed he had no money to pay the bills despite her generous dowry but a few years earlier. Her family had thought he would invest it, but he'd been frittering it away. She'd pawned some of her jewels to pay for an investigation rather than settle the accounts that happily were her husband's legal duty. He would be the one to go to debtors' prison, but it was no fun being the wife of a debtor, especially if she had little chance of extracting money out of him before the bailiffs arrived. 'I'm not sure what good the truth will do her.'

'If he's catting about, then at least she can deny him the marriage bed – save herself all sorts of nasty diseases that way,' said Susan philosophically.

'The law won't protect her.' It was nearly impossible for a woman to gain a divorce; separation was the best she could hope for.

'But the husband doesn't seem the violent sort, just weak. You can tell from the chin.' Susan pointed to her own firm jaw. 'If she has any brain, she'll work out an arrangement with him.'

'Perhaps we should send you to counsel her,' said Jacob. 'She might appreciate the voice of experience.'

Susan, a widow, scowled. 'I'll have you know my husband never strayed – he didn't dare!'

'But you've seen plenty who have done – that's all I meant,' said Jacob, quickly trying to dig himself out of the offence he had unwittingly caused.

Dinner eaten, schoolwork marked, everyone departed, Dora and Jacob were finally left alone in the office.

'Well, darling,' said Jacob, folding his arms. 'We appear to have a Ruby-shaped problem.'

'You don't have to keep to the engagement,' said Dora quickly. She had been thinking about it. She had barely got used to the idea that he was serious about his offer and was expecting it to fall apart at any moment, so this didn't come as a surprise. Someone of Jacob's exalted social status did not marry a bastard daughter of a Liverpool merchant, especially not one who had made a profession for herself on stage.

Jacob shook his head. 'You said you would consider marrying me, which from you is almost as good as agreement, and I'm not letting you back away from that – it was hard enough to persuade you.'

'But if your brother—'

'My bloody brother has nothing to do with it.'

'But he does. Ruby! The child!' The more Dora thought about it, the bleaker she felt about their situation, trying to go against the wishes of everyone they knew. What good could arise from a marriage under those circumstances?

'Your friend should be thinking of you for once.'

'I can't do this to her!'

'Why not? I can't understand why you are even friends with her. All I've seen is that she takes from you while offering scant back.'

How to explain the years of surviving together on the northern circuit, the laughter in rehearsals, the shivering together in winter, the dusty walks in summer sweating through the last item of clean clothing? Ruby had saved her life once, sending fishermen out to save her when she got in trouble in the water. They were comrades in hardship. For all her selfishness, Ruby would be there if Dora needed her, she was certain of that. And Ruby needed Dora now – needed her not to mess up the situation she had found for herself with a gentleman who was prepared to look after another man's child. 'I don't expect you to understand.'

Jacob looked like he was biting back several choice responses to that. Instead, he said:

'I refuse to live my life to please others. I suggest you do the same.'

He was right, of course, but how exactly was one to achieve that when aware of the cost? 'Maybe after the baby ... when things settle down.'

'Settle down? Dora, look at our last few months. When will things ever settle down?' He paced to the map and scowled at England. She knew what he was thinking. They had gone up and down the country several times recently, grieved for lost loved ones, hunted killers or been hunted by them – they hadn't chosen a profession that promised peace and quiet.

She really didn't want to hurt him, but neither did she want to hurt Ruby. 'I'm sorry.'

He turned on her, real anger in his expression. 'No, Dora, you don't get to do that. You don't get to spoil what we have because my brother is keeping a woman while he has a perfectly decent wife of his own. I save my pity for Diana.'

'But Ruby has nothing—'

'The fact that his mistress is a friend of yours is neither here nor there. He is the one at fault, not us.'

'But Ruby—'

He ran his fingers through his hair, tugging at the roots in a frustrated gesture. 'I'm not blaming your friend, Dora. I do realise that a woman in her situation has few good choices. But Arthur? He can bloody well reform and be the upright model husband and father he pretends to be and stop preaching at me for loving someone of a lower social standing!'

'This isn't about the quarrel you have with your brother,' said Dora.

'Oh, but it is. If he is prepared to throw over Ruby because I marry you, then that is on him, not me.'

'We have to acknowledge that what we do has consequences.'

'Yes, it does, but we aren't responsible for all of them. We offered to support her in town before all this, remember? That offer still stands. We're not sending her to the workhouse.'

Ruby wouldn't want that now, not swimming in silks and jewels with a house to furnish. That was the height of her dreams and she wouldn't recover from having that ripped away from her. Intellectually Jacob knew about poverty, but he hadn't lived it. Dora could tell that the gap between her and Jacob on this was too big to bridge at the moment. Yes, she had agreed to consider marrying Jacob, but she had not said if or when she would go through with it. That should give them enough time for second – and third – thoughts. Time for a change of subject.

'The Austens.'

With a sigh, Jacob accepted they were moving on and took a seat. 'The Austens – and chaperoning the spinster.'

'Shall we have the usual division of labour: you do the checks on the *comte* and *comtesse* in the court and high society, and I take the opera singers and the servants?'

He nodded. 'We play to our strengths. What about Miss Austen?'

'If she wants us to solve this quickly, then she will just have to swallow her pride and her prejudices against people of my station and come along in her observer capacity.' Dora grimaced. 'Quite what my connections in that world will make of her, I do not know.'

'I'm afraid I can't smuggle her into my club or the Houses of Parliament so I can't offer to swap places. You'll have to come up with a story to explain her presence with you.'

Dora came around the desk and sat on his knee, hoping he understood the signal that they were signing a truce between them. 'Do you think she'll wear a disguise?'

He snorted. 'Remember that I'm in debt to her brother. Please return her to the Austens unchanged.'

'I can promise unharmed but not unchanged,' said Dora. She smoothed a finger over his very kissable lips. 'Now, how about letting me show you my new room? I've finally got around to unpacking.'

He grinned and lightly bit her finger, sending delighted shivers up her spine. 'Oh, yes, show me your shoebox. I can truly say I've been looking forward to that all day.'

Chapter Seven

Dora had sent a message to Sloane Street that Miss Austen should meet her in the office at ten the next morning. She had instructed that the lady should wear her most fashionable clothes – no 'country cousin' looks if they wished to go into the world of opera singers and actors. Jacob had already departed for his club when on the stroke of ten the lady arrived, interestingly without a maid.

Dora held open the door to wave her into the office. 'You came alone?'

'I hardly think either of us requires another female companion,' Miss Austen said acerbically. 'I'm sure the staff at my brother's house have better things to do than trail after me.' She held out her arms to display her gown. 'Will I do?' She was wearing a red-spotted muslin trimmed with red braid – a stylish choice. Her attitude was daring Dora to criticise and Dora felt she would not come out well from that skirmish.

'You will do well,' said Dora, thinking her own muslin was

looking very dowdy by comparison. When she had some time to herself, she really must unpick the seams and turn the gown to extend its life.

'I understand you will need to explain my presence,' continued the lady, laughter lines at the corners of her eyes crinkling. 'I don't believe you are in the habit of taking a companion with you when you do your work?'

'You are correct.' Dora revised upwards her estimate of Jane Austen's intelligence. Eliza and Henry had not been merely flattering her when claiming she was the cleverest among them. The lady had a talent for wrong-footing her company and seizing the initiative. 'Do you have any suggestions? I confess I was at a loss when I was thinking about this last night.'

'I can imagine.' Was Miss Austen struggling not to smile?

'Do you by any chance have any musical skills? How is your piano playing?' Most ladies could play a few tunes on the pianoforte.

'Tolerable but nothing to boast of,' said the lady. 'I would not attempt to pass myself off as skilled before a real proficient.'

'Then what story can we present?'

'Are you going to explain to those you interview that you are looking into the death of the late *comte* and *comtesse*?'

'Word has got around among those in my world that I am working with Dr Sandys so yes, I was planning to do so.'

'The truth? Never a bad idea.' Miss Austen nodded thoughtfully. 'There is no chance of getting caught out that way. In my case, I suggest you tell them that I am an authoress researching characters for my next novel, but I wish to keep my identity private as ladies of my station do not put their names to their publications.'

Dora frowned. She supposed it was plausible – at a stretch. Authoresses were normally more colourful characters, well known in town like Miss Edgeworth or Madame D'Arblay, not spinster ladies from Hampshire. 'What shall we say you've written, if they ask, or is this your debut work?'

'I think I shall lay claim to the novel *Sense and Sensibility* – yes, that would do. It came out last year and the author is anonymous.'

'*Sense and Sensibility*! Oh, I loved that story.' Dora had borrowed the book from a lending library in York and devoured it in three delighted bites, rushing offstage to pick up where she'd left off. She'd almost missed a cue as she had reached the part when Marianne met Willoughby at the evening party in London.

'We Austens also enjoyed it very much. I consider I know it well enough to answer questions should anyone care to ask.'

'I hope the real authoress will not mind us taking her name in vain?' Dora gathered her notebook and pencil, preparing to go out.

'She sounds an eminently sensible lady and will not mind as it is in a good cause.'

Dora certainly hoped Miss Austen was right.

The only one of the big theatres open at present was Covent Garden, so Dora decided to start there to make a connection with the opera crowd. Many performers would be taking the summer to tour, but if they were in luck, there would be some rehearsing for the beginning of the season or for private concerts. After asking the porter what rehearsals (if any) were taking place, she led Miss Austen to the stage door on Hart Street and knocked.

A grizzled old man answered – the day shift. He was practically bent double with arthritis. They put beefier men on the door during performances to deter the admirers of the leading actors, but there was an unwritten rule in the theatre that retired stagehands should be accommodated with work where possible.

'Good day, sir,' said Dora offering her hand and a shilling. 'My name is Miss Fitz-Pennington—'

Before she could go any further, the man opened the door and grinned. 'Miss Dora Fitz-Pennington!' He still pocketed the shilling.

'You've heard of me?' Dora doubted very much the positive notices she had received for her Viola and Polly Peachum in the provinces had reached London.

'Oh, yes! You're the one who took on Susan, Ren and Hugo. They think they are being so discreet, snooping around on the tail of ne'er-do-wells, but they've been spotted – oh, yes, spotted!'

Naturally, employing people from the Shakespeare's Head Tavern a few doors away would not be missed by the theatrical crowd who went there to exchange news and grab a drink before and after the performance. Watching the agency's employees going about their new work had likely developed into a new spectator sport.

'They have proved to be splendid hires.'

'And that business in the Egyptian Hall!' The doorman tapped the side of his nose. 'We've all kept our tongues from wagging, but it's appreciated, miss, very much appreciated.' With the help of the theatre folk, Dora had walked into the hall with a booby-trapped cart to foil the plot laid by a French spy and to save Kir. What the doorman was appreciating she wasn't sure. Saving the boy, stopping the French gaining a piece of Elgin's Greek marbles, or perhaps delaying the opening of a rival entertainment establishment – all were possible.

'Fascinating,' murmured Miss Austen, gazing at Dora with renewed interest.

'We thank you for your discretion. May we come in? We'd like to observe a rehearsal,' said Dora, attempting to get back on the trail of their purpose for being here.

'But of course. Please go in.' The doorman did not so much as spare a second glance for her companion. 'The ones in today are in the Green Room, fourth door along that corridor.'

Dora felt an odd pang of homesickness as she made her way past the dressing rooms with that odour of the theatre that was partly grease paint, partly powder, and a distinct hint of sweat. Nowhere she had ever performed matched the splendours of Covent Garden, of course; this was the pinnacle to which all others aspired. It was exciting to get backstage here, even if it wasn't with a mind to performing.

'I do love the theatre,' sighed Miss Austen, looking about her with lively attention.

Jolted out of her reverie, Dora glanced at her companion. 'You attend?'

'Whenever I can – though I've never been behind the scenes. This is wonderful – faded grandeur, exactly as one would expect.' She patted the fringe of a frayed velvet curtain over an alcove with fond delight, like an aunt admiring the ringlets of a favoured niece.

'I thought you lived in the countryside?'

'Even country mice are allowed to visit their family in town from time to time.'

Thinking how quickly Miss Austen had come up with the story to explain her presence, Dora grew suspicious that she was in the company of an aspiring actress. The woman didn't have the stage presence to make a go of that, being neither beautiful nor memorably characterful – perfectly pleasant didn't get you cast. 'Did you ever want to go on stage?' She hoped she wouldn't have to be the one to let the lady down if that were her dream.

'Only in private theatricals. My father ran a school when we were growing up and we would often entertain ourselves with putting on a play – even so, they did tend to get out of hand as we youngsters took them to heart. It was easy to fancy yourself in love with a young man spouting fine words written for him by someone else, do you not find?'

'It is a hazard of the profession, to mistake the illusionary character for the reality.' At least Miss Austen talked about it in the past tense. Dora wouldn't have to tell her that the stage wasn't for her.

'Yes, I can well imagine that.'

Dora could now hear the chatter from behind the door of the Green Room and the trickle of notes from a piano. The original actors' waiting room in the sister theatre of Drury Lane had green-painted walls, but the name had now stuck as the communal space backstage in all British theatres, even little ones up north, no matter the colour of their decorations. She knew better than to knock and went in with all the confidence her five years treading the boards had given her. Two men and a lady stood around a piano with a seated accompanist, sheet music in hand. They turned on hearing the interruption and the female pianist's introduction tinkled away into nothing.

'May we help you?' asked the nearest man, a gentleman with a beak of a nose and flushed cheeks, likely in his fifties. He had a stature worthy of an alderman overly fond of mayoral banquets.

The lady arched one expressive brow – she was the epitome of an Italian beauty with her dark hair and eyes, the sort of heroine Lord Byron liked to immortalise in his love poetry. 'No autographs – we are working.' Her accent was distinctly Italian too, which told Dora who she was. She had seen prints of the woman from her younger days, though she was still a fine-looking personage in her early thirties. Occasionally Dora's work brought her into contact with her heroines and here was one of them.

'Madame Catalani, sirs, please forgive our interruption to your rehearsal. My name is Dora Fitz-Pennington and this is Miss Austen.'

The second gentleman, another well-padded singer with greying locks and smiling eyes, snapped his fingers. 'By Jove, the actress who has turned her hand to investigation – oh, yes, we've all been following your exploits with interest.'

Dora sighed inwardly that her hopes to go about incognito in Covent Garden might be ruined due to growing notoriety. 'Tis I.' She gave a theatrical bow.

'And your companion?' asked Madame Catalani.

'She—' Dora hesitated, not wanting to give the lie unless necessary.

'I am the author of *Sense and Sensibility*. I'm researching my next novel,' said Miss Austen happily. 'I must say, accompanying Miss Fitz-Pennington as she goes about her work is turning up some stimulating material.'

The soprano, famed for her three-octave range, who could command any price she named for a private performance, rushed over and kissed Miss Austen on the cheeks three times. '*È una bellissima storia!*' She showed the self-labelled novelist to a chair. 'Please, sit down. What do you want to know? Anything for the writer of that charming book. Will you write about an opera singer, yes? Someone who gives all for *amore*?'

'Something like that,' Miss Austen said with a sly smile.

With silent apologies to the real authoress, Dora took another chair at the table, pushing aside scripts for the next plays.

'Are you writing anything else?' asked the soprano, her attention all on Miss Austen.

'How kind of you to enquire. Indeed, the reception of my first work has encouraged me to try a manuscript I wrote some years ago.'

'Oh? And what is the theme?' asked the singer.

Careful, thought Dora, don't give the game away. She hoped Miss Austen could think on her feet.

'It's about first impressions,' said Miss Austen, 'and how they can so often be mistaken.' She shot a glance at Dora.

'*Perfetto!*' Madame Catalani was reminded of her manners when one of the gentlemen cleared his throat. 'Ah *sì*. This is Mr Incledon.'

The beak-nosed man bowed.

'You have a very fine tenor,' said Miss Austen. 'I heard you sing at a concert last year.'

Dora looked at Mr Incledon questioningly. 'I thought you

had gone separate ways with the management of Covent Garden?' The papers had been full of him severing his relationship acrimoniously with the theatre.

He winked. 'Don't tell them I'm here. It is dashed convenient for rehearsing.'

'We are practising for a concert at Vauxhall Gardens and this piano was available,' explained the other man. 'Charles Dignum.' He bowed and looked hopefully to Miss Austen in expectation that his fame had also preceded him.

This time Dora was able to satisfy his vanity. 'I've heard that you and Mr Incledon are leading members of the Glee Club?' This jolly set sang ballads and popular songs in the higher class of taverns of the city, an excellent way to swell the earnings for male singers.

The two men exchanged a grin. 'If you have a song you want sung, we'll oblige…,' said Mr Dignum.

'For a contribution to the drinking fund,' finished Incledon.

Miss Austen laughed. 'How splendid.'

'How may we help you, Miss Fitz-Pennington, Miss Austen?' asked Madame Catalani. 'I'm afraid our time for conversation is short as we are expected elsewhere, and we must practise.'

'Of course,' said Dora, grateful for the help steering them back to the matter at hand. 'I'm afraid it is a rather shocking case. We are seeking information on the late Comte and Comtesse D'Antraigues. Our client wishes to find out why they died – what drove their killer to take that step and if he acted alone.'

Madame Catalani looked stricken. 'Their poor son, Julien. He must be full of questions why such a terrible thing could happen to him.' She had leaped to the conclusion that the son was the one asking for the investigation – a logical deduction, and one which helpfully kept the banker out of the picture. 'And poor Antoinette! Why would anyone want to do such a terrible thing to her? To go from being the top of the bill at the Paris Opéra to … to that.' She turned to Miss Austen, providing the fictitious authoress with the background she was supposed to be collecting. 'Her career came before my time, but it was said even the late King Louis admired her. I have been compared to her on many occasions, and I have always regarded it as the highest of compliments.'

'I heard something about a singing school?' said Miss Austen.

The lady smiled slightly. 'I believe that was the idea of Her Grace the Duchess of York, but the *comtesse* no longer had the voice or the persistence to make much of the idea. Besides, I never saw them struggle for money. Why work? I would not if I did not have to sing for my supper, as you English say.'

'Indeed. I visited their house,' said Miss Austen. 'They lacked for nothing – servants, fine artworks, and they were beautifully dressed as only the French know how.'

'You were there?' asked Madame Catalani. 'Then you know as much as or more than I do.'

Her comment reminded Dora that she had not yet gained Miss Austen's full impression of the couple they were investigating. As a woman with a sharp eye, she was a valuable source of information that Dora must not neglect.

'I met them only once,' demurred Miss Austen.

'If not from performing or teaching, does anyone know where their money came from?' asked Dora.

Mr Dignum shrugged. 'I always assumed they had family

money or jewels, enough to set them up in style when they fled the revolution.'

There were only so many gemstones one could sew into a hem or smuggle in a packing case. The family estates would have been confiscated and Dora doubted they would have been able to retrieve their wealth if, when Napoleon's regime allowed some nobles back in favour, they had stayed away in London.

Incledon opened his mouth to say something, then snapped it shut.

'Dear sir, anything you tell us will be in confidence,' said Miss Austen, doing Dora's job for her.

'Perhaps I should not say this as the gentleman is dead, but I would not be the first to notice that the *comte* had many friends,' said Incledon. 'He was known to tip well for any gossip about the goings on in the government or in the households of people of influence.'

That did not look good for Henry Austen's hopes that they could separate the double murder from any treasonous activities.

'We saw him often at the Glee Club. My impression – my *first* impression', Dignum made a bow towards Miss Austen, 'was that he was a rackety gentleman, used to living on a lavish scale and determined to continue to do so even without the family estate to supply his spending. He was keen on entertainment and parties. It was always something of a wonder that he and the *comtesse* could afford to move in such exalted circles.'

'Put it like this, if he was short to cover a round, neither of us would've lent him any money,' said Mr Incledon.

'Lord, no,' chuckled Mr Dignum. 'You'd never see that money again.'

They were helpfully creating a picture of an aristocratic couple who got by on the fumes of reputation long after the oil in their lamp had been exhausted.

'We all like gossip, but were you ever worried that he was making enemies by collecting so much?' said Dora.

'You are asking if anyone would kill him over it?' said Mr Incledon.

'That was one of my questions, yes.'

'Not to my knowledge. He collected gossip but I never heard that he passed it on indiscreetly. You wouldn't kill someone for what they knew about you, would you, only for what they repeated.'

You'd be surprised, thought Dora.

Chapter Eight

Brooks's Club

There was a familiarity to a gentleman's club that Jacob knew many men found comforting. It was a mixture of a donnish high table and college library with a whiff of a father's study. Many romped up the steps in delighted anticipation of membership as soon as they were of an age, believing it signalled their entry into adulthood. No more being taken to task on the carpet before the parental desk; now they could sit behind it and opine, berating their own sons when the time came. There were also no women to be seen, no petticoat government, as members disparagingly put it. Jacob had always disliked such sentiments, but since meeting Dora and hearing her views on a woman's place in society, he'd come heartily to despise the arrogance of his sex. They would call him a radical but he thought it natural justice that the scales be rebalanced between the sexes one day, perhaps even allowing women to enter clubs like this, though they might have better things to do with their time.

He kept these thoughts private as he sat in the quiet Reading Room, flicking his way through the newspapers while on the lookout for a friend he could pump for information. He needed someone who had a foot in wilder circles as well as the tame ones of court and Parliament – and he had the very person in mind. The only issue was whether his old schoolfriend was still in the country, as so many were, or if he had returned to town. He should check the society column to see who was coming and who was going.

Fortunately, his watch was rewarded before he turned to that column.

'Knighton!'

Ben Knighton turned on hearing his name called. He grinned at Jacob and hurried over. A stocky man who would've made a good docker had he been born working class, Knighton had married well and was enjoying the substantial income of his family's manufactory in Derby. Schoolmates since Eton, Jacob had last met him a few months ago when he was investigating the Hellfire Club. Knighton had hung around on its edges for a while before coming to his senses, and had helped Jacob with some crucial information.

Knighton shook his hand vigorously. 'Thank goodness there's someone worth speaking to in London. The capital is dead – dead! Not a decent party to go to until Parliament returns in the autumn. Shall we have breakfast?'

They removed to the dining room where the waiter served them a full English breakfast and coffee made to Jacob's taste – strong and black. Knighton grimaced and added three spoonfuls of sugar to his cup.

'Sorry about the old pater. I'll be at the memorial,' Knighton said, taking a sip.

Jacob twitched the sleeve of his black jacket, conscious that his clothes advertised the loss and would continue to do so for the period of mourning. His father had been buried in Westmoreland at their country seat with only local dignitaries present. Arthur was planning a much bigger commemoration at Westminster Abbey once the ton returned to town. 'Thank you.'

'I heard he left you and your siblings well set? Looked after the family coffers so that the girls have dowries and you won't be hard up?'

A nobleman didn't talk specifics about how much money he had, though everyone knew, of course. Being from trade, Knighton had fewer reservations about raising the subject. 'I am some way from begging on a street corner.' Then Jacob guiltily remembered the disabled serviceman to whom he'd tossed a coin the day before. Now he thought about it, it struck him that it was possible he himself had done the amputation in some field station in Portugal that had left the man with only one leg. He should've stopped to ask – it was no excuse that there were so many begging soldiers on the streets and highways.

It was wretchedly inconvenient to have a conscience sometimes.

'And what was this about the Hellfire Club going up in smoke? Your name was mentioned.' Knighton waggled his brows. Jacob's attention was drawn to the scar on Ben's lip that he had given him when they were at school. They had fought then over a schoolboy version of the club – Knighton had been in favour of naughty irreligious drinking parties where guests dressed up as lascivious monks and nuns; Jacob had found the tone cruel and crude so had been against. Boys being boys, this had led to a scrap behind the cricket pavilion. 'I believe you've put paid to the club once and for all?'

'I had very little to do with it,' he murmured. Dora had been the one to set fire to the dangerous secrets held by the corrupt leaders of the club. The Hellfire Club, if it still existed after that shock, had gone very quiet. Jacob suspected it had just gone even further underground as you couldn't stop people exploring their darker urges.

'Hmm,' said Knighton but he let the subject drop – he had so many more he wished to raise. 'But have you really gone into business with an actress, private enquiries or some such? I have to say I was dubious when I heard the rumour.'

'Her name is Miss Fitz-Pennington and yes, we are investigating private matters, discretion guaranteed.'

He could see Knighton filing away the information. He didn't mind because it might drive new custom to their office. 'Such as?'

'Return of stolen items, infidelity, fraud.' He could have added murder, treachery and spying, but Knighton didn't need any more fuel to add to his speculations.

'Very useful, if somewhat surprising. Then again, you surprised us all by going into medicine so perhaps I should always be prepared for the unexpected when I seek news of you.'

'That would be wise.'

'I must bear your agency in mind. Not that I suspect my dear wife of anything immoral – she's rather Methodist in her tastes and will never give me cause to doubt her – but you can't let the servants take advantage now, can you?'

'Quite so.' Jacob attacked his bacon, enjoying the salty taste in contrast to his coffee.

Knighton wasn't finished. 'I hear your brother is less than pleased by your choice of profession.'

'He has made no secret of the fact, but I do not feel inclined to live my life to please the viscount. He has so many others to do that for him. My turn: what brings you to town at this time of year?'

Knighton grimaced. 'I am in the cotton trade as you well know, so you can probably guess.'

'Business?'

'Exactly. We don't take the summer off for parties and making a tour of the country like you blue bloods – present company excepted. It's very tedious really but I had to see our bankers to arrange credit for a new loom we are setting up.' He cut up his sausage into tiny circles, swiping them through the egg yolk before eating. He chewed meditatively. 'This steam power business is expensive. The mechanics are always claiming we need the new and improved version so here I am, trying to persuade the city that I know what I'm talking about.'

'You should've brought one of your mechanics with you.'

Knighton looked at Jacob with shocked surprise. 'You know, that's a dashed good idea. Why didn't I think of that? If they discombobulate me with the engineering talk, then why can't they do the same to my manager, Brighouse, at the bank?'

The waiter topped up the coffee pot. 'Will there be anything else, sirs?'

'Not at the moment. Thank you,' Jacob waited for the waiter to retreat. 'Knighton, there's something I want to—'

'Uh-oh, it seems this isn't just a chance meeting.' Knighton helped himself to a slice of toast which he slathered with butter and marmalade. 'I require fortification against whatever it is you want to ask.' He took a bite. 'Go on.'

Jacob smiled, remembering he'd always liked Knighton, even when he was an idiot at school for admiring secret societies and hellfire antics. Jacob wouldn't have bothered to fight him if he had cared less. 'The Comte and Comtesse D'Antraigues.'

Knighton swallowed with difficultly. 'Lord, Sandys, you do know how to put a man off his breakfast. Messy business. Stabbings, weren't they? Gushing blood all over the pavement like an awful Jacobean revenge tragedy. I heard that a crazed servant went after them with a knife. Must say I looked askance at my man for a few days after that – asked him if he ever felt driven to slit my throat while he's shaving me.'

'And what did he say?'

'He said "Frequently, sir, but never to the point of taking action."' Knighton mimicked the low voice of his valet.

'How extraordinary – a truthful servant.'

'He's been with me since I was a boy. I made sure I gave him an extra day off and a rise in his wages after that.'

Jacob sensed Knighton and his valet enjoyed this kind of banter frequently. 'It is a shame the *comte* did not have such a faithful retainer.'

'Indeed.'

'What have you heard about the murder?'

'You mean why it was done?'

Jacob nodded. The details of how it happened would be available in the account of the inquest and Dora was following that up. He wanted to know what people were saying was the motive, because it was this aspect that worried Henry Austen. If Knighton, a man with his ear to the ground, was linking the banker to the crime then it might be too late to keep their name out of it.

'On the surface of it, it looks like a disgruntled man who quarrelled with his employer,' said Knighton. 'Wouldn't you say?' He glanced at Jacob for confirmation.

'On the surface, yes.'

'But to kill two people – the wife as well, a lady with whom the manservant had far fewer dealings – that is strange.'

'Indeed.'

'Was it a fit of madness? I believe the coroner concluded something to that effect.'

'That is what he ruled.'

'Then why not go after the onlookers – there were several, according to the newspapers, other members of the household. And the son survives.'

'True.'

'Instead, your red-handed murderer quietly goes upstairs and shoots himself. Peculiar.'

'I agree. It was a showy murder. Why not take yourself out in front of the aghast audience?'

Knighton pointed his triangle of toast at Jacob in agreement. 'Yes! I've heard people wondering if it was a crime of passion – he loved the *comtesse* but knew his affection was hopeless. Killed the man who had her, killed her so no one else would enjoy her charms, then killed himself when all hope was over.'

That was exactly what Henry was hoping people would believe. 'That is a possibility.'

Knighton snorted. 'Hardly! The *comtesse* was old – fifty-five at least! She was a charmer in her youth. Word is that she was the *comte*'s mistress before being his wife and neither was very loyal to each other in the bedroom. But fifty-five! I think she was well past her season of inspiring such jealousy. No, I don't believe that for one second.'

Henry Austen's hopes of deterring society's interest from his bank's involvement vanished like a popped soap bubble.

'What do you think happened?' asked Jacob.

A knowing glint entered Knighton's eyes. 'If you are asking, then there is more to it than madness.'

Dammit. Henry Austen was reigniting a fire that had begun to go out. By asking these questions – and how could he do his job without raising the subject? – Jacob could not help but spark interest in the minds of men like Knighton – well-connected, gossiping gentlemen. He'd gone too far to back away now.

'I honestly don't know. I've been asked to find out what happened and that's what I'm doing.'

'What do you think you know?' asked Knighton astutely.

Jacob shook his head and laughed softly. 'I thought I was the one asking the questions. I don't know much about him, other than what is generally known, that he was an émigré and his wife a former opera star.'

Knighton looked grave. 'That was the flash and glitter that was meant to distract the eye. Did you know that they had two houses? Two! One in town and another at Barnes. You don't get to have two houses without money coming from somewhere.'

'And you know where the money came from?'

Knighton nodded, leaning closer. 'I have a friend in the Foreign Office. For all his aristocratic airs and graces, D'Antraigues only survived with a roof over his head because he had a generous government pension. We Brits were keeping him in luxury. Can't say I'm in favour of that kind of thing, giving money to a Froggy foreigner.'

'And what did he do to earn that favour?'

'What indeed?' He sat back. 'I'll leave you to work that one out.'

Jacob had been entertaining the theory that the *comte* might have been feeding information to the French, acting out that he disliked Napoleon to disguise the fact that he was spying for the old country. He and Dora had met a Frenchman like that very recently in the Elgin investigation, and Monsieur Percy would not be the only one in the émigré community. Yet if the money was coming from British government coffers, it suggested the *comte* had been trusted by the administration or provided a service they thought valuable.

'Do you know how much he was worth to them?'

Knighton smiled, delighted to be asked. 'One thousand a year. My friend in the FO was outraged when he compared it to his salary.'

The amount shocked Jacob. 'Well, that explains at least one of the houses, doesn't it?' he said dryly.

'Small change for a Sandys, I've no doubt,' said Knighton with a wink, 'but yes, his fine words must have buttered a few parsnips.'

Chapter Nine

Covent Garden

Miss Austen pulled on her white cotton gloves as they left Covent Garden, a prim gesture that was out of place in the district known for its theatres, whores and cabbages. The lady was behaving as if they'd just emerged from a church service, which got on Dora's nerves.

'That was very informative,' Miss Austen said, looking back at the pillars of the theatre's classical façade, a smile hovering on her lips.

Dora wasn't feeling so sanguine. She hadn't gained many answers from the opera singers, only more questions. 'You think so?' She headed towards Long Acre.

'To see what life is behind stage, how they speak and behave – yes, I'd say it was very informative.'

'I think you are taking your story about being a novelist rather to heart.' Dora hailed a cab. The banker was footing the bill and she doubted he would like his sister to walk all the way to their next destination.

'Where to, love?' asked the jarvey, pulling his carriage up beside them.

'Barnes, please.'

His eyes widened. 'You got enough for that fare? It's a long way.'

'I do, sir.'

'Fair enough.' He glanced at Miss Austen. 'Want me to get down and help you in?' Cabbies rarely descended from their seat behind their horses, but he must have realised he had a real lady as a customer.

'We will manage,' said Dora, helping Miss Austen into the carriage compartment.

'All right, ladies,' the jarvey declared, flicking his whip to tickle his horse into motion. 'We're off to the country.'

'May I enquire as to where we are going next?' asked Miss Austen, trying not to sound put out that Dora had not consulted her on their next move.

'To the scene of the crime.'

'Ah, Barnes Terrace. Of course.' Her hazel eyes watched the world passing by, seemingly missing no detail.

'You visited them there?'

'No, we called on them in Queen Anne Street. I remember that they had an excellent collection of paintings, but the *comte* would insist on speaking French so our communication was somewhat limited, Eliza having to translate. The son is very musical. I wonder what will become of him now?'

'It's good he has a talent to fall back on.' Dora let a few minutes of quiet thought pass as she debated whether or not to raise what was concerning her. It niggled away like an itch that had to be scratched. 'I wasn't comfortable when we were in the Green Room.'

'Oh?' Miss Austen turned to face her. 'In what way? You looked perfectly at home to me.'

'I wasn't comfortable with the way you took credit for another woman's success.'

Something closed down in Miss Austen's expression, her friendliness going inside like a maid whipping in the washing as a rain cloud threatens. 'I don't think it matters. We have a greater cause we are pursuing.'

'I wonder if it is the same one.'

'What do you mean?' Miss Austen could summon a haughty tone when she felt affronted, Dora noted.

'Dr Sandys and I are after the truth. Your brother said he relied on you to spread fictions.'

Miss Austen rolled her eyes. 'Oh, Henry!'

'We won't be involved in misrepresenting the facts about two people who are unable to defend themselves, and neither should you, pretending, as you do to care about what becomes of the son. Think of him if you decide to spread falsehoods.'

'I'm not pretending—'

'Are you not? You get admiration from your favourite opera performers by stealing another woman's reputation, even making claims for her next work. What happens if that gets back to her? She might already have another novel about to come out... What if someone influential like Madame Catalani claims she is disappointed that it wasn't the story she was expecting, or Mr Incledon says the authoress herself had promised but not delivered?'

'You are taking this too seriously.' Miss Austen folded her hands and stared out at the passing trees of Hyde Park.

'Only someone who has never had to worry about where their next meal is coming from would say that.'

Miss Austen snorted, adding fuel to Dora's temper.

'What if the writer is depending on her literary success for her living?'

'Few people can earn enough from writing to live on.'

'That's what your sort think. All the people you know have safety nets spread under the tightrope; nearly everyone I know will break their necks if they fall because there is nothing to catch them.'

'What an excellent image,' murmured Miss Austen, but that only further inflamed Dora's temper. 'Like Lucy Steele, the unprotected female stealing Elinor's chance, morality go hang, because she is desperate.'

'This isn't a story! You can't go stealing someone's reputation without a thought of what it means for them. I regret I agreed to let you come.'

Her piece said, Dora folded her arms and glared at the back of the cab horse. Miss Austen would likely leap out and complain to her brother at her treatment and get them thrown off the job they had been given. She wouldn't mind, pleased to be shot of the annoying Austens, but Jacob would feel his honour had been impugned.

Blast. The client had to be humoured. She was going to have to apologise, wasn't she?

Before she could speak, Miss Austen cleared her throat.

'Thank you.'

'Thank you for what?' grumbled Dora.

'For caring about the writer's reputation. I will be more circumspect in future. My excuse is that my excitement at meeting the opera singers made my tongue run away with me. I wanted them to approve of me.'

'I can understand that.' She felt herself relenting a little.

'It is far more exciting to be the mysterious writer of a novel than plain Miss Jane Austen from Hampshire.'

'There's nothing wrong with being…' Dora struggled for a polite way of saying an ordinary woman from a village.

'Being a spinster whose brothers and sister-in-law are much more interesting than she is? Miss Fitz-Pennington, I know what I am and how others see me. Occasionally, it is pleasant to surprise people to be something else, someone of note.'

'You're talking to an actress. I know all about worrying where one's name appears on the billing.'

'I imagine you do. Families are the same. I'm not expecting you to like me, or even understand me, but I do think we can work well together if you allow it.' She held out her slim gloved hand. 'Are we agreed?'

Dora hesitated, running back through what they had said and realising her main issue had not been addressed. 'Will you misrepresent our findings to save your brother's bank?'

Miss Austen pursed her lips. 'I am more likely to be silent on the subject than lie about it.'

'That's not an answer.'

Miss Austen sighed and dropped her hand. 'I suppose it is not.'

Arriving at Barnes, they descended from the cab and sent the jarvey on his way with a handsome tip. Dora had a quick word with a crossing sweeper and then headed for the nearest tavern, the White Hart. According to the lad, the inquest had taken place in the inn and it was likely the landlord would be taking a personal interest in the case, not least because talking about it would drive customers to his taproom. The sweeper had earned himself sixpence with that intelligence.

Miss Austen trailed in her wake.

Dora went up to the bar and tapped a shilling on the counter in front of the russet-haired pub landlord, his face and hands speckled with freckles to match his locks. One of his eyes wandered, giving him a boss-eyed gaze. He wouldn't be winning any prizes in a beauty contest. 'A glass of gin and information please.' She turned to her companion. 'What's your poison?' She knew her tone lacked civility, but irritation had that effect on her.

'A little wine wouldn't go amiss.' Miss Austen's tone was humble, but Dora wasn't buying what she was selling.

Dora relayed the order and waited for the landlord to present the two glasses. 'Why don't you go and sit over there.' She gestured Miss Austen to take a seat in the window. She had had enough of having the woman hanging on her apron strings all morning, and landlords were better tackled one on one.

With a nod, Miss Austen took her drink to the table and drew out a notebook.

The landlord jerked his head in her direction. 'What's her deal?'

'She's a writer,' said Dora.

'Do I know her?' He was wondering if he had a customer he could boast about to future patrons.

'Not famous. You won't have heard of her.'

He wiped the clean top of the bar. 'All right. What

information is it that you're after?' He flicked his gaze up and down her, trying to judge her social standing from her clothing. 'Husband run off? Sorry – can't help you there.'

'Do I look married?' He smirked. 'Nothing like that.' She put one of her calling cards down on the counter. 'I work for an agency making private enquiries for our clients. I've been asked to find out as much as I can about the double murder that took place here in July.'

His interest sparked. 'Now *that* I can tell you about. But it's worth more than a shilling.'

'Naturally.' She placed several more coins on the counter.

He huffed. 'I don't come cheap.'

She laughed and put another down. 'That's my limit or I'll have to walk home.'

He swept them into his apron pocket with a grin. 'They had the inquest in here.'

'I know that.'

'I had to speak before it.'

'That I did not know. What did you say?' She sipped the gin to put him at his ease. See, they were just settling into a lovely little gossip about things he would probably talk about for free.

'I told 'em how that Lorenzo – he was an odd fish of an Italian – came in here on the very morning around eight o'clock and downed a glass of gin just like the one I served you. Then he went off and killed his master and mistress.'

Dora wondered if the killer had resorted to the gin to screw himself to the sticking point, or perhaps he was a drunkard and that was part of the reason for the violence. 'An Italian? I thought he was a deserter from the French army.'

'He was – but he was recruited in Italy for Bonaparte's

army. If the newspapers have it right, Old Boney has gobbled up most of Europe and, like them Roman Emperors, he takes all nations into his army. But never you fear, we'll beat him in the end. Rule, Britannia, eh?'

That didn't feel very likely with Napoleon striding across Europe, heading for Russia, but Dora wasn't here to talk military campaigns. 'Had Lorenzo been in here before?'

'Oh, yes, he was a regular what with the house only being a couple of doors down. Regular bit of trouble he was too. Temper like a tiger and proud as anything. No wonder he deserted from the French army. That weren't principle; that was not liking being told what to do, if I know anything about a man's character.' His expression turned pensive. 'Some of my girls thought him handsome, but I didn't see it. We all knew to walk softly around him, if you know what I mean?'

'I do indeed. Were you surprised to hear what he had done?'

''Course I was! He wasn't drunk – I wouldn't've let him go out of here if I thought he was a danger to anyone.' He said that quickly, to shield himself from any of the blame. 'It was morning – he came in, one drink – then off to commit carnage. Talk about unexpected!'

'But not unimaginable, if he had a temper?'

The landlord scratched his chin. 'Now that's a trickier question. In the inquest it sounded like he'd planned it. He knew the lord and lady had weapons in their rooms, primed pistols and daggers. The maid, Susannah Black, nice girl, said he'd fired one of their pistols two weeks earlier, and was told off for doing so.'

'They had loaded pistols in both bedrooms?' Now that was a telling detail.

'Must've been terribly afraid of burglars, mustn't they?' He gave her a hard look suggesting he had his suspicions. 'Or old enemies.'

And the couple didn't sleep together. That wasn't unusual in high society, but if they were fearing an attack, they hadn't joined forces for defence. That suggested a rift in the marriage. Were they seeing other lovers?

'Leaving loaded pistols lying around does seem like a recipe for disaster,' said Dora.

'You're right there. I prefer a cudgel – doesn't need loading and sorts out the unruly.' He drew one from under the counter.

'You are very wise.' But if they still had loaded pistols in the house several weeks after Lorenzo had fired one, it sounded as if they did not suspect he would turn the weapons on them. If old enemies were after them, they thought the danger would come from outside. Had they feared reprisals from Napoleon? It wouldn't be the first time a despot had sent people to kill his enemies abroad. 'You mentioned Susannah Black, the maid. Do you know where I can find her?'

He nodded. 'She's still at the house. Julien, the new *comte*, has asked her to shut the place up. He don't want anything to do with it. Who would? The owner is going to have a devil of a job letting it again with that blood staining the doorstep.'

'Thank you. Is there anything else I should ask you, so that I get my money's worth?'

He chuckled. 'So many things, love, but none of them about that murder. Good luck to you.'

With a nod to Miss Austen, Dora headed back out onto the street. Her companion joined her, putting her notebook away.

'Helpful?' Miss Austen asked.

'Yes. The maid who gave evidence at the inquest is still at the house, so we go there next.'

It was only a few doors away, which gave Miss Austen no chance for further questions. Dora wished she could demand the lady stay in the tavern, but had no authority to do so, not when the client was paying for this. She had, however, to establish some rules.

'I anticipate Susannah Black will be deeply upset over what she witnessed and likely to retain some loyalty to the family she serves. We had better not mention your cover story of you writing a book or she will think we are muckrakers digging for scandal to sensationalise in the press.'

'Then we should tell her the truth – that my family are friends of the *comte* and *comtesse*. It is possible she will remember my visit last year; she will know my brother and sister-in-law.'

Dora nodded, much happier with this solution than spreading yet more lies. 'Agreed.'

She knocked on the door of a fine terrace house which looked out over the brown waters of the Thames. The retreating tide was leaving the muddy banks bare, barges and pleasure boats huddled in the deepest parts of the channel. The air was rank with the weed baking in the sun and the distinct odour of drains. After a pause, she could hear footsteps inside and the door opened a crack. A young woman in a mob cap peered around the edge, chain still on.

'Yes?'

'Susannah Black?'

The woman's pale blue eyes grew cold with suspicion. Her skin had the papery pallor of someone who had been indoors too long, like a house plant starved of sunlight. Dora had the odd sensation that she was talking to a ghost. 'Who's asking?' she whispered.

Dora introduced herself and her companion.

'My brother and Eliza want to find out what really happened to your mistress and master,' said Miss Austen, bumping Dora to one side. Dora didn't bump her back but it was a close-run thing. 'I hope you don't mind us coming to you for help?'

Unbending a little, the maid pushed the door closed, but only so she could release the chain. 'You'd better come in then.'

She opened the door wide enough for them to slip inside. The foyer was full of packing cases, all neatly labelled.

'It's only me now,' said Susannah. 'The carrier is coming for these tomorrow and then that's done.' Dressed in black with a white apron that hung off her bony shoulders, she looked as if she had missed a few meals.

'Do you have a place to go to?' asked Miss Austen, placing a gentle hand on the young woman's forearm.

'I'm going home – to Dorset. I've had enough of city life.' She waved them to take seats on the cases. 'Sorry – the chairs have already gone to the auction house.'

'Do you remember me, Susannah?' asked Miss Austen. 'I was a guest of the late *comte* and *comtesse* last year at a musical evening.'

Susannah wrinkled her nose. 'Truth be told, miss, I don't, but I remember your sister-in-law. Pelisse of green merino cloth, gold buttons, ermine tippet?' A little life was returning to the wraith-like girl.

'You have an excellent memory. Yes, I remember she wore that – very becoming.'

'Madame Antoinette', Susannah's voice shook a little at the

mention of her mistress, 'asked me to change the buttons on hers when she saw how well it looked.'

'Susannah, we understand that you've told the inquest everything you knew about the incident, but would you mind repeating it to us now, along with anything else you've remembered since?' asked Dora, thinking it was high time she, the professional, took over the questioning.

The maid swallowed and looked away up the empty stairs, eyes brimming. How often this grand house must have echoed with company and music and now it was home only to the shades of the departed. 'Do I have to?'

'Of course not – we are friends, not the law; however, it might help your late mistress if we can understand what really went on. It would give us the ammunition to counter any slander against them.'

Sharpness returned to Susannah's expression, drying up her tears. 'What slander? She was a good woman, she was!' Her voice now had the snap of a birch rod to it.

'We know that,' said Miss Austen calmly, butting in again – that really had to stop, 'but unfortunately the ton has not yet had time to dig into the crime as it happened right as the season ended. When they come back, the gossip will flare up again and we wish to douse the flames before they spread.'

With a nod, Susannah acquiesced. 'It was a normal morning. Hah!' She rubbed her hand over her face wearily. 'I suppose that's the way of this kind of thing – it blows up out of the blue, the storm that sinks the ship. Like the one that killed my brother off Portland.'

'You were on duty?' prodded Dora when Susannah looked as if she'd run out of words, wandering in memories of those she'd lost.

Susannah forced her spine to straighten. 'Yes – very busy, in fact. We were about to move to Queen Anne Street and were on the point of getting into the carriage. I'd packed her favourite gown – she was going to a p-party.' Her voice hitched and she trembled, hugging her arms to her sides.

Dora shot Miss Austen a look, warning her not to interfere. 'Then what happened?'

'Hebditch had brought the carriage round, so I came down the stairs with the mistress. I saw Lorenzo just there.' She pointed to the entrance. 'So I asked him to open the door for madame, you know, like he normally would. He ignored me – just brushed past us as if we weren't there.'

'He didn't attack the *comtesse* when he had the chance?'

'No, not then. He went upstairs as if he owned the place. It weren't right – I knew something was off about him, but what could I do? Then we heard gunfire. The *comte* came to the top of the stairs, staggering – he wasn't a young man so I thought he'd had an accident with his pistol when packing it up for the journey – but then Lorenzo appeared behind him and … and stabbed him in the back. When the *comte* fell, we saw that Lorenzo had a pistol in the other hand – the one he'd fired, I suppose, because he didn't use it.'

Dora gazed at the top of the stairs, imagining the ghoulish tableau playing out. 'What did you do?'

'Nothing.' Susannah gulped. 'We all stood here like statues, shocked to pieces. It felt like a play – like they'd staged it and the *comte* would get up and laugh at our faces – but it was real.' She repeated it in a lower tone. 'It was real.'

'And then?' said Dora quietly.

'Lorenzo stepped over the *comte* and rushed down the stairs. I thought he was going to make a run for it, but he came at us and stabbed the *comtesse* in the breast.' She touched the place on her chest reflexively. 'Why? What harm had she ever done him? If he had a quarrel with the *comte*, then that's a matter between men, but to stab a woman who had no weapon, who did nothing to provoke him? The savage – the bloody, beastly savage!' She fisted her hands on her lap. 'I wish I'd had a knife to kill him myself – I would've rammed it in his throat – but the coward turned tail when we all started moving out of our shock. He ran back upstairs, got the other pistol from the *comte*'s room – it must've been already loaded because seconds later he shot himself in the mouth. Blew his brains out – I know because I had to mop up after him, though, thank God, I didn't see him do it.'

Three bodies in less than five minutes, thought Dora. The Jacobean playwright, John Webster, would've been proud of that bloody denouement. 'Did the *comtesse* say anything, about why he did it, I mean?'

Susannah shook her head. 'She never had a chance. We called in two surgeons to aid them but neither the *comtesse* nor the *comte* spoke. They just died quietly, which if you knew them you would understand was out of character. If she could've done so, she would've cursed Lorenzo, or asked for a priest, something. She wouldn't have wanted silence.'

The rest is silence, thought Dora, reminded of *Hamlet*. No wonder Susannah had found it like a play – it had the choreography of a staged death, a fittingly operatic ending. 'Then I'm sure she would appreciate you speaking up for her now. Tell me, Susannah, was there any sign that Lorenzo was going to do this? The inquest said a fit of insanity, but what do you think?'

The maid shivered. 'Don't you believe them. He wasn't mad. He knew exactly what he was doing, planned it even.'

'What makes you think that?'

'I caught him firing a pistol a few weeks before, didn't I? When I asked him what the hell he thought he was playing at'—she glanced at Miss Austen—'pardon my language…'

'Do go on,' said Miss Austen. 'It sounds like an occasion where strong language is warranted.'

'Too right it is.' Now she'd got the story off her chest, Susannah was rallying. The wan maid was transforming into an avenging one. 'He told me it was an accident. An accident? Pig's swill! No, I think he was practising – I think he'd already decided to kill the *comte*. Did they tell you he brought a can of oil with him and put it inside the carriage? I think he was going to burn us all alive in there if he got the chance. Vicious bastard.'

'Why would he do that?' asked Dora as Miss Austen looked away. That curse was a little strong for the lady.

''Cause he hated everyone – hated the *comte* for telling him off when he didn't do his job properly, the *comtesse* for scolding him – me as well for when I took him to task for firing that pistol indoors. I was lucky he didn't stab me. No, he wasn't mad. He was angry, so very angry.'

Perhaps it really was the case of a servant who snapped and ran amok in a killing rage? The inquest might've been broadly right in seeing it as an isolated incident.

'It is strange for anger to burn so slowly, to plan and plot,' said Miss Austen softly.

She was right, thought Dora. Killing in a red rage was one thing. Letting a scolding fester for a couple of weeks, buying oil, not striking out at the *comtesse* at first but returning to finish the job, that all sounded like premeditation. And he fired the pistol before all of that happened. He did that first.

The loaded pistols were a piece of the puzzle that she needed to understand. 'Susannah, did you think it odd that your master and mistress kept loaded weapons in their bedrooms?'

She shrugged and looked away. 'It weren't my place.'

Which meant she had thought it strange.

'Who were they afraid of? Not Lorenzo, clearly, as he had the run of the house.'

'I don't know, miss, but the *comte* did say he had enemies "over the water". He became afraid in the last few months, told us all to take precautions and not to talk to strangers.' Susannah grimaced. 'It seems I didn't learn that lesson 'cause I'm talking to you, aren't I?'

Chapter Ten

Brooks's Club

As the breakfast plates were cleared away, Knighton gave Jacob the name of his friend in the Foreign Office and said he'd send a note to smooth the way for Jacob to approach him.

'Much obliged,' said Jacob.

'Consider it payment for the amusement you provide me with in between my boring business meetings.'

As they emerged from the breakfast room into the library, there was a distinct change of atmosphere: the murmurs of conversation died away, newspapers dropped, and monocles were fixed to get a good look at the pair.

Knighton smiled nervously. 'Well, old chap, one of us has blotted our copybook.'

'I think they're looking at me,' murmured Jacob, giving the room what he hoped was a hawkish stare.

'I think they are too. Let me find out what this is about.'

Knighton scurried off to talk to his acquaintances over by the fireplace. Jacob would have preferred to make a dash for the exit, but Knighton hadn't given him a chance to say his farewells. There was nothing for it but to brazen it out. He nodded a good morning to the Duke of Grafton and his cronies and received a stony glare back. He wandered to the nearest bookshelf and feigned an interest in back numbers of the *Edinburgh Review*.

After a few minutes, Knighton returned, a newspaper tucked under his arm. 'Come with me,' he whispered. Then more loudly: 'Let's go see that carriage horse at Tattersall's, the one I told you about.'

Accepting the excuse, Jacob followed him to the cloakroom to retrieve their hats.

'What's going on?' he asked.

'Outside,' said Knighton, beaming at the footman as if nothing was the matter. 'How's the family, Clive?'

'Very good, Mr Knighton. Thank you for asking.' The footman opened the door onto the street.

'Let's take this into Green Park,' Knighton said to Jacob.

Jacob didn't think his friend had been struck with a sudden desire to see the cows being milked, or admire the herbaceous borders, the usual entertainment in the park. His friend had something big to tell him that might need space to be absorbed away from the curious. With an inward groan, he hurried after Knighton, wondering what disaster was about to strike him.

Once they were beyond the ears and eyes of anyone from Brooks's, Knighton passed him the newspaper that he had purloined from the Reading Room against the rules of the club. 'Society column.'

Heart beating with trepidation, Jacob unfolded the paper:

BERKELEY SQUARE
The latest on dit *from the square last night is that an altercation took place in the ton's favourite patisserie. The respected war hero, Dr S—s, was heard to declare that he was marrying a lady of the acting profession, a Miss F—P—, against the wishes of his brother Viscount S—s. The very person to object was none other than the Viscount's latest amour, the divine Miss P—. Hearts are breaking among the marriageable ladies as another eligible bachelor falls for the charms of a person from the lower classes. Will there be none left for respectable girls to marry this season?*

'Damn it all to hell!' Jacob threw the newspaper onto the bench. 'Bloody scandalmongers!'

Knighton picked up the paper and smoothed it down. 'Careful with that. I'm supposed to return it.'

'Chuck the thing in the fire.'

'But that won't stop the gossip.'

Jacob sat on the bench, let his hat fall to the ground, and leaned forwards with his head in his hands. 'I really don't have time for this.' The worst thing was knowing he'd brought this on himself. He shouldn't have let Ruby bait him into blurting out his intentions before an audience.

Knighton sat beside him. 'Do you want me to deny it? I have the ear of those that matter. I could sort it out before it goes any further.'

Jacob gave a frustrated sigh. 'It's too late – and I don't want to deny it. I consider myself engaged to Miss Fitz-Pennington and believe myself very fortunate to have won her hand. It wasn't easy, believe me.' She couldn't back out now it was in the papers, he hoped. He truly believed she wanted it too if she just stopped thinking about everyone but herself for a moment. The rush of love he felt recalling that she could soon be his relieved some of the anguish. Faint heart never won fair lady. She was worth every second of trouble and annoyance he experienced as he battled through the obstacles to their union. 'The only part of this I regret is that I haven't had a chance to announce this to my mother and the viscount before they read it this way.' He flourished a hand to the offending column. 'Too late to steal it from the post bag. My brother will have read his copy at breakfast and my mother will be getting the London papers by the mail coach in a day or two. I'd better write and hope my letter reaches her before she thinks to read the papers.'

'And your brother?'

'I imagine he is laying siege to my office already. I'd better go and see what he has to say for himself.'

Knighton slapped him on the back. 'Need moral support?'

The gesture melted the coldness that had seized Jacob on realising the world knew about his marriage plans before he was ready to tell them. His old schoolfriend was prepared to risk the viscount's displeasure to stand in his corner. 'Thanks, Knighton, but this is something I have to do alone.'

'Thank God for that!' With a rueful grin, Knighton got up. 'Best of luck, old chap.'

Jacob put his hat back on. 'I'll see you at the club – if I survive.'

When Jacob arrived at the office, he found Susan alone at the desk. He came in, half expecting his brother to leap out from behind the door.

'Where is everyone?' he asked.

Susan's lips curved, twitching her beauty spot, a style from yesteryear that she still sported. 'We are all busy as bees. Alex is meeting his friend in the River Police, something about identifying a body they pulled out of the water at Putney.' Susan grimaced at that. 'Ren and Hugo are taking the day off after following the faithless husband last night. I'm going through their report now. I believe we have enough for the wife.'

Nothing out of the ordinary then.

'However—' She put down her pen and mock-scowled. 'I will have you know that I won't put up with any rudeness. I'm too old for that kind of thing.'

He blinked at her, not comprehending. 'I'm sorry. Have I done something to offend you?'

'Not you, love, your pain-in-the-arse brother.'

'Bloody hell.' Jacob sank into the visitor's chair. 'What did he do?'

'He stormed in here about an hour ago and demanded that I produce you as if I were a conjuror with you stashed in my hat like a rabbit. When I told him you were working and would he like to leave a message, he told me that he was a viscount, that I was a bloody nobody, probably of immoral persuasions, and that his disgrace of a brother must present himself at the family mansion at once or suffer the consequences.'

Jacob let his head fall back as he gazed hopelessly at the ceiling. 'Did he spell out what the consequences would be?'

'Funnily enough, I didn't ask. I told him I didn't like his

tone, viscount or no, and that he should make an appointment if he wants you to meet him because you are very busy earning your living.'

'Oh, Susan, thank you.' Jacob knew that was a reply that would have only infuriated his brother further, but he would've loved to have heard that put-down. 'Did he make an appointment?'

'What do you think?' Susan smirked. 'What's he in high dudgeon about in any case?'

'The newspapers announced that Dora and I are getting married.' He just had to persuade the reluctant bride to go the last inch.

Susan gave a squeal of pleasure. 'Oh, I do love a wedding. Does Lord Muckety-Muck not approve?'

'You got it in one.'

'Well, he can shog off. Dora's a fine lass and you're lucky to get her.'

'Exactly my sentiments on the matter.' Jacob's first response had been to go immediately to the family home on Grosvenor Street, but now he thought better of it. Susan was right; he had his damned living to earn and a job to do. The viscount would have to get in line and be polite about it.

His other brother was another matter. He owed William an announcement in person at least, because William and his wife, Charlotte, had welcomed Dora into their home during the investigation of the Earl of Elgin's case. He would do that before he went in search of the Foreign Office contact of Knighton's.

But first, his mother. Jacob quickly wrote a letter to her and dropped it in the bag for Kir to take to the Post Office.

'Thank you for sending the viscount away with a flea in his

ear,' he said to Susan. 'If he returns, or sends a messenger, say that I'm out on calls but will get to him when I have an opening.'

Susan chuckled. 'I think I can do that.'

'I'm off to see my other brother—'

'That'll burn the viscount's bum, to be second in line.'

Vivid but accurate. He grinned. '—then to Whitehall so don't expect me back before you leave for the day.' He picked up his hat. 'Any news from Dora?'

'She was heading to Barnes so I'm not expecting her back until later this afternoon. Do you want me to tell her?'

'Ah, yes.' What was the probability Dora would hear about the article before he had a chance to warn her? She was unlikely to have had time to read the newspaper and there was no reason to think anyone she was meeting today would make the connection. He certainly didn't need to send messengers running after her to warn her because that would only alarm her. 'Use your discretion. Tell her if she needs to know, but otherwise I'll explain this evening.'

Susan tapped her forehead with a military salute. 'Righto, doctor. You'd better cast your hook into fresh waters before his noble bossiness comes back.'

He saluted her back and headed out the door for Mount Street.

William was at home. That was a good sign, thought Jacob, as the butler showed him up to the family parlour. If William had refused him entry, then he would know that the consequences threatened by Arthur were already being imposed.

William was alone, standing by the window and looking down on the street. He turned as Jacob entered.

'Is it true?' he asked.

'Good morning to you too.' Jacob looked about him. 'No Charlotte?'

'She's taken the children to visit her mother.' William must've realised that a frontal attack wasn't going to be welcomed so reverted to his more usual pleasantries. He couldn't be rude for long – it just wasn't in him. 'Please, sit down. I'll ring for a tray. Hungry?'

'I could eat,' admitted Jacob, though breakfast wasn't that long ago.

William rang the bell and ordered a pot of coffee and sandwiches. He sat in the winged armchair, so Jacob took a place in the other one across the fireplace from him.

'In answer to your question, yes, it is true. I didn't think you would be surprised.'

William slouched back and dropped his chin to his chest, contemplating his hands linked in his lap, avoiding Jacob's gaze. 'I was optimistic it would blow over.'

'Blow over?'

'That you and Miss Fitz-Pennington would settle down to being … something else.'

'She isn't mistress material.'

William cleared his throat awkwardly. 'Evidently not. You wouldn't have introduced her to my wife if you thought that, but I hoped that perhaps…'

'Perhaps we would be persuaded to toe the line and live together quietly not challenging you all by giving our relationship religious sanction?'

He jerked his head in a nod.

'Do you know how bad that sounds?' Jacob didn't want that. Marriage mattered to him, dammit, and it should to his brothers.

The butler entered at that fraught moment and placed the tray on a small table between them. William waved him off.

'We are not to be disturbed,' he ordered.

The man retreated without a flicker in his expression indicating that he knew what was going on, but of course he did. Servants always knew.

'Shall we start again?' said Jacob in a light tone. 'I was going to tell you myself but the newspapers got there first. I'm delighted to announce that I have asked Miss Fitz-Pennington to be my wife.' That was if he could persuade her to say 'yes' and stick to that plan now Ruby had lodged a protest.

'Congratulations. I like her – I really do. She's brave and unconventional, and I think she really does love you. I want that for you.'

'But?'

'But I just wish it didn't come with a cargo-hold full of trouble. What's this about Miss Plum?' Rallying, William passed him a plate and offered the sandwiches.

Jacob took two that looked like cheddar and pickle. 'To be honest, that's the part I most regret. Diana will surely read the column – she's no fool. Do you think she knows what Arthur gets up to in his house in Marylebone?'

'I don't know. I find her … inscrutable.'

'Has Charlotte ever said?'

'My wife is friendly with Diana but not an intimate. The new viscountess plays her cards close to her chest.'

And that reserve was part of the reason Arthur had given

Jacob in their last conversation as to why he sought warmth and friendship from a mistress.

Jacob swallowed his mouthful, enjoying the tang of the cheese which was like a slap on the cheek. 'I find it annoying that I am the one treated as if I'm breaking the rules when no moral code is infringed by marrying Dora – in fact, the Church rather demands it of us. I want a family with her, children I can acknowledge. I want to be able to go out and about with her and not have her cut by those who aren't fit to tie her shoelaces.'

'There will still be those that do that even with a wedding ring.'

'Well, they can go hang themselves. I want to be her husband, not her bloody protector. That would break what we have between us.' It was fragile and beautiful, so why did society so delight in crushing it?

William picked up his sandwich, looked at the egg and cress filling that was peeking out, then put it down, his appetite appearing to vanish. 'You are in the right, I do recognise that. Morality is on your side. Arthur has no say in this, and you have every right to happiness with Dora.'

'Thank you.'

'But it is going to be difficult. As your older brother, I feel I must caution you about this. If Arthur is being particularly pig-headed – and I've no reason to think he won't be – he'll try to cut you out of the family, disassociate the Sandys name from you and your wife. He'll claim Evelina and Felicity will be damaged by it.' Their sisters were on the marriage market, one about to be wed, the other looking for a suitable spouse.

'Whereas they aren't hurt by his mistress's name being in the society columns?' It was unfair, but Jacob and William both knew that to be true. Society was breathtakingly hypocritical in that way. 'We can't control what Arthur does, and Evelina will soon be married.' Jacob recalled his sisters' reaction to the news that he was in business with Dora. When they had gathered for their father's funeral, his sisters had taken him to task for making the Sandys name notorious in the ton. Ladies seeking to attract the right kind of suitor wanted not a hint of scandal to touch their families, so marriage would be a much bigger step in the wrong direction in their eyes. But could he live his life to please his sisters? That would be ridiculous. 'Felicity will hate me for doing this, I've no doubt, but I hope she'll come around when she falls in love herself and understands why I'm behaving in this way.'

William sighed. 'I think Felicity is only hoping to fall in "like". She doesn't believe in love after having seen what society considers a good marriage.'

Jacob grimaced. 'She's no fool then, but perhaps I can educate her back into hope? I'd hate to see her in a loveless match.'

'She'll claim you are ruining her chances of even that by being the centre of this scandal.'

'So, according to you, it's a scandal now to marry a single woman, not because I have to but because I want to? The world is mad.'

'Don't be obtuse, Jacob. You know full well what the problem is: Dora is illegitimate, an actress and has been seen unchaperoned with you, so it is assumed, correctly I would guess, that you are lovers. She isn't a sweet virgin from an impeccable family gliding down the aisle untarnished – that's the only kind of bride that would get their approval.'

'If people spent less time speculating about the doings of

others and looked to their own behaviour, then we'd all get on much better. Don't they read the Gospels? They whinge about the speck of dust in a brother's eye when they have a plank in their own?' He knew the complaint was pointless. Society lived to skewer and scoff at those it had decided to tear down. 'The only saving grace about this whole business is that Dora couldn't care tuppence about what other people think, unless they are her friends.' Which was exactly why Ruby was such a threat.

He put his empty plate on the tray, conscious he had a Foreign Office man to catch before he went home for dinner. Time to get to the nub of the matter with William. 'Will you receive us when we are wed even if Arthur tries to forbid it?'

William didn't leap in with his assurances as Jacob had hoped. Instead, he rubbed his face wearily. 'I will talk to Charlotte. You know me – I like to avoid conflict within the family.'

If Arthur pushed matters so that it was a choice of sides, it would harm William's little family if they lost the favour of the viscount. Jacob was disappointed but he understood.

'Send Charlotte my regards. I must go.'

William accompanied him to the door, grateful that the subject was put aside for now. 'What are you investigating this time?'

'A double murder.'

'Lord! How grim!' He wrinkled his brow. 'Not that Frenchman and his wife, the opera singer? It's the only recent double murder I know.'

Jacob nodded. 'It is. What have you heard?'

'Nothing definite but everyone agrees that they were not quite the thing. Oh, they had their own crowd – the musical and artistic lot – but they weren't received in the strictest circles. At least she wasn't because of her past as his mistress. He was more often seen with people of influence.'

'Anyone in particular?'

'Government types – those in military procurement and foreign affairs. I'd heard he was close to the Russians, spent some time with them on the continent somewhere – one of the German states, though I don't believe I ever knew the details.' He shook his head. 'No, I can't remember anything more about them.'

'In what capacity was he with them?'

William smiled wryly. 'Dear brother, isn't it your job to find out?'

Chapter Eleven

Downing Street

The Foreign Office, 15–16 Downing Street, was identical to the town houses occupied by the ton when in London for the season, being at first glance two four-storey domestic buildings with the usual black railings and modestly sized front doors giving out onto a cobbled street. It was only when you got inside that you discovered the houses had been knocked through to create offices for the government servants dealing with matters from Brazil to Borneo, from Novaya Zemlya to Van Diemens Land. Adapting a house meant oddities, with some rooms too big for their purpose and some too small. Jacob was therefore not surprised to find Knighton's friend occupied a room that would be regarded as inadequate for a boot room in his family's castle in Westmoreland. A circular window set high cast a weak light over the desk.

A porter showed Jacob into his audience with the Second Senior Clerk to the minister.

'Mr Thornbury, I've a Dr Sandys for you.'

Thornbury, a prematurely bald man of about Jacob's age, looked up from the paper bed on which his egg-like head nestled. His eyes held a friendly expression of expectation which told Jacob that Knighton had prepared the way for him.

Jacob bowed. 'Mr Thornbury, I'm very grateful you can make time for me.'

Thornbury got up and stretched, a bounce in his movement. 'Make time? My dear sir, you can consider your presence here more as a rescue. I'm positively drowning in paperwork!' He came out from behind his desk and offered his hand. 'Ever been in government?'

Jacob shook his head. 'Though I've had dealings with the military authorities running a field hospital. I have some idea of the mountains of paperwork involved.'

'I've reports coming in from all over the world and I'm supposed to make sense of them – a hopeless task, as whatever action we might've taken is likely out of date now. You have to hope the man on the spot is up to snuff and can take the initiative.' Thornbury reached for his hat on the hatstand. 'Chop?'

It took Jacob a second to realise this was an invitation to go to a chophouse for a bite to eat. Some days when investigating he could find himself skipping meals; today appeared to be making up for that.

'An excellent idea.'

'Let's go to the Silver Cross.'

They marched quickly up Whitehall, past Melbourne House where a few months ago Jacob had met Lord Byron at one of Lady Caroline Lamb's fashionable daytime dancing parties. He was struck now by how close the two worlds were – the serious business of running the British Empire next to the frivolous one of flirtation and balls. Thornbury didn't even spare the house a glance, paying as little attention to the glittering sons and daughters of high society as they paid to him.

The Foreign Office man pushed into the fug of beer and smoke, fighting his way through to a spare table near the back of the tavern. A waiter, a sly fellow with eyes that were everywhere but on the customer he was serving, approached.

'Two chops and two pints of my usual,' said Thornbury.

'Right away, sir.' The waiter sloped away to fill the order. Places like these liked to serve quickly to maximise the number of customers they could seat in the dinner hour.

Thornbury slid into the bench seat, the high back cutting down the buzz of noise. 'Hope you don't mind me ordering for you? I don't have long.'

'Not at all.' Jacob gave the room a swift survey. The majority of customers were government servants like Thornbury. Nobody spared them a second glance, heads down over their plates, newspapers folded on the table in front of them as they scanned the houses for sale, auctions to be held, books published and coroners' reports. 'Did Knighton explain why I wished to speak to you?'

Thornbury nodded. 'The D'Antraigues murders. Terrible business. Why do you want to dig all that up? The servant did himself in before we got to him – saved the hangman a noose, I suppose.'

Jacob agreed with Thornbury but he had a client to satisfy. 'The person who asked me to investigate is worried that wild tales about the late *comte* will begin to circulate once the ton return for the season, that speculation could harm the living.'

The waiter slapped two tankards down with little ceremony, froth spilling over the side to ring the pewter mugs. 'Be right back with your chops, sir,' he said as if he hadn't just created a wash of ale on the table.

Thornbury grinned, amused rather than annoyed by the casual service. 'They're busy.'

'So I see.' Jacob moved his mug out of the puddle.

'As for wild speculation, D'Antraigues was one of those characters who lived a life stranger than anything you could read about in a gothic novel. If rumours are spreading, then I suggest they might be true.'

That wasn't helpful, but before Jacob could remark on this, the waiter was back. This time the gravy went flying when he banged the plates down. Prepared, Jacob grabbed his elbow before he could retreat.

'Cloth?'

The waiter looked at him as if he were speaking Greek.

'For the table?'

With a harrumph of annoyance, the waiter tugged a rag from his belt and ineffectually wiped the surface, leaving a good smear of beery gravy behind.

Thornbury's eyes were laughing even if he was too polite to snigger. 'My advice is don't rest your elbows on the table. Let's set to. They'll want the table in a quarter of an hour.'

Warned, Jacob began carving up his chop. At least this was cooked well, not overdone so that the meat resembled boot leather; rather, it melted in the mouth after a few chews.

'Good?' asked Thornbury.

'Surprisingly, yes.'

'That's why I put up with the service.'

'If many rumours are circulating, perhaps you could help

me to distinguish fact from fiction. What do you know about the *comte*?'

Thornbury chugged his beer then wiped his mouth. 'I glanced at the file before you arrived to refresh my memory, but I'm not sure that we know everything. I do know that he had a falling out with Bonaparte in 1797, when the emperor was still a general.'

'They met personally?'

'Oh, yes, D'Antraigues had that dubious honour. Napoleon arrested the *comte* in Trieste and interrogated him. You should remember that the balance of power was shifting in France at that point. None of us was sure who was going to come out on top. The nobility who had lost everything in the revolution were wondering if it was their moment to come back and reassert their claims, D'Antraigues among them. That wasn't welcome to the new men in the military like Napoleon, who didn't want their gains to be squandered. The generals saw a chance to take over from the civilians in Paris.'

'I remember. We had wondered if the revolution was about to collapse in on itself.'

'Napoleon stopped it, or at least forced it to change direction, so France dropped into his hands like a ripe plum.'

'What did he do?'

'He made the classic move of a would-be dictator. He discredited his opposition, the old guard, claiming they would reverse all the advances the people had made and set the clock back to before 1789. Bonaparte needed proof they were plotting against France so he claimed to have found material damaging to the royalists in exile in the *comte*'s possession. Old Boney is nothing if not a good sophist for his own cause. He used it to ruin D'Antraigues's party's chances in regaining a foothold, and turned the royalists against D'Antraigues, who many believed had betrayed them.'

'Betrayed them in what manner?'

Thornbury leaned closer, almost put his sleeve on the table, then thought better of it. 'It was suspected that the so-called dossier against the royalists was concocted by D'Antraigues in a bargain for his life.'

'The bargain being one made with Napoleon?'

'Correct.'

'So how did he go from that to being a British government pensioner? Surely you wouldn't trust him after suspecting he betrayed the royalists?'

Thornbury's smile was sardonic. 'Why blame a man for what he had to do to survive? There was no love lost between a prisoner and his captor, believe me.'

Jacob recalled the bitterness of Lord Elgin, another of Bonaparte's prisoners, who left by making a bargain with the French emperor. 'That I can believe. Then how did he travel from prison in Trieste to a fashionable house in London – *two* houses, in fact?'

'I'm not the expert on his movements. With a man like that, you are always going to be left with questions.'

'What can you tell me?'

Thornbury polished his plate with a crust of bread. 'He went to Austria where he approached several European governments for work.'

'What kind of work?' asked Jacob as Thornbury made sure he caught every scrap of gravy. Jacob felt he was doing the same in terms of the conversation – trying to gather every crumb the man could offer.

'Reporting on the French for their enemies, claiming to use

his old contacts to have privileged insight as to what was going on inside Napoleon's regime, that kind of thing. War makes us all hungry for information and he was willing to feed us.' He chewed his crust as if to underline the point.

'But if his relations with the royalists were ruined, and he had been arrested by the regime, who were his trusted sources?'

Thornbury smiled cynically at him. 'Who indeed? I think there were those that understood his compromises, and his wife still had her friends. Add too that he was persuasive; he could make a whole cloth out of the patches of information he gathered, so much so that the Russians took him on as an analyst of French affairs. He was attached to their legation in Dresden, their tame Frenchman who could explain the machinations in Napoleon's circle. It helped that he'd published an excellent anti-Bonapartist tract in 1805, proving his writing talents.'

'I can imagine he was very helpful to the Russians. We were all astonished by the meteoric rise of Napoleon and needed someone to explain it to us.'

'Quite so. Unfortunately for the *comte*, the Russians were embarking on one of their periodic rapprochements with the French, deciding they weren't so bad after all and we British were the enemy. It became embarrassing for the Tsar to host an outspoken critic of the French emperor in his legation. That made things too hot for D'Antraigues in Dresden, despite the fact that Prince Czartoryski backed the *comte*.'

'Czartoryski? Tsar Alexander's foreign minister?'

'He certainly had the Tsar's ear on such things. But the Russian court, like the French, is a merry-go-round. The prince fell from favour in 1806, taking his protégés with him.'

'Including the *comte*?'

'Exactly. Prince Czartoryski is loyal to his people, though, and he called in several favours to get the Comte D'Antraigues and family to London. Czartoryski made a kind of gift of D'Antraigues to us, in fact, knowing we would find the *comte* useful. The file gets more detailed from then on, fairly voluminous in fact.'

'Who writes all these reports?'

'Poor fools like me,' Thornbury said wryly. 'Do you not think it a strange state of affairs when D'Antraigues got more time with our foreign ministers than some of their wives did? He fairly haunted the place. Mr Canning wanted to be shot of him when he was foreign minister, but even he couldn't get rid of the man as the *comte* proved too useful.'

'Doing what, for heaven's sake?'

'Reporting, analysing, writing critical articles about Napoleon in French for dissemination – whatever was asked of him, he did.'

'And yet his sources were suspect?'

Thornbury tapped his fingers on his mug thoughtfully. 'Are you wondering if they were fairytales spun out of moonshine and cobwebs? Not always. D'Antraigues was astute enough to read international politics expertly, keeping abreast of the whole European picture, not just fragments. That made his analysis worth reading. His predictions were spot on.'

That was very interesting. D'Antraigues wasn't a charlatan then, but someone who was worth listening to, because what everyone in charge of the conduct of the war wanted to know most of all was what was going to happen next. 'What did he predict for the war this year, Napoleon's push east and Wellington's campaign in the Peninsula?'

'Ah, now that's an interesting question. We were waiting with bated breath to see what he would say. In the file it said that we were expecting a report from him the very day he died, but it never arrived. What arrived was news of his murder.'

'And the report?'

'Not a trace.' Thornbury stood up to go, the waiter back to clear their plates even before they got out from behind the table. 'Funny that, wouldn't you say?'

As they left the inn, they passed an acquaintance of Thornbury who was just entering.

'Vorontsov! How are you settling in?' asked Thornbury, shaking hands. He turned to Jacob. 'Dr Sandys, this is Count Ivan Vorontsov, aide to His Excellency, Pavel Sukhtelen, the special envoy from the Tsar. I'm happy to report that they have been charged with opening the embassy again.'

Jacob bowed. 'An honour, sir.'

A striking-looking gentleman in a navy uniform and epaulets, curling black hair and muttonchop whiskers, Vorontsov returned the greeting with a smart click of his heels and head bob. 'Your friend said this place serves the best lamb cutlets in London. Is he correct?' He graced Thornbury with a wry smile.

'Yes,' said Jacob, 'if you can forgive the lamentable service.'

With a couple of further pleasantries, the Russian proceeded into the inn. The meeting put Thornbury in high spirits.

'I'm so glad the Russians are finally listening to us, even if it is only about where to dine. You heard of the Treaty of Örebro, I'm sure?'

Jacob had been busy on other cases but had followed the newspapers. 'That's in Sweden is it not?'

'Exactly. Both the Swedes and the Russians have fallen out with Napoleon and are coming over to our side. We in the Foreign Office have great hopes – great hopes!'

It would take more than cracks in the old alliances Napoleon had cobbled together to defeat the emperor. 'We've been jilted once by them already in this war and ended up fighting both Russia and Sweden. Do we trust their change of heart? Isn't the de facto king of Sweden, Marshall Bernadotte, Napoleon's old favourite?'

Thornbury grinned and rubbed his hands. 'That is where old Boney made a serious mistake. You can't give your top general independent power then expect him to let you walk all over him. The fool of an emperor occupied Sweden's island of Rügen and Pomerania – naturally, Bernadotte would seek peace with us, the great naval power in the world, to get them back.'

It sounded too close to a tactical game of chess for Jacob's liking, especially when he'd seen the lives lost in the process. 'How can you stand all this tangle of alliances and counter-alliances, Thornbury?'

'Stand it? My dear Sandys, it is why I'm in the service. I find it fascinating.'

They parted on Whitehall. Jacob decided to vary his route home and walk along Pall Mall. Carlton House, beloved London residence of the Prince Regent with its white pillars and porticos, dominated the street. This newly built area was an elegant part of the capital, unlike the higgledy-piggledy slums not that far away in St Giles, which reeked of human misery. Barouches and phaetons rattled past and gentlemen exchanged nods as they hurried to their clubs. This part of town gave the illusion that things were under control, Britain heading in the right direction with its spreading empire and naval dominance, all ugliness and poverty hidden.

Jacob didn't share that confidence. Too many people were being left behind.

A carriage with the royal coat of arms went by, possibly holding the prince, or perhaps his daughter, Princess Charlotte. With George separated from his wife and no more royal babies, it looked like Britain was going to get a queen after George died. Jacob joined the other pedestrians removing their hat as a sign of respect. The country would have to survive the regency first.

Personally, Jacob thought the Prince Regent a disaster. In theory, George no longer had time for the indulgent life of parties and pleasures that he had conducted for the past few decades as the Prince of Wales, not now he was Head of State. He was nominally in charge, though more as a figurehead; his prime minister, Lord Liverpool, did the day-to-day running of the war and made the decisions. Jacob suspected that the regent wasn't that much changed and gave no sign he had risen to the new responsibilities. George also hadn't stuck to the few reforming principles he had professed to support when it hadn't cost him anything. His accession had been a grave disappointment to people like Jacob who wanted to see change.

Musing on the state of the nation as he was, Jacob didn't see the attack coming at him from behind. He did, however, feel the shove between the shoulder blades that sent him tumbling onto the road in front of a coach and four.

Chapter Twelve

Carlton House

Dora rushed up the portico stairs, past the Greek statues in their niches, and into the palatial hall of Carlton House. She shouldered her way through the gaggle of men who had gathered, all discussing the accident that had just been cleared up by the grooms from the Prince Regent's stables. She grabbed the elbow of the nearest footman.

'You can't come in here, miss,' he said with all the portentousness of his over-six feet of height, royal livery and white wig.

'Dr Sandys? Where is he?' she asked, ignoring his attempts to keep her out. Her voice echoed around the space, drawing attention to her. The gentlemen turned to stare.

'And you are?' the footman said coldly, disengaging her fingers from his sleeve.

This was one moment when she wished she and Jacob were

already married. 'His business partner, Dora Fitz-Pennington. Please, just tell me where he is. Is he badly hurt?'

The men returned to their conversation with renewed vigour, no doubt discussing her effrontery for bursting in, but the footman relented. Perhaps he heard the note of genuine distress in her voice. His grip gentled and he steered her away from the onlookers.

'He's in the kitchens, miss. He said he didn't want to bleed on the marble.'

'That sounds like him.'

Following the servant's directions, she made her way into the domestic parts of the Prince Regent's house, barely noticing the sage walls, white plaster and gilding – thousands of pounds' worth of government money going on keeping the regent in the opulent style he preferred. Her heart was still galloping, and she wouldn't be happy until she saw with her own eyes that Jacob wasn't badly injured. The last ten minutes had been a nightmare. After she had dropped Miss Austen at home, she had made her way to the office only to arrive at the same time as the messenger bearing the news from Jacob that he had been run down by a carriage in Pall Mall and wanted money for a surgeon. Jacob had none on him because an enterprising pickpocket had stripped him of his purse while he was lying in the gutter. The fact that Jacob had had enough presence of mind to demand a message be sent was the only thing that had prevented her from panicking.

With the help of a maid dusting a bookcase, she found the kitchens, a cavernous series of connected chambers that added up to a temple to fine dining. The Prince Regent's chef was world-famous. She had never seen such a display of copper pans and jelly moulds.

Then she saw Jacob – and time stopped still for a moment. He was sitting on a wooden chair at the end of the scrubbed kitchen table, a cloth to his head, and his foot up on a stool. A medical gentleman had stripped to his shirt sleeves to examine the back of Jacob's neck. The staff had retreated to the other end of the kitchen to continue their work, though from the low level of activity Dora surmised that the regent himself was not in residence. That was a blessing. She would not fancy her chances of barging in if he had been at home.

'You've a nasty contusion, Sandys,' said the surgeon. 'You're lucky the horse didn't break your neck.'

'Luck was with me. The hoof just clipped my shoulder and I managed to scramble back to the pavement before the wheels ran me over. The coachman was damned good at controlling his team. I think he chose to collide with a wagon rather than with me.' Jacob groaned as the doctor felt his ribs. 'I'm eternally grateful to him.'

'Hurts?'

'What do you think?'

'I have laudanum if you need something for the pain.'

'No, thank you,' he said in a harsh tone, then composed himself. 'I'll manage without.' Dora smiled to herself: her injured warrior was not going to let the little matter of being trampled by horses overset his decision never to take opium in any form again. Good for him. 'Though I have to say,' continued Jacob, 'the poor horses might need something to calm them. They got as bad a scare as I did, bowling along the street at one moment then finding someone under their hooves the next.'

Dora shuddered at the thought. Jacob sounded surprisingly

calm about the whole thing, but then again, he had been in battle. Perhaps he was inured to shocks?

'What on earth were you doing throwing yourself in front of Lord Southwell's coach in the first place?' said the medic, feeling the back of Jacob's head. 'There's a lump there. Watch out for signs that you have a concussion – I don't need to tell you the symptoms.'

Dora came to Jacob's side and took his hand in hers. He gave her fingers a squeeze.

'My love.' He gave her an apologetic look to say all was well and that he was sorry for the scare. 'Did you bring the money?' he asked. 'Dr Beverly was kind enough to drop everything and come to my aid.'

The doctor, an elderly gentleman with pepper-and-salt hair and a bushy beard, harrumphed at that suggestion. 'Good God, Sandys, I don't need paying! You can stand me a drink next time we meet at the club.' He darted an interested glance at Dora from under white brows. 'So, this is the lady, is it, your intended?'

Dora gave Jacob a startled look. Had Jacob been talking about her while Dr Beverly tended to him?

'This is her.' Jacob flushed, though whether from embarrassment or pain was hard to tell. 'Dora, darling, I'm all right. Sit down. You look terrified.'

She sank in the chair next to him, her knees trembling. 'I was – still am. What happened? It's unlike you to have an accident.'

'I'll tell you later, my love. First, would you be so kind as to see the wagoner is compensated for damage and the coachman given something? The servants on the door can show you where they are.'

Dora nodded and stood up. She got the message that he didn't want to discuss it in hearing of one of his peers. She wagged her finger at him. 'Listen to what the doctor says, Jacob, and don't you dare move until I get back.'

Dr Beverly smiled grimly. 'Ah, I see you know what doctors are like as patients. We are the worst possible people to take our own advice.'

'Then I expect you to convince him to be the exception.'

Dora returned to the entrance hall and sought out the footman who had allowed her entry. She explained her mission.

'They're in the Red Lion, miss, steadying their nerves, if you know what I mean.' He gave her a wink, indicating exactly what the steadying entailed.

'Right then, I'll make sure they have the funds for that.'

She found the pub in an alleyway that ran between Pall Mall and King Street, a dirty black-timbered building that had none of the spruce Palladian pretensions of Carlton House and surrounding buildings. The coachman and the wagoner were huddled together at a table. It looked like adversity had resulted in them striking up a friendship.

'Gentlemen,' said Dora, approaching them. 'Dr Sandys sent me to see if you are both well.'

'Dr Sandys?' asked the coachman. He was smartly dressed in navy livery and looked none the worse from the incident. 'Who's that?'

'The man you almost ran over.'

The coachman pulled out a stool for her. 'Hah! He's a lucky beggar. Is he going to be all right?'

'He is right enough to be thinking of you both. A surgeon is seeing to him now.'

The wagoner, distinctive in his country smock and nankeen breeches, raised a mug of ale to her. 'Thank the good Lord for that. I thought he was a goner when I saw him tumble off the pavement.'

'He didn't tumble,' said the coachman. 'He was pushed. I saw it as clear as day. That gave me a second to steer away. I'm only sorry that I clipped your wagon.'

'Better my wagon than a man's leg.'

'He was pushed?' Dora felt sick. 'Did you see by whom?'

The coachman shook his head. 'Not so I would recognise him again. There were several gentlemen on that side of the road. You have to notice in case one of them takes it into his head to try to cross before the horses. Those flash gents can't be trusted when they've had a skinful. All I can say with any certainty is that a man in a dark brown jacket and brown hat, smart like, hurried up from behind him, then deliberately came alongside and shoved.'

'You were coming up from behind too?'

'Yes, that's me. Trotting along after dropping his lordship at his club, not a care in the world, then, bang, there's a man under Jill's hooves and not a damn thing I can do about it.'

'Were you coming in the other direction?' Dora asked the wagoner.

'That's right, miss. I had just unloaded some kegs in Jermyn Street and was thinking about what I was going to have for supper, and then this one comes crashing into me.' He grinned at the coachman.

'The man who pushed Dr Sandys would have been facing you – the one in the brown jacket. Did you see him?' asked Dora.

'No, miss. I was too busy stopping Bernie and Tucker from

making a run for it. My Clydesdales could've dragged his lordship's carriage with us where we'd locked wheels, taken it all the way home to Kent.'

Dora passed over a purse containing what she guessed was generous compensation for a cartwheel and any resulting loss of earnings while it was fixed. 'Dr Sandys doesn't want you to be inconvenienced for getting caught up in this. If that isn't enough for repairs, you can find us at our office.' She slid him a business card.

The carter squinted at it. 'What does it say? I was never very good at reading curly writing.'

'Fitz-Pennington and Sandys, Private Enquiry Agents.' At his blank look, she added: 'We investigate crimes that the usual authorities can't or won't handle.'

'Bet you make a few enemies along the way,' said the coachman, pocketing the money she had passed in his direction.

'If we are doing our job correctly, I'd say that's inevitable,' she agreed. And who had tried to murder Jacob was another mystery they would now have to solve.

Leaving the coachman and the carter to finish their drinks, she returned to Carlton House. The doctor had departed but his patient had stayed put. Jacob was drinking a cup of tea and eating a scone provided by kitchen staff. She pressed his shoulder lightly.

'I take it as a good sign, that you feel up to eating?'

He passed her the untouched half of the scone. 'To be honest, I've eaten so much today, I can't manage another bite, but it felt churlish to refuse.'

She hadn't had a chance to eat so polished off the scone gratefully. 'We have a lot of catching up to do,' she said between mouthfuls.

'Indeed. How was Barnes?'

She shook her head. 'None of that. Someone just tried to kill you. That's the most urgent matter for discussion. Did you see them?'

He frowned as he attempted to summon up the memory. 'No, but I felt them. It was no accidental elbow in the side but a firm shove in the back. The next few moments are a blur of hooves and cobbles, and then I was back on the pavement with people crowding around me, patting me down. I thought they were trying to ascertain if I was injured, and it was only later I realised they'd gone through my pockets and lifted my purse.'

'The same person as the one who pushed you?'

'I suppose that would be a good way to pick a pocket if you don't mind the violence.'

'But highly risky. You'd swing for sure if you were caught.'

'How risky would it be? If I were dead, or even dazed as I was, it was unlikely I would be able to identify them.'

'But an onlooker might – the carriage driver did catch a glimpse of a man in a dark brown jacket and hat. If he'd been quicker to grasp the situation, he could've started a hue and cry after the person before they vanished. We were unlucky that he didn't think to do so.'

They sat in silence for a few moments, the noises of the kitchen filtering back into Dora's consciousness, the turning of the spit and the clattering of pans in the scullery. The smell of roast chicken flavoured with thyme made her mouth water.

'If the pickpocket and the attacker are the same person, and if we think such a crime in broad daylight near a place as well guarded as Carlton House is unlikely for an ordinary thief, it does raise the possibility I was targeted,' said Jacob. His expression turned sombre. 'They might try for you too.'

'You think it is associated with the case?' Dora couldn't think of anything she had discovered that would justify such a murderous attack.

Jacob took her hand and brushed his thumb over her knuckles. 'I have two theories.'

'Only two?' She smiled affectionately at him. His busy brain was always working on problems, coming up with ideas and angles on the cases they tackled together.

'When it happened, I was walking home from meeting a contact at the Foreign Office, a middle-ranking official called Thornbury – he's a friend of Knighton, a school fellow of mine. He told me D'Antraigues was a government pensioner in receipt of a thousand a year.'

'That explains a lot, like how they could afford two lavish houses. What did he do for his money?'

'From Thornbury's description of the situation, the *comte* had few contacts left in France, certainly no one close to the emperor, but he kept abreast with events through the chatter of the émigré community and by following events closely. You could say he made himself an expert and had sound instincts as to what developments meant for the war. Many of us only hold a piece of the puzzle; he was skilled at putting it all together.'

'Doesn't the government have their own people to do that?'

'He also wrote fluent anti-Bonapartist pieces for them.'

'That I can see as a unique skill. A Frenchman addressing the French is much more effective than anything an Englishman can write. I gather that they found him useful and were prepared to pay for it?'

'Yes. Before coming to London he lived in Dresden and worked for the Russian delegation there; he knows the Swedes too. He has good connections with our major eastern allies.'

'The Russians, the Swedes, and many of the German states fighting against Napoleon with us?'

'Exactly.' Jacob sighed. 'I found all the changing alliances were enough to make my head ache before the accident, but now it is ten times worse.'

'My poor love,' said Dora with a wry smile.

'That Thornbury chap said he liked all this international intrigue! Thrived on it! He went on to say that they were expecting a report from D'Antraigues but instead received news of his death.'

Now that was interesting! 'The implication being that, if the report was written, it has gone missing?'

'That's what he thought.'

'I wonder.' Dora tapped her lip, reviewing what she had learned from Susannah Black. 'That does fit with something odd about the crime.'

'Go on.'

'When we questioned the maid who witnessed the murder, she told us how Lorenzo didn't take the chance to kill the *comtesse* on first arrival but went upstairs to the *comte*'s room. If he was in a murderous rage, why not lash out? I wonder if he went in looking for something and was interrupted.'

'By the *comte*?'

'That would make sense. They clearly argued, or something happened, because a shot was fired. They heard that in the hall. Next the *comte* staggered to the top of the stairs and Lorenzo came up behind and stabbed him to death to finish the job.'

Jacob shuddered. 'That shove felt very like a stab in the back. I'm grateful my assailant didn't have a knife.'

He'd had a very narrow escape – it hardly bore thinking about. 'Unfortunately for the D'Antraigues, Lorenzo did. But it was only after killing the *comte* that he came down and stabbed the *comtesse*. He didn't try to kill the witnesses but went back upstairs and killed himself with a second loaded pistol.'

'He didn't say anything, didn't shout anything, nothing to explain his motives?'

'No. And neither of his victims had a chance to speak. Do you think the government searched the house for the *comte*'s report?'

'I'm sure of it. He was their man – at least, they thought he was. They would've sent discreet people to the house to clear out anything embarrassing for government officials. His last report would've been noted in the file Thornbury consulted.'

'Then, if it is missing, it doesn't sound as if Lorenzo had a chance to destroy it.'

'That goes to my theory. What if someone staged the accident to search me for it, or at least information as to where it might be?'

'How would you have got hold of it?'

'If they are following us, they would know we saw Henry Austen and that I had talked to Thornbury. They might have been after my notes or any papers I was carrying.'

'Then they don't know we write things in our case book in the office and don't generally travel with information like that on our person.' Dora grimaced. 'I hope they weren't watching Miss Austen going about with me today because she did nothing but write things down.'

'We should warn everyone at the agency that we might be

targeted for a break-in, as well as the Austens.' He rubbed his jaw. 'And Thornbury.'

Dora saw a chance to get rid of her shadow. 'We should suggest Miss Austen stays out of harm's way.'

'Indeed. Though I think neither of us should go about alone while the threat lasts. We both need someone to watch our backs.'

Hopefully they could investigate together, rather than in separate teams, if he felt well enough to get out of bed tomorrow. She would then be able to keep an eye on him. 'So, to return to your thinking, your first theory is that it is this missing report of the *comte*'s that has got someone interested in us?'

'Interest is a mild way of putting "want to kill".' He gave her a sardonic look.

'And the second theory?'

'I'm not sure I want to say anything.'

'Jacob!'

'I know, I know.' He held up his hands in surrender. 'Look, something else happened today.'

What else could possibly have happened? 'Go on.'

'That unpleasant scene with Ruby in Gunter's made it into the society column. My intent to marry you is public knowledge and it has not been met with universal approval.'

She snorted at that understatement, then realisation dawned. 'Your brother must be furious.'

'Oh, he is, believe me, but not as angry as I am with him for his presumption that he can rule my life.'

Where was Jacob going with this? 'Jacob, he might be angry, but he would never push you in front of a carriage!'

He laughed then held a hand to his ribs. 'No, even I don't think that of Arthur.'

'Then what would be the connection?'

'One of my peers on the way to their club might have decided to take me down a peg or two.'

'So angry that they pushed you into the gutter – with me?'

He winced. 'Well, yes. The assailant might not have cared if I got badly hurt or not. It was the impulse of a bully. Having my pockets picked was the action of an opportune thief.'

'Hmm. I'm not sure which theory I prefer: dangerous secrets or prejudiced bully?'

'Whichever it is, neither of us is safe until this is resolved. But you know what this means?' His eyes twinkled with some of his usual humour.

'No?' she asked suspiciously.

'We must solve the case *and* get married.' He grinned with boyish charm. 'Even an almost-fatal carriage accident has a silver lining.'

Chapter Thirteen

Bruton Mews

After some debate, Jacob and Dora agreed that in his injured condition he should not go back to his usual residence which was a hotel room in Albemarle Street. He was known to lodge there while in London so he would be too easily located both by enemies and his brother – neither of which he was up to facing. That left them with a ticklish problem. Dora's landlady might wink at the occasional male visitor, but they couldn't officially put him to bed there without awkward questions arising.

'Don't say it,' muttered Dora, as he pressed her ring finger on the left hand as they held hands in the carriage home. 'I know. But we're not, so that's that.'

Jacob was determined to carry the day on this point, but right now, with his head pounding, a concussion hovering, and his ribs aching, he did not feel it an opportune moment.

Besides, he hadn't yet organised for the special licence that would be required because they were not settled in parishes where they could arrange for banns to be read. His home parish was in the Lakes, and Dora's? He supposed her parish church was now St James, Piccadilly, but it would take weeks for the banns to be read on consecutive Sundays. He wanted to get a licence, a minister and have done with the business.

That didn't sound very romantic, but he was desperate not to let her slip between his fingers only because worry for others stopped her doing what was best for them both.

'You could turf Alex out of his bed,' said Dora, still pondering the issue of where he should go, 'but I think a better plan would be to ask Yarton.'

Yarton, the efficient butler of Lady Tolworth, had an answer for every domestic crisis. He would not turn a hair at being asked to provide refuge for an injured man who was afraid someone was after him. In all good conscience though, as the search of Jacob's person would've turned up no leads on the missing report, he did not think the assailant would come after him again so soon. They were more likely to go for the Austens, or the office, or Thornbury. He would not be endangering Lady Tolworth's household.

'I think Yarton is a good idea,' he agreed. 'But first we should make sure everyone knows the threat. Let's send Alex to the Austens with a message and warn everyone else to be on their guard. We should have at least two people staying overnight in the office.'

'And Kir must not be one of them.' Dora cushioned his jolt as they went over a pothole. 'He'll want to stay in his usual bed, but we can't risk it. We'll ask Yarton to find a safe place for him as well.'

Jacob was touched to see that all their people were waiting for his return, having gathered when news got out about his injury. As Dora helped him out of the carriage, Alex hurried to take the other side. Kir darted off to the big house to send word that Jacob had survived in one piece, more or less. Susan pulled out the desk chair for him while Ren and Hugo hovered anxiously in the background. This evidence of their concern for him moved him. Their little team was solidifying nicely.

'What happened, sir?' asked Ren, his voice deeper than one might expect from such a small man. He had large features – big eyes, dark brows and a Roman nose – and moved with a rolling gait to make up for his short legs.

'I went up against a carriage and the carriage won,' said Jacob, easing back into the chair.

'That is not a fair fight,' said Hugo in his rich baritone. He travelled through life with his stomach going before him like the rounded prow of a battleship. He leaned a little back to find his centre of gravity. Despite his girth, he could be nimble on his feet and was courageous when the decisive moment arrived. He would make a good watchdog tonight. 'You'd get better odds going up against Tom Cribbs in the ring.'

Kir returned with Yarton and then, to Jacob's surprise, Lady Tolworth followed. The Dowager Lady Tolworth was a beautiful woman in her late forties. Tonight she was decked out in the latest fashions and glowing in her status as a society favourite. Jacob thought he had become used to seeing her since they established their office in the mews across from her house, but he couldn't stop the stray memory of their tempestuous time as lovers coming to mind, Ginnie's long naked limbs stretched out next to his. Though she no longer tempted him, he felt decidedly warm remembering it in Dora's presence so he squashed the recollection, stuffing it back in the box of all memories of erotic encounters prior to meeting his love. Everyone stood on the lady's entry, Jacob struggling to his feet.

'Oh, do sit down, you foolish man!' she declared, entering in a swirl of light blue silk and a fringed shawl. Seed pearls snaked through her blonde tresses. Sapphires glittered in her ears and around her neck, far too fine for a workaday place like the office. 'What's all this I hear about you trying to do yourself in?'

'I was pushed—' began Jacob.

'Not the carriage accident, you dunce, but marriage. Marriage!' She snorted, then turned to Dora and said in quite another tone. 'Congratulations, my dear. I hope you will be very happy.'

Dora raised a sardonic eyebrow. 'Thank you … I think. I really have no intention of doing him in.'

'Not you, dear, society will do the job. The knives are out! Though, in my experience, after the honeymoon is over, you will probably wish to do away with him at regular intervals. Husbands are very annoying.'

Jacob was feeling too weary to tackle the storm of energy that was Lady Tolworth. 'Dora, would you mind?'

'Of course, Jacob.'

Resting her hand lightly on his shoulder, mindful of his bruises, Dora explained what had happened and the two theories as to who had attacked Jacob. 'We must all be on our guard,' she concluded. 'Lady Tolworth, would it be convenient for Kir and Jacob to stay with you while the danger lasts?'

'I wouldn't have it any other way,' the lady said. She

twitched her shawl around her shoulders. 'The Comte D'Antraigues, interesting. A valued government informer, how … unsurprising.'

'You knew him?' asked Jacob. Of course Ginnie would know him, seeing how she moved in impeccable social circles as well as a few of the more scandalous, her widowed status giving her that freedom. He'd momentarily overlooked what a good source they had on their doorstep.

'I wouldn't say I knew him, not in the biblical sense, though he did once make a play for my favours.' Ginnie's blue eyes sparkled at the memory. 'Frenchmen – they can be so devilishly charming, can they not?' she said to Dora in a confiding tone. 'I think it is the language – it quite undoes one.'

'He wasn't faithful to his wife?' asked Dora, looking amused by the confidence.

'Nor her to him, but they were faithful in so much as it was understood they would always stand together when it counted. I know many couples like that: you'd swear they hate each other, until they join forces and attack.' Lady Tolworth examined him with a frown. 'Jacob, you're fading. We need to get you into bed. Yarton, please see to it.'

The stately butler bowed. 'At once, my lady.'

'Kir?' The lady looked around the office to spot the boy. He was hovering close to Dora, hoping to be forgotten so he could stay put. 'You, my boy, are coming with me. You can open the door to the carriage and then ride with the coachman.' This was a rare treat for Kir who liked nothing better than accompanying the lady's driver while he took her ladyship about town. 'Yarton will have a bed made up for you in the servants' attics for when we return, and you must promise us all you will use it.' The lady was as clever as she was beautiful. When matters became dangerous she knew it was important to keep Kir busy, or loyalty meant he would drift back into harm's way as he had done during the Elgin investigation. Believing he was protecting Dora by following her, Kir had been kidnapped by a rogue French agent and it had been the devil's own job to rescue him.

'Yes, milady,' said Kir, overawed, as well he might be when faced with one of the ton's most powerful women.

Leaving the details to be settled by others, Jacob hobbled on Alex's arm across the courtyard and upstairs, following Yarton to a guest room.

'Send a note to Thornbury,' said Jacob.

'I will.'

'You'll make sure Dora—'

Alex cut him off. 'You don't need to ask, Sandys. We'll make sure no one gets near her while you're out of commission.'

The bed looked like heaven, already turned down for him to slip between the sheets. How did Yarton do it? The man had a knack for anticipating what was required. Alex helped him undress, hissing in sympathy when he saw the damage.

'I'm surprised you're still on your feet,' he said.

'So am I.' Toppling like a felled tree, Jacob stretched out on the sheet and felt rather than saw Alex draw up the light coverlet. 'Call me early.'

'I'll do no such thing. Rest, Sandys, or you'll be no good to anyone.'

The door shut softly and Jacob began the tumble into sleep. Just before he succumbed, he remembered that, thanks to the complicated, busy day, he hadn't found time to call on, or send word to, Arthur. The viscount would not be pleased to find himself pushed to the back of the queue, even if the excuse was a rather dramatic carriage accident.

He would have to deal with it, thought Jacob. Tomorrow.

Chapter Fourteen

Once Jacob was safely put to bed in Lady Tolworth's house to recover from his wounds, Dora couldn't rest. Sitting at the office desk, it was hard to know what to do first. It had been so close, and she had almost lost him. Her insides still felt cold and her hands trembled at the remembrance. Ink splattered over the blotter, and she was annoyed by her own weakness.

'Buck up, Dora,' she murmured.

She and Jacob were used to dealing with threats – indeed, the last three months had seen people come at them many times, but usually they had known they were targets, and why. This was different.

If his second theory was right, were they facing a life of not-so-veiled contempt for daring to cross social lines to marry? Would people come at them from all sides to show their disapproval, jostling, pushing, sneering? Did that not weigh in the scales with Ruby's protest and suggest Dora should release Jacob from the engagement?

That did not feel like something she would do. Dora put away the casebook in which she had finally managed to update their findings in her worst handwriting. She turned the key in the desk drawer for an added layer of security. Unlike Ruby's objection, which at least had the weight of friendship on its side, Dora found opposition from people whom she heartily disliked only made her more bloody-minded about going ahead with the wedding. She did not have a character to bow to bullies. Putting it crudely, they could bugger off.

That thought cured her of the trembles, thank heavens.

Resolve bolstered, she went to the scullery to make a sandwich to take with her. Her day had not given her many opportunities to eat, and half a scone did not a stomach fill.

As for the other theory, she mused as she sliced the loaf and added some ham, that the attack was connected with the case and the missing final report by the Comte D'Antraigues – something which the pickpocketing seemed to confirm – they had a duty to ensure their client was warned. Better that than sitting quivering in the office like some small furry animal driven back to her burrow. She wrapped and pocketed the sandwich. Time to face the world.

'I'm coming with you,' Dora told Alex as he picked up his hat to call on the Austens in Sloane Street.

Not keen on that plan, he revolved the brim in his hand. 'Dora, Jacob would prefer it if you stayed here – in safety. I do too.' With his soft smile and sincere blue eyes, he really was too handsome for his own good, with his long lashes that many a debutante would sigh for.

She held up a hand. 'That look won't work on me. I'm immune. If the next sentence out of your mouth is "let the menfolk deal with this" then you will regret it.'

He swallowed the very words he was about to speak and said instead: 'But you don't need to come. Only one of us is required to take the message.'

'Fine. Then you stay here and guard the office. Hugo and Ren will appreciate the company, I'm sure.' She cast a look at their employees, who were wisely keeping out of this.

Susan was putting on her shawl in preparation for going home. 'Listen to her, love,' she told Alex. 'You men might think you're invincible, but even you need someone to watch your back. Go with her – I'll feel better for knowing she has company.'

The army had taught Alex when to sound the retreat. He gave a put-upon huff and tapped his hat into place. 'Very well.' He held out an arm. 'Miss Fitz-Pennington?'

'Alex,' Dora replied, placing her hand lightly on his forearm. 'I have a pistol in my reticule.'

'And I a sword in my cane. I think we might brave the streets of London together.'

When they emerged onto Berkeley Square, they could hear popping and shouts from the direction of the river. It was either a riot or a very exuberant party.

'What's going on?' Dora asked, intrigued. 'The crowds seem headed that way.'

'It's the Illuminations for Wellington's victories in Spain.' Alex steered her around a drunkard lying outside a tavern, insensible. Someone had started their celebrations early. 'He's been made a Field Marshall. I think people are relieved to have something to applaud after years of defeats and retreats.'

'You can't blame them.' The rapid patter of a firecracker split the twilight, followed by screams. 'But it sounds as if it is getting out of hand.'

'Fortunately, we are headed away from it. Let's hurry.' He hailed a cab. 'Fuelled by drink and a fine summer evening, I don't think it is going to die down for a few hours, do you? I'd like to be back before they really get going.'

They arrived at Henry and Eliza Austen's house and were quickly ushered into the drawing room.

'Thank goodness you came so quickly,' said Henry, striding towards them. He glanced over Dora's shoulder. 'Where is Dr Sandys?' He turned back. 'And who is this?'

'Mr Alexander Smith,' said Dora, 'our righthand man at the agency. I'm afraid Jacob met with an accident. Do I take it from your words that you sent for us?'

'You must've crossed with the messenger. Yes! Let me ring for Jane and Eliza. They are up in Jane's room putting it to rights.' Henry went to the bell and sent a maid to fetch the ladies. 'What's this about Dr Sandys and an accident?'

Dora wanted to say 'What's this about Jane and putting her room to rights?' but knew she would have to satisfy the client's curiosity first. She quickly explained the events of the day and how it might connect with the case. His wife and Miss Austen arrived during her account and listened quietly until the end.

'That makes sense of what was senseless,' said Miss Austen, taking a seat next to her brother. He put his arm around her in comfort.

'I'm sorry, Jane. You should be safe in my house. Anything taken?' he asked soberly.

She grimaced. 'Only some letters. Lord knows what anyone wants with my news to Cassie about the cost of muslin and plaiting lace.'

'Everything else is … in one piece?' He cast a look at Dora

and Alex as if fearing to divulge family secrets before an audience.

Miss Austen folded her hands demurely in her lap. 'P and P is intact. I had left it in the bottom of my valise, and they did not rifle through to find it. If they had, they would probably have dismissed it as my laundry lists,' she said with a droll smile.

He chuckled. 'Indeed.'

There was something going on here that Dora did not understand. What could Miss Austen have that Henry would worry about, and what was P and P? Pounds and Pence? Was she holding on to some secrets involving the bank and the *comte*'s accounts? Did she have his transactions secreted in her luggage? That would be very irresponsible of the banker.

'I don't suppose you would care to explain?' Dora asked, looking directly at the lady who had dogged her steps all day. It was annoying to feel one step behind especially when Miss Austen was supposed to be following her lead. 'We can't do our job properly if we aren't in possession of all the facts.'

Miss Austen knitted her fingers together and squeezed. 'I suppose it will not harm to say and childish to hold on to what is not so very great a secret. Henry, what do you think?'

Her brother nodded. 'We hired Dr Sandys and Miss Fitz-Pennington as confidential agents. They won't divulge any of our private information – it states as much in the contract. I assume the same goes for Mr Smith here?'

'It does,' said Alex.

Miss Austen gave an unexpected laugh, suddenly looking much younger and mischievous, twenty rather than nearly forty. 'Miss Fitz-Pennington, I apologise. I lied about lying.'

Dora could feel a headache hovering. Why did no one

speak plainly in this household? 'I'm afraid I don't understand.'

'I am in truth the author of *Sense and Sensibility*. My reference was to my next novel, the manuscript of which is in my valise, and I would hate to lose it. Not that the world need share the opinion of an ignorant and prejudiced writer. However, Mr Egerton, my publisher, is hopeful that it will be approved by the public.'

'You are talking about *First Impressions*?' asked Dora, realising the lady had played her for a fool that day. Why had she not suspected when the lady had such a ready story to tell the opera singers?

'I've decided to call it *Pride and Prejudice*. It fits better with the title of my previous work and the meaning is less obvious. If I keep the original title everyone will guess that first impressions are wrong and will distrust my heroine's opinions on the people she encounters.'

'And we wouldn't want anyone to distrust Elizabeth Bennet, would we?' said Eliza with a fond smile. 'I'm going to be fierce in defence of my namesake.'

Dora had the unpleasant experience of challenging her own first impressions. The lady, far from stealing another woman's credit, was modestly hiding her own, allowing herself to be underestimated and slighted as an uninteresting spinster from Hampshire. For all Dora's advanced views on the role of women, she too had been guilty of assuming the lady couldn't write such a sparkling novel as *Sense and Sensibility*.

Miss Austen's cheeks flushed. 'I apologise, Miss Fitz-Pennington, for the subterfuge. In my defence, you will be aware that society does not like ladies to advance their name in public and many of us choose not to make ourselves a target.'

She gave a self-deprecating laugh. 'I think my publisher likes the speculation. If I were Lord Byron, he would naturally trumpet my identity from the rafters, but this way my readers can wonder if I am not a much more exciting personage than I am, some lady with access to the highest circles in society, a scintillating hostess, like Eliza here.'

Her sister-in-law waved that remark off. 'Jane, that's nonsense. No one would suspect someone like me of writing your books. You are far too clever for all of us.'

Dora had to agree. The writer of *Sense and Sensibility* was not to be underestimated again.

'Miss Austen, I owe you an apology, not the other way round. I am the investigator and yet I did not pause to wonder even for one second about you. Now you have been attacked—'

'Not I, but my private papers.' Miss Austen saddened at the recollection. Though she was making light of it, she clearly did not like losing her letters.

'That can feel like the same thing – a violation. It does, however, put to rest the question as to who was behind the attack on Dr Sandys and warns us to expect the same might come the way of all of us involved in this case. The evidence appears to be pointing to someone looking for the *comte*'s last report, or other information that he held and on which he based his work. He knew something that still presents a danger to the attacker.'

'But the man who killed him is dead,' protested Eliza. 'Surely the danger has gone to the grave with him?'

'He is, but he might not have acted alone. Today's events bear this out.'

'Someone put him up to it?' asked Miss Austen. 'And when

Lorenzo did not deliver the report, they decided to go after us, thinking we had it?'

Alex spoke for the first time in the debate the women had been dominating. 'Dora, this is all very well, but why would the servant kill himself in that case? Why not make a run for it, or carry on looking elsewhere?'

'Indeed, you have a good point.'

'I did notice something, if I might be so bold?' said Miss Austen.

'Be bold,' said Dora, waving her to continue. She wanted to hear what the observant novelist might've noticed that she had missed.

'Did Susannah Black ever tell us exactly who else was in the house? I can imagine how it would be possible for someone to slip past witnesses during the confusion of that fateful morning.'

'You're right. She told us she didn't see Lorenzo shoot himself; she only cleared up the mess. No one saw him commit suicide, so what if it wasn't suicide?'

Miss Austen nodded. 'And there is something else that is bothering me. Susannah described Lorenzo as proud and forceful, not depressed and desperate. Why go back upstairs after achieving his aim of killing his employers?'

'I can think of two reasons. One: he knew there was a second loaded pistol there and was thinking there was no other way out. Two: to look for something else.'

'The first is likely only if he was ready to commit self-slaughter and I don't believe from Susannah's description of his state of mind that he was,' said the writer. 'It sounds like he could easily have fled the scene.'

'Which means he went back upstairs to continue his

search.' Dora felt like she and Miss Austen were thinking with one mind, completing each other's thoughts. 'And he might not have been alone.'

'Whoever was up there could well have taken that moment to shoot his accomplice and escape, leaving the blame all with Lorenzo.'

'And yet the *comte* outwitted them both. He has hidden what they were searching for – or sent it away. And where do you send something you want to keep safe?'

'To the bank,' said the writer. Both Miss Austen and Dora turned to look at Henry. 'No wonder they are suspicious of our involvement in this. Henry, you must make sure your office in town is guarded and your partners know of the danger.'

'Henry is at risk?' squeaked Eliza, rushing to her husband's side. 'Darling, you must take precautions.'

'Indeed, he must,' said Miss Austen. 'I assume they have a list of people who might conceivably have the papers they are after. I am hardly the top of that, but they saw the opportunity while we were at dinner to break in, my room being the least defended and I had been with Miss Fitz-Pennington all day.'

'Writing everything down,' said Dora. 'If they were watching, they would assume you were something in the way of a secretary, recording what we saw. Your notebook?'

'I keep that with me at all times.' She patted her pocket then frowned. 'When was Dr Sandys attacked?'

'Around six o'clock,' said Alex.

'Then we have more than one person involved, because that was about the time my room was searched. I'd got back from my day with Miss Fitz-Pennington, changed for dinner and went down at around five-thirty.'

'They took letters, you say?' asked Dora.

'They were on the desk and in the drawer, not hidden. They cleared those out. They tossed a few clothes and books around but were disturbed by a maid coming to turn down the bed.'

'Did she see them?'

'Only the back of a man in dark clothing going out the window. I'm on the second floor but he used the drainpipe to climb in and out. I'd foolishly left the window open and lingered in the window before dinner, thinking.' She shrugged. 'Country habits.'

'You aren't foolish, Miss Austen. You weren't to know. It sounds to me like they were instructed to take all writing matter without staying to read it. That raises the possibility whoever is behind this has hired others to help them.' Dora turned to address their chief client. 'Mr Austen, I believe word must be sent to your bank's premises immediately, if it's not already too late. The thieves will realise we are aware of their interest, and they only have a brief window of opportunity before we double our defences.'

'I'll see it done.' Henry rang the bell to summon a footman.

While the message was composed and dispatched, Dora went up to Miss Austen's room to see the damage. As the lady had said, no major harm had been inflicted; it was a focused search by a professional. Miss Austen didn't have much in the way of fencible valuables but even the turquoise bead bracelet on the dressing table had been left unmolested. A normal thief would've pocketed that. Returning to the drawing room, Dora went to the window and watched a postboy collect the letter and sprint off down the street. Dora realised that she was lucky not to have been targeted. Perhaps this was because she had given them no opportunity, having got out of the hackney cab in front of the office and having taken another here. Running across town to go to Jacob had been unpredictable and they would have struggled to intercept her.

Miss Austen came to stand beside her. How Dora's opinion of the lady had undergone a revolution in the last hour! The annoying shadow now felt like someone of substance.

'You realise that none of us are safe until we solve this case,' Dora said softly. 'We wouldn't want the author of *Sense and Sensibility* to come to grief by being foolish and insisting she involve herself in the investigation.'

Miss Austen smiled, her hazel eyes full of mirth. 'You really liked my novel?'

'I fell in love with Elinor – she is who I want to be when I grow up.'

'Don't we all,' said Miss Austen wryly.

'I wanted to shake Marianne while also feeling her passion and pain, and I thought John Dashwood a ridiculous cipher to his poisonous wife. Why didn't you punish Willoughby more?'

'Oh, Miss Fitz-Pennington, I expected better of you.' Miss Austen folded her arms and gave her a schoolmistress look. 'In life, do you see cads getting their comeuppance or do you see them sail on, causing yet more wrecks?'

'They sail on.'

'And the women who fall for them, do they pay ten times over or get away scot-free?'

'They pay.' Miss Austen was right: the Willoughbys of the world never got punished, whereas their victims ended up on the town.

'But he did pay, in a way,' Miss Austen added in a thoughtful tone. 'He had believed himself a man of sensibility, but he chose callousness and avarice. His true punishment was seeing Marianne married and in love. Think what he would see in the mirror each morning, if he dared look.'

'You talk as if he existed.'

'He does – and he doesn't. To me my characters are real – I see glimpses of them in portraits and people. I imagine what happens to them after the close of the novel. And we all know Willoughbys and Mariannes, Elinors and John Dashwoods.'

'Indeed, we do. You have an astute grasp of people. I must ask you, what kind of character do you think our attacker is?'

'Miss Fitz-Pennington, you flatter me. How would I know? My world is a village. I have no expertise in international affairs, or in places where matters are settled with assassination. Drama in what I write comes from cross words or lost reputations.'

'They can be deadly too. And what are villages but a microcosm of all that lies outside them?'

'True.' She thought for a moment, teeth worrying her bottom lip. 'Then I would say it is likely that the *comte* might've known his killer. To be allowed upstairs suggests someone with access to the family rooms, a confidante.'

'A lover?'

She nodded slowly. 'No one mentioned a woman upstairs at the time but shooting someone can be done by either sex.'

'Indeed, it takes no strength to pull a trigger, but you do have to have some skill not to miss.'

'And the art of allurement to get so close that it seems like suicide.'

She made a very good point. Dora could see a female springing that surprise on Lorenzo. He would surely have pushed a man away. Unless Lorenzo had a male lover? Perhaps it was best not to mention that to Miss Austen. Dora's world of the theatre was more liberal in that regard than the villages of England.

'Miss Austen—'

'Please, call me Jane.' She touched Dora's wrist, a clear gesture of offered friendship. '"Miss Austen" makes me think of my sister. Do you have a sister?'

'No.'

'A brother?' Jane looked fondly over at Henry. 'I have six.'

'Only one, and he died a few months ago.'

'Oh, I'm sorry.'

'He was murdered.'

The lady's eyes filled with tears of compassion. 'Oh, my dear! I cannot imagine anything worse.'

'Some things are best not imagined.'

'How true.'

Dora examined the brilliant woman standing beside her. She too could read character: it was part of being an actress and investigator. 'You aren't going to keep out of this investigation, are you?'

'I am not, Miss Fitz-Pennington.'

'You will insist on coming with me tomorrow?'

'I will.'

Dora sighed. 'Call me Dora. If we are going to risk our lives together, we had better do so as comrades-in-arms, Jane. So tell me: can you fire a pistol?'

Chapter Fifteen

Bruton Street

Sleep eluded Jacob. The fireworks popping and crackling outside didn't help, jolting him awake each time he managed to coax rest a little closer. Then he heard voices downstairs – angry booming ones in the hallway. It was too early for Lady Tolworth to be back so that left Yarton to defend the door against all boarders. Unfortunately, it sounded like the pirate trying to swing aboard in this raid was none other than Viscount Sandys. It would perhaps on another occasion be amusing to find out who would prevail in a swashbuckling fight between the finest butler in England pitted against the most headstrong brother, but Jacob decided it wasn't fair to make Yarton verge on being impolite to a leading member of the ton. It went against the grain of the man's training.

Wrapping up in a borrowed silk dressing gown, he shuffled to the top of the stairs, feeling every single one of his bruises.

'I will repeat, my lord, Lady Tolworth is not at home and

her guest is asleep. You must return tomorrow if you wish to call on your brother.' Yarton was using his most stentorian tone. It rarely failed – except in the presence of Arthur.

'I will not be prevented from seeing my own brother by a jumped-up major-domo who doesn't know his betters when he meets them! I'll have you arrested if you try to stop me!' Arthur tried to push past Yarton but the butler bravely held his ground.

'You have no such rights in my lady's house, Viscount Sandys. Call the Watch if you must, but the Charlies will tell you the same thing.'

Looking down over the banister, Jacob was tempted – oh, so tempted – to let his brother humiliate himself by trying and failing to carry out his threats, but his better nature prevailed.

'Arthur, you really should listen to Yarton. An Englishwoman's home is her castle and you are being unmannerly trying to force your way inside.'

'Jacob!' Arthur, to his credit, did look genuinely relieved to see that Jacob was standing and able to talk cogently. 'You are well?'

'Not exactly well, but alive. Yarton, I'll see my brother in the library if you would be so kind as to show him in there. It might take me a few moments to come down the stairs.'

'Very good, sir.' Yarton gave a flick of a finger towards a doorway out of Jacob's sight and a waiting footman bounded up the stairs to assist Jacob in his descent.

Jacob arrived in the library to find the butler serving his brother a brandy for all the world as if they had not come close to a tussle in the hallway.

'Anything for yourself, Dr Sandys?' Yarton enquired.

Tempting though it was to dull his pain with strong spirits,

Jacob knew better. 'If a camomile tisane was available, I would be most appreciative.'

'Of course, sir.' Yarton retreated in search of the tea. Jacob knew that if Lady Tolworth did not stock it in her kitchen, the butler would find a way of supplying it, even if he had to sally forth and pick the flowers himself.

Jacob lowered himself into the chair facing his brother. 'You tracked me down then.'

Arthur didn't say anything, merely gulped his brandy. They resembled each other in their dark hair and blue-grey eyes, but Arthur was solid and broad-shouldered to Jacob's leaner frame. The viscount had been annoyed when his younger brother had grown a few inches taller than him in his teens, because Arthur had not wanted to cede even this advantage. He felt the brother destined to hold the title should also be the most imposing. Nature had had other ideas. Their relationship had followed a similar trajectory a few years later. Odd now to think of it but until ten years ago Arthur had been the model older brother looking out for and guiding the younger and Jacob had sincerely admired him for that. Then Jacob's choices – some good, many bad – meant that 'looking out' had become invigilation and his 'guiding' more like herding Jacob into the sheep pen Arthur preferred. But Arthur was no collie, nor Jacob a sheep, for all his attempts to force them into those roles.

'As you may have heard,' said Jacob, 'I was involved in an accident. Otherwise, I would have sought you out tonight.'

'You would? I would've put good money on your avoiding me. That awful woman in your office was very rude.'

'You were in the wrong – and you owe her an apology.

Mrs Napper is a respectable woman and deserves gentlemanly treatment.'

Arthur gave a harrumph to that, which was as much of a concession as Jacob could expect.

'As for avoiding you, it is tempting, but I'm not a child in fear of a scolding. We must speak to each other like adults – like brothers – on this subject.'

Before Arthur could reply, Yarton returned triumphant with a steaming cup of camomile. 'Will there be anything else, sir?'

'No, thank you, Yarton. I'll ring when the viscount is leaving.'

Yarton bowed and retreated, closing the doors behind him. It had proved a useful interruption because Arthur regrouped and decided on a less hostile approach.

'Are you going to tell me what happened to you?' asked Arthur.

'Someone pushed me in front of Southwell's carriage. Fortunately, he employs a skilled coachman and I escaped with only a battering. I've had worse falling from a horse in a steeplechase.'

'You're telling me someone tried to kill you?'

Jacob blew at the surface of his tea, enjoying the calming scent. 'It wasn't you then?'

'Don't even joke about it!' Arthur's expression sharpened. 'Do you think it was one of us?'

'One of us what?'

'One of our class in society?'

'It happened in Pall Mall – hardly the resort of the ruffians of the rookeries.'

Arthur ran his fingers through his hair in exasperation.

'Oh, Jacob, can't you see? What you are doing will put both you and Miss Fitz-Pennington at risk!'

'It is likely nothing to do with that, but a case we are working on, and no, I cannot give you any details.' He risked a sip, but the tea was still too hot.

'That is no better! If you get yourself caught up in such murderous situations—'

'Correct me if I'm wrong, but wasn't it you I dug a bullet out of a couple of weeks ago when some madman tried to murder you? How is the wound, by the way?'

Arthur touched his chest and winced. 'That's beside the point and you know it. That was an aberration, and he was aiming for Lord Furness, not me. But you… You will be constantly dragging the Sandys name into the gutter! I won't allow it.'

Jacob struggled to hold on to his temper. *Breathe. Count to ten.* Finally, when he felt in command of himself, he replied, 'Tell me, Arthur, is the Sandys name one that belongs solely to you, or are all of Father's children allowed to use it, at least until marriage in the case of the girls?'

'You know the answer to that,' growled his brother. 'But I am the head of the family.'

'You are the head of your branch of the family. I am a sideshoot, establishing my own branch, and this one chooses to define itself as one that is active in the pursuit of truth and justice, making itself useful to our clients.' Jacob wondered with wry amusement why he was sounding so self-righteous; he blamed his brother for driving him to this. 'We've been useful to the government and we've saved lives – that is nothing to be ashamed of. And if I choose to graft Miss Fitz-Pennington on to my branch, what is it to you?'

'Then you will only produce bitter, despised fruit, if you want to persist in this ridiculous imagery!'

Jacob wanted to strangle his brother. Surely no jury would convict him; Viscount Sandys was a sanctimonious ass.

'What fruit do you refer to?' he said, studiously keeping his tone polite. 'Our results so far have revealed the culprits in three murder cases and justice has been served upon them. Or perhaps you are referring to what offspring Dora and I might have once we are married? Then I will tell you that no children of ours will be bitter and despised; they will be loved and cherished. If anyone dares show them the least disrespect, then they will be cut out of our lives.'

'You say that now—'

He interrupted his brother. 'The same goes for Dora – if anyone scorns her then he will answer to me.'

'How many duels are you prepared to fight for that woman?'

'That *lady* – and as many as it takes until people understand I am in deadly earnest about her.'

'Would you even fight me, your own brother?'

'Are you going to scorn her?'

Arthur scowled at his empty glass. 'I cannot accept her into the family. I cannot.'

'Then that is your loss. Your branch of the family will be weakened for it.' Jacob thought it was high time he went on the attack. He had taken one too many batterings today. 'But I would look to your own conduct before you judge mine. Can you imagine how mortifying it is to Diana to see your mistress mentioned in the newspapers?'

Arthur looked away, taking solace in a bust of Aristotle that perched on the philosophy shelf. 'That was unfortunate. I will instruct Ruby to be more circumspect.'

'But you won't give her up and live as a Christian husband should? Are you not aware of the hypocrisy of your position?'

'I can look after my family and the lady under my protection.'

'Show me in the Bible where such an arrangement is approved – I'm talking about the New Testament, not the Old.'

'Don't be such a child, Jacob. It is what we men do – men of our station.'

'You don't get to ignore the Ten Commandments just because you are rich.'

'Who's the hypocrite? I'm well aware that you once kept Lady Tolworth as your mistress.' Arthur gave a sneering look around the comfortable library. 'Or did she keep you?'

If Arthur was resorting to insults, then he was nettled. Had Jacob been feeling less bruised, he might've flung insulting remarks back, but weariness had knocked the fight out of him. What was the point in continuing this argument?

'Thank you for calling on me, Arthur. Please assure those that care about my welfare that I survived the accident without major injury.' He used the arm of the chair to lever himself up. 'I will invite all the family to the wedding. I do hope you are able to come and celebrate my happiness.' Reaching for the bell, he rang. Yarton stepped in before Arthur could reply with more insults. 'The viscount is leaving now.'

'This way, sir,' said the butler firmly.

Arthur thumped his glass down on the side table. 'This isn't over, Jacob. I'll make you see sense one way or another.'

'Goodnight, Arthur. I send my love to Diana and the

children. Do think about what I said.' Jacob sat down again as Yarton whisked his brother away. He cradled his cup. It was going to take a lot more than camomile tea to calm him down after that merry little interlude.

Chapter Sixteen

Sloane Street to Long Acre

Dora felt more nervous on the return journey than she had on the way to the Austens. She kept her hand on the stock of the pistol in her reticule as she sat poised for trouble on the bench seat of the hackney cab, scanning the street for any sign of their enemies. The houses and public buildings that lined the way were joining in the Illuminations for the victory at Salamanca and to celebrate Wellington, several going so far as to spell out the names in lights. With hundreds, perhaps thousands, of people out to admire the spectacle, it was hard to see where danger might come from.

Alex, by contrast, was more at his ease, giving every indication that he was enjoying a warm summer's night trotting through streets bedazzled with flickering candles and lanterns. 'A novelist? Who would've thought the lady had it in her?'

'Who, indeed,' said Dora absentmindedly as her attention was on the passers-by.

'Then again, from the picture in my edition of his plays, Shakespeare looks more like he could tell you the price of corn on the Exchange than be the man who wrote all those wonderful characters.'

'He has a play about that too. *The Merchant of Venice*. "All that glisters is not gold."' Was that man under the tree looking too intently at them or was he just admiring her companion?

The jarvey sitting behind them flicked the whip over the flank of the mare in the traces, just a tickle to keep her steps lively with all the distractions dividing her attention. 'Ho now,' the cabdriver crooned. 'Steady on, Sally.'

The horse frisked and side-stepped, not liking the explosions of the distant fireworks.

'Meaning the opposite is true?' asked Alex. 'That plain packaging can hide the most precious of diamonds?'

'That is the point of the casket game in the play. Distrust first impressions, as Miss Jane Austen would say.'

'And isn't that what we do too, dig down to find out the real story behind events?' said Alex, sounding well pleased with his new life working with her and Jacob. Dora took it as a favourable sign that he was recovering his spirits after the death of her brother, who had been his lover and friend. After being ejected from the army in disgrace, he was regaining his sense of purpose. 'Do you think I'd like her novel?'

'I think you'd like it very much.'

The words had barely left her lips when someone threw a firecracker under the hooves of the horse.

'Hell!' cursed Alex as he threw his arms in front of Dora to stop her being catapulted off the bench seat.

The rapid, percussive bangs spooked the poor beast. It gave a shrill neigh and bolted, forgetting it had a carriage attached behind it. That became yet another thing to alarm the mare as the cab rattled and clanged as it found every rut and every kerb in their wild career. Dora held on for dear life as people screamed, shouted and dived out of the way. A cart selling oranges went flying, then a tinker's barrow loaded with pots and pans.

'Do we still have a driver?' she shouted.

Alex glanced behind them through the window in the back of the passenger compartment. 'Can't see him. Hold on.'

The jarvey had likely been thrown in the first charge. Piccadilly went by in a blur, pedestrians scattering, vehicles driving up onto the pavement to clear a way. People shouted and cursed, but there was little they could do to stop this.

'We have to get the horse back under control,' said Dora. 'Hold me steady.'

'Dora—'

'Just do it, Alex.' She could see the reins flapping about because they were still attached to the brackets on the roof that fed them to the coachman behind. If she could just get up and reach them, she could pull them down and she might be able then to stop the horse.

'We're almost at Haymarket,' warned Alex. 'We might have to bail out.'

She knew what he meant. With the Illuminations at the Little Theatre being one of the chief locations of the celebrations, the broad road would be full of revellers. People would die if the hackney carriage mowed into them. She and Alex would likely be killed or seriously injured in a collision if they stayed inside. No more time to think.

'Brace me.' She struggled up, feeling his firm grip around her thighs as he used his long legs to push against the compartment walls. The horse swerved and she would've been thrown out if it weren't for Alex. She jerked forward then righted herself.

'Can you reach?' he shouted.

'Almost.' The reins danced at the end of her fingertips. 'Damn these blasted things!' She pushed up another inch, Alex lifting her a little. 'Got them!' Hauling them down with her, she shortened the straps, winding them round and round her hands and sat back on the bench. 'Steady, girl! Steady, Sally!'

The poor mare, sweat dripping down her flanks, pulled and frisked. Alex put his arms around Dora, doubling his hands over hers, and helped keep the pressure up on the reins. Feeling the familiar tug on her bit, the mare began to slow. Exhausted, she stumbled and almost went down, but recovered to a walk, then staggered to a full stop, lungs going like the blacksmith's bellows, neck drooping to the cobbles.

Alex leaped out and went to the horse's head to seize the bridle. With Dora holding the reins, they slowly guided the mare to the side of the road just a few feet short of the junction with the Haymarket.

But the danger wasn't over yet. Dora clambered out and reached back in for Alex's swordstick and her reticule. A crowd was gathering, but it was hard to tell if they were the curious or the enemy. Jacob had had his pockets picked by someone pretending to help.

'Are you all right, dearie?' asked one buxom lady with a flower-decked straw hat, out for a night enjoying the Illuminations. It was hard to imagine her as part of any conspiracy involving French *comtes*. 'That poor 'oss looks like it's gonna keel over and die.'

'It had a scare. Someone let off a firecracker,' said Dora, her heart still racing like the cab but a moment ago.

'They should be 'anged, they should, scarin' the poor 'oss like that!'

'Let me help you to a chair,' said a gentleman, a sleek-looking gentleman of fashion with his hair pomaded and primped. He was wearing a dove-grey jacket, but Dora didn't want strangers of any description near her.

'No, thank you. I am quite well, I assure you.' She ducked behind Alex. Past him, she could see two men were running towards them from the direction they had come. It could be innocent – friends of the cabdriver come to rescue his vehicle and horse. Or it could be someone with quite different motives. 'Mr Smith?' She flicked her gaze behind him. He turned to look, then addressed the man in the grey jacket.

'My good man, would you mind holding on to the horse while we seek assistance from the Watch? A man might've been injured by the idiot throwing firecrackers and my wife should go indoors to recover.'

'Very good, sir,' said the man, taking hold of the bridle. 'See to the lady.'

Alex took a grip on her elbow and they made their escape down Coventry Street, the direction keeping up with the story that they were heading for the nearest Watchhouse.

'Are we really going for the Charlies, husband?' asked Dora as they ran.

'What possible good would that do? Let someone else sort out the hackney; we've got to get away before those pursuers catch up with us.' Alex glanced behind. 'Bloody hell, they're still following us. Dark brown jacket. Black jacket.'

'Any ideas where we can lose them?' They dodged between the people but with Alex's height they were difficult to lose in the crowd.

'I have an idea, but I don't think you'll like it.' Alex grimaced.

'Go on.'

'How about Long Acre? No one will question a man taking a woman into one of the bagnios and if we pay the men on the door, they'll keep others out.'

It was a good idea. Pretend to be a whore and a client and they would look like the myriad other couples finding cheap accommodation for an assignation at the bathhouse.

'I'll leave you to explain this to Jacob,' muttered Dora, adjusting her dress to make herself look less reputable. She let her hair tumble around her shoulders. 'All right, 'andsome, I charge five shillings. I'm no daggle-tailed jade.'

He grinned at her. 'No. You, my dear, are in your prime and you really should charge more.' He walked with confidence and knocked on the door of a house with a mermaid over the door.

'Do I want to know how you know this is a house of ill-repute?' She slouched against the ornamental doorway, hip cocked, scanning the crowds with the hard assessing gaze of the professional streetwalker. She could see the heads of their pursuers bobbing at the back of the crowd, trying to push their way through, hats obscuring their features, but she didn't think they'd spotted her and Alex yet.

The door opened.

'That's a story for another time, Sally,' said Alex. He dug into his pocket and passed over a handful of coins to the beefy man who guarded the door. 'We don't want to be disturbed, Colin.'

'Oh, it's you. She's not your usual type, is she, sir?' leered the guard as they bustled past him.

'You know me – always ready to experiment with something new.'

'Third door on the left is free,' said the man, getting down to business. 'Unless you want to share and engage one of the house lads? Then you can go into the main chamber where the baths are – or watch from upstairs.'

'Not today, thank you.' Alex ushered her further in.

Dora span, walking backward to give the doorman a saucy smile. 'But another time, eh?' she said with a wink.

The door to the unoccupied room closed behind them and Alex gave a sigh of relief. 'Safe – for the moment.'

'Do you think they saw us go in here?' Dora checked the walls for spy holes, then dropped her pretence when she decided they were in the clear.

'Perhaps, but they won't see us leave.'

'How so?' The sideboard had a tray of wine and biscuits so she helped herself then poured a glass for Alex. A gulp proved it a cheap and cheerful blend that drove away the chilling memory of the last few minutes.

'Cheers.' Alex tossed his back in one go. 'This is one of those houses that is friendly to Molly. I happen to know there is a back exit in case of a raid.'

She patted his shoulder. Molly houses catered for men who loved men. 'How very useful of you.'

He caught her hand and gave it a squeeze, both relieved beyond words still to be alive. 'Anthony will be pleased that my education with him is not wasted. Let's give them a moment to look for us and draw a blank, then we can make our escape.'

Dora looked around the room with new eyes, thinking of Alex and her brother coming here in happier days. It wasn't a mean establishment and smelled clean – or as clean as a bagnio could be with the passing trade of people after sex. Music played somewhere close by, a fiddle and pipe, and masculine laughter rang out accompanied by some feminine giggles and cries of delight. Someone was having a good time. The squeaking of a bed in the room above came as no surprise, though that encounter sounded less fulfilling for the partner involved. She hoped Anthony had been happy here. There had been precious little happiness at home for either of them.

She sat down on the sofa to wait. How long would it be before the people who were following them gave up their search?

'That was a reckless attack,' said Alex, refilling their glasses. 'If it was an attack and not coincidence.'

Dora rubbed the base of her spine. Some of the jolts had driven right through her. 'The chances of them being able to get to us to search us was slight. Perhaps they were watching us and followed when the horse bolted, but I don't like coincidences, not when we already have had two attacks in one evening.'

'What do you think they were doing then?'

'We might need to reconsider. Perhaps their aim is not so much recovery of the *comte*'s last report, as disruption of our investigation.'

'And what better disruption than killing or maiming the investigators?'

'Exactly.' She nibbled a biscuit. 'Sally? Really, Alex? Do I look like a horse to you?'

He laughed and settled down to wait with her.

Chapter Seventeen

Bruton Street

Jacob woke late the next morning with a single thought in his brain.

They hadn't spoken to the son, Julien, now Comte D'Antraigues.

True, they had only just begun their investigation, and that had turned out to be a very full and dangerous day, but how could they have neglected this obvious line of enquiry? Could the new Comte D'Antraigues be in danger? That oversight needed rectifying immediately.

There was a soft knock on the door before he could throw back the covers and Kir appeared in the doorway carrying a tray that looked almost as big as himself, Yarton at his back to remove obstacles from his path.

'Dr Sandys, your breakfast,' said the boy, placing the tray on his lap with the minimum of rattles and only a slight spillage from the coffee pot.

'Very good, Kir,' said Yarton. 'Now ask if that will be all.'

'Will that be all, sir?' asked Kir, his dark eyes bright with excitement at his first attempt to deliver breakfast to a gentleman. So far it was going swimmingly – Jacob's saucer was certainly swimming in coffee.

'Yes, unless there is any news?' Jacob addressed this comment to Yarton, who was discreetly mopping up the spill.

'There were some disruptions, sir, but everyone is well. Miss Fitz-Pennington said she would tell you about it as soon as you were in a fit state to receive visitors.' Yarton turned to leave.

'Please tell her to come over. We need to go out at once, so I require some clean clothes.' His coat and breeches had not come out well after his altercation with the carriage horse.

'I took the liberty of sending to your rooms, sir. They are waiting for you in the dressing room. Come along, Kir.'

'He can stay,' said Jacob, guiltily aware that he and Dora had been too absent recently from the boy's life. 'I dare say he will nobly volunteer to help me finish my muffins.'

Once Yarton departed, Jacob took a sip of the coffee. It was tempting to call Yarton back and ask him to add a few drops of laudanum to the cup to dull his pain, but he knew where that would lead. Having Kir here was another way of distracting himself from his bruises. Part of breaking a habit was not to dwell on the appetite when it arose.

'What's been going on, Kir? Yarton sounded very mysterious.' He forked up some scrambled eggs, deciding they looked the easiest thing to eat.

Kir flopped back on the end of the bed and kicked his heels, making the springs bounce.

'Careful, I'm eating here.'

'Oops, sorry.' Kir rolled onto his tummy and propped his chin on his hands. 'It's been very exciting, sir. Miss Dora said that the bad men broke into Miss Austen's bedroom, but as she had her notebook on her, they got nothing. Miss Dora told me that was a lesson in keeping private things private – locked away or somewhere no one would think to look.'

'They went after Miss Austen?' Jacob hadn't expected that. Henry's office and business – yes; but his sister? These were desperate people they were dealing with, grasping at straws.

'Miss Dora said something about Miss Austen being more interesting than she seemed – a pearl in an oyster or something. Can't say I understood half of that, but I think Miss Dora now likes her.'

That was a change of heart from his Dora. What had gone on while he was in bed?

'What else?'

Kir resumed bouncing so had to be ordered off the covers. 'Oh, sir, it was so clever of Mr Smith and Miss Dora!' he said from his new post on the rug.

'What was clever?'

'Getting away from the bad men. The rotters made their cab horse – she was a grey mare called Sally – they scared her so she ran wild down Piccadilly – there was almost a fearful smash but Miss Dora stopped it with Mr Smith's help.' The boy jumped up to mime some daring moves of whip and reins. 'Like that! Sally was all right. But the bad men were after them so they ran off and hid in one of them flash bagnios that I'm not supposed to go near if I'm running messages.' That sounded like something Yarton would say. 'They waited till their hunters gave up and sneaked back in late last night when the coast was clear. Miss Dora said they'd had a bit of a scare, but they were unhurt. All of us have to take extra care when we go out and nowhere is to be left unguarded.'

'That sounds'—*alarming*—'exciting.'

'Oh, it is. Mr Yarton put footmen on all the entrances, including to the mews. I could hardly sleep a wink watching them patrol up and down like soldiers.'

'It sounds like I need to get up.'

With Kir's help, Jacob struggled into his clothes. It was very hard to bend so Kir made himself useful rolling stockings over Jacob's bare toes, holding out his breeches for him to step into, and passing braces over his shoulders so he could fasten them to their buttons. A pint-sized valet. Jacob was contemplating the pain of slipping into his jacket when Dora knocked and entered without waiting for a reply.

'Really, Jacob, you should still be in bed!' she exclaimed, seeing him upright. She was neatly dressed in a cream muslin gown and her hair tidied up under her hat, no sign of any damage taken from her adventures.

'Good morning to you too, darling.' He opened his arms. Kir made way so that he could hug Dora. 'Kir's been telling me of your heroics.'

'Hardly heroics. But at least we now know that the attacks are connected with our case and not that other matter.' She flicked a glance at Kir. Yes, it was best not to speak about marriage in front of one of the household's best gossips. Kir was so artless that he would repeat everything to Yarton or a kitchen maid and everyone would know their business.

'And what's all this about you and Miss Austen?'

'She is downstairs.'

'You haven't shaken her off yet?'

'No, though I wish Jane would stay where it is safe.

She revealed last night that she wrote *Sense and Sensibility* – in truth and not just as a lie to explain her accompanying me about town.'

'Did she indeed?' said Jacob, noticing the ladies were now on first name terms, a sign of the new intimacy between them. 'We will have to be careful with Miss Austen or find ourselves skewered in her next novel as an insufferable bore or outrageous flirt.'

'I should've guessed what she was up to. She was too clever, too quick to be an ordinary banker's sister.'

He laughed at that. 'I, by contrast, am not surprised. The women in my life are continual surprises to me. And I know Frank. There is a strain of the extraordinary in the Austen family.' He reached for his jacket.

Dora held it out for him. 'If I can't persuade you to spend the day in bed, then where are we going?'

'To find Julien, the new Comte D'Antraigues.'

'Of course. I should've thought of that. Any idea where to start?'

'If he has given up the house in Barnes, then Queen Anne Street is our best bet.' He waggled his eyebrows at her. 'Fortunately, we know someone who has already been introduced there and can pave the way for our introduction.'

Dora groaned. 'She won't let me forget this. Jane told me she would be useful to the investigation, and she is right.'

Music was playing as they knocked on the door of the D'Antraigues house in Queen Anne Street. It was a jarringly perky military march performed on a piano in what should be a house of mourning. A sullen footman opened the door.

'Comte D'Antraigues is not receiving,' he intoned.

A gust of convivial laughter came from a nearby room.

'Play it again!' boomed a man's voice, vowels rich with a Russian or Polish accent.

The march began again.

'Clearly,' said Jacob in a clipped tone. 'However, this is not a social but a business call. One of our party he already knows.' He gestured to Miss Austen. 'Please give him my card and say the matter is urgent.'

With a sceptical look at the two women behind Jacob, the footman allowed them to wait in the hall while he went in search of his master. Jacob studied with interest the collection of paintings on the wall. If he was any judge, there was a Watteau and a Zoffany hanging here. Both painters had a theatrical style that suited the house of a former opera star. Dora and Miss Austen were heads together over a collection of prints displayed on a marble table, including one of Vesuvius and another of the Fountains of Versailles. Compared to the paintings, they were rather dull pieces. The piano music broke off and there was a murmur of voices. The footman returned.

'He will see you now. Come this way.' The footman wasn't very good at his job. He hadn't even asked for the names of Jacob's companions. Standing at the door, he announced: 'Mr Fitz-Pennington and guests.'

Jacob strode into the room, making for the young man sitting at the piano. 'Actually, my name is Dr Sandys. The lady there is Miss Fitz-Pennington, my business partner, and I believe you've met Miss Austen?'

Seeing the females in the party, Julien, the new Comte

D'Antraigues, sprang up and straightened his coat tails. He shook Jacob's hand and bowed to the ladies.

'Forgive my man. He is still in training. Carl, please ask the cook to send up refreshments for my guests.' He retained only a hint of his French upbringing in his accent. No doubt he had spent almost all his life outside France thanks to the revolution booting his parents out in 1789.

While Julien was correcting the footman's error and instructing him what he should know to do without asking, Jacob took a quick survey of the company gathered for the musical morning. The host Julien was tall and thin with a pronounced nose. One would think that would make him ugly but there was something mesmerising in his dark eyes and sleek black hair that lessened the impact of his nose, somehow making it the perfect feature for his striking face. He was Gallic through and through, from his hand-waving gestures to his shrugs and exclamations of frustration at the quality of the servants he had been able to engage since the collapse of his family and, presumably, his finances. Jacob wondered how much longer Julien would be able to continue in this house. Only until the end of the lease, he would guess. As Julien's father had been the government pensioner, that would have stopped immediately on his demise. Julien had no obvious motive to be a party in their deaths because he must now be far worse off and without an income. Hopefully, the art collection that adorned the walls in this room and the hallway was his and he could sell it to survive a little longer until something else turned up.

Turning his attention to Julien's company, Jacob realised he had met one of them the day before: Count Ivan Vorontsov, aide to the Russian envoy, last seen at the Silver Cross. He bowed.

'Count Vorontsov, how was the chop?'

The count's confusion at this greeting cleared as he got a good look at Jacob. 'Ah, the friend of Thornbury! It was excellent. Delighted to meet you again.'

Jacob introduced Dora and Miss Austen without explaining their presence. He hoped they would get a moment alone with Julien, but the count looked very at home in the music room and made no sign of leaving. In his turn, the Russian introduced his wife, Countess Vorontsova, and her companion, Yekatarina Petrovna. The elegant countess was small and blonde, a complete opposite to her bluff, curly-haired husband. Miss Petrovna was about Dora's stature and had the lively expression of one who found much to mock in life. She was finely dressed and had her brunette hair styled in intricate ringlets which indicated she was no impoverished lady's companion but had her own maid.

Julien invited them all to take seats.

'I cannot tell you how distressed I was to hear of the deaths of your excellent parents,' said Miss Austen, settling into the chair near the piano while he perched on the stool. 'Please accept my heartfelt condolences.'

Julien gave her a nod as if words for his grief were too difficult. He said instead, 'Your brother and his wife have been very kind.'

'They feel it is the least they can do, considering the circumstances.'

Julien looked again at the card in his hand. 'Fitz-Pennington and Sandys? What business do you have with me?'

Jacob shot Dora a look. She was keeping quiet, her attention on the Russians, and gave him no indication how to play this. It was up to him to take the lead. 'Would you care to step outside so we can talk in private?' suggested Jacob.

'No, no, the count and countess are family friends. They know all my business. Indeed, I wouldn't have survived the last month without their support.' Julien tucked the card into his breast pocket.

'Very well. Miss Fitz-Pennington and I run an agency looking into sensitive matters for private clients. One of them has asked us to ascertain the motive for the attack on your parents.'

Julien frowned. 'It was a fit of insanity – I thought the coroner had decided?'

'Indeed, but our client has heard rumours that threaten to tarnish your parents' reputation posthumously and he wishes to have a cast-iron story to lay before the ton when it returns in September.'

'What kind of rumours?'

'That your father was working for the enemy.'

'Impossible!' Julien slammed the piano keys in a crashing discord.

Jacob held up a placating hand. 'Which is why we want to scotch any such rumours and circulate the truth. That may well be that the killer was mad. If we can prove this wasn't an isolated incident on the part of the perpetrator, that he was ill, then that would silence the gossipers.' Indeed, that was an angle they were yet to explore. The Italian was little but a name to them at this point.

Vorontsov gave a snort of disdain. 'You cannot stop

rumours. You can only wait for them to die out. Everyone is dead. It no longer matters.'

'Unfortunately, Count Vorontsov,' said Dora, speaking up for the first time, 'that is not true. Reputations matter to the living. I am sure the *comte* would not want to let his parents' memory be injured when he can prevent it?'

Julien could not say he did not care after she had phrased it that way. 'Indeed, Miss Fitz-Pennington. My parents deserve better. They deserve to have lived, but if they cannot have that, then they deserve to be respected.'

'You weren't with them that day?' Dora asked gently.

'No, I had gone ahead. I was here, preparing for a party – a musical party. *Maman* did so love a—' He broke off and got up to walk off his distress.

'*La comtesse* was a lady of great talent,' said Countess Vorontsova, taking over from their host. She languished on the sofa and fanned herself prettily. 'We adored to hear her sing. Ivan, remember that New Year's party *chez nous* in Dresden? She sang all evening, her powers undiminished.' She turned to Julien. 'Do you remember, Jules? I think you played your first piece before an audience that night.'

He smiled bitterly. 'If only we could turn back the clock.'

'I take it, countess, that you knew the *comte* and *comtesse* well when they lived in Dresden?' asked Jacob, remembering Thornbury had said that the *comte* had been attached to the Russian Legation in 1805 until the then Russian Foreign Minister and the *comte*'s sponsor had fallen out of favour.

'Knew them? *Mon cher* Dr Sandys, *en effet* we lived together, in and out of each other's houses. *Petit* Jules was friendly with our own son, Grigory.' She pursed her rosebud lips, managing to look childlike despite what he estimated was at least forty years of age. 'Is war not a terrible thing? Thinking of the suffering of the mothers of Europe! The continent is awash in tears. Grigory is serving in the army now under Prince Kutuzov. I thought he would be the one in danger, not *mes chers amis* living in London. You remember the party, don't you, Katya?'

Miss Petrovna chuckled sadly. She had a deep voice for a woman, likely an alto if she sang. 'That was a good season. I believe that was the winter I made my debut. It is cruel of you to remind me how many years have passed.' She twirled her hand. 'See, Dr Sandys, seven years have passed and I am still unattached.'

The countess seized Miss Petrovna's fingers, gaze intense. 'You must marry Jules, Katya, and then we can all smile again.'

Julien rolled his eyes, suggesting this was an old tease by someone he knew well and that no one was offended by the shameless matchmaking.

'You know Julien is married to his music,' said Miss Petrovna, patting her friend's hand. 'You must give up your schemes, Marta.'

'I will not give up until everyone is happy and this war is over,' said the countess with every indication that for her part she was not joking.

'Count Vorontsov,' said Jacob, 'I'm sorry to return to the subject of the murders, but if this were a simple case resolved by the death of Lorenzo then there would be wisdom in leaving it there. However, since we began asking questions a day ago it has become clear that someone is dangerously invested in making sure we get no answers. All three of us were attacked yesterday, unlikely though that may sound.'

'Not to mention ungentlemanly,' muttered Miss Austen.

'We've upset someone and now we must know why, else we will not know for certain if the danger has passed.'

'Do you English not say, never disturb the wasp nest?' said Vorontsov, the gold of his epaulets shining with military splendour. He was a strange messenger to preach avoidance. Jacob rather thought his appearance more suited to charging directly at the guns.

'That is all very well if the wasps are settled, but in this case I think they are swarming and ready to sting anyone who dares ask questions,' said Miss Austen with a hint of impatience. 'My room was searched and letters stolen merely because I was seen accompanying Miss Fitz-Pennington as she visited Barnes Terrace.'

'I was pushed in front of a carriage, and Miss Fitz-Pennington's hackney cab had fireworks thrown at the horse, almost causing a serious accident last night,' added Jacob.

'There were many fireworks last night,' said Vorontsov.

'You are suggesting it might be a coincidence?' said Dora. 'Then how do you explain the two men who pursued me after I escaped the carriage?'

Julien went back to the piano and ran his fingers over the polished top, pausing on a miniature in an ornate frame that looked as if it could be his mother at the height of her fame. 'But why? I cannot think of any reason why anyone would do such things.'

'Nor can we at the moment,' said Jacob. 'But if we were attacked, then it stands to reason that you might also be a target.'

Clutching the picture, he threw his arms wide, appealing to the heavens. 'But Lorenzo is dead! Cannot my parents be left in peace?'

'He may not have worked alone, sir,' said Jacob.

Julien put the frame down and turned his back to it, a protective gesture. 'Worked? You mean you think he had some kind of reason other than being employed as a servant to live in my parents' household?'

Now he was beginning to understand! It was about time the young man woke up to the danger.

'You should consider the fact that your father was close to the government and his opinion was valued. It would not be surprising to find the enemy planted informers in his circle to find out what he was saying.'

Julien folded his arms, still in denial. 'But Lorenzo was a deserter. He hated Napoleon.'

'Was he? How do you know that?'

'Well, he told us.' Julien swallowed, letting his arms fall to his side. 'You're right – *sacré bleu*, you're right! I'm a fool. We didn't know much about him when Father took him on. He just seemed amusing and personable. My father liked his staff to be handsome. He said it reflected well on the household.'

'I do not understand what this man is saying,' said the countess, appealing to her husband and shooting disapproving looks at Jacob. 'Do you, Ivan?'

Vorontsov went to stand behind her, resting his hands on her shoulders to give a comforting squeeze. 'He is saying, *ma chérie*, that Bonaparte might have infiltrated the D'Antraigues household and engineered an assassination of our friends. As much as I would prefer to think the deaths were the act of a solitary madman, I am forced to admit that no one holds a grudge like Napoleon.'

'*Non! Ce n'est pas possible!*' said the countess, applying her lacy handkerchief to her eyes which brimmed with tears. *'C'est une horreur!'*

Her friend reached over and took her hand. *'Courage, madame.'*

Feeling rather ungentlemanly to have so upset the ladies, Jacob could do nothing but plough on with their enquiries.

'Comte D'Antraigues, did your father leave you any papers, anything to do with the political reporting that he engaged in for the Foreign Secretary?' he asked.

'Me?' Julien looked shocked at the suggestion. 'No! I have no interest in such things. I take after my mother. My passion is music.'

'Have you been through the contents of his study here?' asked Dora.

'Yes, with the help of Count Vorontsov – oh, and some men from the Foreign Office came to take everything associated with Father's work for them. They said it was a matter of national security.'

So the cupboard was bare here, already picked clean. 'You should make that fact as generally known as possible,' said Jacob, standing up to go. 'If you have nothing of that nature close at hand, you are unlikely to be of interest to the people who attacked us. However, I would caution you to be on your guard. Somehow, we have stepped into murky waters and I don't see the bottom of them yet.'

'Very well. Thank you for the warning. I would suggest you give up your enquiry, but I imagine it is too late for that?' Julien conducted them to the door.

'Indeed, it is,' agreed Jacob. 'The hounds have slipped their leashes and are not yet back in the kennel.'

Julien glanced over his shoulder, checking they were out of

the hearing of his Russian guests. 'If you find anything … pertinent, will you let me know? They are my parents first and foremost and I am the one most concerned with their legacy.'

'We understand, sir,' said Jacob. 'And I know our client is as anxious not to damage their reputation as you could be.'

'I would hate people to judge them. They led unconventional lives.' Julien gave one of his magnificent shrugs, a 'what do you expect?' gesture of the generation that danced its way blindly into the revolution. 'But they were both brilliant in their own way. I count myself fortunate to be their son.'

Chapter Eighteen

Leaving Julien and his Russian guests to distract the son from his grief with music, Dora, Jacob and Jane ventured out onto Queen Anne Street.

'I do not appreciate being hunted like a rabbit,' said Jane, glancing up and down the street, looking as if she expected a runaway carriage to come bowling in their direction. It was empty, the shadows cast by the railing shortening as the sun climbed to noon.

'Then I suggest we dive into a burrow and consider who the fox might be,' said Jacob, offering her his arm. He held out the other to Dora.

'Any suggestions as to where we might go?' asked Dora.

'Gunter's?' suggested Jane hopefully.

'No!' said Dora and Jacob in unison, alarming the writer.

'Why? Is there a problem with that establishment?'

'Only with the gossipers who frequent it,' said Dora. 'And besides, it is a longish walk from here.'

'There is another coffee house that I have been longing to

try,' said Jane. 'Eliza is very partial to it, due to her early years in Madras.'

'Where is it?' asked Jacob.

'George Street. Is that close by?'

'Ah, I know it – and it is. An excellent suggestion as we are very unlikely to be followed into the coffee house and will spot our hunters soon enough if they lurk outside. It's a quiet area of town. Dora, you are in for a treat.'

Anything to be out of danger, thought Dora.

The establishment announced itself as the Hindoostane Coffee House. Carved sandalwood shutters and drapes of cotton chintz gave the front windows an oriental appearance in this row of ordinary town houses. The waiter showed them into a private room as befitting ladies, though the main room was almost empty with only a few old Company men playing chess in the window. Dora admired the prints of elephants and palanquins as Jacob ordered coffee and tea for the table. The waiter retreated.

'Is anyone going to try the culinary fare?' Jacob asked, scanning the menu chalked up on the board.

Dora was intrigued by the unfamiliar names for the offerings. 'Everything is served with rice, not potatoes? And all the dishes are spicy?'

'Cayenne pepper, curry powder, cardamon, cumin, turmeric – Eliza says that English cuisine is very tame compared to the meals she ate as a little girl,' said Jane. 'Now we are here, I will try the mildest. No good leaping into the deepest part of the menu without wetting my toes first and seeing if I can swim.'

'How on earth does an Hindoostane coffee house end up in Marylebone?' asked Dora, in wonder. She had thought she would have to travel to find such a thing. The scents from the kitchen were intriguing, none of the hot grease, bacon and bread smells of an ordinary tavern.

'It is owned by Captain Mohamed of the Bengal Army,' said Jacob. 'A brave man, thinking he can make a go of it here.'

'Plenty of us have family who have been to India and who return with their taste buds ruined for milder fare. I wish him luck,' said Jane. 'But I also wish to try the tandoor chicken.'

With their order given, the three investigators sat back and enjoyed the peace of the private room, each lost in their own thoughts.

Three women on the way home from market passed by with full baskets and reminded Dora that the morning was wearing away.

'Where does the case stand?' she asked. 'What have we learned so far?'

'I must admit I find it very perplexing. My brother thought he was only asking for you to uncover the background to the murder, not to awaken danger again.' Jane sniffed her tea. 'Hmm, interesting. Oolong – I rather liked the name.' She sipped. 'And I like the savour.'

Jacob poured his coffee, seemingly delighted by the wickedly dark colour. 'I believe we can rule out a private motive for the murders. There is no suggestion that Lorenzo was enamoured of the *comtesse*. As for money, Julien is the only one who stood to inherit and he is worse off without his father's income as an informer for the government.'

'His grief is genuine. He wasn't acting when he was overcome with emotion remembering them,' said Dora. She had felt sorry for the man. What would he do now with an empty title and only the glimmerings of musical talent, nothing in the class of his mother, the opera star?

'There is one good thing about the attacks,' said Jacob.

'I cannot think such violence bears any good fruit,' said Jane.

'Oh, but it does, Miss Austen. We know they are after something that is written down – letters or a report, as that is what they took from your room.'

'Actually, Jacob,' contradicted Dora, 'I think they are also trying to scare us off pursuing this any further. Alex and I worked that out after the attack last night. There was nothing to gain from that but putting us out of action.'

'They could have a double motive,' suggested Jane.

'I agree,' said Jacob. 'They know something is missing, likely still in circulation, and they want it most desperately. They want to stop us finding it first. Having searched the *comte*'s houses, they think your brother, and those in his family or employed by him, might have it, so they've gone after us. Thornbury mentioned a final report. Is it not possible that the *comte* would lodge such a valuable thing with Mr Austen prior to delivering it if he felt it of particular value?'

'I can see the logic to that, particularly if he wanted to negotiate a bonus payment from the government,' said Dora. 'Remove it from where it can be taken by a sneak thief, and let everyone know it exists so they can bid for it.'

Jacob nodded. 'The Russians included. He used to work for them. He might have been playing us off against them.'

'Which means he thought he was on to something very important, crucial to the war effort.' What could it be? Dora wondered. Jacob had described the Comte D'Antraigues as a man who put the pieces of the puzzle together. Had he secured a critical piece and formed a picture that killed him?

'But would the *comte* be so mercenary? Did he have no gratitude to the country that sheltered him?' asked Jane.

Jacob gave her a sympathetic smile. 'The man burned through his money, Miss Austen – entertaining his friends, two houses, an art collection to which he regularly added if I'm any judge of these things, not to mention his wife and son. A thousand pound a year would soon vanish in London.'

Dora and Jane exchanged a glance on that statement from a man used to wealth. Both of them could live very comfortably indeed on so much.

'But I thought he hated Bonaparte. Why withhold information that could lead to his downfall?' persisted the writer.

That was a good point. Dora looked to Jacob for an answer. 'Ditto to what she said.'

'I doubt very much he was going to withhold it to the point that it was of no use. He was using the window of opportunity to get well paid for his insights,' suggested Jacob.

'Then what did he foresee, and who is after that report?' asked Dora.

'We must add the Russians to our list of suspects as they are sticking close to Julien. The Vorontsovs could be sincere friends, but they could also be hoping to find the report themselves. Top of the list of suspects must be the French, and then any other governments whose agents were asked to bid for the report – the Swedish, even the Americans might want it.'

Dora gave a huff of frustration. 'That hasn't narrowed

down our suspects. Which of them is willing to commit murder for this?'

'Men are dying in their thousands on the battlefields,' said Jacob matter-of-factly. 'Most government agents would be able to justify the death of a couple of people in London if it got them what they wanted for their country's war effort.'

That was a grim thought. 'I take it your brother has nothing like a report, or letters mentioning one, in his possession?' Dora asked Jane.

The lady paled at the suggestion. 'We must ask him directly, but I don't believe so or he would've mentioned it earlier.'

'Perhaps there is something in the bank's vault?'

Jane laced her fingers around her cup. 'That is a possibility. I simply don't know.'

'It looks like our next stop is the bank,' said Jacob. 'I'd like a look at the D'Antraigues account in any case, to see if that tells us anything.'

Jane drained her Oolong to the dregs and put the cup down with a decisive chink. 'Then I believe we should ask them to put my order in a basket so I can take it with us. I for one do not want to wait to find out what answers may lie in Henry's bank.'

The banking house was in Henrietta Street to the south of Covent Garden. In the hackney cab on the way, Dora decided to ask for more information about Jane's brother's profession as she didn't think she'd ever met a banker before.

'How did your brother end up with a bank in London?' she asked.

Jane smiled. 'Henry is full of surprises.'

'I understand it is a small concern with only three partners?' prompted Jacob.

'That is correct. Henry has had the most unsettled of lives of all my brothers. He first tried the army life but found he enjoyed handling money more than marching in formation.' Jane gave a soft laugh. 'He probably misses the young ladies going into raptures over his red coat. He did look very gallant.'

'Every girl loves an officer,' said Dora, echoing the popular sentiment.

'Quite so. He has opened a little branch of this bank near my home, where people know and trust him, but the main office is here.'

'And how does he make his money?' Dora knew it was a crude enquiry, but she wasn't a lady like Jane and needn't worry about offending anyone.

'I'm afraid I... Well, in the usual way,' said Jane delicately.

'He will be the kind of banker who started with a pool of money from what he and his partners could gather from their friends and acquaintances and then they lend it at a high interest rate to rich men wanting to cover their debts or make investments,' said Jacob, revealing his familiarity with the workings of the world of finance. 'These small banks tend to take on more risk than the large ones because the rewards are commensurably bigger.'

'I can understand better now why Mr Austen is so anxious that no bad associations are attached to his bank,' said Dora. 'If those original investors come asking for their money back because they got the jitters, they might find the pool too shallow as it has been siphoned off to their debtors.'

Jane was looking worried by all this discussion of moneylending. Dora could sympathise. It did sound a very shaky foundation on which to build a life in London, nothing as tangible as the army commission Henry had once held, or the living his father had had in the Church. It could all vanish like a fairy feast. How it must irritate him that his brother Edward had been adopted by a rich family and come into an estate and wealth beyond a man's imaginings! Perhaps that was driving him to try to rival Edward by making his own fortune?

Henry received them in his private office. The first room was occupied by two clerks sitting at high desks, making entries in the bank's ledgers. They looked up curiously as the visitors passed before returning to what looked a mind-numbing task. Henry's office was plain but elegant, without any of the feminine touches of his home. He offered them chairs as he returned to his seat behind the desk.

'Am I to understand from your visit here that you have news? I asked you to try to be discreet and turning up here in force is hardly that,' he said gloomily.

'Henry, dear,' said Jane, 'I believe after three attacks yesterday we are beyond being primarily interested in saving appearances.'

'You can say that, but I have all this to protect.' He flicked his fingers at their surroundings. 'I've already had four customers enquiring if they can withdraw their money.'

'The good news, sir,' said Jacob quickly before Henry and Jane could argue further, 'is that nothing we've discovered indicates there is any truth in the rumours that the Comte

D'Antraigues was disloyal to Britain and her allies. Far from it. It appears the *comte* was a trusted source of information on foreign affairs and was in receipt of a pension from His Majesty's government.'

'Was he indeed?' Henry folded his hands on the ledger, looking a little relieved. 'He never said. Do you think the government would admit to that, should we need to put down rumours of him working for the French?'

Jacob looked sceptical. 'It is a sensitive subject because there are many in Parliament and the press who will take issue with paying a foreigner so much when there are many demands on the public purse.'

'It was ever thus.'

'Indeed, but I think they would prefer not to say anything, and we have no leverage to make them speak the truth in public. I was told this in confidence by someone in the government and they will not thank me for bruiting it about. Am I to understand from your ignorance of the arrangement that the *comte* did not bank that pension with you, meaning you have no proof of where his funds came from?'

'No. He would occasionally lodge sums with me or borrow to buy an artwork that came up for auction, but I was under the impression he didn't have large investments anywhere in London.'

'Did he ever miss a payment?'

'I… He always paid eventually.'

The man was likely close to being bankrupt and kept going from pension to pension, thought Dora, knowing all too well what it was like to live from hand to mouth. His life sounded a gilded version of the same.

'Did he ever say where the money came from, sir?' she asked.

'He said from his writing, Miss Fitz-Pennington. I knew he wrote tracts against Napoleon and assumed that he was exceptionally well paid for them.' In other words, Henry hadn't wanted to ask too many questions, which might be why he had been worried enough to start this enquiry.

'He must have been paid far more than what I get for writing novels,' mused Jane.

'But his writing was more dangerous – as events have proved,' said Henry.

'I'd like to see everything you have on the *comte* if you would oblige,' said Jacob. 'The present *comte*, Julien, is aware we are making enquiries.'

'Then of course. I will send up the books.'

'You have no other holdings, no private papers or strong box?' asked Dora.

'We aren't well placed to store clients' valuables, Miss Fitz-Pennington. He would likely use one of the larger banks with an underground vault for matters like that.'

'Any idea who?'

'I'd try Coutts. I believe he had some dealings with them.'

Jacob went to the inner office to look through the Comte D'Antraigues accounts, leaving the ladies with Henry. Jane produced her basket and placed it on his desk. The wonderful smell of the Tandoor chicken filled the room.

'I brought something to cheer you up,' she said.

'Jane, what would I do without you?' Henry said, giving her a boyish grin. He sent a clerk off to find some plates and forks and divided the contents of the basket into four small helpings.

'We met some Russians at Julien's house,' said Jane, picking cardamon pods out of her rice. 'Do you know anything about them?'

'Which ones?' Henry held a piece of chicken spiked on the tines.

'The Vorontsovs.'

He chewed and swallowed. 'Heavenly. Not personally, but I believe they arrived in the spring. Once Napoleon succeeded in alienating his old allies, the Russians have decided we aren't so bad after all and have come to set up shop again in London.'

'Can you think why they might want the *comte* and *comtesse* dead?' asked Dora.

He swallowed a second mouthful awkwardly and coughed. 'Good Lord. You don't pull your punches, do you, Miss Fitz-Pennington? No, I cannot. The Russian delegation would regard the Comte D'Antraigues as an asset, a Frenchman writing against Napoleon, useful in putting across their arguments against the emperor. And if he were writing valuable reports, why kill the goose laying the golden eggs?'

Jane had a meeting with her publisher that afternoon, so they left her with her brother. Dora wished she had the leisure to stay and hear how the negotiations were going, but murder was a more pressing concern.

'Did you find anything in the accounts?' Dora asked Jacob as they walked quickly back to the office, her with her hand on her pistol in her pocket, Jacob ready to use his walking cane to drive off anyone who dared approach.

'Nothing that would cast light on our case. I've moved

away from the theory that he was taking bribes or acting as a double agent in receipt of money from the French. It seems more straightforward: he was a skilled political commentator and governments were prepared to pay for his analysis.'

'And one was prepared to kill for it?'

'Yes.'

'The French?'

'That would be the obvious conclusion. The killer had been in the French army and we only have his word that he deserted. I think we need to dig into his background and find out who he really was.'

Dora fully agreed with that plan. 'I think I might know where to start.'

'Where would that be?'

'He was Italian so would not the Italians in London be more likely to know him? He might've preferred to spend evenings with people who spoke his language.'

Jacob smiled, getting the hint. 'Is it time for dessert?'

'I believe it is. But let's go to the kitchen door this time. I don't want to find myself in the papers again tomorrow.'

Chapter Nineteen

Gunter's Ice Cream Parlour

Giovanni, the waiter who had served them two days ago at Gunter's, was standing by the kitchen door smoking a cigarillo when they arrived. He immediately tried to hide it behind his back and adopt his customer demeanour, but Dora slapped him on the shoulder. Dora's ability to shift character had always fascinated Jacob.

'It's only us, Giovanni, and not in our front-of-house character. We're backstage now and can drop the act,' she said.

Talking about backstage, the rear of the patisserie had no garden but was used for outbuildings. Milk churns stood by the gate, ready for collection. A door to one windowless brick shed at the northeastern corner had 'Ice House' written on it. Jacob was pleased to see that it looked a well-managed establishment with swept cobbles and everything neat and tidy. He would not think twice about ordering at the front again.

'But signorina…!' protested the waiter.

'I'm Dora and this is Jacob. We're working.'

The waiter looked confused. 'But you are a lady and gentleman.'

'He is. I'm an actress – and no, I'm not his mistress,' she said quickly when a knowing glint entered the waiter's eye. 'We solve mysteries for our clients.'

'*Non ci credo!*'

'I swear it's true. Our office is in Bruton Mews if you want to check.'

Jacob offered his hand, which contained some coins as well as their calling card. 'We're after information.'

Giovanni perked up on the offer of a tip; that was something he could believe. He pocketed the money and took the cigarillo out from behind him. He gave it a puff to keep it lit. 'Very well. But I will not discuss our customers.'

'Glad to hear it,' said Jacob. Unlike the clientele, the waiters at Gunter's were more discreet. 'We are looking into an Italian by the name of Lorenzo.'

Giovanni spluttered a laugh. 'That is all? *Ma dai*, I can point you to six Lorenzos in London at once.'

'Do you have a smoke?' Dora asked, pointing to the cigarillo. 'I always wanted to try.'

'Filthy habit,' muttered Jacob. 'In Spain, half the army is addicted to them.'

With a grin, Giovanni produced another of the small cigars from his breast pocket and snipped off the end with a pair of grape scissors. He then held it to his own lit one until the fresh one smouldered. 'For the lovely lady.'

Dora put it to her lips then paused. 'What do I do?'

'You suck – like this.' His eyes danced wickedly as he demonstrated.

Dora laughed and flicked a warm look at Jacob. 'I do so love sucking.'

Jacob felt a blush rise from his neck and travel up his face. 'Dora!'

'Sorry.' She turned back to Giovanni. 'He's easily embarrassed.'

Jacob could tell she was teasing him to get the waiter on her side and convince him that she was his kind of people, but, damn, she could make him suffer. Only the thought that he would persuade her to carry out her love for such things when they were in bed later made him feel better and left his breeches uncomfortably tight.

'You want to know a Lorenzo? Which one?' asked the waiter.

'Well, Giò, this one was a very bad lot. He killed the Comte and Comtesse D'Antraigues.' Dora leaned beside him and tentatively puffed on the cigarillo. She made a moue of distaste.

'It will grow on you, as you English say,' said Giovanni. '*Sí*, I know that Lorenzo … *purtroppo*. Lorenzo Stelli. He came here with his master and mistress. While they ate ice cream, he would come out here and talk about the old country. He missed speaking *Italiano*.'

'Can you remember anything about him?'

'He could talk, that one.' He made a yapping gesture with his free hand. 'He came from *Milano*. He said he was persuaded to join the emperor's army because they were winning. He wanted to be a winner. If he did not join army, he would have no work and they would kick him around as a peasant.'

That pride went with what they knew of the man.

'Did he say why he left the army?' Dora asked.

Giovanni nodded. 'He was proud of doing so. He said he hated how the Italians were always given the worst jobs. They were sent to face the guns while the French waited behind the hill, saving their powder so they could make a bold advance when the enemy was worn down and they could claim credit for the victory.'

'I suppose it stands to reason that the French might want to spare their own.'

'*Sí, ovviamente*. Also, Lorenzo hated his commander who did not like him. He was given lash for … how do you say? … insubordination?'

Jacob nodded. 'Army discipline can be brutal and if your commanding officer doesn't like you then your life does become unbearable. What happened next? Lorenzo absconded?'

Giovanni nodded and waved the cigarillo in a circle. 'He ran away and took a boat from Genova.'

'How did he end up working for an émigré?' asked Dora.

'I have to go soon.' Giovanni dropped the end of his smoke and ground it out with his heel. 'He said he arrived in London and asked for the man who hated Bonaparte the most. An Italian who plays in the Theatre Royal orchestra pointed him to the Comte D'Antraigues.'

If you were in fact an informer for the French, would you not cook up a story exactly like this? thought Jacob. Why else carry your political views with you and let that influence who you wanted to work for if you were running away from all of that? 'Would you say that Lorenzo truly hated Napoleon?'

'Oh, yes. He would spit every time anyone said the emperor's name. He swore that he would stab him if ever he got the chance.' Giovanni made stabbing motions. 'Like this, he said.'

Instead, Lorenzo stabbed two people who had befriended him and who stood against Napoleon. 'Would you say that he was mad?'

Giovanni shrugged. 'I do not know. We can all break, no? He was passionate, but he made sense. He was *tipico uomo Milanese*.'

'What does that mean?' asked Dora.

'He was quick to take offence. I would not pick an argument with him.'

'And what did you think when you heard he had killed his employers?' asked Jacob.

A man appeared at the door of the kitchen and beckoned Giovanni back inside. The waiter brushed off the ash that had drifted onto his sleeve.

'I thought everyone else had a lucky escape. Lorenzo Stelli was boiling with anger – hot, hot fury like Vesuvius – and someone was going to get burned.'

Jacob updated the casebook while Dora retired to her room. She was on her monthlies, and though as a doctor he was aware of the mechanics of the process, he was vaguer on the methods women used to pad the flow. Even his bold Dora was reticent when it came to normal bodily functions, as most of his female patients were. She had merely said she needed to get changed and he had not pressed her to stay, despite the fact he really didn't want to let her out of his sight while the threat still hung over them. Biology, though, trumped even safety concerns.

Jacob dipped his pen in the inkwell. Lorenzo Stelli, a bomb with a lit fuse – that was the impression Jacob had taken away from the helpful waiter. Either he was a convincing actor or a fanatical opponent of Napoleon. His murder of his employers could have been for personal motives – a slight that he felt he must repay or some other grudge – but with the missing report in the middle of this it felt more than ever as if there was a key piece of information lacking to make sense of the crime.

Why would a man who hated Napoleon kill someone who was aiding the allies in the fight against him?

Alternatively, why would an informer for the French, successfully undercover in the *comte*'s household, blow that all to smithereens in a fit of temper?

Who else could possibly have been there?

He looked back through Dora's notes. Lorenzo had been a favourite of the ladies so that suggested he might have been susceptible to a female, someone who could get close enough to kill him and make it look like suicide. Dora had eliminated the female servants as they were down in the hall to see their mistress to the carriage. A woman, or perhaps a man who was trusted like a brother? Italians were more exuberant in their greetings and would hug and touch each other without shame, unlike the English. He added that addendum to the notes. They must not get fixed on looking for a woman.

Alex came in from the street and hung his hat on the hatstand. He took a quick look around the room.

'How's Dora?' he asked.

'She's in her room and will return soon.' Jacob pushed back from the desk. 'What do you make of all this, Smith? We've found out more about the killer. The story he told about himself fits with the idea that he was a disgruntled deserter who hated Napoleon and objected to army discipline.'

'Most of the ordinary soldiers do, no matter the army,' said Alex wryly.

'So why then turn on his employer, the man who had helped him?'

At that moment, Dora rushed back in. 'Jacob, I've had an idea—Oh, Alex, good day to you.'

'Dora,' said Alex with a grin. 'Your idea?'

'What if Lorenzo snapped because the *comte*'s report concluded that Napoleon would thrash the allied armies? Wouldn't that drive the government to make peace if they lost hope of victory? Lorenzo hated the emperor so much that he couldn't bear it and struck out to silence the *comte*.'

That was a thought, though a bad report from a source was unlikely to sway the conduct of the war, no matter how trusted. 'And the *comtesse*?'

'In his killing frenzy he went for her too – hating them, the world, his fate that brought him to this point.'

'A murder-suicide?' asked Alex. 'As the coroner found?'

'Exactly,' said Dora. 'And Lorenzo wasn't a French informer, but a hater of Napoleon.'

'Then why are people after us now?' asked Jacob.

'Because the report still exists – because we were right that the *comte* was asking for the highest bidders. It is hidden and everyone is after it. We've had the misfortune of stumbling into the skulduggery of international politics resulting from the murders.' She looked at them both, eyes bright with excitement. He wanted to sweep her off her feet and spin her in a circle, however…

Did it tie all the parts of the mystery together? Jacob wasn't sure, but it felt like a strong possibility. 'Well done – that's a good theory.'

Her face fell. 'Why, thank you, kind sir,' she said, deadpan. 'You don't sound convinced.'

'I'm … open to the idea. I think we must test your hypothesis.'

'How?' She flopped down into the visitor's chair that Alex had vacated for her.

'It would help if we could eliminate the possibility of there being someone else in the house at the time of the murder. If he acted alone, then your idea becomes our front runner. I'd like to go back to Barnes and look at where the suicide took place.'

Dora pulled a face. 'The maid knows me. I doubt I'd get back inside again. She'll think I'm vulgarly curious.'

'Then Smith and I can go and ask the owner of the property if we can see it with a view to leasing it as my summer residence. How do you fancy being my solicitor, Smith?'

Alex grinned. 'I imagine I can string together enough legal Latin to be convincing. *Caveat venditor*.'

'Glad to see the army hasn't driven out all your schooling.' Jacob locked the casebook away and kissed Dora's cheek in farewell. 'You'll stay here? Yarton's footmen are keeping a watch so you should be safe.'

'I'll stay for a bit, but then I thought I'd go and visit Ruby. We need to clear the air between us.' He was about to object but she put her finger to his lips. 'And yes, I'll take a footman to accompany me.'

That would have to do. He couldn't ask her to make herself a prisoner.

'Forewarned is forearmed,' he said, more for himself than for her.

'And good luck to anyone who dares attack me at Ruby's. She'll make mincemeat of them.'

Jacob gave Alex a look.

'I'll wait for you outside,' Alex said.

Once he was gone, Jacob pulled Dora to him. 'Remember, when Ruby presses her case, I want to marry you.'

'I know.' She pressed her forehead against his cheek and kissed his throat.

He stroked her back, enjoying the long line of her spine. 'We must live our lives for ourselves, not for others. We do them no favours by letting them ride roughshod over us.'

'That would be a bad habit to encourage,' she agreed.

'So?'

'Jacob, I'm looking for a path forwards that will be acceptable to my friend as well as to us – and perhaps even to your family.'

'I'm not compromising on the fact that we should marry. What if we have children? I refuse to let them suffer the stigma of bastardy.'

She tapped his chest in understanding. 'I know. Believe me, I know how ugly it is to be someone's bastard. But we have time. I'm not pregnant, and Ruby is. Let me see what talking to her will achieve.'

He kissed her and let her go. Despite his smiles, he left feeling a cloud of doom hovering, waiting to envelop them.

Chapter Twenty

Wimpole Street, Marylebone

The maid showed Dora into a handsome drawing room on the first floor. Rococo furniture curved and bowed fussily in armchairs, sofas and side tables, upholstery a mannish navy blue. Hunting scenes galloped across the walls, red-coated riders after a startled streak of a fox. Definitely not Ruby's taste, decided Dora.

'Madame will be down immediately,' said the maid, bobbing a curtsey.

Dora chose a seat on the end of the sofa, glad to sit down. She had cramps, her period uncomfortably heavy. The cloth pad secured by a belt around her waist was snug and fresh, but she would have to use Ruby's closet before returning home or risk an embarrassing accident.

Women's bodies were annoyingly inconvenient. Men didn't understand the half of it.

With that thought, she sprang up, worried she might be

inadvertently leaving a spot on the sofa cushion. She checked the back of her skirt.

Ruby wafted in, dressed in a flowing white gown secured under her bust but leaving her body free of stays.

'Whatever is the matter with you, Dora? I've not put pins in my cushions.' She came over to kiss her on both cheeks.

'It's the visitor,' said Dora, returning the affectionate greeting.

'Poor you; you always do suffer in the first few days. At least I don't have to worry about that for a few months.' Ruby patted her stomach.

'I was worried I might ruin your furniture.'

'Oh, don't be so silly. It's horrid old stuff in any case. I've ordered a whole new set from Thomas Sheraton and it arrives in a few weeks. Do you know you can pick what you want out of a catalogue and it arrives like magic? Who would've thought? Sit down and rest. You appear quite fatigued, not in your best looks at all. Is it just the visitor or is something else the matter?' Ruby sank gracefully into an armchair and put her feet up on a stool. 'Cook will send up some refreshments. Can you stay long?'

The mantelpiece clock, a gilded affair of Atlas supporting the dial, showed it was approaching dinnertime. 'Are you expecting company?'

'Arthur isn't coming until later if that's what you are worried about. How about cards? I do get so bored here on my own. There is only so much shopping one can do to pass the time.'

Dora carried a card table over to set it between them 'Where is the deck?'

'There's a box on the bookcase – the silver one.'

Dora returned with the playing cards and shuffled. 'Piquet?'

Ruby nodded and yawned. 'Sorry – I was napping when you arrived.'

'How are you? All well with the baby?'

She rubbed a circle over her tummy. 'I believe so. She dances around like her mother. Perhaps she'll try for the ballet – plenty of work in that for a few years and it is suitably scandalous. Have you seen how the prudes in the periodicals get in a lather over a girl pirouetting? They don't understand the difference between art and prostitution.'

Dora dealt. 'Still convinced it is going to be a girl?'

Ruby shrugged and picked up her hand. 'Call it a mother's instinct.' She discarded a card and selected another from the undealt pile. 'I'm sorry about the newspapers.' She avoided Dora's eyes.

'It was a bigger problem for Jacob than for me.' Dora rearranged her hand to see what runs of suits she held.

'I hope you can be bothered to score the tricks because I never can be.' Ruby set a king of hearts down. 'Perhaps we should have picked a simpler game.'

Dora responded with a knave. 'Let's see this one through.'

'Arthur arrived here in a fury last night. He'd seen Jacob and been given a firm rebuff.' Ruby collected her win. 'I can say one thing for him: anger makes him a more interesting lover.'

Dora scowled. 'Really, Ruby, I do not want to know. He could be my brother-in-law one day.'

'You still mean to marry?' An edge developed in Ruby's tone.

'Is there any reason why I should not – a reason that does

not concern your own interests? What do you think you would do in my place?'

'Look around for a richer man?' A little of Ruby's old mischief returned. 'Arthur wants me to hold a party to introduce you to some dukes and earls. I think he has it in his head that you are after a title and riches and would accept being a mistress of a higher member of the nobility and jilt a younger son.'

'He doesn't know me very well.' Dora won the next point as Ruby could never concentrate on remembering the cards.

'He is merely judging as he sees. Most women would think like that.' She played a low diamond that was bound to be beaten by Dora.

'Would they? Don't you think most women would prefer to marry for love?' Dora thought of the choices of Jane Austen's characters. For Elinor and Edmund, it was love in a cottage – albeit a decent vicarage. The loss of his fortune was presented as less of a tragedy than the possibility that he would have to marry the awful Lucy Steele. 'Besides, Jacob is independently wealthy. I'm not choosing poverty if I marry him.'

'You've been reading too many novels,' grumbled Ruby, showing she must've tapped into Dora's thoughts, or more likely, watched her in too many green rooms waiting to go on stage with the latest novel in hand. 'The playwrights have it right. Love leads to death, betrayal or comedy.'

'You are not a romantic then?'

'Romance is the icing on the cake. If you don't have the cake, what good is the icing? It leaves you holding a sticky mess in your hand.'

Dora laughed at that. It was for comments like this that she loved Ruby.

'If the viscount says he will continue to keep you even if Jacob and I marry, will you be content?' Dora played a low card, hoping to give Ruby the win.

'You did that on purpose.' Ruby collected the point. 'I would rather not risk his rejection.'

'But Jacob and I cannot live our lives to please you.' She placed a high card down.

Ruby conceded the trick. 'Why not?' But she said it with a laugh, knowing she was being outrageous. 'Can you not wait until I have secured the viscount's affections? He likes me well enough, but I wouldn't say it's a strong attachment, not yet. I don't want to be out on the street with the babe on the way – that's what you might bring about.'

'Do you really think the viscount would do that?'

Ruby rubbed her stomach. 'Oh, he'd pay me off, I've no doubt, but I've not yet earned more than a diamond bracelet or something of that nature.'

'And you want the whole Crown Jewels? How about we agree that Jacob and I will not be precipitate. Things will change when you have the child, you must realise that? The viscount might decide that he does not want a mistress who is more concerned with her baby than him.'

Ruby shook her head at that. 'I'm no fool. I'll hire a nurse and keep the child out of the way when Arthur calls. He will barely know she exists. He is paying for a fantasy – a dream of a woman who lives only for him and is raising a perfect family of pretty little by-blows who think he is wonderful, children who will beg sweets from him and call him Papa. I intend to provide him with his dream.'

Dora cocked her head to one side. 'Do you love him, Ruby? Are your feelings the least bit engaged in what you have with him? It sounds to me like you are approaching this as though you were playing a role.'

'Perhaps I am. If I were you, I would tell me that that was wise.'

'It sounds a loveless existence.'

Ruby shrugged. 'I'll have the children to love. You know me – I'm not sure I have any strong feelings for men other than fear and annoyance. I can desire them, find them amusing in bed, but if I could live my life without relying on one, I'd be truly happy.' Ruby dumped the rest of her cards. 'You win. Let's look at the ladies' magazines together. You can help me pick out a gown for my first party.'

'Oh, Ruby…' Dora felt sorrow swamp her. The abuse her friend had suffered as a child had turned her into this cynic.

Ruby swatted her with the rolled magazine. 'Stop it. I will not be pitied. Why don't we agree that we will attempt not to ruin each other's happiness?'

'Agreed.' Dora sneaked a look at Ruby. 'If we do marry, I'll invite you to the wedding. That will put the fox in the henhouse.'

Ruby chuckled. 'For that, I'd almost say go wed your doctor immediately. We two actresses, veterans of the northern circuit, live for nothing if not to set the world arsy-varsy.'

Dora did not give Ruby a firm answer as to whether she would attend Ruby's first party. It sounded like the viscount would veto Jacob's presence, so that made it awkward for Dora to attend. She returned to the carriage that the footman was holding ready for her, grateful to have escaped the house before Arthur arrived. Encountering him on the doorstep would be deeply awkward.

That was an odd relationship, she thought, as the carriage rocked away over the cobbles, Arthur wanting the façade of a family but none of the commitment. Did he realise it was a husk, that Ruby had no real loyalty to him? He probably did at some level. It was as though they had both consented to play their appointed roles and were angry when anyone else broke into their bubble and questioned them. The viscount was using his money to hold life's complications at bay, playing it safe in a relationship he could control.

How different was her own arrangement. Jacob could have petitioned her harder to accept a similar place in his life, she realised. Her feelings were engaged so he might have been able to wear her down, she was not sure. Yet he had not pressed once he was aware that she held herself to her own standards, ones of independence and choice. If she married him, by law she would be surrendering some of those choices, the most important ones. Her body and children would no longer be hers. Any money she had would become his – not that that was a problem, considering the disparity in their fortune. She would as far as the law was concerned cease to exist independently and could not detach herself from him if things turned sour. Ruby had more choices than she did in that respect. She would have to flee the country and become someone else, if that happened with Jacob.

But would it? She knew in her bones that Jacob was fundamentally decent. He loved her and would use those powers to protect her. That would be annoying, of course, but what if they negotiated the limits of what he would ask?

He might not be bound by the law to respect her wishes but he would keep his word, as he had proved time and again.

It meant taking a chance on a man. Ruby wouldn't, but would Dora?

Pondering these things, Dora let the carriage sweep her back to Mayfair.

Chapter Twenty-One

Barnes Terrace

The agent for the owner of the house on the banks of the Thames did not balk at showing a potential client around even though it was short notice. Jacob surmised that this was because he was aware that the notoriety of a double murder made it a less than restful location for someone looking for a rural retreat.

The dapper gentleman held a lace-trimmed handkerchief in his hand which he flourished like some fop of the previous century. His clothing, however, was sober and worthy of a follower of Beau Brummel. He'd only looked askance twice at Jacob's bruises and the cane he used for his limping walk. Curiosity was eating him up, but he was too well bred to comment.

'Sir will notice that the hall is very spacious, unexpectedly so for a terrace house. The servants' apartments are airy and there is a decent-sized kitchen. The last client'—the one who had expired in a pool of blood, Jacob added silently—'kept a French cook and he was more than satisfied with the arrangements.'

'Pleased to hear it. Make a note, Smith.' Jacob was in his most pompous persona. Alex winked behind the agent's back and muttered:

'Very good, sir. French cook.'

Mr Falconberg jumped neatly over the first stair and the one at the very top, making no mention that he was avoiding the places where the last occupiers had died. The man was obviously superstitious and attempting to avoid the bad luck that came with walking on the spot where someone had expired in violence. 'The house is very well appointed, and I doubt it will remain long on the market.' He didn't think that at all, but he had to give his sales push. 'I believe the best features are the rooms on the first floor. There's a very fine salon with a river view and two principal apartments looking out on the garden at the back, very quiet.'

Jacob obediently followed him upstairs, Alex trailing behind them. He paused inside the empty salon. Without any furniture, and the carpets rolled up, it felt cold and cheerless despite the view of the sluggish Thames and its flotilla of boats. 'As you said, very well appointed. I'm most interested in the bedrooms. My wife-to-be is very particular about noise at night.'

Falconberg nodded sagely. 'A very discerning lady. We have two on this floor. The one decorated to a lady's taste is through here.' He led them to a room decked out with the appearance of Versailles under Louis XIV – white and gold.

If the furniture had been similar, it would have been very striking but overblown for a terrace in Barnes. Dust shadows on the wall denoted where mirrors had hung.

'Very good. And the gentleman's room?'

'Back into the corridor and then the next door.' The agent turned.

'There is no connecting door?' Jacob frowned.

The handkerchief fluttered. 'The … er … last tenants asked for that to be blocked up.'

'Did they not like each other then?' Jacob tapped the wall. It was indeed solid, no hidden doorway that he could detect.

'I'm afraid I really cannot say. They were an older couple…'

'Ah! Hymen's fires were burning low. I understand.' He followed the agent to the room next door. This was decorated to a pleasant masculine taste of forest green and cream, nothing too ornate. 'How did the last tenant arrange his furniture?'

The agent looked taken aback by such a specific request. He had made a misstep, Jacob realised, his interest too pointed. Dora was better at this kind of thing.

'I intend to carry on the business of my estate even while in rural retirement and like to have a desk in my chamber.'

The man's confusion cleared. 'Indeed, the … er … late client had a canopied bed on the back wall, and a desk by the window. Bookshelves on that wall—'

'The one between his room and his wife's?'

'Correct. There's a dressing room through that door.'

Jacob strode over and opened it. 'Very neat.'

'I believe he would have his bath set up there. He was fond of baths,' added the client a little wistfully.

'How did the staff bring up the water?'

'Ah!' Looking delighted that he could satisfy the prospective client's curiosity, Falconberg sprang forward. 'There is a door here to the servant's stairs – very cleverly disguised.' He pushed at the white moulding which was a little more yellowed than the decoration around it and a narrow door opened to a dark stairwell.

'Smith, see where that goes,' ordered Jacob, knowing that a gentleman such as he was pretending to be would not deign to examine the servants' quarters. 'Check if my cook would be as satisfied with arrangements as the Frenchman was.' He turned back to the agent. 'I always found the French too particular over such things. If the fireplace is big enough for a spit for roast beef and the stove for a batch of pudding, then I'll be happy.'

'Quite so,' said Falconberg, though Jacob could tell he now despised him for his tastes. This agent was a man who aspired to ragout and syllabubs.

Getting into the role, Jacob went to the window and whistled the tune Chevy Chase. He wasn't playing his older brother exactly, and definitely not William who was the epitome of politeness and would not turn his back on a man, no matter how menial, but aping the most annoying commanding officer he had known in Portugal, a braggard whose mustachios had more sense than he did.

Footsteps heralded Alex's return. 'Sir, if I might suggest we confer? The house is very promising, but we have others to consider.'

The agent got very hot under the collar hearing that, handkerchief wafting like the pennant on the main mast. 'I can offer a ten per cent discount for twelve months as we are leaving the summer season.'

Jacob folded his arms and gave the bedroom another survey, taking in the details. 'Why did the last tenants give it up?' He was interested to see if the man would lie. It would be easy to disprove as soon as they went into the nearest tavern and stated their business in the area.

'I'm afraid they died, sir,' said Falconberg, clamping the folder of information he had about the house under his arm as if he were afraid Jacob would rip it from him and riffle through the contents.

'What? Together?'

'Yes, sir. A terrible incident – and not the fault of the house at all. It is unfair for the place to be tarnished by association.'

A version of the truth! How refreshing. 'You will find I am not a superstitious man, Mr Falconberg. Thank you for your time. Smith will be in touch if I decide to take it.' He headed to the stairs, unable to shake from his mind's eye the image of the *comte* tumbling down them, poignard in his chest. Falconberg danced along at his side.

'Very good. And if your lady wishes to see the house, I can be at your disposal at any time, sir – any time!'

Aware he was raising the man's hopes unfairly, Jacob turned at the foot of the stair and offered him a generous tip, even though that was not usual for such a transaction. 'For your pains, sir. I am most satisfied by your attention this evening. Come, Smith, let's take a stroll along the bank and familiarise ourselves with the area.'

'Richmond that way, Putney the other!' called Falconberg a little too enthusiastically as they headed for the riverside walk.

Jacob waved. 'Understood.'

Once they were out of sight of the attentive agent, they took a bench under a weeping willow. It was a pleasant prospect here, the river bending towards Richmond. Travel upstream and you shook off London entirely. Go the other way and you would soon be in the smoke and warren of streets. A swan preened itself on the bank, loosening a downy feather so it fell on the shining mud. Its mate glided by with a gaggle of cygnets, nearly grown, following in a line.

'Did you learn anything?' asked Jacob.

'Many things.' Smith showed him a sketch of the ground floor. 'The stairs go directly to the scullery. I can see how it was convenient to bring up the hot water, but it would also allow the gentleman to smuggle in other visitors without the wife being aware.'

Jacob nodded. 'He wouldn't be the first. If there was a second person present on the day of the killing, could they have escaped unseen?"

'I believe so. As Miss Austen astutely observed, if everyone was called to the hallway by the commotion, it would be easy to slip out the rear door and make your escape through the garden gate. That goes out to a passageway down the side, used for deliveries. A brisk walk and you could mingle with the ordinary people on the street in no more than thirty seconds.'

'Then it is still a strong possibility that it wasn't suicide but a third murder by another hand. But until we have any clue who the person could be – a description or even a sex – then we cannot sensibly make enquiries in the neighbourhood.'

'No, but the family and servants might know who the *comte*'s confidants were – who he would let into his room that way.'

'It's a ticklish thing to ask a son.'

'Agreed. How about I seek out the maidservant, Susannah Black, and see what she will tell me?'

That was a thought. Dora had not explored this possibility when she had come with Miss Austen. 'Is she still in the area?'

'I believe so. The agent told me, when I asked if it was unfurnished, that the last tenant's furniture, the belongings he did not want in his new place—'

'We take nothing to the grave.'

'Quite, but he didn't want to come out with that so early. The furniture is being auctioned tomorrow at a local warehouse. She will be there to report to Julien.'

Jacob didn't want to stay in Barnes overnight but that meant splitting up and leaving Alex here alone. Dora would not be impressed.

'I'll see you to your lodgings. I expect the tavern where they held the inquest has a room – you can find out more about that in the bar. Don't go out on your own tonight.'

Alex laughed. 'Sandys, we're army veterans. I'm not going to let these people get to me – and nor are you. They would be fools to come at us again.'

Jacob couldn't have Alex playing fast and loose with his security, not when he and Dora were responsible for him. 'I haven't seen a great deal of sense from them, only desperation, so please heed the warning. I'll take the next coach back from the tavern and will expect you to report in by tomorrow afternoon. Send word if something holds you up.'

Arrangements made, Jacob took an inside seat of the London-bound coach, submitting to being squeezed in between a bony clergyman and a well-padded matron.

He would've preferred a seat on the roof, but they needed to keep as low a profile as possible.

As the coach rattled away, Jacob wondered if he was sitting in the same seat the murderer had occupied, hurrying away from the bloody scene. Or had they had their own carriage? Or left by boat?

There were too many questions, but he could not shake his gut feeling that Lorenzo had been killed by someone else and not his own hand. Would Dora agree?

Dora wasn't in the office but had retired to her room. Jacob slipped past the Argus of a landlady who was fortunately gossiping with neighbours by her stove and paid him no heed. Tiptoeing upstairs in stockinged feet, boots in hand, he tried the door. Locked. Good. Dora was taking her safety seriously. He knocked gently.

'Who is it?'

'Me.'

There was a scuffling on the other side and the door cracked open. 'Me? So you aren't a crazed killer coming to shut me up?'

'I don't think so. I have other far more pleasurable activities in mind.'

'You'd better come in then.' With a smile, she opened the door, looking delectable in her nightgown and robe, hair tumbled around her shoulders. 'What did you find in Barnes?'

Sitting propped up on the bedhead with her snuggled to his side, Jacob filled her in on the details of their visit, including the decision to leave Alex behind for the auction. 'You approve?'

She nodded. 'We have to take some risks, or they will have achieved their aim.'

'I keep running the events of that bloody morning in my head, trying to see which explanation best fits. If it were a plot by the French, would the *comte* not be more suspicious of those who he invited into his home? Would he not use all his intelligence and connections to check that someone was genuinely an ally and not an enemy? He strikes me as having been too wily a man, lasting over a decade as an analyst of foreign affairs, to make such a basic mistake.'

'But love, or passion, can blind a man to a woman's faults. Perhaps his lover, invited upstairs for more intimate matters, was the one planted by Napoleon in his circle?'

Jacob curled his lip. 'It does seem poor taste to have her there while his wife was next door, even if she came and went by the servants' staircase.'

'Then perhaps the *comte* and *comtesse* had an understanding that they could both play with other partners?'

'No servants' staircase in her room.'

'She might have lost the appetite for intrigue and contented herself with her music and her other pursuits. From what I see, men are slower to give up lovers than women, with many a frisky old goat still indulging in amours in his eighties.'

'We'll see what Alex finds out. How was your evening?'

Dora stroked his chest. 'I played cards with Ruby.'

'She's well?'

'Very comfortably settled in her nest.'

'What did she say about us?'

'She apologised for the newspaper article. We agreed not to

harm each other's prospects if we can avoid it.' Dora tapped him. 'And before you say anything, I did not agree to anything, nor did she.'

'Then you will marry me?'

'Still thinking about it.'

If he had to be like the woodpecker, chipping away until he had made a hole in her defences, then he would do so. 'I wouldn't have to creep past your landlady with my boots in my hand if we were wed.'

'Is that so much of a hardship? Does it not add spice to our love affair?'

He chuckled softly. 'You, my dear, are a very Hindoustanee dish of delights.' He moved to kiss her.

She let her lips cling to his before pulling back. 'You know the visitor is calling?'

'I do. I'm a doctor. And when I see a lady suffering from bellyache and feeling tetchy, I am able to diagnose the cause. What a marvel. Have you forgotten I am a bundle of bruises, so hardly up to much myself? Would you welcome my company in bed? I know I'd like to have you in my arms.'

She nodded. 'That I can manage.'

They settled down on the pillow. 'Have you taken anything for your pain?'

'No.'

'Good. Laudanum—'

'Is a slippery slope. I am aware.'

He made to get up again, thinking his bedside manner could do with some work. 'I could make you willow bark tea.'

She pulled him back. 'And risk Mrs Jones detecting your presence under her roof? No, thank you. Being with you will take away the pain as well, if not better.'

They spooned together on the narrow bed. He spread his hand over her lower belly to help ease the cramp. 'Better?'

'Yes.'

'Just think, every night like this if we marry.' Tap-tap. Tap-tap. The woodpecker was not giving up.

'I'll add that to the considerations,' she muttered before they fell asleep together.

Chapter Twenty-Two

Miss Jane Austen arrived at the office the next morning with renewed enthusiasm for the search, looking youthfully pink-cheeked and excited in her blue gown, matching pelisse and chip straw riding hat. It was hard to think of her as a staid spinster in her middle age.

'I take it the meeting with your publisher went well?' Dora asked with a smile as she showed Jane in to where Jacob was hastily clearing away the breakfast things. He rattled away with a tray to the scullery.

'He is taking his time, but I am confident we can agree terms. I do so love having money of my own.' Jane sat down on the visitor's chair. 'Dora, I have to confess, I'm considering a poplin gown. I saw some material at Layton and Shear's that would tempt even the most parsimonious person.'

That made Dora laugh. 'Jane, you have revealed your weakness!'

'I'm afraid so. I am easily led into temptation when it comes to clothes.'

Jacob returned from the scullery where he had banished their plates. 'Dora's weakness is ice cream.'

'And yours, doctor?' Jane said archly.

The good humour vanished from Jacob's expression as no doubt he remembered his trouble with opium.

'He has too many to enumerate,' Dora said quickly. 'Coffee comes high on the list.'

From the flicker of interest in Jane's eyes, she registered the awkward moment but let it pass. 'What are we going to do today? Did you make any progress after I left you yesterday?'

'We discovered that it would have been possible for a person to have been hidden upstairs at the time of the murders and to have left by the servants' staircase without passing through the hall. Mr Smith has stayed behind to question the maidservant at the auction of the furniture from the house in Barnes,' said Jacob.

'While we wait for him to return with news, I think we should give more thought to where the *comte* may have left his final report.' Dora flicked through their case notes. 'Not Barnes Terrace, not the bank. In Queen Anne Street, Julien did not know of anything of that nature and it appears that the government and the Russian friends have been through the late *comte*'s papers.'

'Ah yes, what about those Russians?' mused Jane. 'Count Vorontsov is a fine-looking man, but tough. I can imagine him on a battlefield ordering a charge, sabre drawn. His wife seems like one of those perpetual child women who lie on the sofa and beg to be looked after – no harm in her but no great good. As for Yekatarina Petrovna – she looks as if a day doesn't pass without some chance for mischief.'

'She mentioned a debut. I couldn't tell if that meant as a performer or as a lady on her first season,' said Jacob.

'Performer,' said Jane and Dora together.

Dora laughed at their once more synchronous thoughts. 'I don't know what told you, but I recognise one of my tribe. I would hazard Miss Petrovna is a singer and no doubt very accomplished.'

'Yes, she would walk the line between lady and performer most elegantly,' agreed Jane. 'It was rather vulgar of her to flourish her hand like that, evidence that she is willing to marry into respectability should the right candidate come along, so watch yourself, Dr Sandys.'

'I am already taken,' he said with a fond look at Dora.

'Hmm. A love match? How interesting – rare and precious.' Jane shook herself, returning to their business. 'Were there not a few years when, despite their antipathy, the Tsar and Napoleon gritted their teeth and formed an alliance against us? The Vorontsovs would have distanced themselves from their old friend, the *comte*, as a result.'

Jacob nodded. 'And now that alliance has collapsed and Napoleon is marching east, the Russians find it useful to return to London and revive the old friendship. The *comte* would have understood that the relationship was based on political expediency and not been shocked by that.'

'Would he have trusted them?' asked Dora.

Jacob shrugged. 'I don't know. Would he have trusted anyone? I don't think so, not in his game. If he did take the dangerous route of advertising that he had something valuable to share and was waiting for the best offer, my money is on him hiding it cunningly so equally wily people would not be able to steal it.'

'But he would want it on hand so that he could produce it, surely? The bidding period would be short as the material would lose its value as time passed,' added Dora. 'Indeed, perhaps it is no longer salient and those people attacking us are seeking a stale loaf?'

'They were returning to Queen Anne Street for a party,' said Jane suddenly. 'What party? One they were holding or were they going out?'

'And I wonder, was it a party attended by his political contacts during which he would decide who got the report?' asked Jacob.

Dora checked their notes. 'Julien said it was a musical party. I got the impression they were holding it because he said something about being at the house to make preparations. He could mean he was practising for his performance, but what if the D'Antraigues were the hosts?'

'I went to one of their parties last year,' said Jane. 'They loved entertaining and did it regularly. The *comtesse* did not need any encouragement to delight us all with her arias at great length, and the *comte* got equal pleasure from showing off his art collection, also at great and exhaustive length. I am certain that if they were due to hold a party, Eliza and Henry would have been invited.'

'In that case,' said Dora, getting up, 'I think we'd better go and ask them. Where are they this morning?'

'Henry is at the bank, of course, but I left Eliza at Layton & Shear's.'

'Do you think she will still be there?' Dora took her hat from the stand.

'Oh, yes, she was placing an order for the new season and

will not be rushed over such important considerations as to how much crêpe and how much gauze. The shop is next door to the bank. Henry says that he no sooner gets money in than she trips along to the draper's to spend it.' Jane pulled a wry face. 'Having watched Eliza at the counter besotted by every new delivery from Ireland or India, I don't think he is joking.'

That sounded very convenient for them. 'And if we miss her there, we can bother Henry for an answer.'

'Agreed, though I think he would prefer us not to call again at the bank if we can avoid it. He is still hoping to escape free of scandal.'

'Understood. Jacob, I don't think we need you for this.' Dora shrugged into a light shawl. The morning was fine and she needed no overcoat.

'It's a sad day when you women no longer need us men. Then, as I am superfluous, I'll go to Coutts and see if they will tell me whether the *comte* kept anything in their strongroom.' He took his top hat and tapped it into place.

'On your own?' asked Dora, brow wrinkled in worry.

'It's early yet, villains are hopefully abed, and I'll take care, I promise.'

'No walking near the edge of the pavement.' She kissed him. 'Take care of my doctor.'

He kissed her back. 'And take care of my actress.' At least he hadn't said forger. There were some things Jane Austen didn't need to know about her, decided Dora.

'Will anyone take care of me?' Jane asked with humour dancing in her eyes at their little farewell ceremony.

Dora turned to her, hand outstretched. 'We both will – but this morning it is my turn.' She squeezed Jane's gloved fingers in reassurance. 'Please do as I say. If I sense danger, we can't pause to argue what we should do next.'

'Understood. Navy rules. The captain is always right.' Jane saluted her.

Dora offered her arm so they could walk together. 'As we go you must tell me about your brother Frank. Have you ever thought of writing a book about the navy? You must know an awful lot about it with two brothers in that profession.'

Jane rolled her eyes. '*Et tu*, Dora? If I had a shilling for the many times someone told me what I should write, then I would already be a very rich woman.'

Layton & Shear's was in Bedford House, half the size of the vast Harding, Howell & Co. or not as well stocked as Newton's, but Dora found she preferred it as she wasn't overwhelmed with the choice on show. Bolts of cloth were stacked on shelves with some strategically placed fabrics spilling out like waterfalls. The shopkeepers only risked the hardier dyes and prints in this display with the choicest material kept under the counter and reserved for the discerning customer who could pay her bill. The male attendant was wrestling a bolt of yellow muslin, letting it billow out over the counter, quite an arresting colour that Dora knew would look well on her – if she could afford it. Eliza took one edge and held it up against the pale skin of her inner arm.

'Will it make me look sallow, do you think?' she asked her server.

'Madam looks beautiful in every shade,' said the man untruthfully.

Jane marched over and rapped her sister-in-law on the temple. 'What are you thinking, Eliza! It is a very lucky chance that I returned in the nick of time. You can't wear that – I definitely shan't wear that – and Cassandra ten years ago could have carried it off, but not today. Strike it off the list.'

'But it is so pretty,' sighed Eliza.

'For daffodils and newborn chicks, it is, not for grown English women with too much red in their complexion.'

The server glowered at Jane but rolled up the offending muslin. 'Would madam like to see anything else?' he asked portentously.

'That will be all today, Martin,' said Eliza. 'Please have my parcels made up.'

He bowed and went to the desk to tot up the account.

'Eliza, we were hoping to find you here,' said Jane leaning on the counter next to the seated Mrs Austen. Chairs were provided for paying customers, not for loiterers. 'Miss Fitz-Pennington has a question.'

Eliza greeted Dora kindly and raised an expectant eyebrow. 'How may I help?'

Dora checked that no one was in earshot, but for the moment they were in an island of calm surrounded by seas of silk and satin. 'The day the *comte* and *comtesse* died – had you heard of a party that they planned for that evening, or planned to attend?'

Eliza frowned and then her brow cleared. 'Oh, yes, I had forgotten. The awfulness drove that out of my mind, and it never took place in any case. They were holding a select musical evening to welcome the Russian delegation back to London. Their particular friends, the Vorontsovs, were to be the guests of honour and a Russian singer of some renown was to sing with the *comtesse*. I had been looking forward to it.'

'Yekatarina Petrovna, by any chance?'

Eliza drummed her fingers on the polished counter. 'That might've been the name – yes, I think it was.'

'And the party was to take place in Queen Anne Street?'

'That's correct. I remember that I was already getting ready to go out – Dorcas was pressing my lilac sarsenet with the demi-train and I had such a pretty little cap to go with it – and then we heard news of their murder. You can imagine what a terrible shock that was. Henry went immediately to the house to see if Julien needed any help, but the Russians were already with him and fending off unwanted callers. Henry returned and told me he wasn't required.'

Those Russians kept turning up. They were certainly making up for the lost years by shoehorning themselves in the D'Antraigues's lives again, both generations. Dora could think of no reason for violence from the Vorontsovs. Russia had joined the anti-Bonaparte coalition again and were now Britain's ally. The delegation could woo the *comte* back to report for them if they wished to pay for it. Killing him did not make sense.

'Had you seen the Vorontsovs with the D'Antraigues before then?'

'I've never met them,' said Eliza. 'I've heard the countess is a very pretty woman, but our paths have not yet crossed. Doubtless, when the season starts again, we will meet. It will be very sad that it is a tragedy that gives us something in common.'

'And Henry?'

'He's not mentioned them, but I can ask.'

Jane patted Eliza's shoulder. 'No need, sister; I'll ask him at dinner.' The server returned with an impressive stack of brown-paper-wrapped parcels. 'It looks like you might prefer that to be the subject of conversation rather than your shopping bill.'

Chapter Twenty-Three

Coutts Bank

'I'm afraid we can't divulge any details of a client's holdings.' Mr Jefferson looked resolute if somewhat pained to deny a favoured customer his request. 'I'm sure you would understand as you benefit from the same discretion.'

Jacob sighed inwardly. He wasn't going to get anywhere, was he, with a direct request, and certainly not by standing in the middle of the marble-tiled banking hall in full view of the great and the good who banked here? He would have to ask Julien, but he imagined the young man's finances were stuck in probate waiting for a court ruling to clear him as the heir to all his father owned. That might not get him the answer in time.

'I do understand. I was hoping that an enquiry about a deceased person would be looked on differently.'

Mr Jefferson sniffed. 'We do not serve individuals, but families. We must think of them when we deal with the affairs of a person who is no longer with us. Oh, my lord.' He bowed to the man behind Jacob.

A hand clapped Jacob's shoulder, uncomfortably, like a bailiff's heavy mitt. 'Jefferson. I hope my brother hasn't been giving you any trouble?'

It would be Arthur, wouldn't it? He was probably here to count his pennies as his mistress was draining his ready cash like a plug pulled from a sink.

'Not at all, sir. I was merely explaining to Dr Sandys that I am unable to give him any information regarding another client.'

The viscount rocked on his heels, hands behind his back. 'Oh? Was he asking about me?'

'What? No!' protested Jacob. 'How could you think that?'

Arthur gave him a wintry smile. 'You have always been curious.'

'I was asking after a person who is of interest in a case I'm investigating – a deceased person, the Comte D'Antraigues.'

Arthur curled a lip. 'The murdered Frenchman? Shocking business. What has he to do with anything?'

'When I was here a few days ago Mr Jefferson here mentioned that there were rumours flying about a bank. I'm interested because one of the owners is the brother of a man who saved my life in the retreat from Corunna.'

'How close did you come to death?' asked the viscount with some heat. There were details of his life in the military that Jacob had softened for his family.

'Close enough to make its acquaintance. Anyway, I looked into the matter and discovered the rumours connected to the late *comte*, along with the suggestion that he was disloyal to his adopted country.' The bank manager pursed his lips, clearly unhappy to have been caught out gossiping. 'I investigated and found that, contrary to the rumours, the *comte* was dedicated to the fight against Napoleon, valued by the government and our allies, and no collaborator.' He said this with an eye to Mr Jefferson spreading rumours that would benefit Henry Austen's bank. 'However, it appears that the *comte* did possess something that his killer wanted – and I wondered if it was all the while safely tucked up in the strongroom as I was told he banked here.'

Arthur crossed his arms and looked at Mr Jefferson. 'Is this true? Did the *comte* bank here?'

Jefferson folded himself in half in his agony of torn loyalties, twisting his hands together. The living won out. 'Yes, my lord, he was a valued customer.'

'We are all valued customers,' observed Arthur in his most lordly tone. 'My brother's enquiry seems simple enough. He's not asking you how much money the man had, nor asking you to spill any secrets that would harm the living. He has merely asked whether the unfortunate man had a strongbox here. His heirs would like to know that too, I've no doubt.'

'And I will apply to Julien, the new Comte D'Antraigues, should the answer be in the affirmative,' said Jacob. He stood shoulder to shoulder with his brother, knowing that two Sandyses in a row would have an intimidating effect.

Mr Jefferson crumbled. 'I will check our records. One moment.' He scurried away.

'Thank you,' muttered Jacob.

Arthur was scowling. 'I hope he doesn't fold so early if someone asks after my holdings.'

'You are safe.'

'How do you reckon that?'

'You aren't French and you aren't dead – a living English lord is what Mr Jefferson seeks to serve most faithfully.'

They took a seat on a bench at the side of the banking hall, Arthur pressing a hand to his chest as he sat, Jacob lowering himself gingerly. Arthur gave a grunt of laughter.

'We are a pair of old crocks, aren't we? How are you recovering from your brush with the cobbles of Pall Mall?'

'Much better today, thank you. I only had bruises. How are you? No sign of infection?'

'No, I'm healing well.'

They watched the customers swirl through the doors and out again. Money, the lifeblood of the city, was in its most tangible form, dispensed from the grilled counters and into pockets. Larger sums were carried away in promissory notes.

'Was it coincidence that you are here this morning or were you following me?' asked Jacob.

'You flatter yourself. I have an appointment – for which I am now late.'

'If you need to go—' He started to rise.

'Sit down,' said Arthur. 'They can wait for me. I'm pleased to have crossed paths with you. William has been bending my ear about your future. A private marriage, he suggests, one that we don't have to acknowledge but will satisfy your moral qualms. How about it?'

Jacob tamped down the anger that swelled in his chest. How typical of William to suggest a half measure! 'What good would that do Dora? People would assume she is my mistress, and our children would be considered bastards – two outcomes I am anxious to avoid.'

'You preached that it was your Christian duty. If you are right before God, what matter the world?'

'Unfortunately, the world does matter.'

'But your lady seems not to mind, so why should you?'

'You misunderstand her if you think that.'

Arthur chewed on his lip, struggling to keep what he really wanted to say inside.

Jacob sighed. 'Go on: say what you must.'

'I fear she is only after your money and social rank. This is a test. If she really loves you, she will agree to an arrangement that is in your own best interest.' It came out in a rush.

Jacob laughed at that. 'Really? That is what you think? You think she will fail the test?'

'There's probably some affection in the mix, but it won't last if it doesn't come with benefits. She would be a fool not to care for her future. An actress only lasts as long as her beauty. She must feather her nest now. It's how the world works. She stands to gain by a public marriage, but you will lose.'

Jacob saw Mr Jefferson returning so stood up. It was as well to bring this discussion to an end before he had a public quarrel with the viscount. 'I know you believe that, Arthur, so I pity you.' He took a step forward. 'Mr Jefferson?'

The man was already shaking his head. 'No strongbox for the late *comte*, Dr Sandys. In fact, now I recall it, he kept much of his worldly goods tied up in his art collection, and that he displayed on his walls, not in a bank vault.'

Jacob thanked him and took his leave. He turned to say farewell to his brother, but the viscount was already being ushered away by the head of the bank to a private meeting, younger brothers not invited. He raised a hand to bid him goodbye, but Arthur did not look back.

Chapter Twenty-Four

Theatre Royal, Covent Garden

This was probably a very bad idea, thought Dora as she approached the stage door of Covent Garden, Ren accompanying her so he could watch her back. With Jacob at the bank and Jane gone home to dinner to quiz her brother about the Vorontsovs, she had decided to take on the challenge of finding out more about Yekatarina Petrovna. Remembering the three singers she and Jane had met and their interest in the investigation, tracking them down for more information had seemed sensible in the office; now it seemed in poor taste.

'Well, miss,' said Ren, hands on hips. 'Aren't you going to knock?'

Dora took a step back, half turning to go. 'What if Madame Catalani thinks I'm stalking her, you know, like a hunter after a stag? She must get tired of people thinking up excuses to spend time with her.'

Ren sighed, his disgust at her vacillation evident. 'So what if she does? Have you got a job to do or not?'

'I do. Yes, I absolutely do.' Inside she was cringing. She usually didn't mind offending people, but her heroine…?

Giving up on her, Ren pushed past and banged on the door. It flew open. The porter who had been on duty on two days ago looked at her, then down at Ren.

'Oh, it's you, Ren. No, they don't need a Tom Thumb in the pantomime. Grimaldi has that all sewn up. We're doing clowns.'

'We're not here for a job – though if the wind changes, you'll let me know, eh?' said Ren with a huge wink. 'I dare say Miss Dora here wouldn't say "no" to a Covent Garden audition, would you, miss?'

'What? Me?' Would she? Playing a big role in a play here was the height of everything Dora had dreamed of when slogging her way across the Pennines with the Northern Players. She hadn't even considered that as a possibility, but to do it just once… Ren wiggled his eyebrows at her and she knew then he was teasing and – worse – she had fallen for it. Who was she fooling? There were many hopefuls and many others ahead of her in the profession with better connections and a known record in London. 'In that unlikely event, I would consider throwing my hat in the ring,' she agreed, as it only seemed polite, 'but as Ren says, we are here to talk to the singers, if they are still rehearsing.'

'They've gone over to Vauxhall Gardens for the dress rehearsal,' said the doorkeeper. He handed them a bill advertising the delights on offer that evening, a grand fête to celebrate Wellington's recent victories and newly created title of Marquess. She ran her eye down the programme. Madame

Catalani was singing Thompson and Arne's 'Rule, Britannia!'; Incledon and Dignum were to perform some comic songs, and they were to be joined by a chorus of the allies for martial airs.

'This chorus of the allies, who might they be?' she asked.

The doorkeeper scratched his head, dislodging his cap. 'That would be some German basses, a Portuguese baritone – he's very good, in my humble opinion, worth the price of admission – a Spaniard – don't think much of him, too nasal – a Russian alto, and an Austrian mezzo-soprano. They're reasonable but not a patch on Madame.'

'Would the Russian be Miss Petrovna by any chance?'

'Yeah, that's right. Busy little bee, she is. Flew in here in July and been buzzing around ever since, sweet-talking the management, desperate to make an appearance.'

That sounded about right. 'Do you know where she is lodging?'

'With them Russians at the embassy. Thinks herself a cut above, she does. Looks at me like I'm horse shit.' He shook his head at the madness of the world. 'Don't you think it strange how the Russians can go off and hobnob with old Boney for a few years, *all's forgiven, doesn't matter you chopped the heads off your king and queen, my old pal, yeah, we'll pucker up and kiss your Corsican arse*, then when that little love affair is over, they come back to us and pretend like it never happened? *Oh, Georgie boy, of course we always loved you more, and your armies.*'

A shrewd analysis of the state of politics from an unexpected source. 'In war, you might end up with odd bedfellows,' she offered.

'Yeah, but I just hope they don't fuck us over again, pardon my French, miss.'

'I think that might be old school English, but consider yourself forgiven.'

'She wanted to sing a solo,' the porter added as an afterthought. 'That Russian woman. Madame Catalani shut that down quick as lightning as it's her concert. She's the one arranging it for Wellington and she doesn't want no newcomer butting in to divert the spotlight onto the Tsar or whoever the Russians think is their best hope.'

'That would be Prince Kutuzov,' said Dora. 'He's in charge of the Tsar's army now.'

'Who the hell is Kutuzov when he's at home?' said the doorkeeper. 'I read the newspapers – got sons in the army so of course I do – but I can't keep all these names straight in my head, particularly those Russian ones. Fair jaw crackers, they are. Kutuzov, eh? Well, good luck to him, but he's not the main attraction tonight. That would be the Marquess of Wellington. God bless him and all that fight with him.'

Thanking him for the information, Dora and Ren turned to go. They joined the crowds in Covent Garden market, stallholders packing up after a busy morning; prostitutes taking it easy on their doorsteps, enjoying their few hours of leisure before the evening trade; street urchins loitering in alleyways, hoping for some easy gleanings from the fruit and vegetables that hadn't been sold. A tabby cat with a stub of a tail sprawled on the doorstep of a tavern, risking getting stepped on. That was probably how it lost the other half of its tail.

'Are you going to go?' asked Ren.

'To the concert? I think so.'

'Not alone?'

'I'm not that stupid, Ren.'

'Never said you were, miss.'

He was only implying it. 'I've never been before, but even a northern lass like me has read novels about the dangers of the dark walks in Vauxhall.'

'Best way to experience some things if you ask me – in a book. Vauxhall Gardens are overpriced, and the ham is so thin you can see the light through it – and they make that a selling point! Ham shavings! Bleeding con if you ask me. And if it rains, no fun at all.' They both looked up at the skies which were promisingly fine. 'Though you might be safe on that account. Take Dr Sandys with you – and an umbrella.'

'That was the plan.'

They had reached the fine portico of St Paul's church at the far end of the market from the theatre when they heard footsteps hurrying up behind them.

Ren span round and produced a knife – a knife? Where had that come from, Dora wondered. 'Stay right there!' he growled.

The man came to halt, panting. He looked down at Ren, smiled, then thought better of his laughter when the knife was not lowered. '*Je suis désolé, monsieur*, but I saw Miss Fitz-Pennington and I was ravished with joy to see a familiar face. I have no, how do you say, bad intentions?' He gave an elaborate bow. 'Michel Percy, *votre serviteur*.'

Michel Percy. Dora couldn't believe it. The French agent, last encountered fleeing the scene of the explosion in the Egyptian Hall, had the bare-faced cheek to be strolling about Covent Garden as if he wasn't a wanted man! Dora had regretted letting him escape on that occasion, particularly when it turned out that he was far more than the collector of gossip and art for Napoleon's collection in the Louvre, but at least she had comforted herself that their paths were unlikely to cross again and she wouldn't be reminded of her mistake. Yet here he was, dressed in a well-tailored cream linen long coat and stocking pantaloons that were daringly close-fitting. With his matching waistcoat and cravat, he was a pale column of dandified gentleman foreign to English climes.

'Mr Percy,' she said flatly. 'You are the last person I expected to see.'

He made to kiss her hand, but she tucked them behind her back. He turned the gesture into another bow. 'I live to entertain you with such delicious surprises.'

'Delicious? You must be joking. Or are you going to be apprehended by the runners while we stand here? Now *that* I would find entertaining.'

Ren looked between the two of them, realising who he was. Ren had been part of the team tailing the man during the Elgin investigation. He slipped his knife back under his jacket. 'What do you want to do with this cove, miss?'

'You mean the French spy?' she said tartly.

Percy grimaced. 'I hate to correct a lady, but I'm no spy. You see before you a diplomatic envoy to the Court of St James, legitimately accredited. Even in these times of regrettable war, our governments allow some conversation to happen.'

Dora snorted.

'I'm afraid it is true, *ma chérie*. England would starve without exports of our grain. You could stand on principle, naturally, but why do so when we have a surplus to sell and you a peasantry to feed?'

'I can't believe you are here to negotiate the trade in wheat. Sale of fine art, or erotic paintings, yes.' Her mind was whirling. They had been wondering about the French involvement in the *comte*'s murder and here was a prime candidate for tangling in such intrigue. 'My joy at your return knows no bounds. When did you arrive, *monsieur*?'

Percy made a show of dusting himself down. 'I am fresh off the boat, do you not notice the sea salt?'

They would have to check that. He favoured using his own yacht so he could slip across the Channel on his own timetable. 'I thought you would be in prison in Paris, or at least in disgrace for the débâcle in May?'

'*Au contraire*, that was my triumph! I told you, mademoiselle, that I could explain that all to my people. I stopped Fleury, did I not?'

Dora folded her arms. 'No, I stopped him.' Fleury had been Percy's rival, running his own spy operation in London. He had nearly blown up members of the Elgin circle, and had killed innocent bystanders in his attempt to discredit Percy and find favour in Paris.

'Details, details.' Percy fluttered his fingers, dismissing her part in ending the career of the other French spy who had been loose in London. 'I explained it all most cogently. What is more, I even managed to find a little piece of the Parthenon marbles thanks to my ingenuity – it now sits on display in the Louvre, educating my countrymen about the beauties of the classical age. *Tout le monde est content!* Apart from Fleury, who is dead.'

'You are far too pleased with yourself,' said Dora.

'If I do not celebrate my achievements, who else will do so?'

She had to smile at that. There was something so audacious about his self-love that she could not help but admire him a little bit.

Ren fidgeted. 'Do you want me to call a runner, miss? We can get some of these barrow boys to keep hold of him. Just tell them he's French and they'll do the rest, probably muddy up that stupid white coat of his.'

'What a bloodthirsty little man. I approve,' said Percy.

'Don't patronise him,' said Dora.

'You mean, don't talk *down* to him?' Percy hid a smile behind a cough.

'Not funny.'

'I thought it was hilarious.'

Dora sighed. She had not forgotten how infuriating he could be. 'It's all right, Ren. I think he is speaking the truth when he says he has diplomatic immunity. He is enjoying being able to talk to me in broad daylight far too much for that to be one of his many lies.'

Percy replaced his hat which he had taken off to flourish in his bow. 'As perceptive as always.'

'I do not believe you ran after me merely to greet me. What do you want, Mr Percy?'

He clapped his hand to his breast. 'So many things, but I know your heart is already given to the dear doctor and I must wear the willow. How is he, by the way?'

Recovering from being run over – had Percy been behind that? 'He is very well, thank you. I've no doubt he will be most interested to hear of your return.'

'*Bon!* We must get together, a little party of old friends, and discuss what has happened since we last met.'

'I'm afraid we are very busy.'

'In a few weeks then. I can wait.'

Dora frowned. 'How long are you going to be here?'

He grinned. She knew then that this was what he had stopped her to say. 'Did I not mention? I am permanently attached to our embassy here. I'm staying for the foreseeable future as the trade envoy. You are – how do you say? – stuck with me for good.'

Chapter Twenty-Five

Bruton Mews

Jacob paced between the window and Dora's bed while she got ready behind a small screen for their evening engagement at Vauxhall. He tied a fresh cravat, nothing too fancy, by way of a knot but it was made from silk as befitted an appearance in society.

'There's no mistake? Percy is back in London?' he called to her.

'He is.'

'Is it a joke?'

'If it is, it is in very bad taste on the part of the French. The irony is overwhelming. Thanks to our help in killing off Fleury, Percy is now in good odour with his masters in Paris and they've sent him back.' She threw her day dress over the screen and took down the burgundy evening gown. Jacob was tempted to go round to help her at this very interesting moment between gowns. There was a lot of fun that could be had while buttoning dresses…

'Jacob, are you listening?'

Damn, he must've missed something. 'Sorry, I was contemplating coming behind your screen to help you dress.'

There was a gratifying pause as she considered it, before she said, 'Tempting though that is, I'd better press on. We've got a lot to do. I asked you about the trade envoy post – is it a real position?'

'The trade is real enough. Grain is one of the products that our government allows through the blockade when we don't have enough. We were importing French wheat before the war and that hasn't changed.'

'Buying grain from the enemy? They've had years to sort it out!'

'Even so, with a growing population in the cities, our farmers couldn't increase our production quickly enough to do away with the imports despite all the enclosing that has been going on. The harvest was bad across Europe last year, not just here, so Napoleon suspended exports, keeping the grain for his home market. The government didn't like that, and I imagine allowing Percy in as the trade envoy is part of the attempt to get the grain flowing again.'

'But doesn't that strike you as strange? The government must know that the money we send goes into French coffers to buy the armaments that plants our boys in the ground.'

Jacob grimaced as he checked his cravat in the mirror. 'There is more than one contradiction when it comes to trade. Name me a government minister who doesn't indulge his taste for French wine and brandy, keeping the smugglers in business, while at the same time piously passing laws to prosecute them.' Moving to the bed he picked up his black jacket. He slid his arms into the sleeves, pleased that this was no longer such a painful process. The bruises were now more colourful than troublesome, and he diagnosed himself as healing up satisfactorily. He'd always bounced back quickly from falls in riding and this was very similar.

Dora emerged, looking delectable in her gown, a hand-me-down from Lady Tolworth, that she had remade to fit her. The current fashion to have the bodice lift the breasts and the sleeves start on the top of the shoulders left a field of very kissable skin exposed. 'What do you think?' She held her arms out and spun in a circle.

'Perfect – and why isn't it already time for bed?' She laughed and shook a finger at him in warning. He resumed dressing, attaching his watchchain across his waistcoat, and added, 'As for the trade envoy role, I imagine he is using that as a cover so he can be up to his old tricks informing on us.'

'That's what I thought. He said he has only just arrived. If we take him at his word – never a safe wager, I know – then perhaps he was dispatched once the French heard about the murders? They want to know what that was all about and sent a man to investigate. Would you help me with my pearls?' she asked.

'Of course I'll help. You mean he is doing the same task as we are?'

'Thank you. I wouldn't call it the same as he is on the opposite side. Have we overlooked another French agent running amok in London, killing off troublesome *comtes* and *comtesses*?'

'We haven't eliminated that possibility, but Percy's arrival is the first presence of the French in the whole affair that we've detected.'

'Apart from the victims themselves.'

'True.' He took the necklace from her. Dora didn't have many jewels, and had rejected his attempts to buy her any, but she was proud of her double string of seed pearls, an eighteenth birthday gift from her brother. Coming up behind her, he fastened the clasp and, naturally, had to run his lips over her bare neck.

'Jacob!' she exclaimed with a shiver.

'When does the visitor leave, remind me?' It couldn't be soon enough.

'Two more days.' She turned around in his arms. 'There are other things we can do before then. I think I hinted as much.' Her hand went to the buttons on his breeches and her smile was pure sauce. 'Poor love. We can't have you going out in this state.'

He cleared his throat. She. Was. Killing. Him. He let his head drop back, having just enough sense to move away from the window.

'Hmm? Nothing to say?' teased Dora. The clock in the nearby church struck five. 'We have an hour if you don't mind missing dinner.'

'Dinner? Who the h-hell needs dinner?' He groaned as she slid to her knees and undid him.

Alex arrived back from the auction in time to accompany them to Vauxhall. As an open-air venue with many directions from which people could come at them, Jacob welcomed the extra person on their team. And perhaps it was as well he wasn't alone with Dora in the carriage after that unplanned interlude – but, damn, she could make him blush like a maiden when he thought of what she'd done, wringing throaty cries from him that he hadn't known he could make. Once the visitor had gone, he would repay his debt with interest.

'Everything all right, Sandys?' asked Alex from the backward-facing seat of the hired carriage.

'Just a twinge. From my injuries,' Jacob lied, adjusting his breeches.

'Is that what you call it?'

Dora kicked at Alex from the seat across from him. 'Stop teasing. The poor man was at death's door on Tuesday. You should rejoice he is well enough to come out tonight.'

'Yes, be nice to me,' said Jacob. 'I'm one of the two people paying your wages.' He had to get his mind back on their business and consider what they were hoping to achieve in Vauxhall. They had plenty of time for their discussion as the popularity of the fête meant there was a long line of carriages edging their way over Westminster Bridge. If Dora hadn't been shod in light slippers rather than boots, he would've suggested they got out and walked. Perhaps he would when they got a bit closer.

'Did Susannah have anything to say on the matter of clandestine visitors entering via the back stair?' he asked. See? He could be businesslike.

Alex nodded. 'She did, after much flattery and persuasion. As Dora said in her notes, the maid is loyal to her former mistress, and it took many promises that it wouldn't travel further than me for her to divulge what she knew.' He made a sour face. 'By "me", I was thinking "in my presence". If you happen to overhear my thoughts on the subject, then so be it. I'm not exactly breaking my word.'

'Sophist,' said Dora. 'Please continue. Speak your thoughts aloud. Don't mind us.'

'That I certainly won't – apart from as it concerns getting paid. The helpful maid said it was an open secret in the house that the *comte* had his callers. The interesting new detail that didn't come out in the inquest was that Lorenzo was the one who arranged their arrival and departure.'

'That stands to reason,' said Jacob. 'He was the *comte*'s man and the one closest to him. I've not heard that he had the skills of a valet, so perhaps he had those of a pander?'

'According to the maid, the *comte*'s taste was for a higher quality of goods than might be bought in the local bordello,' said Alex. 'He cultivated amours with classic French gallantry, all of which she swears were platonic and not of the sort you pay for.'

'Of course she did. She would hardly blacken the reputation of either the *comte* or the *comtesse*,' said Dora. 'And was there a special friend in the picture at the time of their deaths?'

'A new lady. Susannah hadn't seen her but caught a glimpse of an emerald-green hooded cloak disappearing down the side passageway a few days before. I asked her if the mystery lady was there on the day itself, and she said she had no idea. Too much else was going on to be sure either way.'

'Hmm,' mused Dora. 'Would the *comte* be so foolish as to fall for a French trap? Was he the kind to flutter to the flame of a lady only to be burned by the candle?'

'Us men are, unfortunately, too often led by the little brain in our breeches than the one in our heads,' said Alex, flicking a knowing look at Jacob.

'Cut it out,' growled Jacob, 'Or it won't just be your pay we'll be docking.'

'Sorry, sorry. I'm merely jealous that I don't have my own Dora – well, not a Dora, obviously.' Alex grinned, then sobered. 'From your interest in Miss Petrovna, am I right in thinking she might be high on your list for the *comte*'s mystery woman?'

'She is,' said Dora, 'but with Michel Percy back in the country we must also ask ourselves if he had a French agent, or someone in the pay of the French, who insinuated themselves into the household.'

'I think it more likely to be someone from another nationality, or even a corruptible Englishwoman. The *comte* would have been on his guard if a lady from France suddenly claimed to have an attachment to him,' said Jacob. 'That would be far too obvious.'

'I will be very interested to see if Percy turns up at the fête tonight,' said Dora.

'A Frenchman at a celebration of their defeat? Would he dare?' asked Alex.

'Oh, he would. It would be exactly the kind of trick he would pull from up his sleeve to prove how debonair he is.'

Jacob squeezed her hand where it rested on his thigh. 'Then we might have that reunion he requested earlier than promised.'

Their carriage eventually was able to drop them close enough to the entrance to the gardens. Jacob and Alex fell into step either side of Dora as they paid their entry fee and emerged from the gatehouse. Strings of multi-coloured lanterns lit the long walks between the trees, enticing visitors to move on and ease the crush near the gate. Many were tempted to stretch their legs after a long wait in the carriages, heading out along the sandy paths, boots and shoes crunching on the dry ground. Music played in the distance with the occasional gust of applause and cheers from those who were already far into their evening of entertainment of watching the tightrope walkers and fire-eaters. The amber glow of the sunset provided a dramatic backdrop to the dark tree canopy. It would be very easy, considering the crowds, to lose sight of each other, but Jacob was determined that would not happen to them.

'How shall we approach this?' asked Dora. 'I've not been to the gardens before, so I bow to your superior knowledge.' She gave him a jaunty bob of her head.

'It's unlike you to take direction,' said Alex, stepping out the way of a portly lady and her arrow-thin companion.

'On the contrary, I have made a career on stage out of doing just that. I thought you were the one who couldn't follow orders?'

'Children, children,' said Jacob, intervening before their sibling tormenting grew too cutting. 'I suggest we engage one of the boxes early and watch the crowds from there.' He checked the bill that the porter had handed Dora. 'The concert is going to be in the orchestra at nine and we will be able to watch the crowds gathering.'

'The orchestra?' asked Dora, looking about her, likely searching for a sign.

'It's that building over there – the one that looks like a very ornate bandstand.' Jacob pointed to the circular pavilion in the middle of the first courtyard of the gardens. 'The supper boxes are in that horseshoe cloister on the far side. The boxes are the best place to listen to the concert.'

Dora squeezed his arm, going up on her tiptoes to catch sight of the attractions he was describing. 'It's hopeless. There are so many people! Who would've thought London held so many?' As they were standing still to debate their next move, crowds rushed past, the patrons coming from all walks of life, from the silken nobility with their liveried entourage to the linen-clad apprentice treating his sweetheart in summer muslin to a night out. 'I know we are here on business but I would love to explore. We should arrange a meeting point in case we get separated.'

Jacob made a mental note that he should keep an eye on her as Dora was always one to throw herself into the thick of things. 'I hope you don't mean to go off on your own?'

She snorted. 'Don't worry. I've read my *Evelina*. Fanny Burney warned me that women on their own are accosted in the dark walks by uncouth louts. But what about the lighted ones?' Her eyes glittered with humour.

'Perhaps we should try to remain together, hmm? Seeing how someone has attacked us on several occasions.'

'While I pity the poor lout who dares accost Mistress Dora, I suggest we let Handel be our refuge, if by unlucky chance we lose sight of each other,' said Alex, gesturing to the statue of the composer who had done so much with his music to popularise the outdoor entertainment offered in the gardens.

'Agreed,' said Jacob. 'Now, let's get ourselves a box before Dora heads off to take on all comers.'

Money opened the door to a supper box in prime position. Jacob paid extra to engage it for the entire evening. Visitors who could not afford the comfort of a box strolled from attraction to attraction, trying to time their arrival for the spectacles, such as the turning on of the cascades or the lighting of the fireworks, but Jacob knew from experience that wandering all evening was tiring and you could miss so much by always being a little late or a little early. Better to hire a box and use that as a base. It did come with the drawback that you had to order the ridiculously overpriced ham and barely drinkable Arrack punch – a small price when it allowed them to watch everyone circulating around the orchestra and heading deeper into the gardens. If you sat there long enough, you could be sure of seeing everyone.

Dora propped her chin on her hand as she surveyed the women. 'I think I missed the message that we were all to come in our regimentals.'

Now she had mentioned it, Jacob noticed that nearly all the ladies' outfits made nods to the victories that were being celebrated, with red, white and blue trimmings or pelisses that had the cut and braiding of an officer's coat. 'You should have worn your redingote.'

'It would've clashed horribly with my gown, which is why I settled on a shawl.'

'What's going on over there?' asked Alex, drawing their attention to the stage where the concert was to be performed.

Dora smiled. 'Now here's something on which I am the expert! They are putting the finishing touches to the backdrop and getting the lights ready. That's the back layer and I expect there will be a gauze curtain in front so they can add some special effects.'

'Looks like a naval battle scene,' said Alex.

'Trafalgar,' confirmed Jacob.

'I would not be surprised to hear some cannon-fire at

strategic moments in the musical programme. That's got very popular recently.' Dora used a pair of opera glasses that she had brought with her to scan the stage. 'Yes! Look! There's a man on the upper storey of the orchestra with a small ship's gun.'

'Let's hope he fires blanks because that thing is pointed our way,' said Alex.

'This could either be a musical triumph, or a disaster,' mused Dora. 'The more elaborate the theatrical effects in a performance, the more likelihood of them going wrong. How long have they been rehearsing? Not long by the sounds of it.' She patted Jacob's arm. 'This is going to be thrilling either way.'

'What about our quarry?' asked Jacob.

'I think you're right. We only need sit here and they will come to us. Miss Petrovna will be singing shortly, and Michel Percy will not want to miss the main event of the evening. We should invite him to join us.' She smiled at Jacob's arched brow. 'No, I'm serious.'

'Keep your friends close and your enemies closer?' said Alex.

'Exactly.'

'Speaking of which, I spy the enemy,' said Jacob, watching Michel Percy stroll along the avenue of trees. 'You were absolutely right about him. Shall I catch him for you?'

Dora grinned. 'Reel him in. I'm far happier knowing where he is so let's invite him to supper.'

Chapter Twenty-Six

Percy gave Jacob an enthusiastic greeting, kissing him on the cheeks in Gallic fashion while Jacob submitted stiff-backed to the embrace. That was not a popular gesture with the people in the Frenchman's vicinity. They edged away from such an un-English display. Dora watched the two men approach with wry amusement, noting the dagger looks they attracted in their wake. Percy was going to get himself thumped before the fireworks even began.

'I think I'll make myself scarce,' said Alex, getting up from the table. 'He doesn't know me and I'd prefer not to remind him of my existence. It might come in useful later.'

'Good idea. Stay alert,' said Dora. 'He's likely not the only enemy here tonight.'

Alex gave her a salute and slid out the back of the box so he didn't pass the new arrival.

'Mademoiselle Dora,' said Percy, bowing over her hand. 'We meet again. How do you say? I am the bad penny who keeps turning up?'

He said it before she could. 'Mr Percy, I admit I am surprised to see you here.' She wasn't at all, but he expected her to be shocked so that is what she would offer him. 'I would have thought an evening celebrating a victory over your country's armies would not be a pleasant experience.'

'Really?' He sat down in the seat Alex had vacated. 'You think I am worried by a few little skirmishes in dusty Spanish towns when the Emperor of France has marched victorious across Europe? Where are the Prussian victories? Or the Russian?'

The waiter arrived with three glasses of punch. Percy took the one ordered for Alex, seeming not to notice that he hadn't put in his own request. Perhaps he was under the mistaken impression they had exceptional service here.

Dora raised her glass. 'To victory.'

'To victory,' Jacob and Percy echoed.

Dora let the sweet and spicy taste of the drink settle in her mouth, smiling as Jacob pulled a face. He didn't have her sweet tooth.

Percy swirled his punch, studying it thoughtfully as the leaves rustled above and shadows flickered across his face. 'I never could understand why you English spoil perfectly decent wine and spirits with sugar and other flavours.'

'What a trial for you then to be sent back,' said Jacob laconically.

'Oh, I wouldn't say that. I must give it a second chance.' Percy sipped and shrugged. 'It does grow on you, I suppose.'

Dora wasn't sure if they were still talking about punch. With Percy, there was always another meaning hidden under the surface. 'Tell me, *monsieur*, why do you want to attend a celebration of a military victory at all?'

'Is not anybody who is anybody here tonight? I thought I would reintroduce myself.'

'That might be so, but at a fête like this? When we last met you said you abhorred the waste of lives in the wars across the continent and preferred to fight your battle in the arena of culture. You said that struggle was one for the centuries, not just to settle who gets the upper hand for the next few years.'

'Ah, you listened so well! How unusual in a lady.' He raised the glass of the punch he didn't like to her.

'You also said you wanted to define European art by collecting the best examples for your emperor's galleries, but here you are as trade envoy dealing in sacks of grain. What has happened to that ambition?'

Percy curved his lips in his secret smile, the one that said he knew far more than his audience. 'Why think I have given it up? Who know what chances the next few years will bring someone of my talents?'

'I think I understand. He's here for the spoils,' said Jacob. 'If you are waiting, *monsieur*, for England to be defeated so you get first pick of our collections, then save your breath to cool your porridge.'

'Oh? You think you will win, you with your armies facing so many enemies?' His brown eyes gleamed with cruel amusement. 'You've foolishly opened a new front in America, taking on an enemy that it makes no sense to fight. I believe that is a fatal strategic error.'

'We didn't start that war.'

'It takes two sides to fight. You could have walked away or negotiated an agreement with the colonials.'

Jacob shook his head but contented himself with serving Dora a share of the ham.

'You make it sound easy,' said Dora, picking up the argument that Jacob had let drop. 'Snap your fingers and say "let there be peace". Perhaps you should get a position as advisor to Napoleon. There would be much less bloodshed if he decided that he really didn't need to control the entirety of Europe and could content himself reigning at home.'

Percy waved his hand to her but addressed Jacob. 'Is it not most alluring for a lady to talk politics?'

Jacob started on his own plate, inspecting the wafer-thin ham as if it held the auguries for future victories like the geese on the Capitoline Hill. 'I wouldn't patronise her, if I were you, or you might find your tenure in London cut short as you seek medical treatment for gelding.'

Percy propped his chin on his palm and batted his eyelashes at Jacob. 'Would you help me, *mon cher docteur*?'

'No, I don't think I would.'

Percy sat back and snorted. 'Heartless man. You two are destined for each other, I can see that. Congratulations, by the way. I saw it in the newspapers on my arrival – such a joy to find two dear friends are to be wed. Do not forget to send me an invitation to the wedding breakfast.'

Was that an accurate report of when he arrived? Hard to know with him. As for what he said about the invitation, Dora was not going to weaken Jacob's standing by explaining she hadn't exactly agreed to be wed. Better to face society with a united stance. 'Are you not worried for your safety, being the sole French representative at this celebration?'

Percy looked around the audience that was gathering for the concert. 'There are bound to be others from my nation in this crowd. Did you not provide a welcome for many who fled the revolution? *Remarquez*, I understand England is a dangerous place for any Frenchman, *émigré* or supporter of Bonaparte. Your murderers do not care to make a distinction.'

He was raising the issue of the *comte* and *comtesse* himself. How interesting. Perhaps he really had been sent to find out what had happened and was coming to them as a likely source of information, knowing they kept abreast of events?

'Oh? Do you have anyone particular in mind?' asked Dora.

'You must have seen it – the horrible double murder of two French exiles.'

'When did this happen?' asked Jacob, looking puzzled.

'Last month. The Comte and Comtesse D'Antraigues.' Percy was watching Jacob's face closely as he was aware Jacob was not the actor of the pair.

Jacob frowned as if consulting his memory. Not bad, my love, thought Dora. 'I believe I did read something about that – but Dora and I were in the north country at the time, enjoying a holiday at my cottage in Cumberland. It's a beautiful area. Have you ever visited?'

'I can't say that I have. Is it not a place where it rains all the time? I don't have the tolerance for wetness that you English have.'

'It is damp, that is true, but we get the reward of green hills, waterfalls and lakes. It may not be as grand as the Alps but it is more congenial to human existence. You might live among these wonders without fearing an avalanche. It is favoured by many of our men of literature – Wordsworth and Coleridge to name but two.'

Percy was not going to accept the change of subject without putting up a fight. He was here to gather information and wanted to herd them back to his theme. 'You really didn't take note of the case? There can't be many murders of this kind even in London.'

'That is true. Normally I would be as interested but if it happened in July that coincided with the death of my father,' said Jacob. 'My mind was not on gossip.' He was playing his most pompous self. Dora would have to be careful she didn't give the game away by smiling.

'Ah yes. I had read…' Percy changed tack. 'I apologise. I should have offered my condolences. You sit here in black and yet I did not enquire or even recall that the viscount had passed. I do so now. My condolences on your loss. Your brother has succeeded to the title, of course?'

'He has.'

'And you are content with the change? It must come as a blow to be demoted to the brother and not the son of a viscount.' Percy was probing to see if he could find any cracks, but it was a half-hearted attempt, thought Dora, not up to his usual subtle line of questioning.

Jacob's chin shot up, the Sandys' stubbornness in his profile. 'I find your line of questioning impertinent, sir. I am not happy that my father has died. What son would be? But as for the rest, it is the natural order of things. The new viscount will doubtless be a credit to the family.'

Mischief peeped out of Percy's expression. If he were a god, he would be Loki, Dora decided, the Norse trickster. 'Despite having a mistress who objects to your marriage?' he asked.

So that was why he led them down this path! Dora jabbed her ham with her fork to express her frustration, imagining it a vulnerable part of Percy's body.

Jacob gave Percy his best supercilious stare, his tone bored. 'I thought you were more sophisticated than that, *monsieur*.

You disappoint me. My brother's amours are not a subject I air in the presence of a lady.'

Percy chuckled. 'Forgive me. I am being impolite, and I know that is a worse sin in English society than … well … sin.'

He was an amusing sparring partner, to be sure. There was movement on the stage, giving Dora a chance to shift them off this subject. She greatly preferred not to discuss the murders with Percy, but it was interesting that he was – or was feigning to be – ignorant. 'Look, the performers are gathering. Have you seen Madame Catalani perform before, sir?'

'An exquisite.' Percy kissed the tips of his fingers. 'Italians so often are.'

Dora flattened the concert bill out on the linen tablecloth, consulting the programme. 'I've heard the Portuguese baritone is excellent, but the Spaniard is too nasal.'

Jacob raised a brow. 'Oh? Who told you this, my dear?'

'I was visiting friends at Covent Garden,' said Dora. 'The doorman is very well informed.'

'Ah yes, the men no one notices but who see all. I will look forward then to…' Percy checked the list of songs, '"É Delícia Ter Amor" and visit the necessary during "Quando el bien que adoro".'

'You should stay and form your own opinion,' said Dora. 'I believe they will be singing with the ladies. I've heard the Russian is an excellent alto.'

A spark of interest lit Percy's eyes. 'Yekaterina Petrovna? Yes, her reputation goes before her. I was told that she was a favourite performer in Dresden for a time. Have you met her?' He was probing again. The fact that he knew about Petrovna's presence in Dresden was evidence that he had done his research into the D'Antraigues's life before London.

Additionally, that he'd offered Petrovna's name freely suggested she was not a French agent, or not one he controlled. Dora and Jacob had experienced the French government running rival intelligence operations in England before, so they could not eliminate that possibility.

'I don't recall. One meets so many people and attends many concerts. Has she been in the country long?' asked Jacob, answering for Dora.

'Only since July,' said Percy. 'Or so I heard.'

'Then it is unlikely our paths have crossed. We have been out of town,' said Jacob. 'As I told you.'

'Yes, yes, of course. I adore Russian women – so fiery and always speaking excellent French. It is the language of the court, of course. I was hoping for an introduction, but I must look elsewhere.' Percy lifted a slice of ham from the platter, looking to see if the light really did pass through the wafer-thin slices as was their reputation. 'How do they do that? Is there a special machine?'

'You mean like a guillotine?' asked Dora dryly.

Percy was saved from thinking up a suitable riposte by the arrival of the Vorontsovs at the railing in front of their table. The count bowed.

'Dr Sandys, how clever of you to find a box for the concert.'

This was not good. Their claim not to know Petrovna was about to be blown to smithereens.

'Early bird, Count Vorontsov, catches the worm, or a prime seat as in this case. Do you know the new French trade envoy, Michel Percy?' said Jacob swiftly.

The Russian went very still for a second, before he said with glacial politeness. 'I don't believe I do. Pleased to make your acquaintance, sir.'

'Your Excellency,' said Percy. 'My lady.' He bowed over her hand. '*Enchanté.*'

The lady, seemingly ignorant of the political undercurrent to the exchange, giggled. '*Et moi aussi.*' She tapped her husband's arm with her fan. 'Do prevail upon Dr Sandys to allow me to sit in his box. I am fatigued by so much walking, walking, walking. People pushing and shoving and the fire-eaters were a great disappointment, *malheureusement.*'

'We only walked the length of one path, *mon coeur*, hardly a Marathonian adventure,' said her husband.

'It felt like it.' The countess was visibly wilting.

What could Jacob do but offer her the spare seat at their table and give up his own to the count? He came to stand behind Dora's chair.

'I have only today presented my credentials at the Court of St James,' said Percy, showing no sign he would give up his seat, though he was the cuckoo in the nest. 'No doubt I will soon become familiar with all my diplomatic colleagues. Such a civilised arrangement, to keep open the communications even during a lamentable time of war, do you not think?'

'Indeed,' said the count coolly. He was interrupted from making any further comment by the arrival of the conductor. This gentleman escorted Madame Catalani to centre stage and applause rang out. The other singers gathered behind her, taking their seats in the second rank. Dora was surprised to see the Comte D'Antraigues, Julien, take his seat at the grand piano. She had not thought his skill would earn him a soloist role. Perhaps Miss Petrovna had pulled some strings for him? The conductor tapped his music stand, the orchestra lifted instruments, all took a breath, and began.

It was truly a fine performance. Even the Spaniard sang

well, and Dora could detect nothing nasal about his voice. Perhaps the doorman had had the misfortune to hear him when he had a cold, she speculated. She particularly enjoyed the duet between Madame Catalani and Miss Petrovna taken from *The Marriage of Figaro*. It suited the mischievous air that the Russian woman carried even onto the stage. Her strength was in the comic opera rather than the tragic. Seeing her trip lightly through the notes, it was hard to imagine her as a killer. Had Dora allowed her mind to run after Petrovna as a possible lover of the *comte* merely because she lacked other suspects? Or was she a very good actress?

One could smile and smile and be a villain, as Shakespeare noted.

Julien did not play a solo piece but was present throughout as an accompanist, turning in a solid performance of that task. It might well be his best hope for a future income.

'Rule, Britannia!' was to be the big finale and Dora sat forward to enjoy the full spectacle that the stagehands had been working on. She did so love a *coup de théâtre* when well executed.

Percy was watching her with amusement. 'Are you expecting something special?' he said in a low voice. 'Something stimulating?' He brushed his fingers over her forearm.

She scowled at him and removed her arm. 'Your skills are slipping, Mr Percy. That was a very awkward *double entendre*.'

He sat back and huffed. 'I believe you are right. Poor me. I am much out of practice. Will you help me hone my skills again? I think you have much to teach about pretending to be what you are not.'

'That's acting, Mr Percy. Buy a ticket to Covent Garden and educate yourself,' she said acerbically.

'Why do that when I can learn from an expert?'

A drum roll brought their snippy exchange to an end. The lights were shuttered and then uncovered so only the gauze backdrop was illuminated. It showed a night scene of a flotilla of naval vessels heading into battle, the moon overhead bathing the waves in silvery light. Madame Catalani, now in a breastplate and helmet, launched into the opening verse. The crowd hushed in awe as her pure voice rang out. Excitement built like a clock being wound to striking point, that tolled when she reached the chorus. As she sang the first 'Rule, Britannia!' the gun fired, the drums beat, and the lights were uncovered behind the gauze, an intense flash like cannon-fire, then were covered again. In time to the music, the stagehands uncovered and covered the lanterns so that the effect on the watchers was to see fire blazing at the mouths of the ship's guns, broadsides against the French. The crowd grew wild with joy, cheering each flash. The people joined in – how could they resist? – their voices swelling under Madame Catalani's heaven-sent one so that the whole garden was swept with the tidal wave of patriotic noise. This was excellently done. Dora leaped to her feet and held Jacob's hand. They shared a smile and roared along to the chorus. Forget war's many complexities for the moment; this was simply a jolly good show. The Russians stood too in respect, the countess leaning on her husband, but didn't sing. Seated, Percy made himself a ham sandwich and chewed with deliberate *sang-froid*.

All was going brilliantly until the last reloading of the gun. The musician took the last shell from his stockpile. As the final chorus began, the cue arrived and the gunner fired but, rather than just noise and smoke, a live shell hit the tree canopy over their heads with an ear-splitting crack. Branches rained down on the supper boxes, some smouldering, the roof collapsing. Head ringing, Dora dived for cover under the table. Jacob dragged the countess down with him as she had been too shocked to move from her chair. The count groaned under the impact of a tree limb that had crashed through the roof of their pavilion and struck him on the back. The diners who had escaped injury screamed and ran for safety. Unfortunately, this last gunfire was the signal to start the fireworks and the pyrotechnics working in the far reaches of the park had no idea that anything was wrong. The screams of the people escaping the burning pavilions joined with the whistle and bangs of the rockets, the bursts of white, yellow and red fire in the sky.

'*Merde!*' cursed Percy, seeing the bunting go up in a string of flame. 'We must move or burn.' He grabbed Dora's wrist and pulled her out of the box via the back exit. Dora would have gone back for Jacob, but the crowd was inexorably flowing in one direction which was away from the fire, a terrifying, suffocating press of people. All she had to anchor herself in the current was Percy's grip on her arm. Someone trod on her heel and she stumbled, losing a shoe and the skin on the back of her ankle. Percy prevented her falling.

'We will be crushed!' shouted Percy. 'Let us get out of this.' Seeing his chance, he dragged her with him down one of the infamous dark walks of Vauxhall Garden and away from the stampede.

Chapter Twenty-Seven

Acting quickly, Jacob lifted the countess over the rail of the box and dropped her to the ground. 'Make for the stage and Miss Petrovna.' The performers were standing aghast on the platform watching the chaotic scenes around them, but their elevated position made it a haven in the stormy seas. 'I'll get your husband.'

The lady clung to his hand like a limpet. 'Oh, but I shall faint. You must help me.'

Irritation flashed through him. Why could the bloody woman not think of her husband before herself? He peeled her fingers off him. 'Your husband is injured. You are not. Now buck up, madame, and get yourself to safety.' He gave her a little shove in that direction and fortunately Miss Petrovna caught sight of her friend and waved her over. 'Look, she's waiting for you.'

Seeing someone else who could look after her, the countess picked up her skirts and bolted for the stage, helped by the fact most of the audience had already cleared the area. She could move when she had to.

Jacob looked up. The trees had brought down the wooden canopy and parts of it were on fire. Still the wretched fireworks exploded, casting bursts of light on the confusion below. Dora had exited out the back with Percy, but he couldn't go in search of her until he had dealt with the emergency at hand. It was too much like the many battlefields he had attended, no good choices and only medical protocol to guide one's actions. He could feel cold sweat trickle down his spine. Now was not the time to indulge in unpleasant memories; now was the time for action.

He moved to the injured man. At least this was familiar.

'Stay still. I'm going to lift the branch off you.' He felt the count's neck. Heartbeat was strong.

A groan greeted his touch. Vorontsov was coming round.

'There was an accident and you've been struck by a tree branch, Count Vorontsov. I must check you for injuries before I move you, but I'm getting you out of here, understood?'

The man groaned again. Good enough.

'Brace yourself.' Jacob did not like the speed at which the canopy fire was spreading. The wooden roof had saved them from most of the splinters from the explosion but now it was threatening to undo that good work by burning them to death. He had to dodge the smouldering slats as they fell. 'One. Two. Three.' Heaving on the branch he could only lift it, not enough to clear the body. He swore. He needed help. 'Hi! You there! Give me a hand!' He called to a shocked-looking apprentice who was staggering across the ruins of the audience area. The boy touched his chest. 'Yes, you, soldier. Get over here.'

Hearing the call to action, the young recruit jogged over and jumped the rail. 'What do you want me to do?'

'Pull that man out when I take the weight.'

'Fuck me, it's burning down!' said the apprentice, noticing the fiery heavens overhead.

'I know that, private, but we've got to do this now. Stop lollygagging and pull!'

On the count of three, he lifted and his recruit pulled. They got the count clear and Jacob let the branch fall with a thump. They needed a stretcher, or they risked exacerbating any injury the count might have.

'Pull the cloth off the table. We'll use the tabletop to carry him.'

'Oh, heck, sir, it's all on fire now.' The young man looked close to panicking like a raw recruit facing the guns for the first time.

'Remember your orders, private. Move your arse! Table. Now!'

The apprentice glared at him while he shoved the plates and glasses off the top and flipped the trestle table over to yank off the legs. 'This isn't a bloody battlefield and I'm not in your army! I'm a cobbler.'

A bit of spirit was better than fear. 'I've been on battlefields, and I don't see the difference. Don't worry, cobbler, I'll see you are rewarded for bravery.'

The young man scoffed at that but stuck with him, some of his normal wits returning with his attitude. 'Who's the cove?'

'Does it matter?'

'Might be the bloody Frenchman who blew us all up, spoiling our fun. Someone said he was in this box.'

That didn't bode well for Percy wherever he was. 'Not a

Frenchman. The count is an ally of England – a Russian. We are friends with them.' For now. 'Take his shoulders and slide him on the table when I tell you.'

Vorontsov successfully transferred to the table, Jacob kicked out what remained of the railing. Seeing some gardeners arriving to extinguish the flames, he commandeered two to help lift the makeshift stretcher.

'Where are we going with this?' asked the apprentice. 'I gotta find my girl.'

So have I, thought Jacob. 'We'll carry it as far as the stage. On my mark – lift!'

Far from being able to go in search of Dora, Jacob found his skills required to attend the injured. The count was the worst hit by the explosion. Jacob feared that there might be a spinal injury, but he didn't want to alarm anyone. Instead, he made it very clear no one was to move his patient until the count's own surgeons arrived and made their assessment. He did not want to spark a diplomatic incident if his negligence meant the envoy emerged from the evening paralysed. As the countess was useless in a crisis, it was to Miss Petrovna that he entrusted the instructions and advised that utmost care should be taken before moving him to their embassy.

'This is a scandal,' Miss Petrovna said, gazing at the ruins of her debut in London. 'Who did this? The French? Are we safe here?'

Jacob had only time to shake his head when he was called away to new patients. Julien moved to assist Miss Petrovna by relieving her of the task of comforting the countess. The other injured included several burns victims and one casualty – a child caught in the stampede. There was nothing Jacob could do. The boy was already dead when he was carried to the stage, his distraught father weeping, the mother with her dress half dragged off her. Their cries of anguish would stay with Jacob long after he delivered the news.

'Who did this?' asked the father, echoing Miss Petrovna's question. 'Who wanted to destroy our happiness? It's that devil Bonaparte and his men, isn't it, doctor?'

That rumour seemed to be spreading very quickly. 'I don't know, sir. It appeared an accident to me. I am so sorry for your terrible loss – please, take your wife home.' Jacob slipped the man some money for a carriage. 'You don't need to stay here.'

'Not without my boy. We stay here until he's ready to come home,' said the father.

Jacob nodded. There was no point arguing with the grieving father and no harm would be done as they sat in vigil for the child who looked no more than Kir's age, until the gardens management arranged for a coroner. Thank God, they had not brought Kir tonight, nor told him where they were going. He would've smuggled himself in to see this show and could now have been the one lying at Jacob's feet.

'What a bloody mess,' he muttered to himself.

Taking out a handkerchief, Jacob wiped his face as the supper pavilion burned down behind him.

Chapter Twenty-Eight

'I think this is far enough.' Chest heaving as he sucked in breaths, Percy led Dora to a stone bench where they could both rest. It was surrounded by laurel bushes, a barrier of dark glossy leaves and dense branches giving the impression of seclusion. The fireworks still occasionally burst in the sky, but the cries were getting more distant, the immediate crisis abating. '*Mon Dieu*, they tried to kill me.' He shook his head in disbelief. 'But I have diplomatic status – that should be respected.'

Dora waited until she could string more than two words together before replying. 'You are hasty, sir. I could claim the gunner aimed at me. It was pointed in our direction long before you came to sit with us. Could it not be an accident?'

He only shook his head, feeling his arms and legs for injuries. As an experienced agent, he would know that some injuries only made themselves apparent after the initial shock had passed. Following his example, Dora checked herself over. Apart from a few minor abrasions, she was unhurt.

'Who would put live ammunition in a pile of blanks by accident?' wondered Percy.

True. With the attempts on their lives recently, it did seem very bad luck to almost die by chance. That wasn't something she wished to discuss with him. She should continue to be ignorant. 'Could it be a mix-up in the arsenal? The gun is no ordinary stage prop. The stagehand charged with firing it might not know the difference.'

'He should've done. There is no excuse. I would not be surprised to read tomorrow that people died in that rout.'

A shiver ran down her spine. Without his quick thinking, she might have been one of the victims. Dora reached down to her bruised heel. It wasn't bleeding, just skinned. 'Thank you for keeping me on my feet.'

He reached into his pocket and took out a fresh handkerchief, acting more like his usual self as he regained his balance. '*Mon plaisir*. Tie that around your foot, *ma chérie*. It is better than going without shoes until we can find a conveyance.'

'We must find Jacob.'

'And how do we do that, pray?'

'We agreed to meet at the statue of Handel if we got separated.' Hopefully the statue would have escaped the conflagration. It stood alone in its little garden plot.

He nodded, accepting that. 'Then when you are recovered, we will limp back in that direction and pay our respects to Maestro Handel.'

The big starburst overhead signalled the fireworks were reaching their crescendo. The flashes cast even deeper shadows in the already dark walkway. Dora tied the knot at her ankle and stood.

'I am ready.'

'*Bon.*' He offered her his arm. '*Allons-y.*'

Speaking in French was fatal. A gang of young men surged out of the shrubbery.

'I thought it was 'im!' cried one, shoving Dora back and seizing Percy by the lapels. 'You French bastard! You'll pay for this!' The thug shook Percy until his teeth must've rattled. His hat fell to the floor only to be stamped on by another in the gang.

Percy held up his hands. 'It was not me! I am the victim in this!'

Dora could've groaned. That was the wrong tactic.

'Victim? Bollocks to that! What's a fucking snail-eater doing at our celebration, eh? You tell me that.' The young man, one of the alehouse toughs who thought themselves the cock of the walk, wasn't going to listen to reason.

'I am a diplomat – I was with English friends. Miss Dora, explain, please!' His eyes rolled to her in desperation like a calf sensing it was heading for the abattoir.

This wasn't good – really not good. Dora couldn't think of an escape, or words to calm the aggressors. They were looking for someone to blame and Percy was it. Still, she had to try.

'Gentlemen, please—'

Her appeal was cut off. 'We don't take the word of a slut who keeps company with a Frenchie.' A second man grabbed Dora from behind, arm across her neck. 'Whoring for the enemy, are you? Well then, you won't mind giving us some of that, will you?' His other hand spread across her stomach and scrunched up the material of her gown.

That was enough! Life on the road had taught her a thing or two about what to do when in a tough spot – swift action was one. 'Get your dirty hands off me, you idiot!' Dora jerked her head back to collide with his nose, seized his little finger and yanked it so he either had to let go or let her break it. She followed up with an elbow to his diaphragm. The man howled and released his hold on her. She darted forward and pushed the oaf off Percy. This gave the Frenchman time enough to recover and pull a blade from his pocket. He held it out.

'Get behind me, Dora. You should know, gentlemen, I'm trained in the art of knife fighting. If you come at me, more than one of you will die tonight.'

Oh, thank you, Percy. What a brilliant way to defuse the situation: threaten them with death!

With a sigh, Dora pulled out her pistol from her reticule and levelled it at the ruffian who had grabbed Percy.

'Step back, gentlemen, or I will fire.'

'You brought a pistol to a knife fight?' muttered Percy with sardonic amusement.

The man thought for a moment, then swaggered, taking a pace forward. He was an unprepossessing individual with a shock of greasy hair and unshaven chin. 'What you going to do, eh, whore? You've one shot and there are many more of us than you.'

Dora lowered the muzzle to point at his groin. 'But do you really want to sing soprano for the rest of your life? Trust me, I can get off the shot before your friends reach me and you really won't care what happens next, will you?'

He hesitated but decided to be stupid. 'She's bluffing. Lads, get 'em!'

Damn. She was going to have to shoot him. She tightened her finger on the trigger.

Just then, Alex pushed out of the bushes, sword already released from his stick. He slashed it across the space between Dora and the louts, halting them in their tracks. Dora pulled up the muzzle and discharged the pistol in the air, barely avoiding getting Alex in the back. Everyone flinched in surprise that she actually had a loaded gun.

'Dammit, Alex, I could've killed you!' She trembled with the near miss.

'But you didn't.' He sent her an apologetic look. 'Gentlemen, as you have discovered, she wasn't bluffing and, fortunately for you, I arrived in time to save you from her ire. I'd rather not waste my evening explaining to a magistrate why we needed to rid the world of you and your idiot friends, but I will if you don't stand down.'

'Who the hell are you?' jeered the lout.

Alex looked magnificent as he made a salute with the weapon. 'Lieutenant Colonel Smith, 1st battalion 2nd Foot Guard, at this lady's service and not yours. Now get going before I teach you a lesson learned on the battlefields of Europe.' Alex cut at the man, slicing a button from his waistcoat.

'Oh, I like this one,' murmured Percy to Dora.

'Hush, you,' she warned.

The leader was still not ready to back down, his blood was up and he wanted his revenge. 'But he's French!' He pointed at Percy.

'Your point being?' drawled Alex.

'He's the enemy. He fired on the audience.'

'He was sitting in the audience in the line of fire, you fool!

Now use that head of yours for something more than putting a hat on. Go home – or go help put out the fires. That's the patriot action needed now, or do you want Vauxhall to burn down? Leave these people alone.'

With a few dirty looks, hunched shoulders, and grumbling, the men melted back into the shadows.

'Have they gone?' asked Percy, not dropping his guard.

'I hope so.' Dora stowed the pistol in her reticule. With all the firework explosions, no one had come running to investigate the shot.

'You do know how to show a gentleman a good time, Dora.' Percy slid the knife back into his pocket but kept his hand on the hilt.

'I don't remember inviting you to any show, *Mr* Percy. You brought this upon yourself. What were you thinking, flaunting yourself at an evening like this?'

'Showing that we the French are not afraid?'

'Well, I don't know about you French, but this Englishwoman was terrified by that little altercation.'

He replaced his hat, punching out the dent but it would never be the same again. 'I might have miscalculated the strength of feeling against my nation.'

'Are you all right, Dora?' asked Alex, coming to her side, sword still drawn.

Finally, a sensible person to talk to. 'Yes. Have you seen Jacob?'

'From a distance. He was tending to the wounded who have been carried to a temporary hospital on the stage. I imagine he's desperate to find you so we'd better hurry back before he sets off to hunt.' He looked down. 'Oh, your foot!'

'Lost a shoe – nothing worse.' They began moving back towards the concert stage. Percy trailed behind them.

'Are you not going to introduce me?' the Frenchman called from behind.

'No,' said Dora.

They arrived at the same time as the Russian doctors who took over the care of the count. Dora hurried to Jacob's side.

'You're bleeding,' she said, noticing a trickle of blood on his neck.

He touched the tip of his ear. 'I think a splinter caught me here.'

'Let me look.' She pulled his head down. There was a nick on the top edge. 'You're hurt here, but not badly.'

'The helix?'

'Is that what it's called? I didn't know. Live and learn. I have the remedy for it.'

His eyes softened in a smile. 'Oh, yes?'

She kissed it better. 'There.'

He hugged her to him. 'Thank God you're all right. There was a boy – crushed. I couldn't do anything for him.'

'Oh, Jacob. That wasn't your fault.'

'Wasn't it? Was someone trying to get us? We've been attacked so many times over the past two days, I can't believe it is coincidence.'

She squeezed him tightly. 'This was planned in advance. Who knew we would be here? Percy thought they were aiming for him, but surely he came on a whim? I imagine Count

Vorontsov might consider he was the target. But perhaps it was a ghastly accident? They are common enough on stage.'

He set her away from him and gave a firm nod. Her Jacob didn't like showing any weakness before others. 'You're right. We mustn't jump to conclusions. Cool heads and all that.'

'Are you finished here?' she looked around at the row of injured people waiting for stretchers to carry them out of the gardens.

'I should stay till all my patients are gone.'

'Then I will make myself useful and ask the stagehands what happened. I think they are more likely to talk to me than to you.'

'How so?'

'The authorities will be looking for someone to blame and the stagehands are in the frame for it.'

'And I seem too official?'

'Exactly.'

'Very well then. But don't leave on your own.'

She kissed his cheek. 'Same goes for you, Dr Sandys.'

Just as she was about to find the backstage crew, Madame Catalani approached, holding a pair of slippers.

'Miss Fitz-Pennington, I could not help but notice you've lost a shoe. Would you like to borrow these? I have a spare pair.'

'Thank you. I am much obliged.' Untying the handkerchief, Dora wriggled her feet into them, finding she took the same size as her heroine.

'Unlike Cinderella, you have found your prince already, I see, without the intervention of a lost slipper.' The soprano's gaze was on Jacob. He made a fine sight, looking rakishly dishevelled, sleeves rolled up to display capable arms, bronzed after their stay in the Lakes. His expression was compassionate as he listened to a girl's account of how she came to twist her ankle while he bandaged her injury. 'Is he the one the newspapers say you are going to marry?' At Dora's surprised look, the singer smiled slightly. 'Yes, I too read the gossip, though one seldom comes across anything good about oneself in that column.'

'Yes, that's him. He said he wanted to marry me – told the world, in fact.'

The soprano gave her an astute look. 'And you? Have you told the world that you said "yes"?'

'I'm still thinking about it.'

'What is holding you back, if you don't mind me asking?'

Now did not seem the time to lie, with death and destruction around them. 'Old loyalties – and fear.'

Madame Catalani crossed her arms, foot tapping. 'That I can understand. But in the end, is it not quite simple?'

'What do you mean?'

'You know what I mean. Think about it. I'd better go and see what we can do for the poor victims of this evening's events.'

With that, she patted Dora's arm and went back to join her friends packing up from the débâcle. It was unfair that her arrangements had been blown apart. Still, the concert would get more inches in the newspapers the next day, so Madame Catalani might not think it quite so much a disaster of an evening when she read flattering comments in the column about her standing strong under fire.

Dora looked around her for the backstage crew. They were

loading the piano onto a wagon to be taken back to the music room. Who was the one to set up the live round for the gun? That was what she now had to find out. She headed for them, brimming with questions.

Chapter Twenty-Nine

Bruton Mews

Dora and Jacob sat in the office, taking a late breakfast in the sunshine that came through the open door. Alex and Kir were outside, playing knucklebones on the step. Alex seemed to get a vast deal of pleasure from revisiting childhood games and was teaching Kir how to maximise his points as they tossed up the little bones and tried to catch as many as possible. Jacob could understand the attraction of something entirely unrelated to murderous plots. It was good to be doing something normal after the upsetting events of the night before and they all found it cleansing to hear a child laugh. Even so, Jacob couldn't help but think of the little boy who would play no more games and the parents who had lost their child in such a senseless way.

Dora brushed his arm. 'You couldn't do anything for him.'

He gave her a humourless smile. 'Reading my thoughts now?'

'They are not hard to guess when you stare at Kir like that.'

He sighed. 'All we can do is go forward – work out what is really going on. Let's go over what we learned about last night.'

'Let's make a fresh pot of tea for me and coffee for you, and then decide our next step.'

Before they could get to that, Miss Austen rushed in, her bonnet ribbons flying behind her.

'Have you read the news?' she asked, waving a newspaper. 'An attack on Madame Catalani! What is the world coming to?'

'Good morning to you too,' said Dora, getting up to greet her. 'It was a little more than that, I'm afraid, Jane. We were at the concert and were just discussing it. I can say with absolute certainty that Madame Catalani was not the target, but we and our investigation might have been.'

'I beg your pardon?' Miss Austen's hazel eyes rounded in shock as she held on to Dora's hands.

'Miss Austen, please do take a seat.' Jacob held one out for her.

'You had better hear the full story.' Dora told their visitor about the events of the night before while Jacob fetched a clean cup from the scullery. He poured the tea for the ladies.

'Thank you, Dr Sandys. I need this to steady my nerves.' The cup did rattle a little in Miss Austen's hand so she put it down on the table. 'They are my old friends when it comes to rude shocks, but today they are in such a flutter hearing how close you both came to death. And the authorities can't trace the gunner?'

'No, unfortunately not. It was a scene of great confusion and many witnesses slipped away before anyone thought to follow up on this. I questioned the stage crew and the musicians who were still there,' said Dora. 'They don't normally have a gun as part of their orchestra, so no one was surprised by a stranger turning up to fire it. They assumed the management had arranged for it, or the singers. The first time they met him was at the dress rehearsal and he only fired the gun once to check it was working. They didn't want to waste the ammunition as it was a crown a pop.'

'Did anyone get his name?' asked Miss Austen.

'No. He barely spoke and kept himself to himself.' Dora looked at Jacob. 'That's one thing we must do this morning: find out who engaged him.'

Jacob made a note. 'Indeed so – the fact that he went missing immediately afterwards is suspicious.'

'Was he scared of getting the blame?' wondered Dora.

He nodded. 'Or conscious of guilt?'

'I think we should call on Julien this morning,' said Dora, coming to a decision. 'He was there, and I didn't get a chance to talk to him as he had his hands full with the Russian countess.'

'Oh, Lord, I can imagine she was no good in a crisis,' said Miss Austen, shaking her head at the picture she was conjuring. 'She strikes me as the sort who would consume attention more worthily spent on alleviating the crisis.'

'You would be right about that,' said Jacob. 'Very well. Let us go and see how the young *comte* is this morning.'

The Russians weren't in occupation when they called on Queen Anne Street. Julien told them that his friends had gone back to the embassy after Vauxhall, the countess had retired to her bed and Miss Petrovna was nursing the count.

'Any news on his condition?' asked Jacob, following the new Comte D'Antraigues up the stairs.

'The surgeons were worried for a time last night, but they now think he is badly bruised and there are no bones broken. With all the swelling it is hard to tell so he must stay lying down until that goes.'

'No loss of sensation in his extremities?'

'None reported. A few burns but nothing too serious. I'm sure he'll want to thank you when he is recovered. Without your quick action, it would have been very much worse. Please, come in.'

The count took them to the library on the first floor and invited them to sit. A maid brought refreshments. Jacob wondered if Julien had dismissed the footman who had served him so ill on their last visit. If so, that showed he had sense. Poor servants were like internal bleeding: fatal before you knew what was happening. You only had to look at what had happened with Lorenzo Stelli to prove that case.

'Sir, we were wondering if you had any idea who the man firing the gun was?' asked Dora. 'No one in the orchestra or among the stage crew knew him.'

Julien tapped his long pianist fingers, making a steeple against his chest. 'I'm afraid I didn't pay him much attention. What did I notice? He was ten or so years older than me, dark hair, pale eyes – grey perhaps, like the doctor here. I don't remember him saying anything except the occasional grunt of assent when given orders. I don't even know if he was English.'

That was an interesting detail. They'd never identified their two assailants, known in the case notes only as brown jacket and black coat. Could one of them have taken up the gunner's post?

'Would you recognise him if you saw him again?' asked Jacob.

'I believe I would.' Julien beat out a little rhythm with his fingertips. 'Now you mention it, I do remember one thing. There were grumbles from the percussion players that he was on a separate contract and rumour had it that he was getting paid more than them for his participation, the same rate of pay as me, in fact.'

'Do you know who holds the contracts? That would surely name him,' said Dora.

'If he used his real name,' added Miss Austen.

'That would be Madame Catalani's stage manager,' said Julien. 'He was responsible for hiring the extra talent for the evening. A Mr Pierce.' He gave an address convenient for the theatre in Covent Garden.

Jacob met Dora's gaze, and from what he saw there he assumed silent agreement that they now had a lead to follow up.

'Sir, when we were here last time, we told you we were looking for something your father might have left behind, a report that another party is desperate to get their hands on,' said Jacob. 'You mentioned that the Vorontsovs and the government have both searched the house. However, nothing has turned up and from the fact that the attacks are still occurring, it suggests that the hidden item is still believed to be missing.'

Julien looked up sharply. 'Am I to understand that you think the incident last night is connected to this?' The thought had not occurred to him, which was telling. The *comte* had no idea of the deep waters in which he was wading. 'I thought it was just very bad luck.'

'The missing gunner, the fact that the box where we and the Vorontsovs were sitting was the worst hit, the recklessness of the attacks – that all suggests it is a possibility.'

'There may have been other targets, of course,' added Dora. 'We were seated with a French diplomat who assumed it was aimed at him. It could have been done to ruin Madame Catalani's concert, or diminish Wellington's victories, or it could have been an accident. We are considering all these theories too.'

The *comte* looked distressed, as if hoping that this would all go away. 'It seemed pure accident to me.'

'There was nothing pure about it, unfortunately.'

Julien grimaced in acknowledgment. 'That poor child. Not a sight I will forget in a hurry.'

'Indeed. Running with the theory that connects to your father, do you mind telling us about him?' asked Jacob. He noticed that Miss Austen was scribbling all of this down, her face alert with interest. It was unnerving to have one's actions monitored by so astute a writer, but so far Julien had not objected.

'My father? No, I do not mind talking about him. In fact, it is good to talk about him. So many people avoid the subject with me as if him being murdered meant I should somehow feel ashamed of him.' He crossed his legs and brushed off the thigh of his immaculate breeches. 'He was a brilliant man, quite the cleverest person I've ever met. My mother was the more talented, if you understand the difference, but when it came to judging the outcome of events, or anticipating moves in stocks and shares, my father was always a step ahead of the game.' Julien gestured to the room. 'That is how we could afford to live in style in two houses. He invested wisely.'

That was an interesting development on the question of their finances, and one Henry Austen was not party to. Jacob should've realised the D'Antraigues had more money than rumoured, because an account at Coutts was not available to everyone. The late *comte* clearly had played his cards close to his chest, allowing others to doubt his credit worthiness as it all added to the mystery of his position. He had liked to keep people guessing.

'Before he died, did he mention anything that was particularly on his mind? We are looking for the last thing that he wrote for the Foreign Office.'

'Yes, I know about that. He was in regular correspondence with the government. It was men from that department who searched his study. They were most aggrieved that nothing turned up. I told them what I'll tell you now: the night before my parents died, as I left to come here, my mother was excited for the party and my father said it would be a very lucrative affair as he had something explosive up his sleeve.'

'What did you think he meant by that?' asked Miss Austen.

'It was my father's way of saying he had valuable intelligence, something that many people would pay for. He had been saying for some time that his pension wasn't sufficient and that he could augment it elsewhere.'

The theory that he had provoked a bidding war seemed a good one, noted Jacob.

'Do you think it was something Lorenzo would kill for?' asked Dora.

Julien sighed. 'I don't know, Miss Fitz-Pennington. I thought he'd run mad, that my parents' death was just a horrible, inexplicable tragedy, but since you raised the question with me the day before yesterday, I've begun to wonder. I even discussed it with Count Vorontsov. My father never completely trusted Lorenzo. The Italian hadn't been in service with him long enough to earn the trust, he said, but he found the man useful.'

'You mean by conducting ladies to his room discreetly?' said Jacob. 'Apologies to the present company.' He looked to Miss Austen who kept her head down, pencil moving.

'My father was no saint. I am aware he had his lady friends,' said Julien. 'We French are much more sophisticated than you English when it comes to relationships. Mother had her own amours – or did until I was born. Neither hid this from me. They loved each other and that was enough faithfulness for them both. They were each other's best friend when it came down to it.'

'Was the countess or Miss Petrovna one of your father's special ladies?' asked Dora.

Julien gave a bark of laughter. 'Definitely not the countess. Can you imagine her having the energy to pursue an amour outside of her marriage, or even in it?' A wicked glint of amusement lit his eye, showing the witty man he normally was under better circumstances.

'Miss Petrovna?' asked Jacob.

He shrugged. 'I never saw anything of that nature between them. My father loved music, and she is a talented musician; that was the bond between them, if anything. If there was more in Dresden, I'm afraid I do not remember. But Yekatarina had only been in England a few weeks before they died so it doesn't seem likely. Besides, the countess keeps throwing her at me. If that had been a known affair, it would not be in very good taste to suggest her as my wife, now would it?'

'But not impossible?'

Julien spread his hands in a hopeless gesture. 'Does it matter now?'

It might matter very much but there was nothing to be gained in distressing him with their suspicions. Jacob looked to Dora to take up the questioning.

'If your father had something he wished to hide but keep close at hand, what do you think he would have done with it?' asked Dora.

Julien got up and paced to the mantelpiece. Jacob thought for a second that he might be going to open a secret compartment and solve the mystery for them, but instead he rubbed the dust off the clock which wasn't ticking. 'I need to wind this. The servants are cutting corners.' He turned to look at Dora. 'My father would never have forgotten to wind the clocks. He had a mind that noticed details. He loved playing games with me when I was little to encourage me to develop the habit of paying attention. It has helped with my music and in so many other areas of my profession, I can tell you.'

'What game did he play?'

'Oh, the usual one. No doubt you've played it yourself. He would invite me into his room and ask me to take note of where everything was, then ask me to leave and come back again a minute later. I had to pick out what he had moved or changed.'

'We used to play that with objects on a tray,' said Miss Austen. 'Never with anything as challenging as a room.'

Julien smiled sadly. 'My father liked a challenge.'

'If we were to ask you now, what is different about the rooms your father used from how they usually were, what would you say?' asked Jacob.

'What? All of them?' Looking thankful for the excuse to be moving, Julien didn't wait for an answer. He got up and prowled the library. 'I can't see anything. I've moved a couple of books but that was over the last few days.'

'This was his study?'

'Yes, when in town. That's his desk. We searched it thoroughly. There are hidden compartments, but I emptied those.'

'What did they contain?'

'His will – before you ask, I'm the only child so everything comes to me. Some coin. Nothing in the nature of a report or recent letters.'

'Perhaps you should look downstairs in the room where the party was to be held,' suggested Jacob.

'The music room? Very well. Ladies?' Julien opened the door for Miss Austen and Dora, and they descended the flight of stairs, through the hall and into the room where they had first met him with his Russian guests.

'I see your father liked his theatrical works,' said Jacob, noticing the Zoffany and the Watteau again.

'He loved anything in that line,' said Julien. 'It was how he met *Maman*.' He stood in the doorway of the music room and scanned it attentively. 'Funny, doing this is like having him with me again. I can hear him telling me to look, *really* look.'

'And?' asked Miss Austen. 'What do you see?' Her pencil

was poised over her notebook. She evidently found Julien fascinating.

'On the day they died we'd cleared all the furniture to the side to make way for the guests. We had hired chairs for the concert and those were stacked over there.' He pointed to a space along one wall. '*Maman* insisted we clear the small pictures as well. She said her admirers might steal her likeness – it had happened before, at the height of her fame.'

He was describing a room with many changes and footmen coming and going with the chairs and furniture – not an ideal place to conceal something.

Jacob stepped back into the hallway and considered the paintings. Would the late *comte* hide a report behind a canvas? That was too unwieldy to be useful, surely, and taking it on and off the wall cumbersome, requiring other people's involvement. 'How about those?' He pointed to the prints on the side table.

'Those are relatively new,' said Julien. 'Vesuvius and the Fountains of Versailles, my father's new toys.'

Dora, who had been studying the portraits, came over. 'A volcano. Could that be a pun on explosive?'

They had stood out as being very dull, Jacob remembered thinking when he'd seen the prints the first time. He then recalled the Battle of Trafalgar of yesternight. The man was passionate about the theatre and theatrical effects...

'Are those transparencies?' he asked.

Julien smiled. 'They are. How clever of you to spot that, Dr Sandys. I was going to surprise you by holding one up to the light. My father got endless amusement from displaying them to his guests and teasing them that their assumptions about the picture were wrong.'

'First impressions,' murmured Miss Austen with a glance at Dora. 'Please do show us,' she said more loudly.

Julien took the one of the fountains. 'It is best with a strong lamp in a darkened room, but this window will do as the sun is coming through it.' He held it up and the dull dribble of a fountain shot into sparkling light. 'My mother said it was very like the real thing when *le Roi et la Reine* were alive. After the revolution'—he took the picture away and the fountain vanished—'and before!' The fountains gushed again with the light behind them.

Dora brought him the one of Vesuvius. 'Will this do the same?'

'*Mais oui.* You will see what the poor people of Pompeii experienced in the terrifying moment before death.' His French accent was becoming stronger as he enjoyed the little show he was putting on, memories of the best times with his parents. 'My father had a very dramatic speech he would give on that explosion and then, *voilà!*' He moved the picture to the window. It did not change. '*Quoi?*' He turned it over, then stared at it again.

Jacob's heart thumped with anticipation as it did when he was close to solving a puzzle. 'May I?'

Julien passed it to him. 'I don't understand.'

'You will. Your father liked his games. He gave you a hint that it was explosive – it would amuse him to use a volcano print to hide it in plain sight as Miss Fitz-Pennington hinted. We've all been walking past it without giving it a second look – you because you knew the secret and did not feel like playing; we because we thought it a rather dull etching of the Bay of Naples.' He slid the tacks securing the frame out of their pinholes. 'For a transparency to work, there must be a thin layer like gauze over the picture beneath and nothing in between. In this case, something has been placed between the two layers.' He gently opened the back. 'I imagine your father was planning a theatrical denouement just as you were doing, handing the lucky winner of the bid for his report the information at the party before the jealous eyes of their rivals.'

Julien grimaced. 'That does sound like him. Is there something?'

Jacob gently eased out the folded page. 'Indeed, there is.'

'Is that what everyone is killing people to get their hands on?'

'I'm afraid it is.' Hesitating, Jacob then held it out. 'It is yours. What do you want done with it?'

Julien took it, unfolded the sheet, and read. 'Why kill for this?' With a sigh, he handed it back to Jacob. 'Such things do not interest me. I don't even want it in the house. My priority is to stop more deaths and these awful attacks, so I want you to let people know it has been found and handed to the government.'

'You don't want to bargain for it? Demand to be paid?' asked Dora, looking over Jacob's shoulder as they both read the contents.

'I have no wish to repeat the mistakes of my parents. My father miscalculated and that'—Julien's voice hitched—'that proved fatal.'

Jacob's admiration for the young man went up many notches.

'Then we will do what you ask. I'll take this to my acquaintance at the Foreign Office. I suggest you tell all callers about the game we played and pretend ignorance of the contents. Say we whisked it away before you had a chance to read it and that it was addressed to the Foreign Secretary so you had no business reading it in any case. Make it perfectly clear you are out of the business from which your father earned his reputation.'

'Make it clear to whom?' asked Julien, puzzled.

'Everyone,' said Dora.

'Especially the Russians,' added Jacob.

Chapter Thirty

'That was simply thrilling,' said Jane as they got into a hackney carriage. 'I felt privileged to witness how you two work together, like a well-oiled machine. Is your life always like this?'

Dora was tempted to laugh at that description. She could think of many occasions when she and Jacob had rubbed up against each other and produced sparks. 'Sometimes. Much of what we do is patient watching or asking the right questions of those who know our targets.'

'I've always thought the greatest marriages are those between two people who complement each other, whether it be to run a gentleman's household, a ship of the line or a vast landed estate.'

'We aren't married.'

'Not quite on the same page yet?' asked Jane.

'You could say that.' Dora listened as Jacob gave the driver instructions to drop the ladies at the address for the stage manager in Covent Garden and then take him on to the

Foreign Office. They were dividing their efforts, weren't they? She did agree that they had to make haste, but he should have asked her. He saw her expression when he took his seat.

'I thought we agreed?' he said warily.

'When did we agree?'

'When our eyes met and you... You're right. I merely thought I'd understood your intention.'

'Shall I fetch the oilcan?' said Jane archly as she nudged Dora. The carriage began moving.

'I find words are usually necessary to avoid misunderstanding, Jacob,' said Dora dryly. 'It is a good plan, but remember that these people are still at large. We aren't safe until they know they are too late to get their hands on the report. And we will still have to guard against them lashing out in anger.'

'What did the report say?' asked Jane. 'I was dying to ask but thought I should show restraint.'

'I found it rather encouraging,' said Dora. 'Do you want to read it?'

Jane shook her head. 'Please summarise the main points for me. I'd prefer we talk about what we are doing, in the time we have left before we get to our destination.'

'The *comte*'s last report said that Napoleon had made a serious error. The emperor does not understand the general he is up against,' said Jacob.

'Field Marshal Wellington?' asked Jane.

'Not him this time. Napoleon is unlikely to face him as they are in very different theatres of war, one in Spain the other on the border of Russia. The *comte* was writing about Prince Kutuzov.'

'Head of the Russian armies?'

'That's the man. Kutuzov is a general of the old school who doesn't flinch at doing what is necessary. He will burn every building and destroy all the crops between Kiev and Moscow rather than let the French get hold of them. The *comte* predicted that the French armies would march into a desert with a Russian winter approaching. There will be nothing to requisition and the line of supply too long and vulnerable to feed so a huge force.'

Jane wrinkled her brow. 'Napoleon doesn't know this? How can he not?'

'Because he thinks the Tsar is a young man who would prefer to sue for peace as he did before. Napoleon doesn't expect Alexander to sacrifice his own country to stop the invaders. He has not given sufficient weight to the stubbornness of the old soldier in charge.'

'The *comte* predicted that Napoleon will retreat?'

'Not before he goes too far. D'Antraigues predicted that Napoleon will lose – and that means he will lose everything. That was the explosion the *comte* promised.'

Dora had read the same message too. It felt unreal at this time when the emperor's power was at its zenith. But perhaps that was just it – the hubris of a man who had come to believe that he couldn't lose a battle? He had reached a peak and now was destined to decline. He had forgotten that other forces were ranged against him, bloody-minded peasantry and the approaching winter to name but two; these no general could defeat.

'Who had the motive to kill to keep this quiet? The allies must welcome the news. Our government will be encouraged and find renewed enthusiasm for the fight. The Russians too must be very happy with this verdict,' said Jane. 'I know my brothers in the navy would celebrate to hear their contribution to the war has not been in vain.'

'Does this mean the French are back in contention as our killers?' asked Dora, then immediately corrected herself. 'That doesn't feel right. It seemed to me that Michel Percy was one step behind us, or more. We wondered if Lorenzo, hating Napoleon as he did, killed his master because he couldn't stand the report predicting French success, but we have a report saying the exact opposite.'

'I think I know what happened,' said Jacob. 'Or, at least, I have a suspicion of the motive for keeping this report out of circulation. I'm just not certain who.' He shook himself. 'Let's get this report handed over to Thornbury in the strictest confidence. We can say it has been found, but we must make sure no one knows what is in it. That is the best way of unmasking our killer.'

'What are you plotting, Jacob? You know I don't like to be kept in the dark.'

'Visit the stage manager and get confirmation of who put the gunner in the orchestra. If that name is the person I suspect, then we have confirmation. I don't want to prejudice your questions by giving you the name now.'

He was up to something, but Dora trusted him enough to let this play out as he suggested. 'And after we have the name?'

'I'll meet you at the office. You'll know where we are going if I'm proved right. Ah, we're here.' Jacob got out and handed them down to the pavement.

Dora poked him in the ribs. 'You are being tricky.'

He kissed her hard and fast. 'No, I'm being cautious. I need to talk to Thornbury about the international repercussions. I'm hoping to persuade him to work with us so we can decide our next move.' He got back into the carriage and drove off to Whitehall.

Mr Pierce was having a bad day. Dora could tell this from the moment they entered his office as he shouted at his clerk to turn away all callers and deny all responsibility for injuries or lost items as a result of the accident at the concert.

'He's not going to like us asking questions,' said Jane.

'Then we need to make him think we are doing him a favour. Any ideas?'

The clerk hurried over to them, his expression wary. 'Ladies, I'm afraid Mr Pierce is busy today. If it is about the concert last night, you must take your grievances to the managers of Vauxhall Gardens.'

'It is nothing to do with that,' said Jane. 'I'm here on a matter of business.'

What tale was she spinning now, wondered Dora.

'My name is Miss Austen. My sister-in-law is contemplating holding a musical party and was considering engaging Mr Pierce's services to organise it. Are you saying Mr Pierce is too busy to take on new business? If so, I'll got to the next person on my list.' She made as if consulting her notebook.

The clerk's demeanour changed in a trice. 'No, no, please, dear lady. I'll see if he is available. I believe his eleven o'clock appointment cancelled so he likely has an opening.'

He hurried off to the inner office.

'You are a genius,' muttered Dora.

'I do try,' said Jane with a smile. 'I'll leave you to extract the information as I've got us through the door.'

The clerk ushered them in. 'Miss Austen and her ... er ... companion.'

Mr Pierce, a man with the face of a bulldog, small eyes and jutting chin, got up and bowed. 'Delighted, Miss Austen, please do take a seat.'

Jane did as bidden. Dora remained standing, playing the part of chaperone servant as she scanned where the contracts might be held. It was a neat room, everything filed away. Playbills advertising Madame Catalani's most famous concerts were hung framed on the wall.

'Mr Pierce, thank you for seeing me without an appointment,' said Jane. 'I had the very great pleasure of meeting Madame Catalani a few days ago and mentioned her to my sister-in-law. I understand you organise her concerts when she is engaged outside a traditional theatre or concert venue?'

'I have that pleasure. I must mention that she is much sought after and can command the very best prices for her performance.' He was looking askance at the lady who was no sophisticate in her respectable muslin walking dress and pelisse.

'I have no doubt that is true. My brother is a partner in a bank so there is no shortage of funds for the party my sister-in-law has in mind.'

Mr Pierce nodded. 'Forgive me if you thought me unmannerly for raising the matter of money. It is better to check before we progress any further with arrangements, to save later disappointment. What date did your sister-in-law have in mind?'

Time to step in and relieve Jane of the burden of spinning this story any further. Dora put her card on the man's desk. He looked down, surprised to be presented with a calling card by a woman he had dismissed as a servant.

'Private enquiries?' He frowned, holding it between finger and thumb. 'What is going on here?'

'I'm Miss Fitz-Pennington. I almost died last night because the man you hired to fire a gun put in a live round.'

'I haven't got time for this!' Mr Pierce leaped to his feet and opened his mouth to summon his clerk.

'I wouldn't do that if I were you. Your employer, Madame Catalani, can vouch for us and will not like to hear that you manhandled us out of your office. She's rather fond of Miss Austen. My friend here is telling you the truth when she said we made your lady's acquaintance earlier this week.'

He shut his mouth and looked in the direction of the theatre only a street away. Dora wouldn't be surprised if the singers were there to discuss the concert and lick their wounds.

'Madame Catalani was also there last night as my business partner, Dr Sandys, tended the injured,' continued Dora. 'Thanks to his quick actions, he made the number of people calling in your office for recompense much less than it could have been. You might have had a dead Russian diplomat as an added complication, but Dr Sandys rescued him from a burning pavilion. I'm sure you've been told about that.'

The manager sat back down and folded his arms, scowling. The bulldog was close to biting. 'What do you want then? Money?' He thought he'd got her type pinned down.

'We want the name of the gunner and the one who suggested you hire him.'

'But that's confidential!'

'Why?' asked Jane in her reasonable tone. 'What have you to hide?'

'Why, nothing! It is only that … in business, you can't go sharing secrets as to how you make the magic happen.'

'It's nothing to do with trade secrets, let alone magic,' said Dora. 'He wants to keep the books private because he doesn't pay everyone equally but only what he thinks they will accept.' She knew full well this was how the entertainment world worked. She had been paid less than her male colleagues despite being the bigger draw at the box office. The Mr Pierces of the world were everywhere in the profession.

'Well, yes!' He didn't even look ashamed by that fact.

'When it comes to attempted murder, I think such niceties should be abandoned, don't you?'

'Attempted murder? No one said anything about that!'

'They soon will be. If you want to keep out of this, you'd better tell us what you know and be rid of us. If we must sit here and summon a Bow Street runner to explain our case, then things will get a lot more complicated.' She had no intention of calling on the runners, but he wasn't to know that. Gently bred ladies would think the runners were allies, not the obstacles that she usually found them to be.

He stared at her, gauging her resolution. Finding she wasn't to be moved until she got what she came for, he groaned and threw up his hands. 'All right, all right. But this goes no further, agreed?'

That suited her. They didn't want the person in question to get wind that they were on their trail. 'The contract?'

With no good humour, he pulled a file out of his desk drawer and leafed through the pages until he came to the right one. 'John Smith of Barnes Terrace.' He frowned. 'My clerk filled it out but that doesn't sound right. I thought he was German or something foreign.'

'Then it is safe to assume that was an alias. Who suggested you hired him?'

'Madame Catalani, of course.'

Dora could not see the world-famous soprano behind this plot. 'And who recommended him to her?'

He grimaced. 'The Russian woman, Yekatarina Petrovna. She said she knew someone who could fire a gun.'

'I bet she did,' said Dora.

Chapter Thirty-One

Downing Street

In his cupboard of an office, Thornbury was practically dancing on the spot as he read the report.

'We are going to win!' He bumped into a pile of papers but didn't care as they cascaded to the floor. 'Did you read this? Of course you did!'

Jacob watched him with amusement as the Second Senior Clerk to the minister capered. 'If you read on, you'll see that the late *comte* did caution that the American War might endanger that outcome, tying up the armies when we need them most, that we might not win that engagement.'

'Yes, yes, but picture the map of Europe, once Napoleon's for the taking. He has pushed his rule to almost every corner of the continent and now he is overreaching. Look how he is neglecting the Peninsular Campaign where Wellington is making headway in Spain and Portugal while he concentrates on the north, aiming to reach Moscow to teach the Tsar a lesson. Napoleon's grand army will not be so grand once he marches it into the Russian countryside. We had thought as much ourselves. Many of us believe Bonaparte will do the prudent thing and halt once the winter arrives and wait for spring, but the late *comte* thinks he won't be able to resist chasing after the retreating Russians like a hound on a scent that takes him tumbling over a cliff. Wily old Kutuzov knows this and has the guts to bank on it.'

'That's about the sum of it. Thornbury, may I ask why you put so much store in the *comte*'s view? If others are speculating this might be the outcome, why is this report worth killing for?'

The Foreign Office man finally sat down and reverently spread the report out before him. 'It is all to do with his reputation. Have you ever known a man who can predict the rise and fall of the market, the one who makes you thousands and saves you from great losses?'

'If I knew such a man, I'd be much richer than I am today.'

'Wouldn't we all? But D'Antraigues was like this for events on the continent. At first, we were sceptical that this émigré blown in from Germany could know anything, but time after time his opinion proved correct. Why else did we pay him his pension and put up with his ways, calling on the Foreign Secretary as if they were old school friends?'

'Did you know he was shopping this report around and looking for another paymaster?'

Thornbury looked a little uncomfortable. 'The First Senior Clerk did mention something like this to me a few days ago when I asked to see the file. There would've been ructions in the department if D'Antraigues had gone ahead with his stupid auction, calls for his pension to be cancelled, so I doubt he would've done so when push came to shove.'

A gust of irritation blew through Jacob. 'And you only mention this now?'

'It never happened and was only a rumour. I didn't want to slander the dead.'

'Our understanding is that the *comte* wanted to present this at a musical party on the day he died, handing it to the highest bidder.'

Thornbury looked away and up at the high window. 'And if so, we had decided not to get involved in that disgraceful bidding process but press him for our own copy of the report quietly or tell him he could say goodbye to the pension. He would have liked being paid twice for the same information.'

'Who was bidding, do you know?'

'The chief contenders were the Prussians, the Swedes and the Russians. My money was on the Russians winning the bid as he was closest to them.'

'This is good news for them, isn't it?'

'Only after a lot of suffering. I would think it a mixed bag myself. Imagine if it were here instead. Imagine that Wellington was fighting at home and decided that everything between Dover and London could be sacrificed to stop an invasion – crops burned in the fields, great houses reduced to ashes, barns pulled down. There would be a revolution if he suggested such a thing.'

'Whereas in Russia…?'

'The country is so vast, such losses are absorbed like a stone dropping into a deep pool. Besides, the Russians have serfs –

which is another name for slaves – and not our independently minded peasantry. I can't imagine the serfs ever revolting.'

'I imagine King Louis said the same thing. Now we have the information, what do we do with it? I'm sure you will share it with your superiors, naturally, but everyone is sniffing around for the report, even the French. People are willing to kill for it.'

Thornbury drummed his fingers. 'Yes, it is a conundrum, isn't it?'

'It strikes me that if the French put as much weight on the *comte*'s assessment as you do, letting them know what is in this report could be exceedingly damaging.'

'You're right. We must keep it away from them. What do you suggest?'

'I have a plan both to wrongfoot the French and expose the person behind the assassination of the *comte* and his wife and subsequent attacks.'

'That sounds intriguing. Tell me more.'

'It requires the auction to go ahead and for you to play your part. You'll need permission, of course, and I'll need to ask the new *comte* if we can stand in his stead.'

'You?'

'Not me, exactly, but the *comte*'s banker, Mr Austen. He can say that the will has now been read and the late *comte* has entrusted it to him to sell the report on behalf of the estate.'

'Yes, that does sound like something the clever old *comte* would have done.'

'It might be dangerous, but if we get this right we will have honoured the *comte*'s final wishes.'

'And what did he wish?'

'The defeat of Napoleon, of course.'

Returning to Bruton Mews, Jacob listened to what Dora and Miss Austen had discovered about the hiring of the gunner.

'Excellent. That is confirmation of what I suspected,' he said. 'The Russians are in this up to their ears. Or at least one of them is.'

'It certainly is looking that way. Do you think Miss Petrovna was acting alone or with her government's approval?' asked Dora.

'Odd business, shooting at your own representative and his wife,' said Jane.

'It looks more like the actions of someone going far beyond their orders,' said Jacob. 'The only way we can find that out is to talk to Count Vorontsov. His near brush with death will likely have made him suspicious that there are dealings in the embassy to which he isn't party.'

'I think you should call on him,' said Dora. 'It would be natural for you to do so as you attended him last night.'

'Agreed. I'll make that a priority. We'll need his cooperation for what we do next.'

'Which is?' asked Jane.

'Use the report as bait to bring them into the open?' suggested Dora.

Delighted that her ideas were running in the same direction as his, he wanted to smother her in kisses and take her to bed, but they had company. 'My thoughts exactly. We should go ahead with the auction and see who comes to bid.'

'But you can't sell this report if there's a chance it might fall into the wrong hands!' protested Miss Austen.

Dora grinned. 'Oh, Jacob, I can tell from your expression that that is exactly what you hope will happen.'

'You know me so well, love. Michel Percy will find it irresistible.'

'What are you two cooking up?' asked Miss Austen suspiciously.

'We need a few unusual ingredients in our dish to tempt our foreign guests to attend. Dora can supply one of them.'

'What spice would that be?' asked the novelist.

'Let's just say I have an accomplishment that might come in very useful,' said Dora.

'Why do I think you aren't talking about painting tables, covering screens or netting purses?'

'Because you, dear Jane, are a lady of great discernment.'

'Do you think your brother will agree to host this auction?' he asked the lady novelist, changing the subject away from Dora's unusual skill.

'I believe so, if it does not put Eliza or anyone in the household at risk,' said Miss Austen.

'I see it rather as a way of ensuring publicity so that no one comes looking for the report again – no more break-ins, no more attacks on us as we go about our business. You can publish your next novel in peace. Dora, what is your opinion?'

'I think it is a brilliant idea if we can pull it off. And if Jane were not here, I would kiss you.' Dora beamed at him.

'Don't mind me,' said Miss Austen.

Jacob grinned at her. 'Would you mind going together to Sloane Street to pave the way for the event? Invitations must be written and other preparations made. You know what you must do?' he asked Dora.

'Yes, Jacob. I'm glad my skills are finally being exercised.'

'Where do you want us to conceal the report?' asked Miss Austen.

'I'm planning to call again on Julien and ask to borrow the transparency. He might wish to be present.'

'I was under the impression he wanted rid of the whole sorry business,' said Dora. 'He handed the report to us like a hot potato.'

'But he would likely want to witness the person behind his parents' death being brought to account.'

'Count Vorontsov is unlikely to be able to attend,' said Dora.

'I will call on him after I've spoken to Julien. As you said, it would not be so odd for me to visit the Russian embassy after being the first person to treat his injuries. It is time we had a frank talk.'

'Then we will bid them all to attend Eliza's musical party tomorrow night,' said Miss Austen. She gave Dora a teasing smile. 'I wonder if Mr Pierce would like to organise it?'

'I think he would like nothing more to do with us. Do not worry, I know where we can get performers at short notice.'

'Oh? Where?'

Dora chuckled. 'Jane, for a lady with keen powers of observation, have you not noticed we employ them, and I have made my living on stage? I even have one of my singing partners here in London. I'm sure she will be thrilled to do something other than shopping for an evening.'

She was talking about Ruby. 'Do you think that wise?' asked Jacob.

Dora tapped his cheek softly. 'Wake up, Jacob! You are holding a party for killers. You need tough, experienced performers we can trust. I think Ruby is the perfect choice.'

He trapped her hand and kissed her fingers. 'I will be guided by you.' He just had to hope she was right about Ruby's trustworthiness.

Chapter Thirty-Two

Hanover Square

Leaving Dora to accompany Miss Austen home to arrange matters in Sloane Street, Jacob took himself off to the Russian embassy. The new arrivals had set up in Hanover Square, a development of elegant townhouses around a garden located not far from their office. He handed his card to the butler and was invited to wait in the foyer.

The house had the hallmarks of a rented property, walls adorned with unobjectionable landscapes and portraits of forgotten people. The only picture the current owners had had time to change was an expansive view of Moscow that hung on the stairs. The city was set low in the landscape, onion-domed churches and the city walls lifting it out of the plains, holding up the huge weight of the cloudy sky, the Moskva River sweeping past its skirts. It was an image created during the days of Catherine the Great, the current Tsar's formidable grandmother.

'His Excellency will see you now,' said the butler, interrupting Jacob's study of the picture.

As they progressed to the second floor, a door slammed at the far end of the corridor on the first, attracting his gaze. He caught a fleeting glimpse of a man hurrying towards them then turning abruptly away to the servants' staircase when he saw Jacob. He wore a brown coat.

Lots of people wore brown coats but instinct told Jacob this was the one he was seeking. Did the man in black lurk somewhere there too? He thought it highly likely.

Count Vorontsov was lying in the centre of a double bed, lightly covered with a sheet. He was staring mutinously up at the ceiling like a very big, disgruntled child sent to bed without supper. Hearing Jacob enter, he waved a hand.

'Forgive me not getting up to greet you. My doctors have ordered me to lie like this. I cannot even sit up to eat.'

'As another of that profession, I am afraid I must echo their advice. We are all worried about your spine, as doubtless you have been told.'

'Yes, yes, they think I will paralyse myself if I leap out of bed – me who has fallen off a horse in a cavalry charge and lived to tell the tale. I am ashamed I have been brought down by a musician!'

'Consol yourself. It may have been no ordinary musician.'

Jacob took a seat by the count's bed and waited for the butler to withdraw.

'Gone, has he?' asked the count.

'Yes, he has.'

'A good man, but he is following the doctor's orders worse than my mother. Pass me the flask in the side table there, be a good chap.'

Jacob did as he was asked. He wasn't this man's keeper, after all.

'*Za zdorovye!*' The count gingerly lifted it to his lips to avoid spillage and took a gulp. He smacked his lips. 'Ah!'

'Better?'

'Yes. Do you want some?' He waved the flask in Jacob's direction.

'No, thank you. A little early for me.'

The count began to screw on the cap but it was an awkward angle for that operation, so Jacob took it from him, sealed it and then slid it under the count's pillow.

'I am pleased you called this morning. I want to thank you for saving my life last night.'

'Think nothing of it. I did what any decent man would do.'

'I beg to differ; there are many indecent men in existence, unfortunately.'

'That is undoubtedly true. Sir, I've been looking into the events of the concert.'

'You do not think it an accident.'

'No, I don't. And neither do you.'

The count gave a grunt of assent. 'Aimed at the Frenchman?'

'I think not, though I've often wanted to shoot him with a cannon, if you understand me?'

'I do indeed. The French can be so … what is the English word? Aggravating?'

'Very apposite. Was it generally known you were to attend the concert?'

'It was.'

That cleared up that mystery. Jacob had been wondering

how the gunner had known in advance that his target would attend 'And did you say that you would sit in the pavilion?'

'My wife isn't one to stand for long. Miss Petrovna told us that it would give us the best view.'

'Do you know if anyone would want to kill you, or get you out of the way at the very least?'

The count's eyes gleamed. He did indeed have someone in mind. 'You are wondering if it was an attack on Russia? A French sympathiser planted in the orchestra perhaps?'

'No, not exactly. Let me explain.' He unfolded his theory as to what had been going on behind the count's back. The injured man was quivering with rage by the time Jacob finished.

'I've got to get up!' He made to rise, but Jacob, who was expecting this reaction, put his hands on the count's chest to keep him flat.

'Don't give your enemy the satisfaction of completing the work they started last night.'

Vorontsov let out a huff of disgust at himself and at the situation. 'You've told me all this for a reason. What do you want me to do?'

So Jacob explained.

Chapter Thirty-Three

64 Sloane Street

Up in Miss Austen's room, after a busy afternoon and evening of organising and rehearsing, Jane sealed the last invitation while Dora finished off her own assignment.

'Good, we are done.' Jane added her card to the basket and rang for a maid. 'Hill, please see that these last ones are sent out at once.'

'Very good, Miss Austen,' said the maid, bobbing a curtsey.

Jane got up and stretched. 'I haven't written so much in one sitting for years. Do you think they will all come?'

'How can they not? They were all asked to the original auction so they will be eager to get a chance to win the bid.' Dora blotted her work and folded it up.

'And the Frenchman?'

'We asked Kir and Mr Smith to talk loudly and indiscreetly about the auction in the mews outside our office while they played knucklebones. Percy will have his spies deployed by now so he will invite himself along, I have no doubt.'

'Then there is nothing more to be done tonight.'

'Agreed, though it is in many ways the most dangerous hour. Someone wanting to circumvent proceedings might well strike tonight. That is why we are all here to guard the premises. The men are downstairs but, if you don't mind, I'll stay in here with you. We know the attackers have identified your room and made use of that drainpipe before, so it is better we be prudent and make sure you are not alone.' Dora did not want the loss of a friend and such a promising novelist on her conscience. Jacob had seconded her in that. Eliza Austen had her husband at her side; Jane had no one in her bedroom, what with her sister Cassandra being at home with their mother.

Jane nodded. 'Thank you. I'd like that.' They'd closed the curtains some hours ago, but now she went to check through the gap. 'It is horrible to think someone might try to break in tonight.'

'Rather than fret your poor nerves, why don't you sit down and read a book to take your mind off things?'

'It is likely that the only thing that would get my mind off what is going on is to work.' She went over to her little writing desk and got out some paper. 'I've been making notes for my novel after *Pride and Prejudice*. I'll work on that.'

'Might I see the book you have in draft?'

Jane looked apprehensive. 'You really did like *Sense and Sensibility*?'

'I really did.'

The author went to her chest and pulled out a ream of paper, holding it close to her heart. 'Cassandra thinks people will like this one even more than Elinor and Marianne, but I don't share her confidence. It was the work of my youth, or begun then, when things were so much sunnier than they are now. I wonder if it is too light, too funny, not serious enough for our present time?'

Dora laughed. 'My dear Jane, it sounds the perfect antidote to waiting for a villain to burst in. We can laugh them out of countenance and kick them off the balcony.'

'That's exactly what Elizabeth would do.' Gathering her courage, Jane handed it over. 'Be kind. Writers ask for frank opinions, but really, we only want praise.'

Dora read until her candle burned down, caught a few hours' sleep, then finished the story in the morning at first light. It felt like she had passed from an old to a new world in that interval. Wordlessly, she handed *Pride and Prejudice* back to Jane for safekeeping before they went down to breakfast. There was no way she would risk this with thieves about.

'That bad, eh?' said Jane with a sigh, locking it in her chest.

'That good.' Dora hugged her friend. 'I stand in awe – no!' She went down on her knees and bowed like a slave to the sultan in the pantomime. 'I bow before your greatness.'

Jane flapped her hands at her. 'Stop mocking me, you silly goose!'

'Mock? Never! My obeisance is sincerely meant.' She hopped up. 'You, my dear Miss Jane Austen, are the Madame Catalani of the pen.'

'What a delightful comparison!' Jane's cheeks went pink.

'It is the best book I've ever had the pleasure to read, Elizabeth my favourite heroine, and if your Mr Egerton doesn't pay you a thousand pounds for it, then he is undervaluing your talent.'

'I was hoping for a hundred and fifty, but Henry warns that I might have to settle for less.'

Dora pulled a face. 'Why do we women always have to settle for less? Byron is said to have got five hundred guineas for *Childe Harold*, and that isn't a patch on your work.'

'I'm no Lord Byron.'

'Thank heavens not, or there would be a string of abandoned lovers and waifs in your wake.'

'Yes, he is a deliciously reprehensible sort, isn't he?'

The breakfast table hosted a motley crew of performers and the Austen family, Eliza and Henry showing their relaxed attitude to social status by joining them for the meal. There was a lively discussion about the bill of fare to be laid before the guests, both the society friends were able to come at short notice, and the diplomatic targets who were there for the secret conclusion to the evening. The theme was 'Music from the Stage'. Hugo and Ren were to do a comic song; Julien, who had agreed with Jacob that he should be present, was to play a piece by Mozart; Susan had suggested she sing a setting of Shakespeare's 'It was a lover and his lass' that she had done to great acclaim in Bath; while Dora herself had picked 'Oh, the broom' from *The Beggar's Opera*. A friend of Hugo's, currently out of work due to the closure of Drury Lane, was engaged to play a piece on the harp. Ruby, expected to arrive later for the dress rehearsal, had sent a note agreeing to join Dora, Hugo and Ren in 'Over the hills and far away', also from *The Beggar's Opera*, in addition to a solo from *Così fan tutte*. They had a programme to which the climax would be the announcement of the winner of the auction in a room set aside for the international guests.

Jacob took his place beside Dora, yawning a little as he had had the watch in the middle of the night.

'All quiet?' she asked.

'Yes. We saw some people loitering but, when they saw us watching, they made themselves scarce. And you?' He heaped his plate with breakfast fuel to keep him going during what was likely to be a long day.

'I could barely sleep a wink.'

He squeezed her hand. 'I'm sorry, love. The danger will be over soon.'

'No, you don't understand! That book – Jane's next one – it is the most wonderful story I've ever read.'

He chuckled. 'I'm glad you liked it. It would spoil your new friendship if you had harsh things to say.'

He wasn't getting it. 'Jacob, she's one of the greats, one of the most talented writers of all time.' He smiled but in a way that was merely humouring her. 'You like Wordsworth? Well, she's my Wordsworth, only better.' She said the last with a teasing smile, knowing he was passionate about his Lakes poet.

'Then I look forward to reading it for myself. When are we to expect Ruby?'

'She has an appointment with a mantua-maker about a new gown and will arrive after that.'

'I'm surprised she agreed so readily.'

'Are you?' Dora twiddled her teaspoon, nervous already about the evening – not her part in it, but the invitation that would put a killer in their midst. 'She's used to working, Jacob. She dreamed of the life of the ladybird, luxury and freedom from want, but now she's living it, she's lonely. Her happiness depends on the whims of a man who can only spare her a little of his time. I think she's grateful I involved her, though she'll claim it is a favour to me, her way of apologising for putting our names in the newspapers.'

Jacob spread butter on his toast, his appetite showing no signs of being blunted by nerves. 'Sorry to put this crudely, but is she good enough for a London audience?'

Dora smiled at his effort to be restrained. He did not like Ruby. 'You saw us perform once? What was it we did in Kendal?'

'*As You Like It* and *Castle Spectre*.'

'I thought so. Neither of us sang then. You are in for a surprise.'

'A good or a bad one?' he asked plaintively.

'You'll have to wait for this evening to find out.'

Ruby came in like a thunderstorm in red silk. She grasped Dora's shoulders and kissed her on both cheeks.

'My first engagement in London!' she said. 'A private party – how delightful. They are so much better than public concerts, do you not agree?' She turned to her hosts. 'Mr Austen, Mrs Austen, charmed.' She dipped a curtsey. She spared Jane Austen only a nod and smile of acknowledgment. 'Lead on, Dora. We must practise until we are perfect!' That had not been her motto when in the Northern Players. There she had been of the school of 'it will be all right on the night.'

As Dora expected, Ruby lost some of her London airs and graces when the door was closed on the practice room and she was alone with her tribe of theatrical folk. She teased Hugo, flirted with Ren and walked carefully around Susan.

Dora drew her aside during the run-through of Hugo and Ren's song and explained the hidden agenda for the evening, without mentioning the details of the report that the bidders wanted. This wasn't because she didn't trust Ruby, but because she knew her friend would simply not be interested.

'I take it that the viscount approves of your participation here?' Dora asked.

Ruby fluttered her fingers, the new rings glittering. 'He said I was to amuse myself in his absence.'

'Oh?'

'He's gone north to fetch his family back for the season. When his wife is in town, he won't be able to spend every evening with me, he explained.'

'Is this what he envisaged as amusing yourself?'

Ruby bit her lip. 'Perhaps not. But as long as no report of this gets into the papers, need he know?'

'We certainly aren't aiming for the society column, or if we make it into it, it will be one of those insipid "Mr and Mrs Austen, a private party at home" remarks with no details.'

'Then all will be well.' Ruby's gaze settled on Julien at the piano. 'That's the new *comte*, I take it? He now must sing for his supper?'

'I'm not sure.' Jacob had told her that the late *comte* might have been a better manager of his money than his reputation among the ton suggested. 'But I think he prefers it to sitting at home in that big empty house of his.'

'Hmm.' Ruby settled herself into her most becoming pose, shoulders back, head tilted so she looked up through her lashes at her interlocutors, winsome and defenceless. 'I will go and introduce myself.'

'Be gentle. He has just lost both his parents in a brutal fashion.'

When she left, Jane, who had been observing the rehearsal from a quiet corner while sewing a costume for Ren, came over to Dora.

'That's your friend, the one you spoke of?'

'It is.'

'A flamboyant person. Would it be fair to say trouble follows her?'

'No more than it does me. In fact, I'm worse.' Dora grinned.

'I meant in the area of love?'

'Ah, well, it has left her in a certain situation, as you doubtless noticed. She means to be good, but most moralists would find fault with her behaviour.'

'Charming but dangerous to gentlemen?'

'Yes, but don't you think we women are in far more danger from them, than they from us?'

'True. Still, the lady adventurer is a curious role. I look forward to hearing her perform.'

'I notice you haven't made yourself known to her?'

It was Jane's turn to laugh. 'She would not know what to do with a woman like me.'

A truer word was never spoken. 'And you?'

'I do. An adventurous female of dubious morals? I'll put her in my next book!'

Chapter Thirty-Four

'Is this how you feel on a first night?' whispered Jacob, as he waited in the wings with Dora. His stomach was churning and he simultaneously felt hot and cold, his body confused as to whether it wanted to fly away or stay and fight.

'Oh, no, that's much worse,' she told him. 'This is a picnic in the park – a few songs, no complicated scenery changes, same costume throughout.'

The dining room had been turned into a concert hall, Henry's study sacrificed as the Green Room. Through the crack in the doorway they could see that the audience was gathering, excited by an unexpected invitation in the doldrums of the summer in London. Professional gentlemen outnumbered the gentry, comprising of the civil servants, merchants and stockbrokers who could not afford to take months off to visit estates outside the capital, but it was a respectable gathering nonetheless, nothing that betrayed the hastiness of the organisation. Thornbury was there with what looked like his superior, the First Senior Clerk to the minister. The latter had a wild head of brown hair as if he had stolen all that was lacking from the bald pate of his underling. Slightly stooped, with glasses perched on the end of his nose, he was peering at the list of songs Eliza and Jane Austen had painstakingly copied out, there being no time to involve a printer. Ben Knighton was there too, thrilled to have scored an invitation to an exclusive event. When Countess Vorontsov entered, leaning heavily on the arm of Miss Petrovna, Thornbury ushered her to a seat in the front row. From the serious expression on his face, Jacob guessed he was commiserating with the lady on the injury her husband had sustained two nights before. In the row behind her, Jacob spotted the blond-headed Swedish envoy – he looked annoyed by the delay before the auction, tapping his programme restlessly on his knee – and the sour-faced Prussian, who sat like he was on horseback, his spine not touching the seat.

Jacob could feel Dora's breath on his cheek. He turned and snatched a quick kiss. It reminded him of the first time he had been close to her, in a stable in an innyard in Kendal. Long before he fell in love with her, he had been keenly aware of her presence as a woman.

She kissed him back. 'Everyone here that you wanted?'

'Except the French. We must have them here for this to work.'

'It is possible Percy will send someone to bid in his stead.'

'True. We will only know when we retire for the private auction.'

'Have you agreed with Henry how that will go?'

'I have. They've been told to bring sealed bids and there will only be one round of bidding. The *comte*'s report goes to the highest bidder, no matter the identity. Henry is making out he is bound by the terms of the will. Percy will see this as an opportunity to snatch it from his enemies. He's going to wedge himself in somehow, but I'm not certain in what manner.'

'Then they have to make their best bid from the outset and not hold anything back?'

'Yes, it isn't really about the money, though that is an interesting sideshow to the evening.'

'What is it about then?'

'The bidding process is about accommodating Count Vorontsov who would have been here otherwise. He has sent his wife with his bid, and one cannot imagine her managing anything as complicated as deciding whether to up her bid or not.'

'Miss Petrovna could.'

'She could, but he has decided he doesn't trust her.'

'Wise man.'

Henry came to the front of the room and greeted his guests. His sister took her place at the piano as she was accompanying the first few numbers. On Mrs Austen's prodding, she had volunteered that she was competent enough to play for the comic songs but would surrender her place to a true professional when they reached the more operatic part of the evening.

'Ladies and gentlemen, thank you so much for accepting our invitation for this evening of music from the stage. I'm sure you will share with my wife and me the thought that August can be a month that is devoid of private entertainments, whereas, in the autumn, you will be showered with invitations. We decided, therefore, to bring our favourite people together'—he smiled expansively at the company before him—'and share with them some of our favourite songs. I'm thrilled to say some of the Theatre Royal's most experienced performers were available, as well as some new talent recently arrived from the northern circuit, so you will be delighted, we hope, by this blend of the novel and the familiar. But that is enough from me. Ladies and gentlemen, prepare to be comically entertained by Hugo Ingles and Goliath Renfrew!'

Hugo and Ren entered from opposite sides and bowed to the company. There was a ripple of laughter at the name for the little man. No wonder Ren had dropped it for his nickname. That joke must have worn thin years ago.

They embarked on an easy bantering conversation, casting themselves as two London gents hitting the town's most popular places, using their little story as a cue for their song. Jacob waited long enough to find that his employees could indeed carry off a merry caper or two, before retreating from the doorway.

Dora was putting the finishing touches to her appearance, fastening pearl earrings and a necklace borrowed from Eliza. She met his eyes in the mirror.

'O ye of little faith!'

He smiled wryly. 'I know, I know. This isn't my area.'

She settled the pendant just above her cleavage where it would drive the red-blooded men in the audience wild with desire – or him at least. 'If Hugo and Ren barged into your hospital and demanded to operate on a patient, I would understand your hesitation; but all of us have been doing this for years.'

'Some of us longer than others,' quipped Susan, darkening her eyebrows with a charcoal pencil.

Jacob stood behind Dora and ran his finger down the chain,

pleased to see she shivered at the ghost of a touch. 'You look beautiful.'

'Why, thank you, kind sir.' She put her hand over his. 'Do not fret about the concert, Jacob. Worry about your plan for the auction. There's much that can go wrong with that.'

He gave her a chiding look. 'Was that supposed to be calming? I now feel ten times worse.'

Ruby glided over, peerless in scarlet. If she was going to be called a Jezebel for being pregnant outside of wedlock, she was going to embrace that reputation without shame. Many actresses had trodden this path before her, the famous Mrs Jordan for one, who had a clutch of children with Prince William. 'Good evening, Dr Sandys. Thank you for the names of the accoucheurs.'

He dipped his chin to her. He had been avoiding her all afternoon, but he couldn't duck out of a polite conversation now. 'Miss Plum. Are you well?'

'I am.'

'Thank you for joining us at short notice.'

She nodded regally to that pleasantry. 'It was the least I could do for my dearest friend.'

Was he the only one hearing her twist the knife in Dora's gentle soul, reminding her not to betray her friend by seeking her own happiness? He could feel Dora watching them in the mirror, her expression guarded.

'I hope you get the reward of enjoying the performance.'

'I hope you do too. You must go out there and watch, not skulk behind the scenes making us all nervous. We have got this under control.'

Dora grinned, tapping him on the leg. 'I agree with Ruby. Try to enjoy it – and keep an eye out for the French.'

Having been given his marching orders, Jacob used the servants' corridor to enter at the back of the dining room. All heads were turned to the stage where Ren and Hugo were completing their act. The Londoners were roaring with belly laughs while the foreigners looked bemused by some of the local references that sailed over their heads. There was one lady who sat pinch-faced. Was she Percy's representative? She had the strong profile that he associated with Gallic beauties.

After enthusiastic applause, the mood changed as Miss Austen surrendered her place at the piano to Julien. He accompanied Susan in her sweet Shakespearian ballad, then played expertly a sonata by Mozart, a clever piece that ran up and down the keys like the pitter-patter of a rainstorm. Once he had finished, Dora entered and stood beside him. With a look between them, Julien gave her the note for 'Oh, the broom'. Then she started singing.

Dear God! He had not known her voice was sublime. He had heard her sing going about the house, or humming, but she had never performed for him. Why had he not asked? She must have thought him severely lacking in interest in her accomplishments. It was a simple Scottish air that suited her voice, a mezzo-soprano. He thought her daring to sing unaccompanied like this after the flourishes of Mozart, but it suited the words. As Jacob listened, he realised that it was about a shepherdess taken out of her own country by a bonnie laird, pining for the flowering broom she'd left behind on the hillside. Was it a message to him? Dora had never been a shepherdess of course, perish the thought, but he had taken her away from her people, the performers who lived simple but rich lives acting on stages across the north country. He'd thrown her into a world of viscounts and diplomats with enemies around every corner, a place where his own family did not accept her.

He swallowed. She was so at home with her fellow performers and he would never be the kind of man who could get up on stage and sing a song, or play out a scene. Would she tire of his more restrained ways and long for the alchemical reaction of a stage play and public applause that produced a golden moment for her? Would he have to let her go back to that?

Michel Percy arrived at his side, a handkerchief flourished in his hand as he dabbed his eyes with false sensibility. His eyes glittered with fiery resolution, belying the Man of Feeling act. 'Very affecting. I did not realise Miss Dora could sing so well.'

Neither had Jacob, but he wasn't going to admit that to the enemy. 'She is talented in many areas.' He joined in the applause. Dora's eyes met his then slid to his side. Yes, he took the bait, my darling, thought Jacob.

'I always thought her a skilful woman. As I'm sure you are enjoying, frequently.'

The *double entendre* was there to be acknowledged but it went against his plans if he planted a facer on the man's nose so early in the evening. Later maybe.

'I didn't know you were invited,' Jacob said instead, thinking he deserved a medal for his restraint.

'My invitation must have got lost in the postbag,' said Percy. 'I understood all diplomatic representatives were summoned.'

'So like Perrault's aged fairy you come to cast your curse on Sleeping Beauty's christening?' said Jacob.

'You read fairytales? How surprisingly whimsical. You

always struck me as a practical man.' Percy tucked his handkerchief away. 'You aren't going to have me thrown out of this christening then?'

'I am not the host,' said Jacob.

'Then I had better go and charm Mrs Austen. She looks like a lady who will enjoy a little French gallantry. She must miss her first husband, being married to a plain old Englishman.'

'Not so plain, not so old,' said Jacob, but he let Percy go off to discover that himself.

Jacob's emotions settled as the harpist played. He might be reading too much into Dora's choice of song. It could be as simple as it being the one she could perform best in this setting. Though Ruby had edged him out of the dressing room with Dora's agreement, that was not the same as evicting him from her life.

Catching his train of thought, he realised he was far less secure in his relationship than he had thought. Did he want to be married because he was grasping after a sense of security rather than because it was what was best for Dora?

Now was not the time to second guess his course of action. His offer of marriage was public. Until she broke off with him, that was the direction in which he intended to travel.

Ruby arrived on stage with the sweeping arm of the opera diva. He hoped Dora did not over-estimate her friend's skills or this was going to be embarrassing. He doubted very much Ruby could speak Italian but the song she had chosen was in that language. He joined in the polite applause for her entrance. With a gracious smile at Julien, she began.

What a relief. She could sing. Personally, he preferred Dora's artless voice with its soaring tones, but someone had taken the trouble to train Ruby in the operatic style. It might not fill a Covent Garden or the Haymarket, but it would do for a small room like this. Her delivery was polished and disarming. He could tell the audience were loving her. The choice of song, 'In uomini, in soldati' was mischievous and apposite. Despina asks if in men, in soldiers, women hope for loyalty. It ends with the phrase '*Amiam per comodo, Per vanità!*', or 'Let's love for convenience, for vanity!' Was that what Ruby had decided? He feared so.

She would be gratified by the applause, particularly as several gentlemen stood to shout 'brava!'. That was the currency she enjoyed the most, Jacob knew, even more than his brother's wealth.

They were coming to the climax of the evening. Ruby was joined on stage for the final number: 'Over the hills and far away'. It was a well-known tune that had the audience clapping along. Eliza Austen was beaming at the triumph of an evening, looking like she would need little persuasion to get up and start a reel. Seeking out her even more interesting sister-in-law, Jacob found Jane at the side of the room, watching the audience as much as she did the performers, a sardonic smile on her lips. She had not forgotten for a moment that this was no ordinary concert; as in *Hamlet* it was a mousetrap to catch a villain. Or two.

Neither should he take his eye off the ball. Affairs of the heart had to take second place to affairs of state. It was time he got into position.

Chapter Thirty-Five

The majority of the concertgoers went to supper with Mrs Austen in the breakfast room. She was ably escorted by Knighton while a select few followed Henry into a little-used drawing room downstairs. It was normally thought to be too dark and cold for entertaining, but it served their purposes well for this auction. The guests upstairs were unlikely to wander down here and it was possible to leave quickly if necessary.

Dora slid into the back of the room, joining Jane by the window. They used the heavy drapes to conceal their presence. This was Jacob's show, with his performer, Henry, about to take centre stage. Neither of them wanted to upstage this carefully laid scene.

'Are you crossing your fingers?' Dora whispered.

'And my toes,' confirmed Jane.

The gentlemen and three ladies who had indicated that they were taking part in the bidding took seats at the front. Jacob had told Dora who they were during the intermission.

The Swede, the Prussian, the two Russian women, the men from the Foreign Office and Michel Percy were all expected to be present. He had been surprised to find Portugal had sent a representative in the comely form of a Miss Rodrigues, a lady that Thornbury had muttered was their head of intelligence, known for her seductive ways. Many a minister and general had got into trouble with her. Jacob stood next to Henry, the print of Vesuvius in his hands.

'Ladies and gentlemen,' said Henry, 'now to the very interesting conclusion to the evening.'

Julien arrived, gave the room's occupants a hard stare, and stalked down to the front. He took the seat that had been prepared for him, facing them. The young man had grown up quickly over the past few days.

'You are all aware of the tragic murder of the Comte D'Antraigues's parents last month,' continued Henry. 'You are also aware that the late *comte* was a man of unparalleled sagacity as far as it stretched to predicting the outcome of political and military events. He was due to submit a report on this on the very day that he was killed, and you were all bidden to pledge what you would give for his insights.'

'Almost all of us,' said the Swede. 'I do object to the presence of a Frenchman in the room.'

Henry spread his hands. 'I am exceedingly sorry, Your Excellency, but I have to abide by the terms of the will. The *comte* specified that all diplomatic personnel were to be invited. He did not foresee that the French envoy would make use of this loophole, and I am unable to go back to get the will amended. I do know, however, that the present *comte* is unhappy at his presence. Monsieur, will you leave to spare a son further distress?'

Percy looked apologetic. 'I am devastated that the *comte* would think my presence here hurtful. I have something to offer that I believe he will want to hear.'

Henry huffed as if he were annoyed that Percy was sticking. 'Very well, then we may proceed. Dr Sandys, the report?'

Jacob stood forward. 'You will have noticed that there was a delay in calling you together. That was because our friend here did not know where the report had been concealed by his father. He had a cryptic clue but did not know how to unravel it. My partner and I were engaged to find out and we located it yesterday. It is here.' He flourished the print. 'The winning bid gets this picture and the report which we believe is concealed inside.'

'You believe?' asked Miss Petrovna. Her eyes narrowed on the print.

'Yes. It is a transparency but look...' Jacob held it to a candelabra. 'No change. The report is folded between the two layers. We have ascertained that it is there but gone no further. The *comte*'s instructions were strict on this point. Only the winning bid gets to read it.'

'And you expect us to believe you?' asked Percy dryly.

'I'm not sure anyone here has a choice but to believe me. You are free to leave if you object. No? What I can promise on my honour is that this print contains a copy of the *comte*'s report in his own handwriting.'

Jacob stood back, letting them mutter among themselves as they absorbed this information.

Henry came forward again. 'Your bids please.'

Each representative placed their envelope on a silver tray that he passed round for the purpose, all apart from Percy who sat back with an amused smile. Henry handed the tray to Julien who broke the seal on each. His eyebrows winged up as he read what were doubtless impressive figures.

'Do we have a winner?' asked Henry.

Julien nodded.

That was when Percy made his move. 'My apologies for my tardiness, *monsieur le comte*, but I could not seal my bid. I can only present it.' He pulled a rolled document out of his inside pocket and placed it on top of all the other bids. 'I have here a letter returning to you all your ancestral estates in France and her colonies. I offer not only the monetary value of those estates, but the return of your honour and prestige in France!'

Dora could have laughed. How like their wily Frenchman! From their past dealings in the Elgin investigation during which he kept wrong-footing them, they knew Percy would have a surprise up his sleeve, something that would help him win the bid, and he had not disappointed them. They had anticipated a heap of gold, not this offer of restoration of the family. They could only hope Julien was not seduced by it into revealing their plot.

The young Comte D'Antraigues unrolled the document. He looked hard at the seal. 'This is valid?'

'It is. Endorsed by the Emperor's Chef de Cabinet.'

'I don't know what to say.' Julien looked at Henry, then Jacob. 'What do we do? It is by far the best bid. No one else can offer me this.'

Henry scowled like he was chewing a mouthful of fishbones and feared to choke. 'The will is clear.'

Percy smiled broadly. 'I adore the uprightness of the English legal system, second only to the Code Napoléon.' He plucked the print out of Jacob's hands. 'Don't look at me like that, *mon cher docteur*. I have no doubt you read the thing. This now puts us on, how do you say, level pegging, *hein*?'

Like an actor who knows when to take his exit before the catcalls and rotten fruit start flying, Percy walked swiftly to the door. '*À bientôt*.'

The door shut behind him. Miss Petrovna shot to her feet, in her hand a stiletto that Dora hadn't seen her pulled from a pocket sheath in her evening gown.

'What are you thinking! You can't let him leave with that!' she shouted, making to follow.

Henry grabbed her arms from behind while Jacob disarmed her.

'I'm afraid we can't have you slitting the throat of a guest,' Jacob said to her. 'That would be terribly bad form.'

She was spitting mad, like a cat that has had a bucket of water thrown over her. 'You imbecile! Do you want to lose the war?'

'How do I know that the French having the report will have that effect?' Jacob said with a laudably puzzled expression. 'None of us knows what is in it.'

'But we do! He predicts that Napoleon will lose because he dares to invade my country.'

'Oh, I see.' Jacob shrugged. 'The French won't like that, but it is too late now. The *comte* has his estate returned fairly. They can't ask for their money back.'

'Urgh!' The lady gave a cry of utter frustration at the stupidity of men. 'Let me spell it out for you. If they are warned by such a reputable source as the late Comte D'Antraigues, they will call off the invasion. They will overwinter in Kiev or Warszawa and march in the spring. Napoleon will keep his army intact and he will win!'

'Oh, dear. That does sound serious,' said Henry.

The Prussian stood up. 'We must stop the Frenchman.'

'I've got men outside,' said the Swede. 'I'll have him followed. We can stop any dispatches before they reach the coast.'

Good luck with that, thought Dora. Percy would be heading straight for his yacht on the Thames if his past actions were anything to go by.

Julien stood up and bashed the silver tray like a gong, startling them all. 'Enough. Yekatarina, tell us. How do you know what was in my father's last report?'

She blinked several times then straightened her spine. 'He showed a draft of it to me, Julien. I didn't know where he put the final version, but I knew what he was going to say.'

'When did he show that to you?' asked Jacob, following up the opening Julien had given them.

She pressed her lips together.

'Then I'll tell you when it was. I have spoken to your senior officer, to Count Vorontsov. He told me that his country was making approaches to employ the *comte* again as a Russian informant, writing reports for him to send to Moscow. You had been delegated to handle him, to persuade him to work again for the Tsar, to woo him, if you like.'

'I did no—' Her eyes were bright with exasperation. She would clearly like to strangle the whole pack of them.

'You did. The count explained to me that Lorenzo Stelli was placed there by you to facilitate your access to the *comte*. Many people would assume an attractive lady visiting the *comte* by the backstairs was there for amorous reasons. Lorenzo knew otherwise. He showed you in on the day that the murders took place. You were upstairs when it happened. Are you going to tell us what he did, or shall I? By the way, Count Vorontsov is now fully aware of the events and your part in them. He had thought Lorenzo had succumbed to a fit of madness, and if you were to blame, it was for a poorly chosen operative. You had not told him you were there that morning, had you?'

The circle of listeners now seemed more like a trap than people who would back her up on the importance of the French not getting the information. Her gaze skittered around the room looking for an exit.

'Please,' she appealed to them. 'This is not important. We must stop Percy!'

The Swede and the Prussian looked half persuaded. The Portuguese lady was quicker to realise what was afoot.

'Tell us what you did,' she said, 'then we can deal with the French.'

'All right!' Petrovna turned to Julien. 'It wasn't meant to happen like that. D'Antraigues was so happy that events would finally lead to the undoing of his great enemy that he did not stop to think of the danger of releasing the information too early. Lorenzo and I told him that he must not sell the report – that he must not even give it to the British government.' She nodded to Thornbury and his senior manager. 'I told him that he had to stop, or we would stop him.' She wrung her hands. 'He laughed in our faces. Lorenzo took that as an instruction to shoot him. That only clipped him – Lorenzo always was a terrible soldier – so he went after him with the poignard our agents are issued for close work.'

'You mean for assassinations,' said the Portuguese woman coolly, sounding like someone who knew exactly how that world worked.

Petrovna nodded. 'I would've screamed but nobody could

know I was there. The diplomatic repercussions were too horrible. Lorenzo left me in the room and the next thing I knew he was back, telling me he had removed the problem of the *comtesse* too in case her husband had told her what he planned to do with the report. He'd even brought oil with him to burn the place down. I was shocked – horrified. They were my friends.'

Julien spat at her feet. 'That to your friendship!'

'Then you killed him,' prompted Jacob.

'Of course! It was the only thing I could do. He was out of control, rabid like a dog, so I shot him and made it look like suicide. Then I left.' She looked down at the ground, but then the righteousness of her actions came back to her. 'I did what was necessary and we must do the same now. We must stop Percy. Napoleon must invade Russia.'

'What is going on?' murmured the countess. 'What is everyone talking about?'

'Murder, ma'am,' said Jacob. 'I'm afraid we are going to deprive you of your companion. Your husband has arranged for the arrest of Miss Petrovna and her two accomplices at the embassy on the charge of high treason against the Russian State. Her desire to protect Russia may have been laudable to her paymasters but the means were not. She was party to the killing of a valuable source of information and then tried to kill her superior when he started asking questions about her mishandling of the affair. It was your husband she tried to kill at Vauxhall Gardens, in order to cover up her mistakes. She will leave here in chains. I hope that is enough?' he asked Julien. 'It avoids further scandal for your family and your friends.' He gestured to Henry. His bank should now be safe from further rumours.

Julien nodded. He looked sick at heart, unable to find the words to express his loss.

'But I'm a patriot!' protested Miss Petrovna as three burly men from the Russian delegation entered.

'What are Igor, Alexei and Dimitri doing here?' burbled the countess.

'They are here to take Miss Petrovna away and charge her with treason,' repeated Jacob.

'He is more patient with her than I would be,' murmured Jane in Dora's ear.

'I did it for Russia!' shouted Miss Petrovna.

'When did trying to kill us, the investigators looking for the *comte*'s report, become patriotic?' asked Jacob.

'When you looked like you would do what you have done tonight – let Napoleon know his mistake!'

'If you had left us alone, Count Vorontsov would not have grown suspicious. Ask yourself this: when you fired on your own senior officer at the concert on Vauxhall Gardens, did you do it for Russia or for yourself?'

Her expression shuttered. 'I saw the opportunity to take out many of my enemies, so I seized it. In war one must make sacrifices.'

'And it had nothing to do with the uncomfortable questions the count was asking about the activities of your two servants? He had begun to get suspicious when I told him about the hidden report and he'd started watching you, hadn't he? You knew he was going to expose you as an accomplice to the murderers, didn't you?'

She folded her arms but found these seized from behind and her hands tied at the wrists, a cloak put over her shoulders to conceal that she was under arrest. Her usually attractive face was now twisted with an expression of cold fury.

'You are all traitors – all of you! The few lives I have taken are nothing to the thousands that will be lost in the war, thanks to you!'

'That's my cue,' Dora said to Jane. She then moved to the front of the gathering. 'You are mistaken, Miss Petrovna. You have not been paying attention. You heard Dr Sandys swear on his honour that the print contained a copy of the *comte*'s report in his own handwriting. That is true. What he did not say is that I made the copy using an aptitude I have for … er … replicating the handwriting of others if I have a sample before me. I copied the report. Mr Percy will think it the genuine article. I may, however, have made a few changes in some important areas, like the fact that Napoleon will win if he invades now and that the Tsar will sue for peace before he reaches Moscow, little things like that.'

'The devil is in the detail,' said Jacob, coming to stand beside her.

Miss Petrovna sagged in the grip of her Russian guards, much of the fight leaving her. 'At least you did that. *Bien*. I do not regret what I have done, and I am sorry for your loss,' she said to Julien as she was led away.

Thornbury went to the front of the room and held up a hand to stop the chatter of the delegates left behind. 'As you see, my dear colleagues, you have been party to a sleight of hand that will hopefully change the course of the war. Miss Petrovna was right about one thing. Utmost secrecy is paramount, at least until Napoleon is too far committed to turn back. I would suggest you keep this information on a strict need-to-know basis and consider twice if you should share it with anyone beyond this room. Hint, if you must, to your capitals, but keep the Comte D'Antraigues's name out of it until his prediction is proved true or false. Do I have your agreement?'

Jacob bent down to Dora's level to say in a low voice. 'I think we can leave the diplomats to their wrangling. Our work here is done.'

She nodded, grateful that the highwire act they had plotted with a faked report and a trick to get the French to buy it, had gone off with no one plunging to their death. 'Will she pay?'

'For the *comte* and *comtesse*? Probably not. However, the count will not look so kindly on her shooting at him and his wife. That will earn her a severe penalty, if not death.' He looked serious, contemplating the aftermath. 'I think it likely there will be no trial, but I wouldn't be surprised if she has an unfortunate accident at sea or a fall from a high window in the Kremlin. Regrettably, the Russians can be ruthless.'

'She was ruthless in her turn,' said Dora.

'Yes, she was. The boy's death at Vauxhall Gardens is on her tally, and it could have been much worse.'

They rejoined the party, the other guests oblivious to the drama happening downstairs. Jacob went off to thank the other performers as well as his friend Knighton, leaving Dora alone with Jane for a moment. The two women stood together watching the people milling around, the flirting, the whispered arguments, the cuts direct, and the teasing.

'Will you put this in a novel?' asked Dora.

Jane snorted. 'No one would believe it. My world is this one'—she nodded to the party—'not that of international plots and murder. I'm pleased, though, that I was here to see the end of the story. I will tell my sister and no one else. Napoleon will hear nothing from me.'

Dora smiled at the idea of the emperor paying attention to the doings of a lady from an English shire. 'Will you stay in London much longer?'

'Sadly, my excuse of a bad cold will not survive much longer. I must return to my mother and sister. You'd like my sister.'

'And your mother?'

Jane laughed.

'I see. Then I hope we will meet again.'

'I will let you know when I next come to town. I have *Pride and Prejudice* to nurse through the printing press.' She rubbed her hands in anticipation.

'And I will make sure I am first on the list of purchasers. You will be working on the next one?'

'I will. I might even mention the navy because, apparently, I could write well about that.' She gave Dora a flat look.

Dora held up her hands. 'You don't need any advice from me.' The spirit of mischief took over. 'I will, however, give you a wager if you care to take it?'

'Oh?'

'You have written three of the most attractive heroines in any novel I have ever read in Elinor, Marianne and the wonderful Elizabeth. I dare you to write some pills – people who it is a real challenge for us all to love. Then I will know you are far better than Byron who only writes about brooding heroes that he sees in his own mirror.'

'That is a difficult task indeed.' Jane made the slashing gesture of a fencer. 'Challenge accepted.'

Chapter Thirty-Six

Green Park

Summer in London wasn't so bad, thought Jacob. Not when you had completed a task to your satisfaction, outwitted a wily enemy, fulfilled your obligation to an old friend and, best of all, were strolling in the sunshine with your lady on your arm in one of the capital's parks.

'There truly are cows?' said Dora, wrinkling her nose.

'Yes, very pretty ones with matching milkmaids.'

The trees rustled in the breeze, the leaves waving their encouragement. He should speak his piece.

'Dora, I have been thinking.'

She smiled at him, the sun gilding her beautiful cheeks, her curling hair. Lord, he couldn't give her up!

'Go on,' she encouraged. 'I'm a captive audience. The only competition is milking time, and you win hands down.'

He smiled at her wit. 'Your song – at the concert.'

'Which one?'

'"*Oh, the broom.*"'

'Pretty, isn't it?' She began humming it again.

'Did you mean it?'

'Mean it in what way?'

'Mean it as a message to me, that you miss where you came from?'

She stopped and pulled him into a little arbour in the shrubbery. 'What bolt has got loose in your noggin? I can hear it rattling around in there.' She tapped his head. 'I sang that song because it was a good choice for the company. I had more to think about than sending opaque messages to my lover, if you recall. We were trying to unmask a killer.'

He let out a huge sigh of relief. 'Good. Excellent.'

She cocked her head. 'You've been worrying about that all night, haven't you? I thought you were acting strangely.'

'I don't want you to feel trapped into marrying me because Ruby blurted it before the world. I want you to want to marry me as much as I want to marry you.'

Dora squeezed his fingers in hers. 'I understand, but you've forgotten an essential element.'

'I have?'

'You asked me, and I told you, on several occasions since, that I am thinking about it.'

'Yes, I remember words to that effect.' He grimaced. 'I've been on tenterhooks.'

'Well, I *have* been thinking about it. I even took advice from Madame Catalani who reminded me that some decisions in life are really quite simple and are nothing to do with anyone else. You said the same to me too. I did listen. I can't be ruled by Ruby; I must be ruled by my heart. I now have an answer.'

His own heart began to race. 'And?'

She shook her head. 'Not like that. Ask me again. I recently came to see that a second proposal is always much more romantic than a first.'

He cast his eyes heavenward. 'It's that damn book again, isn't it? You haven't stopped thinking about it.'

'Is that really what you should be worrying about? Besides, it isn't a damn book; it is a wonderful, heavenly study of a person of wit and intelligence marrying … a lot of money.' She smirked at that description, then leaned forward. 'You have to read it to get the joke.'

'I will, I will.' He looked about him, not that he minded if anyone saw, but some things were better without an audience. The path was clear. 'Dora Fitz-Pennington.' He went down on one knee. 'Light of my life and friend of my heart, will you do me the very great honour of marrying me?'

She looked down at him for a second, keeping him in suspense, until she leaned down and said:

'Yes.'

Acknowledgments

It has been a pure delight to imagine Dora and Jacob's lives crossing that of my favourite author. I knew as soon as I set off to investigate the events of this period that it would be a possibility; I only needed to find the right story. The spark came from asking the question: what was Jane Austen up to in August 1812? There is a gap in her letters (thank you, editor Deidre Le Faye), possibly because these were lost or destroyed. Such gaps are perfect for writers to creep inside and plant our stories.

Then I came across a mention of the real and shocking murder of the Comte and Comtesse D'Antraigues in the biography of Jane Austen by Claire Tomalin. It was the sudden braking moment where my story swerved off the road I was following into a new and fascinating sidetrack. What's this? Jane had tea with a French *comte* and an opera singer who were brutally killed the next year? This led me down the research route of finding out what happened. The *comte* really was dabbling in the world of espionage as described in the novel, playing off more than one side, and for me the account of the murders did not add up. This story is my 'supposal' as to what might have happened, though my cast of involved diplomats is invented, layered upon the presence of the real delegations and the politics of the day. I'd like to thank Geri Walton, Thomas Munch-Petersen and Catherine Curzon for their interesting articles on the murder. You don't agree with each other, details varying just like witnesses of a crime, but that made it even more fun to come up with my own verdict on 'whodunnit'.

You will also notice that there is much about entertainment and eating in Regency London in this book – every establishment is based on a once existing restaurant, cafe or club. I would like to thank Penny Hampson, Rachel Knowles and the Internet Archive – the latter has the Gunter's recipe book which makes fascinating reading. Get cooking that Parmesan ice cream, everyone! I also found *The London Encyclopaedia* (editors Weinreb and Hibbert) invaluable. My clothing notes come from Hilary Davidson's two excellent books on the fashions of Jane Austen's era. Jane gets to wear some of the real garments described as part of her wardrobe in Hilary's book – thank you for those delicious details!

And finally on the research front, I'd like to thank *The Times* online archive, access given by my publisher. When I got stuck in August 1812, I would go and read the paper for the day in question. That gave me so many ideas for this book and future ones. Londoners really did light up the streets for the Marquess of Wellington and there were disturbances and wildly thrown firecrackers. The lesson for the historical novelist is you rarely have to make anything up; life is strange enough!

Bridgerton meets *The Da Vinci Code* **in the most page-turning regency romance book you will read in 2025!**

In Buckinghamshire, the infamous Hellfire Caves house a pleasure palace for the idle rich – a secret society steeped in satanism, opium and debauchery of the highest order.

When the club's warden, Antony Pennington, is brutally murdered, his bastard sister, Dora, must follow the clues to decode who the killer is, aided by an unexpected ally – ex-Army officer, former opium addict and son of a Viscount, Dr Jacob Sandys.

As a shadow dogs their every footstep, Dora and Jacob find themselves in the midst of a shocking conspiracy, caught between the legendary Illuminati and the Hell Fire Club. With time running out, they must fight against both the most influential gentleman of the ton – and the undeniable attraction they feel towards each other…

AVAILABLE NOW IN PAPERBACK, EBOOK AND AUDIO!

'A rip-roaring, helter-skelter adventure careening breathlessly through Regency society… An uproarious delight'
~ **Historical Novel Society**

Lord Elgin's Greek marbles are the talk of London society, so when a death threat arrives, the earl hires actress Dora Fitz-Pennington and the honourable Dr Jacob Sandys to investigate. They plunge into the scandals of society's most eminent members, from the Byron circle to the secret world of collectors.

As danger lurks around London's every corner, in the most exclusive ballrooms and the roughest taverns, Dora and Jacob will face not only what has been left unsaid simmering between them but the threat of silent assassins, traitorous acquaintances and the darkest of secrets…

AVAILABLE NOW IN PAPERBACK, EBOOK AND AUDIO!

Join Dr Jacob Sandys and Dora Fitz-Pennington once again on their latest deadly adventure!

Despite their attempts to keep their forbidden romance away from the disapproving eyes of society, Dr Jacob Sandys and Dora Fitz-Pennington find themselves drawn into the scandals of the British elite once more when William Wordsworth's prized notebook of unpublished poems goes missing.

When news arrives of a disturbing murder in London – a body pulled from the Thames with a shepherd's crook wedged in the victim's mouth – Dora and Jacob are compelled to investigate.

What links a poet's stolen treasure to a high-society murder? And will Dora and Jacob's love weather the storm, or will dark secrets doom their happiness?

AVAILABLE NOW IN PAPERBACK, EBOOK AND AUDIO!

The author and One More Chapter would like to thank everyone who contributed to the publication of this story...

Analytics
Imogen Wolstencroft

Audio
Fionnuala Barrett
Ciara Briggs

Contracts
Laura Amos
Inigo Vyvyan

Design
Lucy Bennett
Fiona Greenway
Liane Payne
Dean Russell

Digital Sales
Laura Daley
Lydia Grainge
Hannah Lismore

eCommerce
Laura Carpenter
Madeline ODonovan
Charlotte Stevens
Christina Storey
Jo Surman
Rachel Ward

Editorial
Janet Marie Adkins
Kara Daniel
Charlotte Ledger
Federica Leonardis
Lydia Mason
Jennie Rothwell
Sofia Salazar Studer
Helen Williams

Harper360
Emily Gerbner
Ariana Juarez
Jean Marie Kelly
emma sullivan
Sophia Wilhelm

International Sales
Peter Borcsok
Ruth Burrow
Bethan Moore
Colleen Simpson

Inventory
Sarah Callaghan
Kirsty Norman

Marketing & Publicity
Chloe Cummings
Grace Edwards
Katie Sadler

Operations
Melissa Okusanya
Hannah Stamp

Production
Denis Manson
Simon Moore
Francesca Tuzzeo

Rights
Ashton Mucha
Alisah Saghir
Zoe Shine
Aisling Smyth
Lucy Vanderbilt

Trade Marketing
Ben Hurd
Eleanor Slater

The HarperCollins Distribution Team

The HarperCollins Finance & Royalties Team

The HarperCollins Legal Team

The HarperCollins Technology Team

UK Sales
Isabel Coburn
Jay Cochrane
Sabina Lewis
Holly Martin
Harriet Williams
Leah Woods

And every other essential link in the chain from delivery drivers to booksellers to librarians and beyond!

ONE MORE CHAPTER

One More Chapter is an award-winning global division of HarperCollins.

Subscribe to our newsletter to get our latest eBook deals and stay up to date with all our new releases!

signup.harpercollins.co.uk/join/signup-omc

Meet the team at
www.onemorechapter.com

Follow us!

@onemorechapterhc

Do you write unputdownable fiction?
We love to hear from new voices.
Find out how to submit your novel at
www.onemorechapter.com/submissions